Jake built a fire in the fireplace and then sat beside Caitlin. Close.

Handing her drink to her, he brushed her hand lightly. The physical contact, while so slight, burned. Soft, warm skin. A startling awareness that increased his desire.

She smiled at him. "Thank you. We're having quite a storm. There won't be any going home the way I came. This kind of downpour gets the river spilling out of its banks."

She slanted him a look that was hot. He wondered if it was deliberate. Maybe he shouldn't be so hasty in getting rid of her.

While he had no intention of selling any part of the Santerre ranch back to her, how far would she go to try to convince him to do so?

"We have plenty of room," he said in a husky voice. "You can stay all night."

Dear Reader,

Our lives are interwoven with our families and as the years pass, no one can predict outcomes. Falling in love involves two people, but their relationship is also affected by the influence of family, which I like to include in my stories.

Family has always been important in my life, and it is consequential in my books. This time it is the world of Jake Benton, a cowboy CEO, a multi-millionaire mogul who loves his West Texas cattle ranch and a cowboy's life. He never expects to cross paths with his beautiful neighbor. Their sizzling attraction plays havoc with bitter feelings from generations of feuding between their families.

Against the backgrounds of Dallas, a West Texas ranch and the French Quarter in New Orleans, the family conflicts give the characters tough choices to make. Each has to cope with events from the past. Caitlin's tenderhearted care for others propels her into a tempestuous relationship with Jake. Ultimately, Jake makes a life-changing discovery that he hopes will win Caitlin's heart. Their story begins…

Sara Orwig

TEXAS-SIZED TEMPTATION

BY
SARA ORWIG

Published in Great Britain 2012
by Mills & Boon, an imprint of Harlequin (UK) Limited,
Eton House, 18-24 Paradise Road, Richmond, Surrey TW9 1SR

© Sara Orwig 2011

ISBN: 978 0 263 89114 0

51-011

Harleq[uin] [Books S.A. uses paper]s that are natural, renewable and
recycla[ble] [products and made from wood gr]own in sustainable fore[sts]. The
logging [and manufactur]ing processes conform to the legal en[vironmen]tal
regulat[io]ns of the country [of origin.]

Printed [and bound in Spain]
by Blac[kprint CPI, Barcelona]

Sara Orwig lives in Oklahoma. She has a patient husband who will take her on research trips anywhere from big cities to old forts. She is an avid collector of Western history books. With a master's degree in English, Sara has written historical romance, mainstream fiction and contemporary romance. Books are beloved treasures that take Sara to magical worlds, and she loves both reading and writing them.

To David, Susan, Jim, Hannah, Ellen,
Rachel, Dixie, Joe, Kristine, Cameron, Anne, Brian,
Colin, Elisabeth, Myles. With many thanks to Maureen.

One

Unless the event had been an act of God, when was the last time a life-changing decision had been taken out of his control? Not for years. And he intended to keep it that way.

Beneath darkening skies in the early October afternoon Jake Benton drove from the private airstrip toward his ranch. From the moment he had left Dallas for the weekend, he had been happy to put distance between himself and his father, who still meddled in his life. They had once fought over which university Jake would attend; later whether he would work in the family business or not. That had brought the first threat to disinherit him. Now when his dad threatened to disinherit Jake, it was over bigger and more important things. Like the most recent demand to get married within the year.

Jake shoved thoughts about his quarrel with his father out of mind. He was on his way to his sprawling West Texas ranch, a retreat where he could get away to relax. The only people for miles were ones who worked for him and his brother. As always when he returned to the ranch, he wondered why he didn't come more often.

He couldn't escape the phone or demands of business, but he could cut back on them.

Jake felt himself relax as the family ranch home that was now his, with its guesthouses, bunkhouse, staff homes, outbuildings, barns, shop, gym and various other structures, appeared in the distance. Irrigated, landscaped yards with beds of brightly colored fall blooms surrounded each house. Jake took in the view, his pleasure over being at the ranch increasing. While clouds hid the sun and thunder rumbled closer at hand, the road divided. Jake took the curve leading to his house. As he turned the corner and drove to the side of the house, he saw someone on his porch. Startled, he stared in surprise. He had a fence and security at the gate leading from the highway. In all the years he had never had any uninvited visitors—until now.

His first reaction was annoyance that someone had breached his privacy and trespassed. Curiosity replaced aggravation. His trespasser, from a distance, looked like a woman. The closer he approached, the more he could see that she was good-looking.

As he pulled to a stop only yards from his house, his gaze raked over her. She stood, walked to the steps and halted to watch him.

Auburn hair piled on her head framed an oval face with prominent cheekbones. Her long legs, encased in pale, slim jeans above Western boots caught his attention. A short leather jacket was cut high, revealing her tiny waist. He was close enough now to experience a skip in his heartbeat.

His last shred of animosity vanished. Searching his memory for a clue to her identity or reason for her on his porch, he remained at a loss. He couldn't imagine why she was waiting for him or how she had known he was coming. Intrigued, determined to get answers, he stepped out of the car.

As his gaze locked with hers, he was startled by a sizzling current of attraction. The chemistry was instant, hot and inviting.

Whatever she was up to, she was audacious. As he approached her, he felt a defiance coming from her that puzzled him.

"Welcome home, Jake," she said in a mellow, quiet voice. In spite of the polite greeting, his sense of a silent challenge increased.

With his gaze still fastened on hers, he climbed the porch steps until he reached the top. Standing only inches from her, he had intended to intimidate her. Instead, he felt ensnared in huge, crystal-green eyes fringed with sweeping auburn lashes. She was gorgeous and he couldn't pull his gaze away.

"I don't often get surprised, but I am now," he admitted. "How'd you get past my security at the gate?"

When a faint smile lifted the corner of her mouth, his attention shifted lower to her full lips. Her mouth made him wonder how it would be to kiss her. Taking a deep breath, he tried to get his thoughts back to his question.

"You don't know me, do you?" she asked.

"No," he admitted. Even more disturbing, she thought he should know her. He never could have gone out with her without remembering. A woman with fabulous looks was not to be forgotten. "You have the advantage. I suspect I should know you. One thing, we've never gone out together," he said, voicing aloud his thoughts.

Another faint smile tugged at her mouth. "No, we haven't," she said patiently. "And to answer your question, I didn't pass your security checkpoint. I came across your ranch from the west."

"There's no gate or road from the west," he said, glancing

beyond her at the land that vanished in a long grove of thick oaks he'd had planted as a windbreak. He could picture beyond the oaks, the flat, mesquite-covered land extending miles to his western boundary. "If you forded the river, it must be mostly dried up now, but rain is threatening," he said, taking a deep breath and smelling the rain that approached. "If you have a vehicle parked in the woods, I better let my foreman know before he calls the sheriff. You're trespassing, which could cause you trouble. I can call the sheriff to have you arrested. I have signs posted."

"This is a desperate effort to talk to you. I haven't been able to get past the secretaries and your attorneys."

His curiosity returned. With an effort he stopped staring at her, focusing instead on who she was. For all he knew, she could be a threat, although at the moment, he would relish a physical struggle with her because he would like to touch her.

An intriguing scent tempted him.

"All right, you want to talk. We can sit here on the porch and have a discussion," he said, motioning toward chairs. He was reluctant to invite her into his house. It crossed his mind that she might be armed. "First though, I'll admit, I don't know who you are."

He received another flicker of amusement. "Caitlin Santerre."

The name was a knife stab. As if ice water had poured over him, he cooled toward her while he stared at her, reconciling his memory of Caitlin Santerre with the beautiful woman standing before him.

"Son-of-a-gun," he said beneath his breath, for once not hiding his reaction to a shock. "You grew up. What the hell do you want with me?"

"You actually don't even know, do you?" she asked, anger

creeping into her tone. "You own our land. I want to buy part of it back."

"You get to the point. Yes, I own it. It's my land since your brother sold it. I was surprised he was willing to sell it to me."

"Will loves money more than maintaining an old family feud, remaining loyal to the family and keeping the home place. All Will wants is to take care of Will," she said.

"I have to agree, but I'm biased. You should have told him to not sell," Jake said, trying to remember the age difference. He had never paid attention to her as a child when he saw her in town. She had seemed years younger and he hadn't given her a thought then or since.

"My brother and I aren't close. We never have been."

"That I can understand," Jake said, a cynical note creeping into his voice when he thought about Will Santerre whom he despised. The litany ran through his thoughts—the first Benton to settle in Texas in the mid-1800s, killing the first Santerre who was trying to divert water. The retaliations followed, which included killing cattle, poisoning water. In the next generation a Santerre son burned the Benton house and barn. The feud continued until his father put Caitlin's father in the hospital after a fistfight. Finally, his generation with the ultimate and most personal clash, made Jake feel the old hurts like a scar. He would always be certain Will Santerre had killed his older sister, Brittany. Will was tried and found not guilty. Will had sworn it was Brittany who caused the car crash, but Jake would never be convinced. His family was guilty of doing things to the Santerres, but his family had always felt justified. While Jake had hated it, Brittany had been in love with Will. Brittany had been Football Queen, Class President, beautiful, popular—Will loved the girls and went after her. Maybe out of both revenge and really wanting her. Maybe just because he had thought she would be a conquest that would make him look good. Jake could never believe anyone as selfish as Will could love another person. As far as he was concerned, Will loved himself more than anybody else. Jake looked at Caitlin. Her beauty now was tempered by the knowledge of her lineage.

The first huge drops of rain fell, slanting to hit along the edge of the porch. "This rain was a twenty-percent chance—most unlikely from the morning weather report. I'll make this short," she said.

"Let me call my foreman about your vehicle—what did you drive?"

She flashed a smile that made Jake forget his hostility again. Her white teeth were even and her smile was a warm invitation as if she were on the verge of sharing a delightful secret. "There's no vehicle. And there's no road," she answered, jerking her head toward the trees. "I came from the west on horseback. He jumped your fence. You might want to tell your foreman I have a tethered horse. I would appreciate getting my horse out of the weather."

"Ah, now I know why no one spotted you. I have men who drive the boundaries, but they can't cover this big ranch all the time. The likelihood of anyone coming across the ranch from any direction other than the highway is minimal to nonexistent. I'm not here most of the time, keep a low profile when I am home, and it's peaceful out here. I don't have enemies—or at least not many," he said, thinking of his former neighbors. Jake glanced at the trees again. "I'll tell someone to bring your horse in so it's sheltered."

"Thanks."

As Jake made his call, more drops fell. He put away his phone. "My foreman will put your horse in the stable closest to the house."

"Thanks."

"This may only be a fall shower. Let's go inside where we

can talk in more comfortable surroundings," Jake suggested, intrigued by her in spite of his burning hatred of her half brother. "Since our grandfathers' days, we haven't had to worry much about trespassers."

"I guess our fathers were less into tearing down fences and stealing livestock from each other than the generations before them. The feud between our families began with the first two men who settled here."

"It may be less violent, but it hasn't ever ended," Jake said, thinking again of Will.

"Where is Will now?"

"He won't ever be back. He's bought a home in San Francisco and also owns a home in Paris. He's into investments. Beyond that, I know little about him. We have virtually no contact."

Knowing they were getting on a bad topic, Jake held the door for her. "This is a turn in the feud—you're the first Santerre to be invited in."

She barely looked at her surroundings as they walked down the wide hall. "So this is where you grew up."

"Yes. The original part of this house is as old as the house where you grew up. I know your dad's house was built later."

"My dad's house no longer exists," she said sharply. "Your crew began demolition last week. It doesn't take long to destroy a structure. Fortunately, Grandmother's house is the one that dates back to the beginning."

Holding back a retort, Jake directed her into a room. "Let's sit in the study," he said.

They entered one of Jake's favorite places, spacious with floor-to-ceiling bookshelves on two walls while the remaining walls were glass. French doors opened onto the wraparound porch and patio, which had been remodeled with an extended roof and comfortable living areas. Beyond the patio, steps led down to a pool with a waterfall, a cabana, chairs and chaise longues. Tropical plants added an appealing touch.

"Have a seat," Jake said. He turned as she sat in a leather wingback chair. In a sweeping glance he took in her blue Western shirt that clung to lush curves and tucked into her snug jeans. Her belt circled a waist that was as small as he had guessed at his first glimpse. The little Santerre kid he had always ignored had turned into a stunning woman. He sat in another leather chair that faced her across a low mahogany table.

She crossed her long legs and he wondered how she would look in a dress. The image made his blood heat. She looked poised, comfortable, unlike someone desperate to get him to agree to something. She also looked desirable. Even though she was a Santerre, there was a red-hot chemistry about her that tempted him to forget who she was.

When he looked up from her legs, his eyes met hers and he was again ensnared. Attraction was tangible. She had to feel it because she held his gaze as invisible sparks heated him. He wanted to know her better. At the same time, the lifelong hatred of all Santerres coated the magnetism with bitterness. Caitlin was as forbidden as poison, yet he wanted to place his lips on her to taste and kiss.

Taking a deep breath he tore his gaze away to return his attention with more composure.

"Have you been waiting long?" he asked. "I took my time flying in here this morning."

"I was willing to wait," she said.

"How'd you know I was coming today?"

Amusement flashed in her expressive eyes. "I've hired a private detective to learn your whereabouts so I could find an opportunity to talk to you. You rarely have a bodyguard with you."

"You're taking a chance because you know I can have you arrested."

"It would be a little more difficult to consider me a trespasser now that you've invited me into your house."

"So you want to buy back part of your ranch. Why didn't you discuss this with your brother?"

"My half brother never gave me the opportunity. It's general knowledge in these parts that traditionally in the Santerre family, the oldest son inherits the ranch. They are raised to protect the ranch, maintain it, keep it in the family. Well, all of that instruction didn't take with Will. He does as he pleases and he has no interest in cowboys, the country or ranch life."

"He told me he didn't," Jake said, thinking about the closing that he hadn't planned to attend and then did just to face Will when he bought out the Santerres. In spite of Will being happy over the sale, the buyout had been sweet revenge—a goal through generations of Bentons to see the last of the Santerres in the area. Jake's attorneys had already informed him that Caitlin wasn't included in the ranch inheritance. Also, she hadn't lived at the ranch since she had graduated from college. He still had thought of her as a child, so he had dismissed her from mind.

"Why didn't Will sell part of the ranch to you since you want it badly?"

"He didn't bother to contact me, either about selling or to ask if I wanted to buy any part of it. Will and I aren't close. He cares only about himself."

"I'd agree with that," Jake stated, remembering the antagonism he had felt toward Will at the closing. Each time he had looked into Will's hazel eyes, he could see loathing mirrored there.

"If it were left up to Will," Caitlin continued, "I would be excluded from the family. Our father felt the same."

"If I remember correctly, your grandmother raised you. She was a Santerre, actually, your father's mother."

"Yes, but unlike him in so many ways. I loved her deeply and she was good to me. Because of her, I'm recognized as a Santerre by everyone except Will."

Jake recalled lots of gossip regarding the Santerre family history—how Caitlin's mother had been a maid for the Santerres, the brief affair...and the resulting baby. And how the baby had been unacknowledged and cut off by Titus Santerre, yet adopted and raised by her paternal grandmother. How Titus Santerre had remained married to Will's mother until her death and did not remarry.

"Why do you want to buy any of the ranch back?" he asked. "You don't live here any longer and you're not a rancher." His gaze drifted over her thick auburn hair that was pinned loosely on her head with a few escaping strands. Looking silky, her hair was another temptation, making him think of running his fingers through the soft strands.

"I adored my grandmother and I loved growing up in her house. The people who worked for her closely were included in her will. Our foreman, Kirby Lenox, Altheda Perkins, who was our cook and now also cleans, and Cecilia Mayes, Grandmother's companion—they all stayed on. Kirby and two who work for him, still run the ranch. They care for the horses and the few cattle we have. Altheda maintains the house, cooking and overseeing the cleaning. Cecilia is elderly now. She devoted her life to Grandmother, first as her personal secretary and later as companion.

"I knew people were still staying there."

"As owner, you could have evicted them."

"I'm not in a rush. I figured they would leave before long. If they didn't, then I planned to tell them they had to go. It is my property."

"I love all of them because they were there when I grew

up. I wanted to keep the house, barn and animals for them as long as they live. I wanted to be able to return occasionally to the ranch house—just as you must do here."

Jake nodded. "Why didn't you tell Will?"

She looked away but he had seen the coldness in her expression that came with his question. "I did tell Will. He just laughed at me and reminded me that my father barely acknowledged my existence so I had no say in what he did with the ranch. He said he would tell me if it looked as if I could come up with more money to buy it and make a better offer than anyone else who bid on it. When the time came, he didn't. I knew nothing about the sale. He didn't legally have to notify me because I had no more part of ownership of the ranch than a stranger."

Jake felt no stir of sympathy for her. Even though she and Will were alienated, Jake couldn't forget that they were both Santerres. The same blood ran in her veins as in Will's.

"You know I can't work up much sympathy for a Santerre," Jake admitted, voicing his thoughts aloud. "Not even a beautiful one."

One dark eyebrow arched as she gave him a level look. "You're honest. I'm not asking you to like me or even see me again in your lifetime. I just want to buy the house and part of the land. Grandmother never owned it. There was a stipulation in my father's will assuring her she could live there the rest of her life and then it would belong to Will. All I want is a small part."

"What advantage for me would there be in doing any such thing?" he asked. "It would mean keeping a Santerre for a neighbor. You surely heard the family histories and know what kind of past we've had."

"Oh, I've heard," she replied lightly as if discussing the weather. "The first Benton killed the first Santerre over water. The river meanders and thus the argument continues about each family's rights and boundary. Our great-great-grandfathers were political opponents. Your family supposedly burned down our barn in the early days, rustled cattle, stole our horses. The list is long."

"You've left out the most recent episode that touched our lives, at least it affected mine. You may have been young enough to miss it. I'm thirty-four. You must be about twenty-two."

Her eyes danced with amusement. "You're a little off. If that were the case, when you were seventeen in high school, I would have been toddling off to kindergarten. No, I'm twenty-eight now."

Smiling, he shrugged. "You were a little kid. You might as well have been five when I was seventeen. I paid no attention to you at that age."

"Mmm, I'll have to remedy that. I have no intention of letting you continue to ignore me," she drawled, making his heart skip because she was flirting with him.

"Maybe I'll have to reassess my attitude toward Santerres," he said.

"You might be surprised by what you'd find," she rejoined, slanting him a coy smile that made his pulse jump.

"You should make me forget you're related to Will. As far as our family is concerned, Will caused my sister Brittany's death."

"When the District Attorney pressed charges and Will was brought to trial, he was found innocent. The car wreck was ruled an accident. Will has been cleared of that charge," Caitlin stated matter-of-factly.

"I'll never feel he was innocent," Jake replied. "Will testified that Brittany tried to run him off the road. But she was in love with him. Will is the one who ran her off the road."

"The jury found Will innocent. Will and I barely speak.

He'll probably cease to do so now that our father is gone. Although, my success in my profession has given Will a grudging mellowing toward me. Not enough to inform me of his decision to sell the ranch, much less of the agreement to sell it to you."

"Will is rotten," Jake said, thinking more about Caitlin's silky auburn hair and huge eyes, still amazed to learn her identity.

"Please think about this. I want to save the house and people's livelihoods that you'll take away. I love them and they're older now. I feel responsible for their well-being because they've devoted their lives to my grandmother and to me."

"Noble, but they also got paid to do so and probably a damned good salary."

"Sure, but it went beyond that. That house holds happy memories. Please rethink my request to buy before you answer hastily."

He smiled at her as he sat in silence and studied her. "All right, I'll think about it, but I doubt if I'll change my mind."

"If so, your decision has to be spite." Her expression didn't change. Green eyes observed him coolly. "You have one of the largest ranches in the state as it is and now you've bought up neighboring ranches as well as ours. I urge you to have an open mind when you give this thought."

"It isn't spite. At least not toward you. It's vengeful where Will is concerned. I was delighted to buy him out. Even happier to tear down Will's home place, turning it into rubble that will be cleared. Eventually, in its place will be mesquite, cactus and bare ground."

Lightning crackled and popped while thunder made the windows rattle. Rain began to drum against the house.

Jake's mind raced as his gaze roamed over her again. Her beauty pulled on his senses and there was an unmistakable physical attraction, but he didn't care to pursue it. She was a Santerre and he wasn't selling land back to her. She should have talked to Will immediately after their father's death about her wishes to keep their grandmother's property. He glanced beyond her through the French doors at the downpour, listening to the loud hiss of rain.

He glanced at his watch; it was almost six o'clock. He wanted her to stay for dinner when common sense said to get rid of her. Tell her no, get her out of his life and keep the property. She would give up and go on with her life if she learned there was no hope of regaining her childhood home.

But, traitorous or not, he was enjoying the sight of her too much. "You might as well stay for dinner. You can't ride home in this and I don't care to get out in it right now. It's a gully washer and you know as well as I do how fast creeks and streams here will flood, so just stay. I can take you home later and you can get your horse when it's convenient."

She gave him another of her long, assessing looks and he couldn't guess what ran through her thoughts. "Very well, thank you."

He nodded. "This place is stocked. All the staff is gone, Their work is minimal since I'm here so little. I give them notice when I want them. My cook lives here on the ranch, and the other house staff live in town. Since you're here, I'll ask Fred to come in the morning. He lives on the ranch, so it's easy for him to do so. Dinner will be what I can rustle up."

"That's fine. You can keep it simple."

"Want a drink? Wine, soft drink, mixed drink, beer?"

"A glass of water would be great," she said.

"Let's go to the family room. It's more comfortable."

"Fine, lead the way," she said, standing in a fluid motion.

She was tall, although a good six inches shorter than he was. They walked into an adjoining room twice the size of the study with windows and French doors with another, more panoramic view of the storm. French doors also opened onto the porch and the covered patio. She crossed to the windows to look out while he built a fire in a stone fireplace. He went to the bar to get her water and get himself a cold beer.

"We can sit outside and watch the storm if you prefer, although it may be chilly. I can build a fire and I'll cook out there."

"I have a jacket."

"And I don't get cold," he said. They walked out to the patio with its comfortable furniture, stainless-steel equipment and a state-of-the-art cooker.

"Even though there are no walls, you have what amounts to another few rooms out here," she remarked, glancing around at a living area, a kitchen area and the cabana and pool.

"It's livable. A fire will make it more so." He built a fire in a fireplace and then sat facing her near the blazing orange flames.

Handing her drink to her, he brushed her hand lightly. The physical contact, while so slight, burned. Soft warm skin. A startling awareness increased his desire.

She smiled at him. "Thank you. We're having quite a storm. There won't be any going home the way I came. As you said, this kind of downpour gets the river spilling out of its banks."

She slanted him a look that was hot. He wondered if it was deliberate. Maybe he shouldn't be so hasty in getting rid of her after dinner.

While he had no intention of selling any part of the Santerre ranch back to her, how far would she go to try to convince him to do so?

"It's already dark out because of the storm," he said. "We have plenty of room," he added in a husky voice. "You can stay all night."

Two

"A Santerre staying overnight with a Benton. It's a shocking invitation that would turn our relatives topsy-turvy if they had known."

"Scared to stay with a Benton?"

"Not remotely. I look forward to it," she said, smiling at him. "It's just that never in my wildest imaginings would I have guessed I would be here overnight. One Santerre is definitely shocked."

"This is a stormy night, so better to stay inside."

"Good. Staying longer will give me more time to try to talk you into selling. You don't live here year round, why would you want so much more land? I know you've bought the ranch to the east of this one in addition to buying ours."

"The first and foremost reason is oil," he answered. "My brother thinks there may be oil in this general area. You have to know that he's already drilling to the west of your grandmother's house."

"I see the activity with the trucks coming and going all hours. A rig is up now. From the upstairs floors we can see the work. They have fenced off the area so the cattle won't roam there. I don't think you'll find any oil. My dad went through this at one time."

"Gabe thinks there may be oil on your ranch, or on the old Patterson place. That's why I wanted the land to the east, partially why I wanted your home place. Mostly I wanted to buy out Will and see the last of the Santerres in Nealey County. The people who worked for your grandmother are not Santerres. They would eventually have to go, but I haven't been in a rush to run them off."

"I have never done anything to hurt you or your family," she stated quietly, but he saw the flare of fire in her eyes indicating animosity was not his alone.

"No, you haven't. Admit it, though, you don't like me or any other Benton."

She glanced away. "I was raised to feel that way. I'm sure both families are at fault." Her attention returned to him. "Your dislike hinges primarily on your sister and Will, even though Will was found innocent."

Jake hoped he hid the sudden clenching of his insides as the old anger stirred again. She had touched a nerve. "I'll always feel my sister's death was due to Will."

"Even though a jury found him innocent?" Caitlin asked. "From what Will said, your sister was the one at fault."

"My sister had the poor judgment to fall in love with your half brother," Jake said, thinking Caitlin should have left the topic alone because she stirred memories of the most abhorrent event in his life. It was the ultimate culmination of his hatred of Will. "Brittany didn't live to tell her side of the story."

"At the trial Will testified that they had a fight and she drove off in a rage. He said he was afraid she would have a wreck and he followed her. He tried to get in front of her car so he could slow her down. He testified that when he tried to pass her, she sideswiped his car. She lost control and crashed."

"I'll always think Will sideswiped her car. Will was the one who wanted her out of his life. She wanted him to marry her."

"That never came out in the trial, although it was common talk. Will admitted to Grandmother that Brittany wanted him to marry her."

"You know a lot about it."

"I was there, even if I was younger than you."

"She was pregnant with Will's baby," Jake said, feeling the dull hurt that came when he thought about Brittany's crash. "Brittany told me. She was in love with him, too. I'm convinced Will ran her off the road and she crashed," Jake said, hurt growing with each word. He hated having painful memories dredged up again.

Caitlin gasped. "I always figured talk of pregnancy was just a rumor. It was never brought up at the trial."

"My mother didn't know about it. My dad didn't want it brought out at the trial and your family sure as hell didn't," Jake said. "I will always blame Will. I don't believe he told the truth about that night, but no one will ever know because only two people were present. At the time of the trial, one of them was dead," Jake stated, bitterness filling him as he sank into dark memories of a painful time. "We better get off this subject if you want to have a civil conversation with me."

Jake gazed into fiery green eyes. Caitlin made no effort to hide her anger. He could feel the waves of antagonism that revealed her flirting was simply a means to try to get what she wanted from him.

"So that's why you hate Will so much," she said.

"Will and I have competed in school in sports and in the

classroom. I was captain of the football team when he wanted
to be. We both were on the baseball team. I had more home
runs than Will. He had more stolen bases. I was my class
president and the next year he was his class president. We
were both on the debate team. Will and I have had plenty
of our own battles. I never put Will in the hospital or vice
versa."

"You broke his nose. Actually, I wasn't too sorry when I
heard that. I thought a good punch was well deserved."

"It definitely was," he said lightly. "It was the loss of
Brittany that tops my list of complaints against Will. I loved
my sister and I hated to see her go out with Will. Brittany and
I fought constantly over that. When she could, she hid her
relationship with Will from our dad. I should have told him,
but I don't think it would have helped. She was eighteen, a
senior. Will was eighteen by then. I was still seventeen. She
would have done what she wanted. I don't think anyone could
have stopped her. Not even that fatal night."

"As a Benton, you'll always think Will was guilty."

"Yes. While you'll always think he's innocent. We're at
an impasse on the issue and it makes even a business deal
between us an emotional event that can't be looked at in a
purely impartial way."

"Will's no angel and we've never gotten along. Grandmother
sat him down and made him tell her what happened. He swore
that was the truth and I don't think even Will could have lied
to her. She could be a formidable woman. More intimidating
than my father."

Jake sipped his beer and listened to the rain, remembering
all the emotional upheaval of that time in their lives. He could
imagine easily Will Santerre lying to his grandmother. He
looked at Caitlin and saw a Santerre, Will's half sister. The
ultimate irony would be to seduce her.

He had no intention of selling one inch of the Santerre place back to her.

How valuable was the land to her? Was trying to obtain it worth the price of seduction?

"That's Will," Caitlin continued. "What he did has little to do with me other than the fact that the same blood runs in our veins. There is no love lost between the two of us, so do not lump me with him." The air was thick with hostility again. There was a fine line between them that kept them civil and caused her to flirt with him. He owned her family home and it was headed for destruction. In turn, he was beginning to want her in his bed. The more he was with her, the more he desired her.

She placed her palm on his cheek, startling him. "I told you. I'm going to make you see me as a woman and not as a Santerre."

"I do already," he answered in a husky voice, letting go thoughts about past history. Her hand was warm, soft against his cheek and he wanted her to keep it there. He longed to slip his arm around her waist and pull her into his embrace, to lean close to taste her lips.

Instead, when she sat back in her chair, he took her empty glass from her. "Want something stronger than water this time?"

"I'll have another glass of water," she said, smiling at him and getting up to follow him to the bar. She slid onto a high bar stool and watched as he filled another glass of water and sat on a bar stool facing her.

With their knees lightly touching, the temperature on the patio rose a notch in spite of the rain-chilled air.

"Now what can I do to get you to pay attention to me?" she asked.

He smiled. "You have my full attention right now," he said. "Should it wander, you'll figure out some way to capture my notice again. Some way as clever as getting into my house and spending the evening with me. You managed that easily."

"Right now we're captives of the storm. We both have to be here." She leaned forward, her face closer to his. "I don't know whether I can ever get you to see me apart from my family."

"I promise you," he replied in a huskier voice, "that I see you as Caitlin, a beautiful woman."

Something flickered in the depths of her eyes and she got a sensual, solemn expression that made his heartbeat race. As his gaze dropped to her mouth, his desire to kiss her grew. He wondered about her kiss, resolving to satisfy his curiosity before the night was out.

"Now we have the whole evening to get to know each other. Do you work, Caitlin?"

She nodded. "I'm a professional photographer."

"You must be good if you're earning a living at it."

Swirling her glass of water, she replied, "I freelance and I do earn a living at it."

One dark eyebrow arched. "Why do you want to stay out here when you have a busy life elsewhere in the world?"

"Same reason you're here, probably," she replied. "I can relax, get away from everything else and have solitude."

He sipped his drink and nodded. "You're right," he admitted. "This is an escape for me."

"What do you need to escape from? Business decisions? Women?"

He laughed. "Never women."

"You think about it—I'll make a nice neighbor and the old feud will die with us. I won't fight with you over the boundary, over water, never over the mineral rights, which I'm certain you won't sell back to me, but that's not my purpose here. I want to keep the home for all those people I told you about. Selfishly, also for my own memories and pleasure."

She sipped her water and turned to watch the rain that still came in torrents. "We're having a record breaker."

"Maybe it'll be a night to remember," he said softly. She gave him a sultry look. He wondered if she hadn't wanted the ranch from him if she would have been far less friendly. She had a convincing act to get what she wanted.

"It already has been," she replied. He took her chin in hand to hold her face so he could look into her eyes.

"Are you playing with me to get what you want, Caitlin?" he asked.

"Perhaps, but you're doing the same thing."

"I didn't come to the ranch wanting something from you."

"You do now," she replied, and his heart drummed. He wanted to close the last few inches between them to kiss her. As if she guessed his intent, with a deft move, she twisted away from his light grasp and sat back, smiling coyly at him.

"What would it hurt to sell a piece of the ranch back to me? You could still search for oil and reap the rewards if you find it. The little parcel you'd sell to me, you'd really never miss."

"You could turn right around and give it to Will. As a matter of fact, how do I know that he hasn't had a change of heart and sent you to buy a piece of the ranch back for him? If I sell to you, it's yours to do with as you see fit."

"You can write it in the contract. I'll swear in front of a judge if you want—I absolutely am not doing this for Will," she said and her expression frosted. "Will and I speak only when necessary. Our father barely recognized me. Will has snubbed me on the street in town before. There's no love lost between us."

"I'd think you'd be glad to be rid of the house and the land that belonged to your father and that Will inherited. That would be a constant reminder of your status in the family when you're here. And a reminder your grandmother couldn't own the house she lived in. The Santerres were not considerate of the women in the family."

"No. When I'm in the house where I grew up, my blood father and Will are an insignificant part of it. My father and Will were at her house for family get-togethers, rarely any other times. Grandmother couldn't own the land or the house, but she had other assets. She left Will a token $25,000, otherwise all her money, savings, stocks, bonds, went to me. One thing, Will had to mind Grandmother and he hated that. Will never took orders well from anyone except Grandmother and sometimes his father. Grandmother made him mind and it irritated him no end, but she was the one person on this earth Will truly feared. He feared and cooperated with his father just to the point to keep in his good graces. Will's mother spoiled him terribly. She may have contributed greatly to Will being the selfish, self-centered person he is."

"Did you ever go to your father's house?"

She shook her head and stood, watching the rain. "No, except for Christmases when I was young. Later my father and Will would travel to exotic places to celebrate. I think they were both frightened of Grandmother. They didn't mess with her. I haven't seen Will since my father's funeral. We talked on the phone after I learned about the sale of the ranch. That's how I know Will is living in California and Paris. I'm my father's daughter by blood only. Since I didn't grow up with him, he had little influence on my life. Grandmother raised me to think for myself and form my own opinions. I keep telling you, please don't categorize me with Will." Caitlin tilted her head, studying Jake.

"I haven't. I can keep you and Will separate in my mind." Jake reached out to touch a stray lock of her hair. "I have a suggestion. Let's set aside business so we can enjoy the next few hours. For a while, let's forget that I'm a Benton and you're a Santerre. We can get to know each other on another level that doesn't involve the past, but is the present. If we'd just met, we wouldn't be into all this family history. I think we'll have a better evening that we're compelled by rain to share."

She smiled. "You feel compelled to share this evening with me?"

"You've already said we're captive for tonight and I never said the time together was a bad thing. I'm just trying to make it better by removing some of the remnants of the family feud for a few hours. We can always return to swords' points."

She laughed softly. "Deal. At least we can try. We'll see how long it lasts."

"Excellent," he said, smiling at her. Again, there was a flicker in the depths of her eyes and his insides tightened. She was responsive to him, willing to flirt. She wanted to kiss, he was sure of it, but he was determined to wait until the right moment.

"So, Caitlin, tell me about professional photography. Do you have a studio somewhere?"

"Yes, I do in Houston as well as galleries in Houston and in Santa Fe. I have homes both places."

"Impressive."

She smiled as she peered over the edge of her drink at him. "You're not really impressed. I like my work. Actually, I love my work."

"And what kind of photography do you do?"

"Don't sound as if I'm playing marbles for a living," she said, her smile taking the bite out of her words. "I take pictures of people, families, children, celebs, pets. I specialize in black-and-white photography of people and children. I already know about you—the CEO of Benton Energy, Inc.

Your father is retired now and you run the company. Your brother Gabe is CEO of Benton Drilling."

"Right. Before hunger sets in, I'll fire up the grill for steaks. I'll put potatoes in to cook." He went to the refrigerator to remove the steaks and put them on the grill.

While he cooked, she helped him get salads and water on the table. When she was finished, she perched on the bar stool nearest him to talk to him. "This is a wonderful patio. You can sit outside, yet you're protected from the elements here."

"I enjoy it when I'm here," he said, glancing beyond the patio at the pool that was splashing as raindrops hit the blue surface. "No swimming in this weather." Lightning streaked the sky in a brilliant flash. "If the lightning worries you, we can go inside."

"I'm fine."

"So what does worry you, Caitlin?"

"Losing the property, not being able to help the people who worked for Grandmother through the years."

"I walked into that one."

"So what worries you, Jake?"

"Business failure. My dad's interference in my life."

"You're a little old for your daddy to interfere, especially since you're running a large company," she said and he detected the amusement in her voice.

"Oh, no. I have a manipulative father. At least he tries and I resist. It's not quite the same for my brother. Sometimes I think Brittany dated Will out of rebellion against Dad's constant attempt to dominate her life."

She laughed. "That's mind-boggling. You are definitely not the type to have someone try to control you."

He grinned, turning from the steaks to sit near her for a few minutes. "I like your smile, your laughter. When you laugh, it's a sunny spring day."

"Thank you. That's a nice compliment," she replied. "Too bad you're not Jake Smith and I'm not Caitlin Jones. The night might be incredibly different."

"For tonight, we can try to be Jake Smith and Caitlin Jones. We've already agreed to forget business. Just stretch it a little more and pretend we don't have family histories."

"That's a giant stretch with pitfalls all along the pathway, but it would have been nice," she added and sipped her water.

He leaned down so his face was closer to hers and her eyes widened. "Try. You have an imagination. See me as someone you just met," he urged, thinking she had the greenest eyes he had ever seen. Her perfume tormented him and her mouth was a constant temptation.

"While it's an exciting prospect, it's the way to disaster. Impossible," she answered breathlessly and he was certain she felt the attraction, too.

"Coward," he teased with a faint smile, wanting to lean the last few inches and kiss her. She tilted her face up another degree.

"Wicked man," she replied, smiling to make light of her words.

It would be so easy to close the mere inches of distance and kiss her and she wanted the kiss as much as he, but he resisted. He wanted her to be eager to kiss with no hesitation. The tantalizing moments were building his desire. Hopefully, hers, too.

"Your steaks may be crispy now," she remarked.

He hurried to flip the steaks. He turned, catching her studying him. "Now, wine with dinner?" he asked.

"Yes, thank you," she replied and he moved behind the bar to get a bottle of Shiraz.

In a short time they were seated near the fireplace with dinner in front of them. She was a dainty eater, telling him

about her gallery in Santa Fe while he mentally peeled away
the blue Western shirt. His appetite for steak diminished. To
his surprise, he wanted to see her again beyond tonight and
he wanted to take her dancing so he could hold her in his
arms.

Common sense told him to forget both things. As a
Santerre, when they got down to business, she was going
to be unhappy with him because he didn't want to leave a
Santerre house standing. The people who had worked for her
grandmother could retire or find other jobs, he was sure. He
would look into hiring them himself.

Out of sentiment Caitlin wanted the house she grew up in,
but she spent little time here. She could move everything out
of the house into another home elsewhere. He saw no valid
reason to sell the place back to her and several reasons to
turn her down. He didn't want Santerres left in the county.
He didn't want to have to worry about Caitlin and that old
house sitting in the center of his property, leaving part of the
property out of his control. If Gabe struck oil, it would be even
more important to own the land. While he had mineral rights,
he didn't want to have to drive around Caitlin's holdings.

Was he being uncooperative because she was a Santerre?
So what? It was his property, legally purchased and he
couldn't help if her half brother had not informed her about
the sale or her father hadn't included her in ownership. From
all he'd heard, her father never had involved her in anything
in his life. It was solely the grandmother who had adopted
Caitlin to give her a Santerre life.

"Your grandmother has been gone now—what—five
years?" Jake asked, trying to recall when he heard that
Madeline Santerre had passed away.

"Yes. You have an excellent memory because I know that
wasn't a date that meant anything to you," Caitlin replied,
looking away. "I loved her with all my heart," she added

quietly. Her emotional answer indicated she probably cared so much for the people who had worked for her grandmother because she didn't have anyone else. Her father and half brother had rejected her all her life. So had her birth mother in giving her up for adoption. "The minute Grandmother heard my mother planned to put me up for adoption, she stepped up and took me in."

"So where did you go to college, Caitlin?"

"To Texas University and then to Stanford. My degree is from Stanford. I had intended to go into law, but by my junior year I was earning a lot of money with photography, so I finished college and became a photographer. What about you, Jake?"

"Texas University, too, but years ahead of you. Then a master's in business from Harvard. Then back to work here. Pretty simple and predictable."

"Sure," she said, smiling at him. "You told me what you don't like, so what do you like, Jake?"

"Beautiful women, slow, hot kisses—"

She laughed, interrupting him. "That was not what I had in mind. Besides women, what do you like?"

He grinned. "Making money and doing business deals, watching the business grow, the usual. I swim, I play golf, play basketball with my friends, I ski, I like snow-covered mountains or tropical islands. I'm easy to please. Your turn."

"I'm even easier to please. I like a riveting book, quiet winter nights, getting just the right picture, little children—"

"That sounds like marriage is looming."

"Not at all. No man in my life, but I hope someday. Don't you want to marry someday?"

"Yes, but not this year," he said a little more forcefully than he had intended.

She laughed. "Okay, so you're not ready. I think I can make the same promise safely. I will not marry this year," she said, mimicking him and he had to smile and was relieved she made light of his comment.

The rain turned to a steady, moderate rain. Jake took her hand, aware of her smooth skin, the warmth and softness of her. "Let's go in where it's warmer. I'm glad we don't have to get out in this," he said.

She looked down at her clothes. "I just have what I'm wearing. If you can stand seeing me in the same thing in the morning, only more wrinkled, I'm happy to stay because water may be over some of the bridges, I'd guess."

"Great." He switched on lights in the living area. The fire had burned low and he added logs.

He put on music and took her hand, pulling her to her feet. "Come here, Caitlin, and let's dance," he said, drawing her to him on the polished oak floor in a space between area rugs.

She came into his arms easily, following his lead. He liked holding her, wanting her more with each hour that passed. Common sense still screamed to keep his distance to avoid entanglement of any kind with her, but it was a losing argument. It would be the ultimate irony to seduce Will's half sister, except Will wouldn't care because he obviously had no fondness or even polite consideration for Caitlin.

Jake tightened his arms around her and moved slowly with her. "This is good, Caitlin," he said quietly, more to himself than her.

"Not wise, but it's good," she added, indicating that she must hold the same view of getting acquainted that he had.

"So you like to dance."

"I love to dance and I'm glad you thought of this," she said softly. They moved quietly, conversation ceasing and he was sorry when the music came to an end.

She looked up at him. He held her lightly in his embrace and he felt as if he were tumbling down into a sea of green, falling headlong without any hope of stopping. He had waited long enough.

Three

Caitlin's heart drummed as she gazed into Jake Benton's eyes. Her afternoon had turned her world topsy-turvy. All her life she had been given reasons to dislike the Bentons. Her grandmother had hated Jake's father for things he had done to her son, Caitlin's father, in the years the men were growing up. They had been thrown together at school as well as in town. Grandmother had disliked Jake because of complaints about him from Will.

During the past month, Caitlin herself had developed hostility toward Jake, which had increased swiftly when she found a stone wall of interference keeping her from contacting him.

He was important, busy, an oil millionaire, but he should have had a streak of common courtesy to at least take a phone call from someone from the neighboring ranch. While the bitterness between the families could have made him unreceptive, she suspected he was never even told that she was trying to contact him.

Growing up, she had disliked the Bentons because she had been taught to. Jake's snubs had added fuel to the fires of contempt. The only way to get the property back from him was to communicate with him. When she had learned he was expected at the West Texas ranch, she had decided to confront him to force him to listen to her request.

He was being as stubborn as she had expected. What she hadn't anticipated was the scalding chemistry the moment they were face-to-face. It was an intense attraction he felt as much as she did. He also probably hated it as much as she did. Except he had seduction in his eyes. She could imagine how much it would amuse him to seduce a Santerre, even one on the fringe of the family. Titus Santerre's illegitimate child whom he only grudgingly acknowledged because his own mother adopted her.

The thoughts swirled briefly and then vanished. Caitlin's gaze locked with Jake's. His blue eyes held a blatant hunger. Her breathing altered while her temperature rose and her heart skipped. She tilted her face up, knowing she should step away and never kiss him, never open a Pandora's box of problems.

The instant attraction had mushroomed with each hour. A kiss might send it soaring out of control. She had no intention of repeating her mother's big mistake in life that had left Caitlin abandoned and hurt.

"Caitlin," Jake said in a quiet, husky voice that conveyed desire and was an invitation to her.

How could she have this intense sexy reaction to him? A man she had disliked her entire life even though she had never known him or talked to him before? *Get away from him,* an inner feeling urged. He was over six feet of danger to her peace of mind. A kiss would only make things worse. There was no way a kiss would have positive results.

"No," she whispered without moving an inch.

He slipped his hand behind her head, cupping her head lightly. "This is something we both want," he whispered, his gaze lowering to her mouth. "I have since we were standing on the porch this afternoon."

Her lips parted, tingled in anticipation. She was lost to his seductive ways and her own desire, the volatile chemistry between them, her own foolishness.

He leaned down, slowly, tantalizingly. His tongue stroked her lower lip and then he brushed her mouth with his own. Electricity streaked as swiftly as a bolt of lightning flashing outside. Her insides knotted while she slid an arm around his neck. She moved as if she were a puppet with someone else pulling the strings.

His arm tightened around her waist, drawing her more tightly against him.

His kiss scalded, teased. Lust burst in her, sending sparks through her being. She wanted him, needing to touch and kiss and make love. Yet the nagging knowledge that she was kissing a Benton persisted for minutes until his kiss demolished her concern.

Her sigh was consumed by his mouth over hers. When he leaned over her, she tightened her arm around his neck, her body molding to his long, hard strength. Her heart drummed as need built. She wanted him to keep kissing her, longed to run her hands over him.

Fireworks burst in her. His spectacular kisses thawed resistance, escalating her longing and response. She pressed against him to hold him tighter, kissing him with all her being, intending to make him melt and give in to her requests. Caution no longer existed.

His tongue stroked hers; she kissed him deeply in return,

slowly thrusting her tongue over his. The faint moans of pleasure were hers. Her hand went to his shirt to twist free top buttons and slip her fingers across his warm, muscled chest.

Running his hands through her hair, he sent pins tumbling and auburn locks falling.

Hot, low inside her, need heightened. She craved him with a hunger that built with each kiss.

Jake's hand slipped down her back to her waist, sliding lightly over her bottom.

His breathing was as ragged as hers and beneath her hand his heartbeat raced. Caressing her nape, he trailed his fingers to her throat, drifting lower lightly down over her breast to her waist.

As he caressed her, the tingling electricity finally sent a warning that broke through her stormy senses. Moving mechanically, she stepped back a fraction to stop their kisses.

"Jake, wait. This is getting out of hand. I never intended this to happen and neither did you."

He framed her face with his hands. "You never expected it to happen when you came to my place. From the moment we faced each other on the porch, we both wanted to kiss. It was inevitable. I still desire you and you still want me to kiss you because it shows in your expression."

With his words her heart raced faster. He was right and it was obvious, but that didn't make it acceptable. He had nothing to lose. She definitely did.

"Okay, so it shows. Common sense tells me to stop. You and I aren't friends. That's a prerequisite to me for someone to be a lover. An extremely close friend."

Her heart raced as she talked and her gaze was held by his that conveyed his desire. She wanted to lean the last few inches and return to his steamy kisses. He was on target totally, but she had some resistance. Reminding herself of her mission and that he was a Benton, she moved away. "I think we should stop dancing and go back to conversation," she said, heading toward a sofa. She turned to glance at him.

He stood watching her. Locks of his brown hair had fallen across his forehead. His tight jeans revealed his desire that hadn't diminished. Even with distance between them, his expression held lust. His gaze roamed slowly over her and his perusal might as well have been a caress.

Tingling, her body sent entirely different signals from what her logic conveyed. Without taking his gaze from hers, he crossed the room to her. Each step closer made her heart flutter faster. He walked up to her, wrapping his arms around her, bending to kiss her. It was a demanding, possessive kiss that seared and made her weak in the knees.

His hand locked behind her head, his fingers tangling in her hair while he kissed her and shattered her resistance. She pressed against him, losing the battle willingly, pouring kisses back while she clung to him with her arm around his neck. Her other hand roamed down his back and then across the strong column of his neck. Her fingers combed through his short, thick hair. She was never going to forget Jake's kisses. The fleeting thought was as unwanted as his kisses *should* have been.

Why did he have such a devastating effect?

She didn't care why or how threatening they were. His kisses made her want more of him, made her respond and moan with pleasure. Kisses that locked in memory as they awakened needs long dormant, exploded longing and imagination.

When his hands began to free the buttons of her shirt, she gathered her wits to take another stand.

"Jake, stop now. I have to." She gasped for air, looking up

at him, fighting the temptation to rake her fingers through his unruly locks to comb them off his forehead.

Giving her a searching look, he released her. "Want a glass of water or anything to drink?" he asked suddenly. When she declined, he turned and left the room.

She didn't know if he had to put distance between them to help them both cool or just wanted a drink. Whatever the reason, she welcomed his absence and was grateful he had left her. While her heart raced, her breathing sounded as if she had just run a race.

Why, oh, why had she found this excitement and magnetism with Jake Benton—literally the worst person she could think of to feel drawn to.

On the other hand, she should seize the moment, take advantage of the heat between them—as he would—and try to win his cooperation about selling to her.

She glanced at the rain that was coming down harder again. She was in for hours more with Jake and she intended to make the most of them without yielding to his seductive lovemaking.

She sat on the sofa, still conscious of the slight brush of their fingers as he joined her to sit near her.

"When do we return to business?" she asked.

"How about next week when I've had time to think about this? You've known you want to buy back the property, but this is all new to me since late afternoon."

"Why do I suspect you're stalling, although I don't know why you would. Maybe the prospect of seduction tonight is keeping you from flinging a refusal at me."

One corner of his mouth lifted slightly. "That's a sufficient enough reason," he said, turning to look into her eyes. Tingling again, she drew a deep breath.

"I don't know why I have this reaction to you," she admitted.

One dark eyebrow arched. "Man, beautiful woman, there it is," he said. "Elemental."

"Not even remotely elemental," she replied. "I hate to admit to you, few men have the effect you've had."

Something flickered in the depths of his eyes and his chest expanded as he drew a deep breath.

"Oh, my, I shouldn't have divulged that to you," she said, her pulse drumming again.

"No, you shouldn't have if you want me to keep my distance. Remarks like that—there's no way in hell I can sit back and say, 'How nice.'" He moved closer. His arm went around her waist and he lifted her to his lap.

Her instant protest ended as his mouth met hers and they kissed again. Her heart pounded while she clung to him, kissing him hungrily. He cradled her against his shoulder, kissing her while his free hand ran over her hip and along her thigh, sliding up to her breast to stroke in slow circles that taunted even through her lacy bra and cotton shirt.

Fiery tingles radiated from his touch. She should have left well enough alone, but the thought was dim and slid away. Desire surged in a scalding heat running in her veins.

His hand slipped down over her stomach, inching lower between her thighs. Even through her heavy jeans, she could feel his touch as if it were fire.

With an effort she sat up. While she gasped for breath, she gripped his wrist to hold his free hand. "You stop. I shouldn't have told you what I did. We've gone too far too fast."

"Not at all," he argued in a husky, gravelly tone.

She slipped off his lap to the other end of the sofa where she turned to face him. His hooded gaze indicated he still wanted her.

"We should get on some safe topic. Tell me about your hobbies. Your brother and your parents. Your controlling father that meddles in your life."

"My father is the last thing I want to discuss or even think about tonight. I've been enjoying the evening beyond the obvious frustrations. I do not need to drag anger back into my life." He stood. "I'm getting a beer. Want something else? Soft drink? How about homemade lemonade? Juice, milk, wine, martini, any mixed drink—whatever you like?"

"I'll have that lemonade, please, which sounds absolutely wonderful."

"I won't tell you what sounds absolutely wonderful to me," he said, his suggestive drawl conveying a double entendre that was as sizzling as his touch.

"Stop that, Jake. No flirting, no more remarks that are personal."

"Aw, shucks," he drawled, making her chuckle. "Where's the fun in that?"

"Humor me. I caused the last crisis, but we can avoid future ones."

"If my kisses are a 'crisis,' then I have no intentions of avoiding flirting with you."

"Go get the beer and lemonade," she said quietly, wanting to end the volatile conversation that could put them back in each other's arms easily.

She watched him walk away, a masculine stride that was purposeful, hinting of the excellent physical condition he must be in.

Her thoughts were filled with guilt. Why, oh, why had she flirted with him so openly when she had known what the consequences would be?

She couldn't understand her reaction to him, couldn't explain it. It didn't happen with other men, but that definitely did not make Jake "Mr. Right." He was Mr. Wrong in so many ways.

She thought about her grandmother who would be shaking her head and frowning at the idea of spending an evening in the company of a Benton. She never could have explained a relationship with a Benton to her grandmother. Grandmother had been furious with Will for going out with Brittany Benton.

If Will knew she was with Jake tonight, he would be disgusted because of the lifelong competition between the two in school and sports. Then again, perhaps he would shrug it off that she was spending time with Jake because Will also held a low opinion of her, as well. She thought Will had been dazzled by Brittany at first. She also suspected he liked sneaking around, getting away with something that would annoy both families because it stirred talk and envy among his peers.

Jake returned with a cold bottle of beer for himself and a tall, frosty glass of lemonade for her, placing the drinks on a table in front of the sofa.

Only a few feet away, he sat, facing her, and taking a drink of beer.

"The lemonade is delicious."

"I can't take credit. I have a cook."

"Does your cook live in town?"

"Nope. His wife cooks for the men on the ranch and they live in a house here on the ranch. Our foreman also has a house of his own. We've got a big complex with several homes."

"I noticed when I came in."

"I meant it when I said you could have been arrested for trespassing if you had been caught."

"I figured since I obviously wasn't coming to steal livestock and I'm a woman, they would give me time to explain what I was doing and at worst, run me off your property. I really didn't expect to get arrested. Besides, the sheriff is a cousin of my foreman."

Jake smiled. "You're probably right then. It's a long ride by horseback."

"Whatever it takes to talk to the untouchable Benton."

"Definitely never untouchable to you. I'll be happy to convince you just how 'touchable' I am," he teased.

"Don't you dare," she answered, smiling at him. He caught a lock of her hair, twisting it in his fingers and causing slight tugs on her scalp that were as noticeable as every other physical contact.

"So, Caitlin, what do you want in your future?" Jake asked.

"To continue my photography. To marry and have a family."

"What happens to the photography when you marry and have a family?"

"I'll juggle them the way others do. I have leeway to set my own hours for a lot of my work. What's your future, Jake? No marriage, no family, continue to make money."

"Right. No change, really."

"You've grown up in basically the same surroundings I have, yet our families have been totally different. You have a controlling father and siblings. My father didn't want to acknowledge my existence and my grandmother raised me. I have a half brother, but I might as well be an only child, because Will cared nothing for me."

"That must have hurt."

She gazed into blue eyes that hid his feelings. He looked as impassive as if talking about the weather. "I was adopted when I was only weeks old, so I have had my grandmother all my life and she showered love on me. I was happy with her and loved her totally. It hurt to be snubbed and rejected, but not deeply. I don't feel scarred from it. I just don't want it to happen again to a child of mine," she said, facing Jake and getting a strange feeling inside. Seduction could lead to an unexpected pregnancy, a baby born out of wedlock, just as she had been. She didn't want that to happen to a child of hers and the one way to ensure it didn't, was to stay out of any man's bed.

"So seduction is out of the question tonight," Jake remarked lightly as if teasing her, but she was certain the remark was made in earnest.

"Most definitely," she answered quickly. How easily she answered, yet how difficult it was to stick by her resolution.

They sat and talked with Jake touching locks of her hair or her shoulder or lightly caressing her nape. Casual touches that she didn't care to draw attention to, yet they were fanning flames. Finally, she stood. "Jake, it's late. I should turn in."

"Sure, I'll show you a guest bedroom."

When she walked with him down a long hall, he pointed out different rooms. She stopped to look at an enormous dining room with a table that would seat thirty, a cathedral ceiling and a stone fireplace. "Do you ever have this many guests to fill this table?"

"Yes. Parties. There are times I have a lot of company out here. Gabe and I will have things together. There are family parties, too."

"Do your parents spend much time here?"

"Nope. Dad has a ranch in the Hill Country where the area is green and scenic. This place was our family ranch, but Dad deeded it to me and gave Gabe another one he owned."

She nodded. "How nice. A father who passes things on to more than the oldest child. Of course, mine wouldn't have passed anything on to me if I had been the oldest child. I told you, I never dreamed Will would sell the place. Neither did our father who would have put binding stipulations on Will had he known. I'm sure he assumed Will would always live there. He left money to me, but nothing else. No part of the ranch."

"I'll have to admit, I'm glad Will sold out. Our family has wanted that ranch for generations. The sale has brought you into my life, which is a bonus."

They strolled down the wide hall again until he turned into a suite. "These are my rooms. You'll be nearby, but I wanted you to see where I am." She looked at the living area that held a desk, an entertainment center, comfortable sofas and chairs, a wall of bookshelves. On a nearby table she noticed a picture of a beautiful brown-haired woman standing beside a horse.

"That's my sister," he said quietly. "We were close."

Caitlin moved closer to study the picture. "She's beautiful." She understood why Will had gotten involved with her. "She's really gorgeous," she said, thinking she was the feminine version of Jake with blue eyes and brown hair. Caitlin had known about Brittany Benton and Will because sometimes Will had made her cover for him when he had slipped away from family gatherings, and she could remember Brittany as one of the most beautiful girls she had known. Caitlin was aware that Will had been happy and seemingly in love with Brittany at first. She never thought Will concerned himself with the old feud or did anything with Brittany out of revenge. Caitlin was certain that Will did exactly what he wanted to do and family history never mattered to him. Since she had to occasionally be ready to cover for him with the family, she knew when he had been out with Brittany.

Brittany had always been nice to her, and Caitlin had wondered how Will could hold the interest of someone so beautiful and so friendly. Except Will could be charming when he wanted to be. He was with his friends. At first, Will had been wildly happy about dating Brittany. The little Caitlin had seen him, it still was obvious how happy he was. Probably, he had been happy until Brittany had made demands on him. Caitlin could imagine Will carelessly getting Brittany pregnant and then wanting no part of taking any responsibility.

Being with Jake had brought back memories of that time as well as the questions about what had really happened.

Had Will really been driving the car that killed Brittany Benton? If Brittany had been pregnant, Caitlin could see Will becoming desperate to avoid an obligation and the wrath of their father. Deep down, perhaps Grandmother had suspected Will had been responsible, but she always tried to hold the family together. They would never have an answer because the only living person who knew was Will, but Caitlin could imagine him going to any length to live life the way he wanted.

Caitlin's grandmother had always wondered even though she only said it aloud once. They had been talking about the trial late at night and Grandmother had gazed out the window into the dark night. "Will is focused on himself," she had said. "He might be capable of wrecking Brittany Benton's car to get her out of his life." Caitlin had listened in shocked silence. After a few minutes, Grandmother had turned back to look at Caitlin. "This family will stand by Will. He has to be proven innocent."

"I remember at Will's trial, Grandmother had gathered the family. We all had to go to support Will."

"Yeah, our family did the same to show support for Brittany even though she wasn't present," Jake said and his tone was cold.

"My dad always insisted that Will was innocent. We celebrated Will's being found innocent of all charges. That was the one time I recall when Will was nice to me the entire evening. It was one of the few times I can remember seeing him at his best."

"Sorry. I can't agree."

Was Jake trying to get revenge by buying the place and tearing down all the structures, destroying everything owned by the Santerres that he could?

Her grandmother would be shocked, certainly annoyed that Caitlin was here, planning to spend the night with a Benton. Not as annoyed as the men in the family. Will hated Jake and Jake indicated the dislike was mutual. She had heard all about Brittany Benton and Will, whispers from Ginny McCorkin, her best friend, as well as her grandmother's side of the story. Rumors were that Will had gotten Brittany pregnant and refused to marry her. Grandmother had been furious with Will, but she seldom saw Will once he was a teen. Caitlin always figured Brittany was pregnant because of carelessness on Will's part. Will was too selfish to worry about someone else, even when he thought he was in love. Will wanted to stop seeing Brittany, difficult when she lived on the neighboring ranch and didn't want to stop seeing him. Then the fatal night when Will and Brittany had fought when she had died in the car wreck.

Both sides had a battery of lawyers, the Santerres' from Chicago, the Bentons' attorneys from Los Angeles. Will was found innocent and released, all charges dropped, but the hatred between the two families had grown stronger and the animosity between Will and Jake had become worse than ever.

She recalled the trial. Grandmother Santerre had insisted the entire family attend to show support for eighteen-year-old Will. The Bentons had turned out, too, all of them looking solemn and angry. Seventeen-year-old Jake and his brother, his mother and father. Will's mother had still been alive then. She had attended with Titus. Caitlin had been there with Grandmother. They had cousins from Dallas and an aunt and uncle who had come to show support for Will. It had been a solemn time. Caitlin could recall feeling sorry for Brittany and for the mess Will had created. Deep down, Caitlin suspected the Bentons had the true story. Will had a cruel streak and he was a wild driver. Before the fatal accident, when Will had wrecked cars, she had heard her grandmother arguing with her father about covering for Will and buying him new cars without involving the insurance company. It was always difficult for Caitlin to think that Will was any blood relation to Grandmother Santerre who was kind, loving and caring.

That weekend after the trial Will had gone out to celebrate. She'd heard he had had a big fight with Jake Benton. She never heard who won, but assumed Will because she suspected he was meaner and he was a year older and bigger, but she'd heard stories about Jake Benton, too, and wondered if he had held his own with Will.

Caitlin closed her eyes for a moment to clear her thoughts, then glanced around the room again. "You have everything you want here," she said, hoping to change the subject.

"Yes, I do. It's comfortable and I come here to relax and get away from the regular work and office. This is my first love."

"Then why don't you ranch? You don't have to work like crazy."

He shrugged. "Yes, I do. I want to make money. I want total independence from my dad and there are accomplishments in the business world that will help me get what I want to stay totally independent."

"Like making more money, owning more property, building a bigger company and a few other things along the same lines," she said.

"Right. Let me show you where my bedroom is," he said, taking her arm. She stood, resisting him slightly.

"I think I can find your bedroom, should I need to. If the house catches on fire, I'd guess you have an alarm system."

He grinned. "You can't blame me for trying to get you into my bedroom. I'd like to remember you in there in my arms."

"It's not going to happen. Not tonight at any rate," she added.

"Very well, I'll show you to your room next. Wait a minute."

He left and disappeared into an adjoining room to return with folded clothes and a robe on a hanger. "You can have these tonight."

"Thanks. Some of that is still in a package," she said.

"I keep extras. I told you, I have a lot of company here off and on. By the way, I have motion sensors and alarms that I turn on in the evening. Don't go beyond the end of the hall without letting me know."

"I won't."

He led her to another suite near his. "How's this?"

"Lovely," she said, looking at a cheerful suite with white furniture and brightly covered floral patterns in the chairs, splashes of yellow and green in the decor. "Thanks for the shelter from the storm," she said.

He stepped closer and slipped his arm around her waist. "One good-night kiss isn't the end of the world."

"It'll never stop with one," she whispered, standing on tiptoe as she wound her arm around his neck again. His mouth covered hers and she placed her other arm around his waist, holding him while she kissed him in return. The impact was stronger. Temptation grew, but she stopped him. "Jake, I'll see you in the morning."

He gave a hungry look before brushing a kiss on her cheek as he strolled out. She followed him, keeping a wide distance between them.

In the hall he turned. "I'm glad you came and we didn't just have this appointment at the office. It turned out better that I didn't know you wanted to talk to me."

"You didn't have the long ride from my ranch or try for over twenty calls to get through to you."

"Sorry," he said.

"You're not really. You'll continue keeping out unwanted visitors. See you in the morning, Jake. You can call me at seven o'clock. How's that time?"

"Perfect. Good night," he said and was gone, closing the door behind him.

She stood staring at the door. His presence was overwhelming and the day had been a surprise. She had never expected to find Jake Benton a man she would be attracted to. Would he talk reasonably next week or had he already made up his mind and was simply toying with her?

Would she see him again after his decision? She should complete their business and get out of his life. He would get out of hers soon enough.

As she remembered his kiss, her lips tingled. He had stirred a storm in her, something totally unexpected.

She ran her hand over the pile of clothing. The robe was dark blue velvet, soft and warm. She picked up a package wrapped in tissue with a seal and opened it to find new dark blue silk pajamas and slippers. There was a package with a small hairbrush and comb, new toothbrush in plastic, more toiletries in the plastic from a store.

Caitlin showered and dressed in the silk pajamas, relishing the smooth, soft material against her skin. She slipped into the robe, turned the television on low and curled up in bed to watch, but her thoughts drifted to Jake and she neither saw nor heard the program she had turned on.

She still marveled over the chemistry between them. How could it happen with Jake? It wasn't anything either of them wanted or did one thing to cause. Yet it existed, all right, as apparent as a Roman candle shot into the night sky.

She could only think he would entertain an offer from her to buy back part of the Santerre ranch. Caitlin expected him to make a profit, perhaps a huge one, but she didn't care what the purchase cost. She was well fixed financially, having inherited Grandmother Santerre's fortune, plus the money she made from her photography that was growing each year.

Unless he simply priced it out of the market to keep her from buying, she would pay an exorbitant fee if she had to in order to get the land back. It had been a final cruel snub by Will, selling the place without informing her. She didn't expect to have contact with him ever again.

Her thoughts shifted to Jake and the moment he had stepped out of his car and strolled to his porch, climbing the steps until he was on her level, to gaze into her eyes.

He was far more handsome than she had remembered, but she hadn't seen him for years and as a child, he had just been an older boy. Now he was an incredibly sexy, handsome, appealing man. She didn't want this dynamite reaction to a Benton. Even if none of the arguments and fights had anything to do personally with her.

When Jake had faced her on the porch, she had barely been able to get her breath. His blue-eyed gaze had been riveting. His smile was a flash of warm sunshine. But it was his kisses that took her breath and set her spinning. Kisses that burned and melted and made her want him desperately.

She wanted to be in his arms in his bed right now with Jake making love to her. It was insanity, a slippery slide to disaster. Never in her life did she want to take a chance on leading the life her mother had—rejection by the man she loved, an unplanned pregnancy, giving up her baby, humiliation and hurt. If Grandmother Santerre hadn't been there, Caitlin's life could have been frightful. She was thankful every day for the blessings she had.

Later, she tossed and turned and fell asleep still thinking about Jake and his hot kisses, knowing next week he had agreed to talk to her about buying back part of the ranch. Would he sell to her?

Four

The next morning Caitlin dressed in the same blue shirt and jeans she had worn the day before. She braided her hair into one long rope that hung down her back.

She found Jake in the state-of-the-art kitchen with its cherrywood walls, granite countertops and large glassed-in dining area. He was dressed in jeans and a black knit shirt and was talking on his phone. When her gaze slid over him, her heart skipped faster. He was handsome, far too appealing.

Glancing at her, he motioned her to come in, but she left to give him privacy, walking to the nearest room, which was a sunroom. A yellow bougainvillea grew in a massive pot and climbed up one wall to curl across part of the skylight ceiling. Its yellow blooms were bright, matching the yellow upholstered rattan furniture.

"There you are," Jake said, striding into the room, his presence dominating it. "I motioned to you to come on in. That was no private conversation. It was my friend, Nick

Rafford. We have fathers with similar traits of being control freaks. I got some sympathy and words of wisdom from Nick over my dad's latest demands."

"Sorry. I've never had that problem in my life."

"Be thankful. Come have some breakfast. You look as fresh as if you had just driven here from your home."

"Thank you. I don't quite think so. You may need glasses."

He smiled and walked beside her to the kitchen. In a short time they were seated in the dining area with fluffy eggs and hot buttered toast, tall chilled glasses of orange juice and steaming coffee.

"In fact," he said, "I'm here to get away from my dad. This ranch is a haven."

"Then you can understand how I feel about ours," she said. "It's a retreat even though I'm not trying to escape from any particular person. Just people in general. Do you have this often with your father?"

"Too often to suit me."

"Can't you ignore him?"

Jake shot her a look. "He always sees to it there's a threat that makes it impossible to ignore him."

"A threat?" she asked, beginning to wonder if Jake's father had a streak of meanness like her half brother Will. "Is he like Will? Will can be mean to get his way."

"Depends on what you call mean. Cruel and unusual punishment rather than anything physical. In this case, I will be disinherited."

"Good heavens! What does he want you to do?" she said, staring at Jake and momentarily forgetting her breakfast.

"Get married within the year," Jake answered quietly and she laughed. Jake gave her another grim look. "I'm not joking."

"Sorry. You have to get married or be disinherited? Well,

that's simple enough. Marry someone. You'll inherit a fortune and then you can divorce."

"Oh, no. I have to marry this year and I have to remain married for five years or the deal's off and I'm disinherited. My friend, Nick, has the same sort of father and he made the same kind of demand and Nick just happened to fall in love and marry. My dad knows Nick's father and thought that was an excellent plan—so now he's foisted it on me."

She stared at Jake. "I can't imagine a parent interfering that much, particularly with someone who is as together as you are. You're successful, have friends, have a full life. You're an adult. That decision is highly personal and yours to make. You can't just run out and grab up a wife."

"I have no intention of 'running out and grabbing up a wife' or even marrying if I fall in love. I have my own fortune and this time he's gone too far," Jake stated in a quiet voice that held a cold note of steel. His blue eyes had become glacial. "I'll be damned if I'll marry just to suit my dad. If I fell wildly in love tomorrow, I wouldn't marry this year, not for any reason. I'm calling his hand on this one. He can go ahead and disinherit me. At this point, I don't give a damn." He looked at her for a moment. "How did we get on this subject?"

She was still staring at Jake, horrified that his father would make such a demand and astounded by Jake's attitude. "I can't believe what I'm hearing. You'll give up your father's fortune just to do your own thing in your own way? That's incredible. Will would marry in an instant to avoid being disinherited."

"Do not compare me to your half brother," Jake said, making no effort to hide his annoyance.

"Of course not, sorry," she said, barely thinking about what she was saying as she mulled over a man who would turn down a fortune in order to be his own person and not yield to a demanding father's wishes. "I have to say, I'm impressed."

Jake paused as he was pouring more orange juice. He set

down the pitcher to look at her. The coldness in his expression melted away. "That doesn't help, but it makes me feel better to have someone appreciate my stand."

"I hope you don't fall in love this year. On the other hand, if you do, you might change your mind about the inheritance."

He gave her a cocky grin. "Not much danger of either, but I promise you, I will not marry this year or next for that matter."

She continued to stare at him, unable to fathom his giving up a huge fortune so easily. His father was on lists as one of the wealthiest men in Texas.

"You're staring," he said with amusement. "I'll admit, if it's this startling, you are making me feel better about my decision."

"It is absolutely incredible. I'm trying to think what I would do in the same circumstances. I'm not sure I'd have the willpower to turn down a fortune. It's also depressing because you will not be swayed by money to sell back part of the ranch."

"No. At this point in my life, I'm not easily swayed by money. There are other things in life that entice me," he said and his tone changed and the words took another meaning. Now when she looked into his blue eyes, she saw desire.

"So maybe it's not money I should fling at you for the ranch, but something else, something more personal," she replied in a breathless voice. She was flirting when she knew better. *Leave Jake Benton alone,* she'd ordered herself, yet she couldn't resist the retort and it had an effect as his chest expanded.

"Try me and see what it gets you," he said.

"Maybe I'll do that, Jake." She sipped her juice and lowered the glass. "I think we should get back on a less personal, less flirty basis. I wish I could view life that way. Even though I had a very comfortable life growing up and have

Grandmother's fortune now, I can't be as relaxed about money as you are."

"You have a normal attitude. Besides, when the dust settles, I expect my father to change his mind. But if he doesn't, I'll stick by what I've said."

"I think, Jake Benton, you are an unusual man."

He reached out to tilt her face up to his. "And you, Caitlin, are a beautiful woman. Go to dinner with me tonight. We can fly to Dallas."

"Won't that take a lot of time?" she asked while her heart raced. Dinner with Jake. Foolish, yet it might help win her the ranch.

"I have a plane here. We'll be there in no time. I'll pick you up at a quarter to six."

"A Benton asking out a Santerre. You wouldn't have done that twenty-four hours ago."

"Life changes. I can adapt. So can you."

"Who's the woman in your life right now and what is she doing while you're at the ranch? Will your taking me to dinner interfere in your relationship with her?"

"There is no woman in my life right now. Not one here or in Dallas. I'd think that detective you hired would have told you that item."

"Actually, he did. I just wanted you to confirm it because he could have missed something. That makes me feel better about going out with you."

"I'll look forward to it." His hand slipped behind her head and he moved closer to brush her lips with a light kiss. "Good morning, by the way."

"Good morn—" His mouth covered hers and ended her sentence. Her heart slammed against her ribs. His kiss was slow, hot, igniting desire instantly. While her heart drummed, she relished kissing him. Negatives with Jake ceased to exist.

The only awareness was Jake and sensations he caused. With an effort to grasp safety, she finally ended the kiss.

"How did we get on this footing so swiftly?" she asked, catching her breath. "This time yesterday, I didn't even know you except on sight. And you didn't know me when you saw me. Now we're kissing."

"It happens. Sometimes even faster. The chemistry is there. You feel it, too." He moved away to get the coffeepot and returned to refill their cups. When he sat down, he sipped his juice. "I'll take you home this morning. I've already called the stable to get your horse ready and we'll put him in a trailer."

"Great. I'll be happy to avoid the long ride home. While you're at the house, I want you to meet Cecilia, Kirby and Altheda. I'll call and let them know you're coming."

"That isn't necessary," he said.

"I know. I really want you to meet them."

She ate her breakfast, but her appetite had diminished. The more she was with him, the less likely she thought he would part with his newly acquired property, yet the thought of Jake coming in and tearing down the beloved house turned her to ice. She wasn't going to dwell on that until he gave her an answer about a sale.

"Stop worrying, Caitlin," he said lightly.

"Does it show that much?" she asked, thinking it was sinful for a man to have such thick lashes and such blue eyes.

"Yes, and at this point, it's unnecessary. I haven't made a decision and I want to talk to my brother, Gabe, and our geologist."

"After breakfast, I'll call Altheda to let her know we're coming. I told you about Altheda last night. She's the resident housekeeper and cook. And you'll meet Cecilia, too. She was Grandmother's companion and secretary and long before that, a nanny for me. She's almost part of the family and feels like an great-aunt. I really might as well have been an only child. I can hardly count Will as a sibling even though, legally, he is."

"I don't blame you. I wouldn't count Will as a sibling either, but then I have strong feelings about Will, just as he does about me. I'm still astonished he sold to me."

"I'm sure all Will was thinking about was the money he would get. He wouldn't have cared whose money it was."

"Actually, I think he thought he was getting the best of me by getting my money while I got the ranch. Besides, I was the highest bidder—by far."

"I'm sure he'd view the sale that way. The money was the best of the deal to him."

Jake reached for his coffee. "So does the photography go on hold when you're at the ranch?"

"At the moment, I'm between jobs and I had cleared my schedule, so this is fine. I have to get back to the city soon. I only intended to be here a few days, mainly to see you and discuss the sale."

"I had to get away from Dallas, as well as make myself unavailable to my dad. Now I'm especially glad I did. I just made this decision at the last minute. Your private detective must be a good one. He also must have access to my office or someone very close to me."

"It's not difficult to learn your whereabouts. You don't hide what you do. You flew in your plane and your pilot had a flight plan filed."

Jake nodded. "Interesting. No, I've never had to hide from anyone, so I'm not overly cautious. I keep a relatively low profile anyway."

She laughed. "Right. How many times have I seen your picture on society pages with beautiful women on your arm?"

"Those hardly count."

"The pictures or the women?" Before he could answer, she

said, "I'm teasing you. I know you meant the pictures." She went on. "I know a few things about you from the detective. You have close friends you play golf and basketball with. Let's see if I can remember, Tony Ryder is one close friend. You mentioned your friend Nick Rafford. Those are the ones I recall."

"They're my best friends. Plus my brother. I have a bet with those guys, not my brother, but the others. When we were all bachelors we agreed to each bet a million that we would not marry. The last to marry wins the pot."

She laughed. "So if you marry, you lose a million dollars in a bet and if you don't marry you lose millions in your inheritance. You'll lose either way, Jake. How did you get yourself into that?"

He grinned. "I think the million is the smallest loss. Also, the least likely."

"And your friend Nick is married?"

"Married a woman who was guardian of his baby nephew and she and Nick had a baby. Now he's married and the father of two."

"May you have such great fortune," she teased and Jake rolled his eyes.

"Actually, Nick's really happy. It's been good for him. His dad is ecstatic, which is why my dad is so eager. Tony's dad is just as bad. I'm a buffer for Gabe. Dad always focuses on me while Gabe squeaks by without as much interference. Heaven help him if I marry and get out of Dad's sights. Enough about that."

"I can't imagine such a thing. Grandmother let me make so many of my choices with little direction from her."

"Be thankful." He finished his coffee. "Did you sleep well?"

"Yes, great," she said, having no intention of telling him she couldn't get him out of her thoughts; or how she had wanted his kisses. She wouldn't admit when she had fallen asleep, she had dreamed about him. "And you?"

"Great, but I wasn't in a strange bed in a strange house. This is home to me. Only one thing would have been an improvement," he added with a huskier note entering his voice.

"I'm not asking about that improvement. You had an undisturbed night's sleep. End of subject."

"We're through breakfast. Fred will clean this, so let's get ready to go."

"I can't shake the feeling you're putting me off about discussing a purchase," she said, knowing she should drop it until he wanted to talk. She couldn't get it out of mind more than a few minutes at a time.

"I've told you that we'll talk, but I want to think about it first."

"It seems incredibly simple to me. Sell me a small chunk of the ranch. Deal done. You'll never miss it."

"Maybe."

"Surely you don't want me out of this area. I have never done anything to hurt you," she said, carrying her dishes to the sink in spite of what he'd said.

He caught her wrist as she set down the dishes and reached for the faucet. "I told you, no cleaning. And no, you've never done one thing to hurt me, nor has your grandmother. It's your father and Will that I have strong feelings about."

"Oh, surely, you can't mean that you would hold that land just because I have the same name as Will." She looked into unfathomable blue eyes and wondered how strong his hatred was.

"No, I don't, Caitlin," he said quietly and something inside her unclenched.

"I'm glad," she said, realizing in first one way and then another, he was gaining her liking and her respect. He already stirred desire. It was becoming a potent and frightening combination because she didn't want to care about Jake Benton or have her heart race when he looked at her. Scariest of all was admiring and liking him.

"With oil hanging in the balance, I just want to give some thought to my decision."

"We both have old demons to get past," she said.

"I agree. We've spent a lifetime hating each other's families. It's difficult to switch that off instantly. You rode over here angry with me all the way, didn't you?"

"Yes, as a matter of fact, I did. I've told you why—all those messages I left for you ignored by your employees."

"I'll have to talk to someone about that. Maybe they need to find out a little more about the person before they turn them away. On the other hand, I don't think anyone would have reported to me that a very gorgeous woman was being told she couldn't even have a phone conversation with me."

"Don't be ridiculous." Caitlin smiled.

He turned her to face him. "I'm not being ridiculous. You wouldn't have stood a chance at getting me to sell any land back to you if we hadn't met in person, I can truthfully tell you that. I've always lumped you in with your father and half brother."

"Big mistake," she said. "But then Grandmother didn't like your family, so there you are. I didn't, either."

"Hopefully, that has changed forever for you."

"Time will tell," she said.

"That's a reserved answer, Caitlin," he said, studying her.

"My guess is, you feel the same way. You can't expect me to be overjoyed with you if you turn me down and I'm definitely not saying that as an ultimatum."

"Let's not get into conflict when it isn't necessary," he said.

His cell phone buzzed and he answered to talk briefly before placing it in his pocket again.

"The car, trailer and horse are waiting. Shall we go?" he asked. As they left the house, they emerged into a clear day with water still dripping from trees and the rooftops.

They reached the truck and Jake held her door while she climbed inside. In a short time they were on the highway and she thought of the long ride to his ranch on horseback and how angry and determined she had been to see him.

As they sped toward her ranch, she studied his profile. His stand toward his father's unreasonable demand, his care for his sister and brother—she envied that slightly because she had never had any love or even much kindness or attention from Will. Those things softened her harsh feelings toward the Bentons. Plus the wild unwanted allurement that had captured both of them.

Jake was turning out to be so different from the man she had imagined him to be. Much more appealing. Yet beneath all the good things lay their past history. He was a Benton who had done unacceptable things to Santerres. Will's dislike of Jake and competition with him in sports and school was legendary. Maybe both had excelled simply because they were each trying to outdo the other.

Soon they were on what had once been Santerre land, and she grew more tense with each mile. She wanted to keep her house, keep the people who had worked for her grandmother. Damn Will and his selfish ways and the ultimate cruelty in selling all this to Jake without giving her any chance to buy part of it.

"In a way, I'm surprised Will would sell you the mineral rights."

"I wouldn't have bought the ranch otherwise, but Will told me there's no oil. His father had geologists study the land, even leased it at one point, but they gave up and said there was no oil."

"What about natural gas?"

Jake smiled at her. "As far as Will's concerned, if there's no oil, there's no gas. Will is into buildings and cities and finance, not oil, gas and wind. Or even water rights. There's a lot of water on your ranch."

"I can't believe Will's lawyers let him do this without giving him a lot of advice that was solid."

"Your brother doesn't strike me as the type to take advice well. Not even from men he hires to give it to him."

She nodded. "You're right. Will is supremely confident. It helps him in many ways, but sometimes it blinds him."

"You're so much younger. I'm surprised you were around him often."

"I wasn't, but we had family gatherings because my father was the darling of my grandmother."

"What about you?"

"Oh, yes. She was wonderful to me. I'm a granddaughter, the daughter she never had. But she loved my father with all her being. He loved her, too, so we were together on holidays where Will made his presence felt. I hated being with him because when I was little, he was mean. He'd pinch me or thump me. When I'd cry, he'd deny he had done anything. He'd say I was pretending until Grandmother lectured him. With someone checking on him, he left me alone, but he was never nice, never a brother. Since she passed, he's barely spoken to me."

"Will is something else," Jake said with disgust in his voice.

When they topped a hill, a tall three-story Victorian house came into view. Trees surrounded it and shaded the steeply sloped rooftops, gables, balconies and wide bay windows.

"See, Jake, it's a beautiful old house built by the first Santerre."

"That wasn't the first house," he said.

"There's a tiny log house that was the first, but in time, this house was built. The family considers it the first real ranch house."

She wanted Jake to see the house, meet the people who worked for her and had devoted years to her grandmother. It should be much more difficult for Jake to displace them if he knew them, rather than faceless, nameless entities.

They drove to the corral where a wiry, sandy-haired man with streaks and sideburns of gray came forward to greet her. His weathered face was tan from years in the sun.

"Jake, meet our foreman, Kirby Lenox," she said when she stepped out of the truck and greeted Kirby. "Kirby, this is Jake Benton."

She watched the two shake hands and Kirby size up Jake. She saw no reaction from Jake except a friendly greeting, but she suspected he was taking in everything he saw to help him make his decision about her place.

"I'll get the horse now. It won't take long and then you two can go on to the house," Kirby told them.

As he backed the horse out of the trailer, Jake watched. "That's a fine horse," he said, looking over her bay.

"This one's a dandy. Caitlin has a keen eye for a horse."

"That's because I learned from you," she said, smiling at Kirby.

He grinned as he patted the horse. "He's a fine one. He's Caitlin's favorite. Nice to meet you, Mr. Benton."

"It's Jake, Kirby. We'll see each other again," he said easily as he held the pickup door for Caitlin.

She felt as if she were walking on broken glass, treading carefully, hoping Jake would appreciate the old house and the people or at least like them even half as much as she did.

"Thanks," she said. In minutes Jake stopped in front of the house and walked around to open her door. He took her arm in a light touch that was a blistering contact.

"Come look around," she said, gazing with satisfaction at the porch with wooden rockers, swings, pots of blooming flowers. Lacy gingerbread spindles formed the posts and lacy curtains were pulled back inside the bay windows. Caitlin sighed, wondering how anyone could resist the house's charm.

"This is too beautiful to bulldoze," she said as they crossed the porch. "I don't think a Benton has ever been in this house," she added, knowing this was another twist in the history of the family feud.

When he didn't answer, she became silent. The door swung open and Caitlin faced Cecilia whose big brown eyes went from her to Jake and back to Caitlin. "I'm back. Cecilia, I want you to meet Jake Benton."

"Mr. Benton, welcome to Caitlin's home," Cecilia said warmly, extending her hand to Jake who smiled as he took her hand.

"Jake, this is Cecilia Mayes. I've told you about her," Caitlin said, studying the two of them. Jake sounded incredibly polite, not the least a hard-hearted owner who would evict them. He towered over Cecilia who was only five feet tall, small-boned and thin. She wore a flowered cotton housedress and sandals. Her gray hair was fastened behind her head in a bun. She looked as sweet as she actually was to everyone and Caitlin loved her deeply and wanted to protect her from harm.

"I'm glad to meet you, ma'am," Jake said politely. "Please just call me Jake."

"Certainly," she said. "Come in, please. We can sit in the front parlor and I hope you'll stay for lunch with us. I told Altheda to plan for that."

"Thank you, but I should get home before then. I can sit a minute and visit."

"Fine," she said.

"Cecilia, I want to take Jake to meet Altheda and show him a little of the house. Then we'll join you in the front parlor."

"Of course," Cecilia said.

"I want you to see some of the inside of this house," she told Jake when she was alone with him. "The original house is over a hundred years old. Grandmother made changes, had closets built in, added a wing, a deck and pool, an entertainment center. I've added an office. Even so, a lot is still the same."

Fresh flowers from the garden were on the dining room table, visible from the wide hall when they walked through the open door. Jake's Western boots scraped the polished plank floor. Tempting smells of baking bread wafted in the air and Caitlin was pleased by the appearance of the house.

Deep red velvet chairs circled the mahogany dining table. Cut glass and silver filled a breakfront.

"This room was off limits to me as a very small child unless I was invited to eat in here with the family. We had holiday gatherings fairly often when I was small. There won't be any now or anytime in the future."

"I remember our family get-togethers, tedious to mind my manners, yet fun in teasing Brittany and Gabe when they couldn't get back at me."

"Will did that anytime he was here. The first few times I told on him, he denied everything and I got in trouble, so I just learned to endure his mischief. Only he was mean, pinching me during the family prayer when he knew I wouldn't yell, mean tricks he could get away with."

"The bastard," Jake said.

"That's what Will called me far too often when no one else could hear him. If he got a chance, he reminded me that

I was born out of wedlock and neither of my parents wanted me enough to keep me."

She hoped she kept emotion out of her voice, but it was difficult even after all these years to be unemotional about Will's accusations that actually were on target.

"Thank heavens for my grandmother," Caitlin added.

"She gave you almost as much as your father could have given you. If he had taken you in, you would have had to live under the same roof as Will and you would never have known your grandmother as well as you did."

"I've thought of that many times. Were I given a choice to live my life over with Dad or again with Grandmother, I would pick my life with Grandmother. It was a happy time growing up and she was loving and wonderful to me."

"She didn't have the same charitable attitude toward my father."

"Definitely not. She disliked him enormously because of the beating he gave my dad."

"Our families have a long and violent history," Jake remarked.

"I don't know if either of us can ever view the other without thinking about our bloodlines," she said.

"I definitely can look at you and forget," Jake said softly. "When I am near you, that old feud is the last thing I'm thinking about."

"I'm not pursuing what you are thinking about," she stated with a laugh. "Let me show you more of the house.

"Here's the kitchen," she said, entering a room she loved with a high ceiling and glass-fronted cabinets. Floor-to-ceiling glass gave a panoramic view of the pool and a decorator-designed deck.

Two ceiling fans slowly revolved. A woman in a black uniform with a white apron turned to smile at them. In her hand she held a tray from the oven with tempting-looking brownies.

"Jake, this is Altheda Perkins who has worked here since she was seventeen. Altheda, meet Jake Benton, the man who now owns the ranch."

"Glad to meet you Mr. Benton," she said politely, her smile fading slightly for a brief moment and then returning. Her white hair was a mass of curls framing her face. "Would either of you care for a brownie and milk? I can bring them to the front parlor."

Jake declined at the same time Caitlin did. "We both just finished breakfast. Perhaps later this morning, we might enjoy a bite."

To Jake she said, "The cabinets in here are the originals. The glass fronts are more trouble to take care of, but Altheda is willing and I love them."

"Nice kitchen," he said, looking around. The appliances were as up-to-date as his own, yet the kitchen retained the charm and appearance of another century and Caitlin loved every inch of it.

Caitlin showed him the new part of the house only briefly, dwelling more on the original and older rooms and areas. She tried to make him see that he would be destroying a treasure if he tore it down.

Beyond a polite interest, she couldn't detect any other feelings about what he was seeing. She loved her grandmother's house more than any other place and couldn't see it as anything except a precious home that should be maintained and enjoyed.

How steeped was Jake in the hatred that always lay smoldering between the two families?

She led him through downstairs rooms and then they returned to join Cecilia in the parlor.

Jake sat, talking politely to Cecilia, laughing at a story

she told that had involved him in town. Occasionally as they talked, Caitlin glanced at her watch or the clock on the mantel and was gratified to see that an hour had passed and Jake not only showed no signs of leaving, but seemed to be enjoying himself talking to Cecilia.

Altheda appeared with brownies, a pot of steaming coffee, mugs and saucers.

Jake made a phone call and let Caitlin talk him into staying for lunch.

It was after two in the afternoon when he said he had to get back to the ranch and Caitlin went out to his truck with him.

He held her arm to walk around to his side. "I'd like to walk off into the woods with you or the nearest shed or anywhere we could be alone."

"I don't need to ask why in the world you'd want to do that," she replied, amused, wanting the same thing herself, which she would never admit to him. "I don't think that's possible. You'll be alone with me tonight."

"I'll be at a restaurant with people everywhere."

"I think you'll manage. I'm glad you stayed today and visited with Cecilia."

"She's sweet and reminds me of my grandmother on my mother's side. She knows a lot about people in these parts."

"Cecilia used to get out a lot, go to town and she had many friends. She's become more reclusive in the last years."

He ran his hand across Caitlin's shoulder. "I'll see you in a few hours. Thanks again for lunch."

"Thanks for taking me in during the storm and hearing my plea finally."

He nodded and climbed into his truck and drove away. She walked to the porch and stood watching the truck on the road to the highway.

Cecilia came out to stand beside her. "Caitlin, watch out. He'll break your heart if you're not careful."

Startled, Caitlin turned. "I won't let that happen. I barely know him."

"He's a charming man. He's also accustomed to getting what he wants. Not one word was mentioned about selling land back to you, so I assume he's put you off with an answer."

"Yes, he has until this week when he can talk to his brother and some people at his office."

"He's dangling you along. He wants you and this ranch. I don't think he's going to sell to you."

"Whatever happens," Caitlin said, growing somber over hearing her own sentiments spoken aloud by Cecilia, "I promise, I'll take care of you and Altheda. Kirby, too."

"We can all manage. Your grandmother left us each a trust that will take care of us financially. We'll get along." Cecilia's gaze ran over the porch and tears filled her eyes. "I love this old house and I know you do, too," she said gently. "It may just be time for all of us to let go and move on. Change is life, Caitlin. You know that. You've done your best to win him over, but those Bentons are a hard-hearted bunch toward the Santerres. He hates your brother. It shows in his cold blue eyes."

"Cecilia, Jake isn't so awfully cold," Caitlin said, having a strange feeling of not being truthful. She had a knot in her throat and hated to hear what she feared voiced aloud.

"Just don't fall in love with him, honey. You're going out with him tonight. You be careful. That man doesn't have your interests at heart. At least not now."

"It's just dinner and I'll be careful," Caitlin promised, looking into Cecilia's worried brown eyes. They both stepped closer to hug each other and Caitlin could feel Cecilia's thin shoulders and hurt for her. "Cecilia, I'd do anything to keep him from uprooting you and the others," she said, fighting tears.

"Don't," Cecilia said firmly, pulling away and holding Caitlin's shoulders. "Do not do anything foolish to get your way. He'll take advantage of you and hurt you. We'll all be fine and stop worrying about us. You've talked to him about selling and you've done your part."

Caitlin nodded. "I better check my calls and emails. I haven't since this morning."

"You'll have to put it off for a few more minutes because here comes Kirby," Cecilia said. "I'm going in. He'll want to talk to you, not me. I'm guessing he's in his fatherly mode. We all want to keep you from getting hurt while you're trying to protect us."

Caitlin saw the foreman striding toward her, a lanky, relaxed walk that still covered ground rapidly. She had a sinking feeling he might want to air his feelings and warn her to be careful around Jake, too.

Cecilia left and in minutes Kirby climbed the porch steps to lean against a post facing her as she sat and gently rocked.

"I saw Benton drive away. I hear he's taking you out tonight."

Caitlin couldn't keep from smiling. "You three have a grapevine that carries news faster than text messaging."

He shrugged one shoulder. "Altheda told me. She had lunch for the boys and me and I was up here to get it and talked to her."

"And she must have just found out from Jake's remarks. Yes, I'm going out with him and I'll be fine."

"Look, you're doing this for the three of us, primarily. Dusty and Red, too, because the outcome will impact them. Jake Benton's a tough man. I've ridden against him in rodeos. I've seen Will come up against him and end up the worse for it. I'd say you forget trying to save this place. I don't want to see you hurt."

"Kirby, you're like an older brother to me—or a dad."

"I believe at my age, dad is a better comparison," he said and she smiled fleetingly, her mind on his warning.

"I'll take care of myself and I don't want any of you to worry. Jake won't hurt me. I'm not getting that involved with him."

"He's broken more than a few hearts in this county," Kirby said.

She gazed to the east, thinking about Jake driving home to his ranch.

"I'll be careful. You stop worrying. I've already been warned by Cecilia."

"You might as well give up on him selling the place. That man isn't going to let you have it back. Trucks are pouring in here at that rig where they are drilling. I've watched them with binoculars from the barn loft. They're busy as can be. I wouldn't be surprised if they do find oil. Your dad never thought there was any here, but that time they drilled it was far over in the eastern corner, not up here near the house. They find oil, you can forget any hope of getting part of this ranch back."

"I know. He retains all mineral rights, so he could go right ahead."

"It's not conducive to raising cattle."

"I couldn't just give up without asking. Just please, don't you worry."

Kirby straightened up. "All right. I've said my say and I'll head back to work." He turned and went down the porch steps.

"Kirby—" She waited until he turned around to meet her gaze. "Thank you. I love you for watching out for me."

"You take care, Caitlin. I can't watch out enough to protect you."

She nodded and he walked away, heading back to the barn. Shortly he was in the truck and drove off on one of the ranch's paths.

With a sigh, she went inside, mulling over the warnings against Jake that reaffirmed her own reactions. Neither Kirby nor Cecilia expected Jake to sell back to her. She headed to the kitchen, knowing she might as well listen now to Altheda, hear her cautions and then she could go back to her work to check on her galleries and orders.

When she finally stepped inside her office, she closed the door. Feeling drained, she was more worried than ever about the future of the ranch.

Caitlin soon gave up trying to work because she couldn't keep her mind on anything except Jake. Memories of his kisses tormented her. Questions about his decision concerning the ranch were as constant a concern. All the time she bathed and dressed, she moved as if only half conscious of her actions. Kirby's and Cecilia's warnings made her view the evening with more caution, big reminders to be careful.

In spite of the warnings, her pulse speeded at the prospect. Her feelings toward Jake were mixed; fear he would destroy the place she loved, attraction, family hatreds, excitement. The dinner date would give her another chance to try to talk him into selling. What was really holding him back? Was he trying to get something from her besides a payment? Seduction? Perhaps tonight would bring answers.

Five

With his thoughts on Caitlin, Jake turned into his ranch road and answered a call on his cell. He talked briefly to his brother Gabe who had flown in and was waiting to see him.

When Jake parked, Gabe came out on the porch. His dark brown hair was windblown. He was dressed casually in jeans, boots and a cotton shirt. His blue eyes held curiosity when Jake climbed the porch steps.

"I brought the geological papers, the maps, the description of the barns and outbuildings used by Madeline Santerre. What gives that you're having second thoughts about it?"

"I met Caitlin Santerre and she's asked me to sell part of the property back to her. I'm dragging my feet to see if you find oil."

"Why would you want to consider selling, oil or no oil? We've talked about the possibilities of oil on that land and we've already started drilling."

"We'd retain all mineral, wind and water rights."

"And she would agree to that and still want to buy back part of it?"

"Yep. She wants it for sentimental reasons and to take care of the elderly crew who have worked there."

"Sentimental reasons? You believe that? A sentimental Santerre?"

"This isn't Will. I've found a Santerre who is not like Will at all. I always heard the Grandmother wasn't like her son or grandson. Let's go to the study where we can be comfortable."

"Sure," Gabe said, holding the door and following Jake inside.

"Actually, Will sold it without telling her. They've never gotten along."

"Caitlin Santerre is Titus Santerre's daughter. I've always heard her mother was a Santerre maid."

"That's right. When the maid had the baby Titus didn't want any part of either mother or baby and paid the maid to go away. When she planned to put the baby up for adoption, the grandmother, Madeline Santerre, Titus's mother, adopted her. Thus Caitlin became a Santerre and was raised by Grandmother Santerre. She's told me that Will was never kind to her."

"That can't surprise you."

"Nope. Will is mean through and through. Caitlin is not one bit like Will. She's worrying about the people who worked for Madeline. As far as I can tell, she doesn't have any meanness or selfishness in her."

"Caitlin Santerre. All I remember is a little kid," Gabe said as they entered the study and Jake sat in a leather chair.

"Not so little. I'm taking her to dinner tonight."

"Caitlin? How old is she? I think of her as twelve at the most."

"When you were having birthdays, Caitlin was having birthdays. She's twenty-eight."

"Damn. Twenty-eight? I don't remember seeing her around these parts since she was little." Gabe hooked one knee over the arm of the chair and let his booted foot dangle while he studied Jake. "Why are you taking her to dinner? Why didn't you just tell her no and be on your way?"

"She's beautiful. I want the evening with her."

Gabe's eyebrows arched. "You've hated the Santerres, particularly since Brittany's death. What's the deal here—a little revenge by seducing a Santerre?"

"No. Will doesn't care a thing about her. No revenge there. I just want the evening with her."

Gabe's eyes narrowed as he stared at his brother. "That one I can't figure. You know plenty of beautiful women. You hate the Santerres with a passion. Is there anything you're not telling me?"

"Not a thing. If you could see her, you'd know why I want to go out with her."

Gabe shook his head. "You're not convincing me. I've seen you fight with Will. I've seen you try to beat him in sports. I've heard you call him names and complain about him. You don't like any of them. There's something else."

"Nope."

Gabe became silent and Jake waited patiently for his answers to soak in with his brother.

"Tell her no you won't sell and get on with your life," Gabe said finally. "You're not going to go out often with the woman or have a relationship with her."

"I'll tell her no soon. Probably this week at the office, but tonight, I'm taking her out. If it goes well tonight, I might put her off for a week and go out with her next weekend."

"I can't believe I'm hearing this," Gabe said. "You're sure she isn't going to talk you into selling back to her?"

"Fairly positive."

"Then why the maps and descriptions and pictures?"

"If you must know, she's gaining some of my sympathy. I started out avoiding a definite rejection because I wanted to go out with her. She's gorgeous."

"So you said," Gabe remarked dryly.

"Now, I'm listening to her. If you don't find oil, it doesn't seem such a big deal to sell a patch of land and the old house to her if we retain rights. If you find oil, that house and everyone living in it will be in the way."

"The more you get to know her, the more likely you are to do what she wants."

"Maybe. Maybe not. I don't intend to sell if you find oil."

"That's good because that house of hers may be in the middle of a very lucrative field. I think it is. Before too many more days, we'll know if I'm right."

"I hope you are," Jake said.

"If I am, you won't want her owning any part of the ranch. We'll want to drill where we can get oil. We have to have trucks able to get in and out. I'm puzzled, but okay. I know you're not going all soft over a Santerre. No way is that happening."

"I'm just thinking about it and waiting to hear something decisive from you," Jake said and Gabe smiled.

"I hope I have news for you soon," Gabe remarked. He stood. "I've got to run. I'm flying back to Fort Worth to meet some guys for dinner."

Jake walked to the porch with Gabe. "See you in Dallas."

When his brother was gone, Jake returned to the study to look at the papers Gabe had delivered to him. He hated Will with a passion, disliked Will's father. Why bother selling to Caitlin? He wasn't ready to get her out of his life yet. Erotic images of Caitlin in his bed set his heart drumming.

He had asked to see the house and property because he was

stalling to hear from Gabe about oil before he was forced to give her an answer, yet she had wanted to show him the house and everything else, playing on his sympathy.

She had tried to familiarize him with the house and property so it would not seem impersonal and easy to dispose of. He had allowed her to because the more he was with her, the more he wanted to be with her and to seduce her.

As she had led the way from room to room, he had watched the gentle sway of her hips. He wanted her in his arms in his bed. His blood heated at the thought of tonight. Seduce her, spend time with her and then tell her no.

Would she trade sleeping with him for an agreement from him to sell the house back to her? Or become his mistress for a limited time? The possibility was erotic, tempting. She wanted the house and part of the property in the worst way. It was leverage to get something in return from her and money meant nothing. If it had been Will who wanted the property back, he would have delighted in saying no, but it wasn't Will. This was an entirely different matter. It hinged on Gabe finding oil.

Caitlin had not won him over beyond it being exciting to be with her.

It was a small matter to sell a little piece of the ranch back to her, but he wasn't ready to do so yet. He was certain when he did, he would see no more of Caitlin.

What kind of evening would he have with her? He glanced at his watch. Only a few hours and he would find out.

Caitlin studied herself in the mirror while her thoughts remained only half on her appearance. The prospect of an evening with Jake both excited and disturbed her. Reactions poles apart like all of her responses since she had first faced him. She wanted to get her property back and be done with him because he was an unwanted temptation in her life.

Focusing on her reflection, she smoothed the deep blue long-sleeved dress over her hips. The dress had a draped neckline with a low-cut back. She stepped into silver high-heeled sandals. Her hair was piled on her head, held with a silver clip with a few strands escaping to frame her face. Blue-and-silver earrings dangled from her ears.

A flight to Dallas to eat and then back, but it would be no surprise if he wanted her to stay the night in Dallas. At the thought, her already bubbling insides gave another jump.

The front door knocker made a clang that she could hear upstairs in her bedroom. Grabbing up her clutch purse, she hurried downstairs. Cecilia had already greeted Jake and was in the front room talking to him.

Caitlin heard their voices before she entered the room. Jake stood the minute she walked through the door. Her breathing altered as she looked at Jake in a charcoal suit with a red tie. Even when she was in high heels, he was still the taller. Wickedly handsome, he presented an enormous challenge: win him over about selling—resist seduction.

Then she saw the perusal he was giving her with approval definitely in his warm gaze. "You're beautiful, Caitlin. I can't believe you're the same little kid I remember."

"Thank you. The same little kid you ignored, is what you mean."

"Cecilia, it was nice to see you again, if only briefly."

"Take care tonight," Cecilia said, following them to the door and telling them goodbye. The minute the door closed behind them, Jake took her arm.

"Cecilia looks sweet, but I wouldn't want to meet her in a dark alley. I think she would gladly do me in."

Caitlin laughed. "I have never heard such a description of her in my life. Next to my grandmother, she's the sweetest person on earth."

"You can't tell me I got approval after my visit this

afternoon. That was a frosty few minutes before you arrived."

"Cecilia? I can't believe it. She is always sweet to people. Even Will—she never trusted Will, but she was always kind about him because she knew Grandmother loved him."

"I'm not going to pin you down on Cecilia's opinion of me, but I'd bet the ranch I'm on target."

"You might be," she said, amused by his reaction to Cecilia. "Now if you sell the land back to us, she'll change her opinion completely."

"Ah, that's what her coldness is about. I was afraid it was about taking you out."

"Why would she worry about that?" Caitlin asked.

Jake shot her a look before returning his attention to the ranch road. "Don't make me sound like someone so run-of-the-mill."

She laughed. "You will never be 'run-of-the-mill.' Stop fishing for reassurance or compliments. If our relatives could see us now, they wouldn't believe their eyes. A Benton and a Santerre together for an evening."

"All I can see is a man and a gorgeous woman. That feud melted away when you appeared on my porch."

She smiled as she watched him drive. She had caught a whiff of his woodsy aftershave. All she could remember when she was a kid was an unfriendly older boy who was a Benton and someone to avoid. Not the breathtaking dream sitting only feet away from her and spending the evening with her.

"A penny for your thoughts," he said.

"No amount of money would wring my thoughts out of me right now," she replied, smiling and received another swift glance.

"Now I have to know. Your thoughts must be personal, must involve me and must include tonight."

"You're enough on target that I think we will change the subject. Do you work all the time in Dallas?"

"A large part, but I travel, too. And you're not getting off the hook that easily. Thoughts that concern us and you won't tell me. That's intriguing. Something you don't want to admit."

"Stop it, Jake," she said with a laugh.

"Not when a beautiful woman admits to thoughts about us that she can't confess. That conjures up all sorts of images—"

"You can stop now. You win—I was merely thinking how handsome you are and that we're headed for an exciting evening. There—very ordinary thoughts that could be expected."

"You're not fooling me. You don't want to admit what you're really thinking—more along the lines of speculation about what it would be like to make passionate love," he said, his voice lowering a notch.

She tingled all over. "You won't believe me if I deny that and of course, now you have me thinking about it."

His hand tightened on the steering wheel. Otherwise, she saw no visible sign of reaction to what she'd just said. "Now I wish I had started this conversation when I wasn't driving."

"You brought this on yourself. Perhaps you should take my suggestion and we change the subject."

"Flirting is infinitely more fun with you than an ordinary conversation," he said.

"More dangerous, Jake. You and I were never destined for any kind of future together. We can ignore the feud for a time, but never completely, and it means some things will never take place between us."

"Not necessarily. A kiss can diminish family histories like lightning striking a tree. I'll show you when we return to this conversation when I'm no longer driving."

His words wrapped around her, making her warm. He wouldn't forget what he just said. Kisses awaited, heightening her bubbling excitement.

"I hope you've thought about Grandmother's house. It is so wonderful, Jake. It's filled with memories. I just can't bear to lose it."

"It is a fine old home, Caitlin. There's no argument about that."

They reached his ranch and drove to park in front of an open hangar. Nearby a dazzling white jet waited, a larger craft than she had expected. The moment she stepped inside, she saw it was a luxury jet that held plush seats, tables, a bar, a screen for films, electronic equipment and phones. "This is an elegant plane, Jake."

"It's comfortable and equipped for me to work while I fly. Or be entertained, whichever I want."

"You get what you want most of the time, don't you?"

"Yes. I suspect you do, too, so it's annoying when we don't."

"We each intend to get what we want involving the ranch. Let's just hope we can move to a point where the outcome is mutually satisfying and fulfilling."

"I intend to do that, Caitlin," he said softly, and she had a feeling he wasn't talking about the ranch at all, but about making love.

In a short time they were airborne. She looked at his ranch below as they circled and headed southeast. "Tell me when we are no longer over your ranch."

He gazed outside and she studied his profile, looking at the firm jaw, his prominent cheekbones and symmetrical features. His thick brown hair was combed from his face. She was frustrated by her helplessness to sway Jake.

With his recent acquisitions of neighboring property, Jake's sprawling ranch was enormous. He couldn't possibly need all the land she saw below.

"There," he said, leaning close to her and pointing below. "Since I bought the Patterson place, that's the southeast boundary now. We're negotiating for wind turbines all along the land you see below."

She lost track of what he was saying. Jake was only inches from her as he moved closer to point out his holdings. His mouth was mere inches away, his thickly lashed eyes adding to his handsome appeal.

As if he realized her thoughts, he turned to look into her eyes and her heart thudded. Her breathing altered and she tilted her face up to his. When his gaze lowered to her mouth, her heartbeat pounded.

He leaned the last few inches to kiss her. His lips were warm, sensual, moving slowly on hers while his tongue slipped into her mouth.

She kissed him in return, steadily thinking no, no, no, yet unable to resist him. Desire heightened, her breathing altered. Jake was the most exciting man she had known.

His arm slipped around her waist and she placed a hand against his warm, solid chest, feeling his heart racing beneath her touch.

She kissed him until his arm tightened around her waist and she realized he might be moving her to his lap. He raised his head. "Unbuckle. I want to hold you."

His voice was deep, gravelly and desire filled his blue eyes that had darkened with passion. Her heart raced while she fought her own desire. She placed her hands on his arms.

"Jake, I won't look fit to go out for dinner if I move to your lap. We should stop this craziness anyway."

"It's not craziness," he answered quietly. "I want you, Caitlin." He looked her straight in the eye and barriers around her heart crumbled.

"Don't," she whispered, placing her fingertips lightly on his mouth, aware of his lips beneath her touch. "You can't become important to me, Jake."

"Just kisses—that's not earth-shattering."

She inhaled and bit back her answer. While his kisses had too strong an effect, she had no intention of admitting it to him.

"I'm going to go straighten my clothes. We're cruising now and I can move around according to the pilot."

As she walked away from him, she tingled, feeling certain he watched her. When she returned, she met his watchful gaze and this time had to get to her seat beneath his scrutiny.

He looked faintly amused, as if knowing that his kisses set her ablaze. "So there's no relationship with anyone right now," he said.

"No. I'm not into casual relationships. You said you won't marry. Well, I don't want anything casual. It's a fine thing we're not in each other's lives. It would not be a happy outcome."

"Most relationships begin casually," he said.

She shook her head. "Nothing I'm involved in because I have to have deep commitment. Which I've never had. Nothing has gone beyond the casual stage so far."

Frowning slightly, Jake framed her face. "Nothing? I find that impossible to imagine. I intend to get beyond the casual stage, Caitlin. I want to know you. I want you in my life. We have a mutual attraction that is spectacular. You feel it," he declared.

"Jake, I can't get closely involved with you. I'm not going to, just know that right now."

"We'll see," he said softly and she couldn't catch her breath. They were on the verge of kissing, only it was more volatile than before. She couldn't understand her escalating reaction to him, nor could she get rid of it.

She pulled away, gazing at him with what she hoped was a cool composed regard even while he sent her breathing and heartbeat into a scramble. "You keep your distance, Jake," she whispered. Her faint voice took all the demand out of her words.

"No," he replied. "I have no intention of keeping my distance because part of you doesn't want me at arm's length. Part of you wants to kiss and make love. You can't stop from revealing it."

With a sinking feeling, she looked away. He was right. He could easily demolish her resistance. How was she going to keep him under control and at arm's length all evening? Did she want to keep him at a distance? She wanted the old house and the people who had worked for her to stay on more than anything she had ever wanted since she was a small child. The house was a tie to all she loved in her childhood. The people deserved to be able to stay, not uprooted when they were becoming older.

Letting Jake into her life, succumbing to the fiery attraction might bind him to her strongly enough he would sell the place to her. It was like selling herself to get what she wanted, yet there was another argument. Jake was the sexiest man she had ever met. What would happen if she followed her desire and let a relationship develop?

She thought about her own life and her mother. That's what her mother had done and had an unwanted baby she had given up for adoption. Caitlin would never give up a baby, but she didn't want to bring one into the world fathered by a man who had no interest in a family or a commitment.

All her life she had vowed any relationship would have to be lasting, filled with love, not lust. What she and Jake had found was lust, spectacular, sizzling, but with no substance.

All through the flight, she flirted, enjoyed him and stewed about the outcome of the evening.

When they landed, a limo took them to a private club on the top floor of a tower in downtown Dallas.

They sat at a table in a secluded corner with a glowing candle centered on the table. Soft piano music played near the dance floor, while she barely noticed her surroundings. Her focus was Jake.

Desire built, increasing from the moment she had opened her front door to greet him. His kisses, his touches, his flirting, his declarations of how much he wanted her, all of it already had her shivering with need, thinking about his fiery kisses and anticipating being in his arms.

As she looked across the candlelight into his blue eyes, he reached out to take her hand. His fingers were larger, tan against her skin. Calluses on his palm were rough, making her wonder what he had done to cause them because he spent most of time in offices and in cities. When he was on the ranch, she couldn't imagine he did manual labor.

"I should look at the menu," she said, taking her gaze from him and reaching for the black menu that had been given to her.

During the time wine was poured and they ordered, conversation became impersonal, revolving around dinner choices and she relaxed.

"What's your next project, Caitlin? Will it take you away from Texas or Santa Fe?"

"No. I have appointments in Houston toward the end of October. I took plenty of time off because I've been working a long, intensive schedule the past two months and I've been in Europe taking pictures for a book project."

Steak and lobster dinners arrived. While they ate, she asked Jake about his life and childhood, discovering that he had lived on the ranch year-round the first six years of his life before the Bentons began to spend more time in Dallas.

After dinner Jake said, "Let's dance, Caitlin."

She nodded, standing when he took her hand, and they moved to the dance floor. She stepped into Jake's arms to dance to an old ballad. Jake was warm, tall, agile. Everything about him was appealing except the most important things: his family, his ownership of her home and ranch, his avoidance of commitment.

The contact from dancing with him fanned her desire. She wanted him and she was vulnerable. There hadn't been any man in her life in a long time and none she had ever been serious about. This fascination with Jake remained a constant danger to her well-being and her determination to avoid the wrong relationship.

When a fast number followed, their gazes locked while they danced. He was sexy, light on his feet and each touch sizzled, combating her efforts to cling to caution.

As he twirled her around, she turned to see blatant lust in his blue eyes. He wanted her and his desire made her heart drum. He pulled her tightly against him. "I want you, Caitlin," he whispered, saying what she could read in his eyes. He spun her away and she danced, feeling desired, seductive, knowing she was flirting with temptation again. The whole evening was building toward seduction, in an unwanted escalation of their relationship.

Later, slow dancing in his embrace while they barely moved around the dance floor, he whispered in her ear, "I have a condo here. Let's go there so we can have some privacy."

This was the moment to say no and go home. As she danced, held close against him, after a dream evening, she didn't want to say goodbye. As if watching a puppet in a play, she nodded. "Very well, Jake. For a while. I still want to fly back to the ranch."

"Whatever you want. All you have to do is tell me."

When the number ended, he took her hand and they returned to their table where she retrieved her purse.

"Now I can show you where I live in Dallas. We'll pass the office, too."

She was familiar with Dallas and had a general idea where they were going. When they reached a suburban area, Jake pointed to a twenty-story building on a business campus with a complex of buildings. "There's the Benton campus. We have a lot of diversification. I'm in the main building. Gabe is in the ten-story one next to the tallest building."

"Will you lose anything concerned with the business if you don't do what your dad wants in the coming year?"

"I'm risking all of this, although so far, Dad has simply threatened my inheritance and what he has in his will. I'm not worried. I'm setting up my own business. Dad can do what he wants."

"I can't believe you would give up such a fortune. You could marry and live the kind of life where you and your wife would never have to see each other."

"No. The day I marry, I will be so in love I can't think straight. I'm not ready for that. I haven't ever had a serious relationship or considered marriage and I'm not about to get into a shallow relationship to please my father. He can have his money, his business and everything else. I'll walk away still being my own person."

"That's amazing. You must have incredible willpower."

"Incredible stubbornness is what he'll call it. I don't care. Here's my condo," Jake said, turning into a gated area. He punched a code and tall iron gates swung inward.

Helping her out of the car, Jake took her arm. "I'll give you a brief tour," he said, leading her into a kitchen that made her ranch kitchen look the age it was. Dark wood was softened by the lighting and splashes of color in plants, jars and copper-bottomed pots. An adjoining sitting room was inviting with plaid-covered furniture.

The central hall held a fountain and pool. The living area

was another inviting room with leather furniture and walls of books. As Jake shed his coat and tie and unbuttoned the top buttons of his shirt, her mouth went dry and she forgot his condo.

He glanced at her, then focused more intently and she looked away, moving around the room to look at shelves holding books, vases and pictures. There were pictures of Jake with his brother and sister.

"Even though your father meddles in your life, you had a family with a brother and sister and that's wonderful."

"You at least had your grandmother."

"That I did and I had more in Cecilia, Altheda and Kirby who were like family to me. No, I will always be grateful for my grandmother who gave me a wonderful life."

"All evening I have wanted to do this," he said, reaching up to take the clip out of her hair. While locks tumbled on her shoulders, he placed the clip on a shelf and ran his fingers through her hair. His gaze held hers and it was difficult to get her breath again.

"This is the way I like you best."

Her heart drummed because he stood only inches from her. His gaze was on her mouth and his fingers still combed slowly through her hair. His arm circled her waist, drawing her closer and then he kissed her, his mouth covering hers while his tongue slipped into her mouth.

Her heart pounded. Unable to resist, she stood on tiptoe, put her arms around his neck to hug him as she kissed him in return. "This wasn't going to happen to me," she whispered, looking up at him and meeting blue eyes filled with desire.

"It's happened and it's fantastic," he said. "Stop fighting me and yourself."

"I don't think I've ever fought you," she whispered in return, lost in a spiral of yearning and hot kisses as she clung to him and returned his kisses.

Desire enveloped her, driving away all reason. She wanted only Jake, running her hands across his broad shoulders and feeling his warm skin beneath the fine cotton of his dress shirt. Then her fingers were at his buttons and she twisted them free to run her hands over his chest, tangling her fingers in his thick mat of chest hair.

He tightened his arm around her waist, kissing her hard while his other hand slipped down her back and over her bottom. She gasped as sensations bombarded her. He shifted while he tugged down the zipper of her dress.

Cool air brushed her heated skin, but she barely noticed, thinking about Jake and his kisses, his hard, muscled body pressed against hers, his sculpted chest.

She turned her head slightly. "Jake, I'm not going to complicate my life."

"Not asking you to," he replied while he kissed and caressed her. "Just kisses and touches, Caitlin."

But it wasn't just kisses and touches. He was more exciting, more intriguing. In addition to the attraction, she had gained respect for him from being with him and for his attitude toward his controlling father.

Each kiss was a link that strengthened her desire for him. The whisper of caution was gone as quickly as it had come.

She wanted to be in his arms, kissing him and being kissed by him. And if this was a way to get him to think about selling to her, so be it. She was not getting into an intimate relationship with him over the sale of land, but a few kisses—thoughts stopped plaguing her as she gave herself to the moment and kissed him with all her pent-up longing for him.

He lightly pushed her dress off her shoulders and it fell to her hips. While he kissed her, he unsnapped the wisp of lace that was her bra and his hand cupped her breast, his thumb caressing her.

She moaned with pleasure, wanting to caress him, to stir him as he stirred her. She tugged his shirt free and ran her hand over his rock-solid chest. Jake held her away to look at her, his gaze hot and hungry.

"So beautiful," he whispered, cupping her breasts and bending down to circle a taut bud with his tongue. She clung to his shoulders, closing her eyes and relishing his loving, wanting all of him, wanting a night of love with him and knowing it was forbidden.

Minutes, seconds, she didn't know. She groaned and stepped forward to embrace him, thrusting her hips against him, feeling his erection and knowing he was ready for love.

She clung to him tightly, kissing him long and hard, her tongue going deep and stroking his.

As he kissed her hungrily in return, his arm tightened around her. Her heart thudded against his and she could barely get her breath. She wanted all barriers between them gone.

Releasing her slightly, Jake pushed the dress off her hips and it fell to the floor around her ankles while his hand drifted down over her belly and lower between her thighs.

Moaning with pleasure and regret, she gripped his wrist and stopped him. "Jake," she whispered, gasping for breath. "We have to stop. I can't go into a night of love or anything casual and at this point, loving between us would be casual."

"I want to make love to you all night long," Jake whispered, caressing her and showering kisses on her throat and ear. "I want you in my arms in my bed."

While her heartbeat raced, she scooped up her dress, pulling it in place as he straightened to watch her.

Her heart still pounded from wanting him. His hair was tousled; his chest was bare, appealing and muscled with a faint sheen of sweat on his shoulders. He was aroused, ready, his trousers bulging with evidence. She longed to step back into his embrace, but a lifetime of promises to herself kept her from doing so.

"I'm not ready for casual loving. You're not ready for a commitment. I want you to take me home now."

He gazed at her without saying a word and she wondered what ran through his mind. Finally he nodded, reaching out to take her shoulders and turn her around. He pulled up the zipper on her dress and brushed a light kiss on her nape before turning her back around to face him.

"I'll take you back if that's what you absolutely want, but I've enjoyed being with you. You have tomorrow off and I have to be in Dallas tomorrow for two appointments. Let's stay here tonight. I have plenty of extra bedrooms and you'll have yours and I'll have mine. We can be together and tomorrow I'll make my appointments and then we'll fly back to the ranch. How will that be? Stay here tonight."

<u>Six</u>

One more time they would be thrown together in close contact, spending the night under the same roof. For her own well-being the answer should be no. Spending more time with him would make it harder to say no to his seduction. But it might make it more difficult for him to refuse to sell the land to her, so that meant a yes. The easiest answer.

She nodded. "I'd like that, actually."

"Let's go get something to drink and we can sit and talk where it's comfortable."

"Same as before, Jake, I don't have anything else to wear. I brought nothing with me."

He gave her a crooked grin. "Here, too, I'm prepared, although I could make a suggestion, but I don't think you'd take it."

"I can guess that suggestion," she remarked dryly, uncertain, but suspecting he was teasing. "No thanks. I'll take you up on what you have, which was very nice at the ranch."

"Great. Let's get something to drink. Cold or hot? Soft or otherwise?"

"I'll take a cup of hot tea."

"I'll pass on that one and have a cold beer."

She walked beside him down the hall, trying to get composed and ignore desire that was still white-hot and making her acutely aware of him, more sensitive than ever to the slightest physical contact with him. He had come so close to seduction—a few more minutes and she couldn't have said no. If they were together often, she wouldn't be able to continue to resist him.

"I have to be in Houston tomorrow night because I have an appointment early Tuesday morning."

"I'll get you back in time to go home. I have to be in Kansas City this week. I'll be gone until Friday. Go out with me again next Friday."

"Jake, what about the ranch? I thought we were going to talk tomorrow."

"I'll get an answer to you as soon as I can. I have people checking out the sale for me. Gabe brought information to me at the ranch. Just a little longer, Caitlin."

She studied him, wondering about the delay. She suspected if he wanted to buy it and she had it for sale, there would be no such delay, study of the situation or long thinking about it. She still thought he was stalling for a reason. So far only one reason came to mind—seduction. Now he had asked her out Friday night. Perhaps that was what he had been waiting for.

"How about Friday?" he asked, his dark gaze steady.

"I'll be in Houston, Jake. Not at the ranch."

"I'll pick you up in Houston and have something planned. Maybe a weekend in a tropical place. How's that?"

She smiled. "Extreme. What about dinner in Houston?"

"Far too short a time with you and too ordinary. Let's get away somewhere."

"Sounds exciting," she answered truthfully. "Very well. Let me know when you decide where, so I can let my friend Ginny know where I am. We keep track of each other because neither of us has a family any longer. Ginny's family had the McCorkin drugstore in town. Another kid you don't remember because you didn't pay any attention to her."

"Hey, you were little kids."

"I know. Actually, Cecilia and I talk every day and she keeps track of me, too."

"I'll give you an itinerary. Tracie, my secretary, will send you a text."

"I'll look forward to Friday," she said, knowing she would and at the same time, she would worry about his decision and wonder when she would hear. She didn't expect to hear from him until after their weekend together because she still felt he was procrastinating while he hoped to seduce her.

"You're quiet, Caitlin. What are you thinking?"

"I'm wondering how I'll be able to resist you the next time."

He turned to face her and desire still burned in his expression. "I hope to hell you can't. I want you. I can't sleep for thinking about you. You're special, more exciting than any other woman I've known. I hope you feel that way about me."

Her pulse jumped with his admission. At the same time, his words locked around her heart, tugging on her. He waited for an answer from her, staring intently at her.

"You know you excite me," she whispered. "You came into my life like a whirlwind and you'll go out like one. I want my heart in one piece when that happens."

"I came into your life when I drove home. You were the

storm waiting to break. I don't know that I'll be gone in a flash. Not since every minute with you gets more interesting. There are some times in life you have to take a chance."

"This isn't one of them. That's what my mother did and the consequences were disastrous."

"You don't have to repeat what happened to your mother. We're different people. I'm not Titus Santerre and you're not your mother. Besides, it brought you and your grandmother together."

"We're arguing uselessly," she said, waving her hand.

He turned to head for the kitchen again and she walked beside him. "It'll set my parents back to know we've gone out together."

"What about your feelings for your sister?" she asked.

"That was different and a terrible time for all of us. My mom detests Will and your dad. I doubt if she has strong feelings about you or your grandmother except they always snubbed each other in town."

"I know that. I lived with Grandmother."

"Crazy family feud," he said. "Maybe we can end it."

"You don't really mean that."

"Sure I do," he said as he heated water for her tea, then got out his cold beer and snapped open the bottle. He got a cup and saucer and a small tray, placing everything on it.

"Let's sit on the sofa. It'll be more comfortable than at the table," he said, motioning toward the adjoining sitting room. She sat and tucked her legs beneath her while he placed the teapot on a table near the sofa. He sipped his cold beer.

"What's your friend Ginny do? I guess the McCorkins still run the drugstore."

"Yes, they do. Her dad always says he'll never retire. He has a big pharmacy and that's what he mostly does. Ginny is a drug rep in Houston for a pharmaceutical company."

"That's easy to figure. She grew up knowing those people. She has the background."

"She studied to be a pharmacist, but she likes sales."

Jake nodded. "Where do you get your clients? I guess now, it's easy, but at first, how did you get them?"

"It's never been hard. People see my photographs and ask me about them and want me to take their pictures. I've been fortunate."

"Plus a few other things. I know about being fortunate. Do you have many employees at your galleries and shop?"

"About eight run the galleries. I have an office staff, my secretary, my accountant, a sales manager—just a small staff of people."

"I'll have to go to Houston, see your office and your gallery there. How about showing me sometime soon? I can fly us there."

"Of course. Whenever you want," she answered, willing to do so, yet thinking it would probably never happen and he was just talking. Perhaps if he sold her the land, but she wouldn't allow herself to speculate on what she would do if she got what she wanted from him. "I don't think it will be so spectacular to you."

"I'll be the judge of that. Did your grandmother see your success?"

"Yes, she saw the success I've had and she was pleased. I have some wonderful pictures of her because she was always happy to pose for me."

"Sorry you lost her."

She squeezed his hand in thanks. "Did you go to work for your dad right out of college?"

"For one year. The next year I switched to a different company because I wanted experience that I wouldn't get in our company. Two years later I was a vice president of that company and then I acquired a small company of my own.

The year after that, Dad wanted me to come back. He was getting ready to retire and wanted me in the family empire and made me an offer I couldn't refuse," Jake said. "I've been there since and I'll stay."

"You sound as if you're happy with your work."

"Very. Speaking of going to work—when I go in the morning, is there anything you need to do in Dallas?"

"There are things I can do," she replied. "Catch up on my emails, my calls, go check out some photographic equipment here."

"If you stay here, there's a pool you can use. You can swim, spend a leisurely morning, work out in the exercise room. Do whatever you want to do. I have an appointment at the office and some papers to sign. I'm talking to our geologist about your ranch. Then I'll be back and we can go to lunch."

"Whatever you and your geologists and anyone else decide about oil, wind, water, gas—whatever on our land—that has nothing to do with what I want, Jake. You've met Cecilia and Kirby and Altheda. They're hanging on your decision."

"They may have to hang just a bit longer. I don't want to rush this. Selling back the house isn't what I planned."

A chill slithered down her middle. She couldn't contemplate that he wouldn't capitulate and let her buy back some land. For the first time she realized he was taking his time and keeping her dangling. If and when he refused—in that minute, she would be out of his life. Was he stringing her along because he wanted seduction? The question still plagued her because that seemed the only possible answer.

"Don't look at me as if I just became a two-headed monster."

"You almost have," she said. "I just can't understand the delay in making this decision. You don't run your businesses in this manner."

"I don't make snap decisions often," he remarked dryly.

She realized she was arguing with him and possibly making him dig his heels in—and the sale less likely. She swirled her tea slightly, knowing she should let go of it and give him time.

He covered her hand with his. "Stop worrying. I'll give you a decision within a few days."

She smiled at him, but it was an effort and her heart was not in it. She suspected it showed.

He tilted up her chin. "You have the most beautiful green eyes, Caitlin," he said. "I'm sure you've been told that before."

"Thank you. I'm glad you think so," she said, aware of the casual touch of his fingers on her chin, yet it made her tingle.

"Why haven't I seen you in the intervening years? You lived at your grandmother's house during your college years didn't you?" he asked. He caught a long lock of her hair and twisted it in his fingers. She felt the faint tugs on her scalp, little pulls that should be nothing, yet were tingling and stirred her smoldering desire. She tried to ignore his fingers combing through her hair, but it was impossible to ignore anything about him.

"Yes, but I wasn't home that often and I doubt if you were, either. You wouldn't have seen me on the ranch, only in town. After I was grown if you had seen me, you wouldn't have recognized me."

"True enough, but I would have noticed you and probably asked someone who you were."

Reminding her that he was all about *attraction*. "You told me you want to make money in the future. What else in your future, Jake? What do you want when you already have everything you want in life?" she said, hoping to change the subject and get him talking about himself while she regained her composure.

"I definitely do not have everything I want," he said with an emphasis on *everything* that made it personal, as if referring to their lovemaking.

"I would guess there are few times you don't get what you want at this point in your life."

"True. If I want something, I hope to get it."

Again, she thought the last was aimed at her and their lovemaking. "Noble ambition," she said, keeping the conversation impersonal.

"And in particular," he said, his voice dropping, "I want to make love to you, Caitlin, to finish what we started tonight. And sometime we will," he added with conviction in his voice. His words were a caress, as electrifying as a touch of his fingers.

"Maybe, Jake. Just maybe. There are too many outside factors."

"I intend to keep you in my life if I possibly can."

"You know one way to do so." She was aware of her own power over him. It was as ruthless as using the ranch for leverage to seduce her. "It's really simple."

"Simple. And not so simple. Just trust that I'm working on it."

It was all she'd get from him until he made his decision. She tried to stop thinking about it. His fingers lightly caressed her nape, a feathery touch that was erotic, stirring desire even more.

She sipped hot tea and tried to concentrate on his conversation and ignore the clamoring of her body or his hand wreaking havoc with her. He was driving away all hope of a peaceful night.

As she talked to him, her voice got a breathlessness that he had to notice. Desire burned in the depths of his blue eyes. On one level they were sitting, chatting, getting to know each

other. On another level, Jake was still working his seduction
with each slight caress.

"What hobbies do you have?" she asked. "You've told me
about skiing, swimming, things you like to do."

"There's not much of anything right now because work has
been demanding."

"I remember seeing you in rodeos. You were a bronc rider
and I think a few times I've seen you bull riding."

"I did a little bull riding, but stopped when I hurt my
shoulder. I did bronc riding and calf roping for a long time.
Gabe and I did the calf roping."

She listened to him talk about his rodeo days, horses he
had owned and they compared notes on horses.

They talked about their college days, growing up on the
neighboring ranches. In all their conversation, they avoided
mentioning the family feud, as well as any talk about the
future.

She finally noticed the time. "Jake, it's two in the morning.
I should go to bed."

"Sure," he said, standing. When she reached for her empty
cup, he shook his head.

"Leave it. Someone will get it tomorrow."

"A housekeeper comes in?"

"Yes. You'll meet him in the morning. I won't leave until
long after you're up. I work out early in the morning and swim
a lap in the pool. You can join me swimming or go in later."

"I don't have a suit."

"There are new suits in the drawer. I'll show you. You can
find something you can wear, I'm sure."

"You're well equipped for a woman to sleep over," she
remarked, wondering how many times he had had to furnish
things for his overnight female guests.

"It's easy to keep extras on hand. I have a lot of company
and my staff takes care of the needed items. I don't deal with

it at all. Also, there are straw bags in the closet. Whatever clothes you wear, just toss in a bag and take them with you because the next person won't want something worn by someone else. I don't keep anything someone has worn."

"That's nice, but you sound as if you have a habit of guests sleeping over."

"Not really. I'm just prepared for company. Sometimes guys stop by and then stay to hunt. Female friends have stayed, married couples. A lot of my friends drop by the ranch because they know they're welcome."

At the door of her room she turned to tell him good-night. Jake's arm banded her waist and he drew her close as he bent down to kiss her. His mouth came down on hers possessively. He wrapped her in his embrace and kissed her, sending her heartbeat racing.

Circling her arms around his neck, she clung to him, wanting him with scalding desire, fighting the pull, unable to break off the kiss that deepened. She was lost, spinning away in a fiery blaze of passion. She combed her fingers through the short hair at the back of his head, holding him tightly, wanting the barriers of clothing away. That was no solution to her problem. Instead, it would only create bigger complications in her life.

She kissed him, returning passion, wanting to melt him and make him hunger for her and try to please her. She refused to fall into his arms completely, to be easy and vulnerable and worse yet, have her heart hostage to him.

"Jake," she whispered, breaking off the kiss. "I can't complicate my life. Good night," she said, slipping out of his arms and entering her room to close the door. She leaned against it, her heart pounding while she gasped for breath. She had seen his heavy-lidded expression, lust clearly consuming him. He wanted her physically no matter how he felt toward her otherwise.

She had no illusions that he had lost his animosity toward her family. Probably not altogether toward her. His deep dislike of Santerres lay smoldering beneath the surface of his friendly facade. She hadn't lost her own feelings regarding the Bentons. They had altered slightly because she liked Jake, but he was a Benton and the Bentons had done some bad things to Santerres through the years. The feud hadn't died completely. It never would between Jake and Will, even if he sold to her, but selling her home to her would go a long way toward mending fences.

She didn't want to think about the possibility that he wouldn't sell the house back to her.

She moved around the room and then began looking for the clothing he had said was available. She found new clothing wrapped in tissue, including a silk nightgown. As she changed, she was once again amazed that she was spending another night beneath the same roof as Jake.

When ready for bed, she found a book on the shelf that looked interesting and she curled up to read because sleep wasn't going to come for a while longer. Her body still tingled and she couldn't get Jake and their date out of mind. In minutes she climbed in bed, switched off the light and thought about Jake.

The next morning when she entered the kitchen, she was dressed in blue cotton slacks and a matching shirt that had been in the assortment of new clothing on hand. She wore her high-heeled sandals and had put her hair in one long braid.

As she entered the dining area, Jake stood. He pulled out a chair and his gaze assessed her quickly. "You look fresh and beautiful."

"Thank you. You look quite handsome yourself," she said, taking in Jake's charcoal business suit, dress shirt and tie. "I met your housekeeper as I came through the kitchen."

"Ah, Fred. He's an excellent cook as you'll see. I have an appointment in downtown Dallas. If you want, you can ride in with me. I moved it a little later so we can ride in together. Then you can have my driver take you wherever you'd like to go."

"Fine," she said, thinking of tasks she could do with time and the resources in Dallas.

"Remember, I need to get back to the ranch today. I have a rental car to return and I have to go to Houston tomorrow."

"And I have to leave town, too."

She ate breakfast with him, hearing more stories about the ranch and answering his questions about her business and life in Houston.

Finally they rode to town in a long black limousine driven by a man named Scotty. She told Jake goodbye and then asked Scotty to drive her to a photography shop. Scotty waited patiently while she spent an hour discussing equipment with one of the salesmen. She bought some necessary items and finally went to a shopping center where Scotty waited while she purchased some clothing. When she climbed back into the limousine, she had shed the clothing she had gotten from Jake and was wearing new green silk slacks and a matching shirt.

At two they picked up Jake and within the hour, they were airborne, heading back to the ranch in West Texas.

Jake drove her back to her house, and as always, her heart squeezed at the sight of the old Victorian she'd grown up in. He walked her to the door, and she turned to face him. "Please think about selling the house to me and remember, it means the world to me. I never dreamed Will would sell without letting me know. If I had known, I would have kept up with what he was doing."

"I know how much you want the place. But you don't live here, Caitlin. If I don't sell it back to you—for *business* reasons—I'll see to it that the residents have comfortable places to go. I won't put anyone out in the cold."

She ran her hand along the beveled glass in the door. "I explained that we all have the means to live elsewhere quite comfortably, Jake. We love this place. I know one shouldn't be so attached to a place, but I guess my roots are here." She had a knot in her throat and couldn't bear to think that he wouldn't sell. "I don't see why you have to hang on to this little patch of land, Jake. I really don't. It's important to several of us, but it means nothing to you. I can't even talk about tearing down this old home."

"Stop worrying. I haven't said I wouldn't sell." He frowned slightly. "Just give me the time I asked for, Caitlin, to make a decision."

"I have no choice in the matter," she said, hating the flat tone of her voice, but unable to hide her emotions where the house was concerned.

"You have some choices," he said quietly, his arm banding her waist as he bent to kiss her. His tongue thrust into her mouth and her worries and fears were pushed away. Anger, desire, determination replaced them. She wanted to melt his resistance, storm the barriers of his heart that he kept so closed away. She wrapped her arms around his neck and kissed him in return, responding fully, thrusting her hips against him.

He groaned as his fingers wound in her hair. She could feel tugs on her scalp until her braid was half undone. Raking his fingers through her hair, he pulled locks free. He leaned over her kissing her while his hand lightly caressed her breast. He raised his head. "Where's your door key?"

As she handed it to him, he continued kissing her. In a moment he walked her backward into her house and kicked the door closed behind them. She heard the key fall to the floor while they still kissed.

"Cecilia and Altheda?" he paused to ask.

"They're sound asleep in another wing of the house. They're never in here at night," she answered and he pulled her close again. As he kissed her, he walked her into the nearest room and closed the door.

In seconds Jake pushed her blouse off her shoulders. While he continued kissing her, he unfastened the clasp of her bra and shoved it away to cup her breasts. His hands were warm, his thumbs circling her nipples making her moan with pleasure. "Jake," she whispered as she ran her hands over his shoulders. She wanted him and each kiss only inflamed desire. He was forbidden, dangerous to her future, desirable beyond all dreams.

She twisted free the buttons of his shirt to run her fingers through the thick mat of hair on his chest.

When his hands went to her slacks and they fell around her ankles, she raised her head. He watched her, his eyes half-lidded, burning with desire that mirrored her own feelings.

"I'm not going to complicate my life. We can't make love."

"Yes, we can," he whispered, caressing her breasts, cupping them in his hands again as he bent down to take one in his mouth, his tongue stroking her. She gasped with pleasure and ran her fingers through his hair, momentarily yielding to the sensual delight before she stopped him and shook her head.

"No," she whispered.

"You're gorgeous," he told her as he caressed her. His touch was feathery, setting her ablaze. She trembled with wanting him. In spite of that, she was determined there would be no seduction.

"Jake, that's enough. I cannot complicate my life. I won't do it."

She pulled her clothing in place, aware he watched her. He

stood in silence with smoldering fires in his gaze. When she was dressed, she faced him.

He gazed at her for a moment. "I'll pick you up in Houston Friday night about six. Send me your address. I have your phone number. I'll talk to you this week."

"Thanks for a wonderful time."

He framed her face with his hands. "Sometime, Caitlin, you won't send me away, you'll be mine," he said solemnly.

"You want me, Jake, but when I go out of your life, it won't take long for you to forget me."

"You're not going out of my life anytime soon," he said gruffly. All his words were as searing as his caresses. She responded to everything, wanting to be back in his embrace, to kiss him. "Sometime, you'll want me to make love to you, to hold you and kiss you as much as I want."

"I already do," she whispered and saw his eyes flicker. "But we're not going there, Jake. You know why I won't. It's been a wonderful time with you. Good night."

He gazed her for another tense moment before he brushed a light kiss on her lips and left, closing the door behind him. She didn't follow him out. She locked the door and headed for her bedroom, knowing she would have one more night where sleep wouldn't come and when it did it would be filled with dreams of Jake.

Jake drove to his ranch and took the plane back to Dallas. He had a busy week ahead in Kansas City. It was almost dawn when he stretched out in bed. He wanted to call Caitlin, just to talk to her, but each time he reached for his phone, he paused and then put it back on the table.

He should leave her alone. They were getting too close. He had wanted to seduce her while he still barely knew her, but now, he was getting to know her, enjoying being with her. She impressed him with her photography, her poise, her determination. She was becoming more than just a gorgeous, desirable woman he might get into his bed. He didn't want to become fast friends or get too close. It would hurt her more when he turned her down for the sale.

He reached again for the phone and his hand stilled. He wanted to talk to her. He already missed her and her sunny laughter, her humor, her perception. Reluctantly, he had to admit that she would be furious and she would be hurt by his refusal to sell to her. He was beginning to really hate the prospect of hurting her. Should he rethink selling?

He surprised himself that he would even give the idea consideration. Here was his chance to get all Santerres out of West Texas for once and for all. He had intended to hold the land and refuse to sell to Caitlin. Yet why was it such a worrisome victory?

"Dammit," he said aloud in his dark bedroom. He tossed restlessly. Caitlin was twenty-eight, talented, gorgeous. She would probably fall in love and marry soon and that would be the end of the Santerre name in Texas anyway, because Will had told him he never was coming back since after selling the ranch, he could afford to live wherever he wanted.

The thought of Caitlin marrying wasn't a satisfying prospect, either. Jake refused to dwell on that speculation because he was the only man in her life at present so no marriage loomed on her horizon.

He missed her. Disgusted, he stared into the dark and thought about telling her that he wasn't going to sell her home back to her. Why was that becoming such an odious, distasteful chore? He didn't want to look closely at the answer to his own question. The old Victorian was one of the few ties she had to someone in her life. She had rejection on all sides except from her grandmother and those people who worked for Madeline Santerre. Why wouldn't Caitlin fight to keep that memory and keep close the people who had meant so much to her growing up?

Jake swore softly under his breath. He was beginning to feel like a villain in the whole picture. It was his land to do with as he pleased. There was no valid reason to sell to a Santerre whose house and animals would be in the way if Gabe brought in oil. *Tell her no the next time he was with her and be done with it.*

He silently vowed he would do it. Could he put her off long enough to get another weekend with her? He couldn't keep seeing her or he would *have* to sell to her. He shouldn't wait because the thought of refusing her was giving him growing qualms and guilt.

Despite promising to get back to her about her request this week, he decided he would make a business appointment to see her a week from Monday at her office so he could leave as soon as he told her. He owed it to her to tell her in person. If he didn't seduce her next weekend—and it looked as if she was going to continue to hold him at arm's length—he would tell her anyway.

The idea of Caitlin going out of his life at this point was totally unsatisfactory. He didn't want that to happen and the minute he refused to sell to her, she would be gone. He groaned, thinking it might be easier just to sell her the house and land she wanted and let her stay. If he did, she might be willing to make love with him.

He had to see his father tomorrow and he dreaded the meeting because they would probably get into another battle over marriage and his inheritance.

Jake made a mental note to call Tony and Gabe to set up lunch plans. They would cheer him up. He glanced at the clock again and wondered how early he could call Caitlin. Yesterday, she hadn't joined him in the kitchen until half past seven, so she must sleep late in the mornings.

Groaning, Jake turned to try to go to sleep, thinking about Caitlin and wanting her in his arms. If at all possible, he would see her again Friday night for a weekend getaway. This time he was going to kiss away all her objections. First, he had to get through another tedious session with his father.

Seven

At eight Jake arrived at the palatial mansion where he had grown up. He greeted the staff as he passed through the back hallway, the large family room, and entered the kitchen.

Trying to remember to hang on to his patience, Jake entered the breakfast room where his father sat in a maroon velvet robe while he read the morning paper and sipped what was probably his third cup of coffee. Dirk Benton was a man of habits and for all mornings Jake could recall, as long as his father was home, he rose at six, worked out for thirty minutes, showered and then went to the kitchen for breakfast which year after year was two eggs, toast, bacon and four cups of coffee while he read the morning newspaper. Jake was certain his mother, a late sleeper, was still upstairs.

"Good morning," Jake said.

Blue eyes focused on him as his father lowered the newspaper. "Good morning. Want breakfast? I know we have plenty."

"No thanks, I've already eaten. I brought some papers for you to sign," Jake said, sitting to the right of his father and opening a briefcase to withdraw a folder. He removed a pen from the briefcase and gave his father a quick refresher on what was involved.

Jake waited quietly while his father signed and then put everything back into the briefcase.

"What's your schedule this week?" Dirk asked.

"I'll be in Kansas City the rest of the week."

"Gabe is off to North Dakota later today. Your mother is going shopping in San Antonio. I'll be rather bored. Who did you take out this past weekend? Anyone we know?"

"As a matter of fact, it was someone you know. Better than I do," Jake said, for a moment enjoying the prospect of seeing his father's reaction. "Caitlin Santerre."

Dirk Benton's eyes narrowed while he inhaled sharply. "A Santerre? Will left town and you own their land. What are you doing going out with a Santerre? It has to be the granddaughter Madeline Santerre raised. Dammit, Jake, what the hell were you doing? Don't get tangled up with a Santerre the way Brittany did with Will."

Jake couldn't keep from enjoying his father's reaction. Let the old man stew a moment with the thought that Jake might be thinking of marrying a Santerre to get even for the demand that he marry or be disinherited.

"She was at the ranch when I got there last Saturday. She wants me to sell a little piece of her grandmother's ranch back to her. Will Santerre never let her know he was selling the place."

"Will Santerre is a selfish bastard. Actually that girl is the bastard child. Titus Santerre never wanted to claim her, but Madeline stepped in and adopted her and gave her the Santerre name. I'm not surprised about Will. He wouldn't care what she wanted. I'm sure he wouldn't share a nickel with her if he didn't have to according to Titus's will."

One of his father's eyebrows arched sharply and he studied Jake. "You're not selling it back to her, are you?"

"Of course not. She doesn't want any rights, just the old house and barn and the land they're on. She's sentimental about the house and wants the people who worked for Madeline to be able to live on the ranch for the rest of their lives."

"Well, you don't run a charity. So you told her no."

"Not yet. I will next week. I enjoyed going out with her," he stated honestly.

Dirk's eyes narrowed again. "Don't you marry her out of spite because I demanded you marry. That would be cutting off your nose to spite your face—as the old saying goes."

"No. I won't marry Caitlin Santerre. You can relax on that one. I am not marrying anyone this year."

"You'll come around to my way of thinking before the year's out and a fortune slips through your fingers. Otherwise, you'll regret your actions for the rest of your life."

"I can tell you now—I will not marry. I'll get along."

"Gabe can't give you the share you'll forfeit when he inherits it all."

"Dad, stop meddling in my life. Let me live my life in my own way. I'm not going to change my life because of your threats. Have you told Mom this latest one?"

"Yes. She knows you'll come around."

"You mean you told her that I'll come around and marry and not to worry. Well, you will see at the end of the year when I'm still not married. If I fell in love, I wouldn't marry. I won't be coerced into matrimony to suit my father. You might as well get accustomed to that notion. I better go. I have appointments this morning."

Dirk frowned. "Don't get too involved with a Santerre.

They are bad blood and bad for Bentons. Tell her you won't sell and stop going out with her. She'll cause you trouble one way or another, Jake."

"I'll remember. I think I'm going to be the one to cause her trouble this time. I'll see you, Dad," Jake said. He left, glad to get out of the house, thankful he could put distance between himself and his father.

Jake drove to the office and spent the morning so busy he forgot his dad and the thought of telling Caitlin he wouldn't sell to her. He couldn't forget Caitlin's beautiful face or lush body, though, and several times stopped what he was doing to think about holding her in his arms until he realized time was passing and he was lost in thought.

Midmorning he called her and talked briefly about nothing in particular. At noon, just as he approached the restaurant where he would meet his brother and his friends, he talked briefly to Caitlin again.

Tony, Nick and Gabe were already seated, drinking tall glasses of iced tea.

"Did you see Dad this morning?" Gabe asked as soon as Jake had ordered.

"Yep. He was his usual demanding self. It gave him a shock to learn about Caitlin."

"Did he say anything to you about getting married?" Gabe asked.

"Deal is still on. He's certain I'll marry within this year."

"I hope to hell my dad doesn't try this ploy," Tony said. "Even as big a control freak as he is, I can't imagine him demanding that I marry within the year. I don't know that he's that eager for me to marry anyway."

"I hope Dad doesn't try this one on me," Gabe said. "I can't do what you're doing, Jake. I don't even want to think about it."

"I'm not marrying to please him. There's only one reason to

marry—you have to be crazy in love. You were just fortunate, Nick."

"Damn fortunate to have found Grace. Dad's been gloriously happy with two grandchildren. He hasn't tried to tell me to do anything since he learned he would have two grandchildren. They take all his attention. You guys might think about that one," he said and the others laughed.

"I told Tony and Nick about Caitlin Santerre," Gabe said, sipping tea and crunching a small piece of ice.

"She must really want to keep her family home," Tony remarked. "Will Santerre was always bad news."

"How'd she take your refusal to sell to her?" Gabe asked.

"I haven't told her yet," Jake replied and Gabe's eyebrows shot up as his eyes widened.

"Why not?"

"I'm going out with her this next weekend. I figure as soon as I tell her, I've seen the last of her. I had a fun time with her."

"That's amazing," Gabe said. "A Benton and a Santerre out together. Of course, Will and Brittany went out together."

"Is she good-looking?" Tony asked and Jake gave him a look.

"That's what I figured," Tony answered. "She must be damned gorgeous."

"So when will you tell her?" Gabe persisted.

"A week from now. I know I can't keep putting her off. I'll have to give her an answer."

"She'll be bitter, but I can't imagine her causing you trouble. Now if you were dealing with Will, no telling what kind of grief he would try to cause. The fight would be back on between the Bentons and the Santerres."

"No, she won't cause trouble. At least I don't think so."

To his relief, conversation moved away from his problems

and they talked about business, about the next basketball game. Later, Gabe turned to Jake.

"Did you tell Dad about going out with a Santerre?"

"Yes, and you know his reaction. I ought to marry her out of spite, but I'm not giving him the satisfaction of a marriage, even one he doesn't like."

"I don't know when you got so stubborn," Gabe said.

"I'm not a kid and I'm getting tired of his interference."

"Amen to that one," Gabe said, pushing back his chair. "I've got to run. I have an appointment in thirty minutes and then I fly to Dakota. See y'all soon." He left, his long legs carrying him out quickly.

Nick placed a tip on the table. "I need to get going, too, Jake. Rethink turning down your dad. That's a huge fortune to pass on just to get satisfaction. There are millions of ways to get compensation if you get your dad's inheritance."

Jake shook his head. "I'll survive. Millionaire instead of billionaire. That's not a bad life. I have had it with his taking charge of what I do."

"Nothing will give you independence the same way inheriting your dad's fortune will," Tony remarked after Nick had gone. "As for Caitlin Santerre, that one should be easy. Tell her no deal, and she's gone forever. End of problem." Tony stood. "I should go now, too."

"I'll go with you," Jake said, leaving a tip before walking out with Tony.

"Guess I'll see you two weeks from now for basketball, right?" Tony asked.

"Sure. Usual time."

Jake headed to his car to drive to the office. *As for Caitlin Santerre, that one should be easy. Tell her no deal, and she's gone forever. End of problem.* Tony's words rang in his ears… *gone forever.* Jake didn't care. It couldn't be any other way with Caitlin, but he wanted to seduce her first. The thought of making love to her made him hot, aroused. He was leaving for Kansas City and he couldn't see her until the weekend. She'd go, because he still hadn't given her an answer, putting her off one more time. Friday night, he wanted to kiss her into losing all caution. Friday night—he was already looking forward to the evening with her.

Caitlin studied her image in the full-length mirror while her thoughts were filled of memories of Jake and his kisses. Excitement kept her tingly. Another weekend with Jake. It had been four long days since she had told him goodbye. And though her work and appointments had kept her very busy, she'd never stopped thinking about him. They had talked on the phone each day and every night. Every hour she chatted with him forged a tighter bond. Was it the same for him?

This week he would finally tell her his decision. He'd finally made a definite appointment for her to come in to his office in Dallas on Monday morning.

She still wondered whether he was holding out for this weekend with her before telling her he would not sell to her. Otherwise, why wouldn't he just tell her now?

Jake moved in exalted business circles with mega-deals. She couldn't imagine he had any trouble getting information about the Santerre ranch from his staff. Every hour of the past week had strengthened her guess that he would not sell.

She straightened the skirt of her red crepe dress. This one had a high neck, long sleeves and a skirt that came below her calves, with slits on either side of the straight skirt that revealed glimpses of her legs. She wore high-heeled matching sandals. Her hair was pinned up and she hoped she looked sophisticated, cool and poised. She didn't want Jake to see how much effect he could have on her so easily. Since they were in Houston, she had no idea what they would do. Stay here? Go to some close tropical place for the evening?

The doorbell rang and her pulse jumped at the mere prospect of seeing him again.

She hurried to the door to open it. The jump in her pulse when the doorbell chimed was nothing compared to the thud of her heart at the sight of him. She wanted to walk into his arms and kiss him. Instead, she smiled, while noticing the approval in his expression as he looked at her. How could she guard her heart against the handsome, commanding charmer who looked at her as if she were one of the greatest sights he'd ever seen?

She would have to remind herself almost every minute of the night that Jake was a Benton, an enemy and a threat to the well-being of her heart. In spite of that knowledge, she was breathless.

Tonight she was committed to spending the evening with him. She just had to remember that beneath the handsome facade was a tiger.

"You look gorgeous."

"Thank you. Come in while I get my purse."

Stepping into the entryway, he closed the door and reached for her. "Caitlin," he said in a husky voice that was its own warm caress. "Come here. It's been too long without you."

"Jake, it can't be—" she started. Her words ended abruptly when she saw the fires in his blue eyes. He drew her into his embrace swiftly, his mouth covering hers. She stepped into his arms, willing, eager. Clinging to him, she returned his passionate kiss.

"Damn, I missed you," he whispered, raising his head slightly and then coming back to kiss her again. She closed her eyes and gave herself to hungry kisses, wanting to agree with him that it had been too long, that she had missed him terribly, but she held back the words because they shouldn't be said to him. They could only lead to more heartbreak later.

They kissed until they were both out of breath, their hearts pounding. She could feel the beat of his heart as he held her tightly.

Finally, she stopped the kiss. "Jake, we must—"

"Shh. I had to kiss you. That's all I've thought about all week," he admitted. Her heart drummed and she stood on tiptoe to kiss him again. How else could she react after what he just said to her?

She didn't know how much time passed, but finally she stopped again. "Jake, you made plans for the evening."

"I can ditch them," he said in a gravelly voice. She shook her head.

"No. Let's not do that. I've told you, I'm not into seduction."

"You kiss like you are," he replied instantly and his statement took her breath.

"I missed you, too, but I want to go on with your dinner plans. Let me get my purse."

He followed her into the living area where she picked up her purse. When she turned, he was looking around the room.

"Very nice, Caitlin. Are these your pictures?" he asked, looking at framed black-and-whites of a bridge in Central Park, of the Grand Canyon, of a whale. He moved on to another wall with a grouping of pictures of people of various ages in different settings.

"I'm impressed. You're very good, but then I already knew that."

"Thanks." She glanced around the contemporary living area that had blue walls, with white furniture and touches of red in decorative pillows. "My place is a different style from yours."

"That makes life interesting," he said. "And entirely unlike the ranch house you love so much," he added.

"I like the change and this works for me. I still love the ranch house just the way it is."

"I'm surprised you don't try to duplicate it in your own place since you love it so much."

"No. That style belongs there and this change is satisfying, as well."

"That's surprising. So shall we leave now for New Orleans? Flying time is short and we can have a fun evening."

"Absolutely," she said, smiling at him over the thought of being in New Orleans for the evening.

She locked up and they got into his black limousine.

Jake reached over to take her hand and hold it in his. His fingers were warm, strong.

"New Orleans is one of my favorite places," she said.

"Next time I'll find a place you've never been before."

"New Orleans lends itself to fantastic snapshots and interesting people to photograph. Some of my favorite shots were taken in New Orleans. You ought to let me take your picture. You'd be an expressive subject."

"Expressive?" he asked, sounding amused. "So what shows in my face?"

"Wealth, arrogance "

He chuckled. "Neither wealth nor arrogance can show in a face. Now if you take all of me and my suit, shoes, handmade monogrammed shirt—that's different."

"Just your face. They show. You've got that in-command-of-your-part-of-the-world expression in your eyes and the lift of your chin. It shows, Jake. A zest for life softens the harshness of the other two."

"Ridiculous, Caitlin. You see all that because you know me."

"If you'll let me take your picture, I'll show you someday. I know what people's faces usually reveal."

"We'll make a bet on the outcome. Make it worthwhile because I intend to win," he said.

"You're so sure of yourself," she said, amused by his smug tone. "That's what will show in your photograph."

"I've had a lot of photographs taken of myself and I can't recall ever thinking those attributes show."

"Of course, they won't to you. A bet—I'll think about that one."

They were soon airborne again on his private jet and just as he'd said, it was early evening when they arrived in New Orleans.

As they stepped out of the limo in the warm air of the French Quarter, the low wail of a trumpet by a street player assailed her, the sounds of people laughing and talking while four sailors passed them, turning to look briefly at her, then at Jake and away.

Jake whisked her inside a restaurant in a building that she was certain was well over one hundred years old. A maître d' greeted Jake and led them through a busy, darkened restaurant with soft lighting, blues being played. They passed a small dance floor with the band playing blues. The music became muted slightly as they followed the maître d'. They emerged onto an empty patio with one table set with white linen, a candle in a hurricane class encircled by a doughnut-shaped crystal vase holding gardenia blooms. Banks of pink oleanders, ferns, tall trees with hanging wisps of Spanish moss formed a border to the patio, enclosing it, giving them privacy while flickering torches furnished the lighting.

"Jake, this is beautiful," she said. "No one else is seated out here," she said when she was alone with him at their table

"I've reserved the patio for us tonight. We'll be undisturbed."

"This is all ours," she said, looking around again. "It's gorgeous out here."

"I agree about gorgeous," he said, gazing intently at her and her attention returned to him.

"You look ravishing tonight, Caitlin," he said in a deeper voice.

"Thank you," she answered, her pulse racing as it had since he had come to her door. "Do you have a condo here? Is this another night you'll want me to stay over until tomorrow?"

"I don't have a condo here. I rent a hotel suite. As far as staying over—that, Caitlin, is up to you."

Another tingle taunted her while his blue eyes held unmistakable desire. "Want a glass of wine?"

"Yes," she said, looking at the wine menu and trying to focus on words in front of her, anything to tear her gaze from his. He saw too much. He knew the effect he had on her. She was flying back to Houston tonight. That was a promise to herself, but even as she made it, she hoped she had the willpower to live by it.

After they had ordered lobster dinners, he stood to take her hand. "Let's dance," he said, walking inside with her to the dance floor. The restaurant was warmer, the band belting out another blues number. She stepped into Jake's embrace to dance with him, more conscious than ever of the scent of him, the masculine aftershave, the faint, clean soapy smell. His strong neck was warm beneath her fingers, his short hair brushing her hand lightly.

She cared more for Jake than any other man she had ever known. Did she really want to part with him without intimacy? If she did, would she regret it forever? The question continued to disturb her. She had always feared an unplanned pregnancy, a repeat of what had happened to her mother, something she wanted to avoid at all costs. Make love to Jake? Was that so impossible? So fraught with hazard? Birth control was readily available. People made love now with no reason except lust. One night. She wouldn't lose her heart forever over one night with him. A memory to keep—making love with a man she might already be in love with.

The questions badgered her. She desired him, constantly, day and night. His kisses set her ablaze and right now, she wanted to kiss him and be kissed. One night with memories to hold forever.

As if he discerned her thoughts, he tilted up her chin to look into her eyes. "We could go to the hotel suite I've reserved—and eat in private."

"Jake, we have lobster dinners ordered," she whispered, tempted to yield, to take the risk for what she wanted.

"We can get lobster dinners there. Let's eat at the hotel, Caitlin."

Her mouth was dry and she couldn't answer. She merely nodded, her heart pounding. She held his wrist. "Jake, I'm not making a commitment to stay the night."

"I didn't ask you to," he whispered. "Let's go. I'll tell the maître d', pay the bill and he can surprise another couple with free lobsters."

Soon enough, they were back in the limo. As soon as the limo was moving through the quarter, slowly because of the crowd, Jake closed the partition and turned to take her into his arms.

She went swiftly, holding him tightly as she let go all the pent-up desire and poured herself into her kisses. Passion made her hot and eager. She ran her fingers through his hair, combing it back.

Pulling her onto his lap, he cradled her against his shoulder while he kissed her and tangled his hand in her hair to send pins flying. He was aroused, hard against her and his kisses swept her away until his hands were at the neck of her dress, starting to pull her zipper.

While she gripped his wrists, she sat up. "Jake, we've got to walk into the hotel. I won't look presentable."

"You look breathtaking. Every man tonight has turned to look at you. It would be impossible for you to look unpresentable," he whispered, leaning toward her, but she stopped him again.

"How far away is this hotel?"

"Not far. We'll wait to make you happy, but it is definitely difficult. Even more so than when we arrived in the Quarter. You look ready for love, darlin'," he drawled softly, his words pouring over her like warm, sweet honey.

She scooted off his lap, moving away from him slightly while he watched her with a smoldering look that kept her heartbeat racing. She took the rest of the pins from her hair and shook her head, letting the thick auburn locks tumble down on her shoulders.

Finally the limo slowed and stopped. They stepped out beneath a canopied awning in glittering lights to enter a lobby with crystal chandeliers, tall fountains with sparkling water splashing, and an atrium that swept up more than twenty stories. She went with Jake to the desk where they welcomed him.

He had the suite waiting so this was what he had expected to have happen. She was tempted to stop now, but she thought of her earlier arguments with herself.

This night, she would take Jake as a lover, the first man in her life and becoming more important to her each day.

Eight

As Jake held her arm, they took an elevator reserved for the penthouse suite. His pulse pounded. He had the suite reserved for tonight, but he had intended to ask her to go there late tonight after dinner and dancing.

He hadn't planned on how much he wanted her. She had flirted with him, set him on fire with her kisses, given him looks that kept him stirred and hot. When he had suggested leaving for the hotel, he half expected her to flatly refuse for the night.

Instead, he had been surprised, pleased even more by her response and willingness. Seduction tonight became a possibility. The prospect alone aroused him, kept him on edge. In minutes, he would have Caitlin all to himself.

They emerged from the elevator and he ushered her into the penthouse suite and switched on lights. "I'll get champagne to celebrate."

"Celebrate what?" she asked with a slight sharpness in her tone.

"Our friendship," he answered easily, seeing her visibly relax. He shed his coat and tie and crossed the room while she prowled like a cat.

"Jake, this is beautiful and there's already champagne, wine and a huge platter of tempting-looking hors d'oeuvres."

"Help yourself. They spoil me when I stay here."

"You must be a valued customer," she said with a hint of question.

He smiled. "I haven't brought a woman here before."

"Why not?"

He laughed at her question. "This is a private place where I can get away and people don't look here for me."

Caitlin canted a hip to one side and cocked her head to study him. "So why did you bring me, then?"

"Because this is a special night and I wanted to take you to one of my favorite places."

That earned a smile.

"I'll be forever glad you came to my ranch, Caitlin." She was so beautiful she took his breath away. Her hair was silky, thick and soft. As she moved, the slit in her dress revealed her long, shapely legs.

With an effort he walked away to switch on music that he turned low, blues by local artists. He went to the bar to pour two glasses of champagne and picked up the flutes that held the pale bubbly liquid. When he turned, Caitlin was nowhere in sight. Then he saw the door open on the darkened balcony and he walked outside where the night air was still warm.

"Jake, it's beautiful out here," she said. "The view is amazing with the river below us with all the varied boats. I can see the Quarter, even the music carries slightly. What a great place."

"I like it. It relaxes me to be here."

"There, that's how I feel about the house I grew up in. Even more so. I love that place beyond measure. You think of that when you make your decision. Jake, what you intend will involve more than business results. It's people and love and history and roots for me. You'll break my heart if you don't sell to me," she said bluntly.

He lifted his champagne flute. "Caitlin, here's to mending fences between a Santerre and a Benton. You and I can bury that past."

She gazed at him intently without raising her glass. "We can if you cooperate. Otherwise, it may grow worse. But for now," she said solemnly, raising her glass in a toast, "here's to mending fences." And she touched her glass to his with a faint clink.

They both sipped, watching each other. He could see desire plainly in her eyes. She had to see the same in his.

He took her glass and set it on a table beside his and drew her into his arms to dance.

"This is a dream night, Caitlin. I've been thinking about this all week, eager to get home to be with you."

Her perfume was exotic, another temptation. He didn't want to rush her. He wanted to take time, to weave a web of seduction so Caitlin would have the same desires that he did. From her signals, she already did.

His heartbeat raced and he was hot in spite of the pleasant evening temperature. He danced her inside and switched off lights, moving slowly with her, aware of her softness and her sweet smell, her silky hair against his cheek.

The song ended and another began. They continued dancing straight through the momentary silence, into the next song. He wrapped his arms around her, holding her close and dancing slowly with her.

Her soft curves were driving him over an edge. Monday was eons away. He had put it out of mind when he left to pick her up and it crossed his mind only dimly once in the evening. That was tomorrow's worry. Tonight he was with an intoxicating woman. He wanted to hold her, make love with her. He desired her with an intensity that shocked him. He turned to look at her and she gazed up at him, her green eyes sending a lightning bolt of electricity in him. "I want you, Caitlin. I want you to be mine," he whispered.

Jake's words set Caitlin's heart pounding. She was aware of their bodies pressed together, her thighs brushing his as they danced, of her being held close against his muscular chest, his strong arms around her. Seduction was in his every look and move.

For once in her life she was actually contemplating tossing aside her rules and promises and fears. A tremble shook her. Lamplights from the balcony shed a faint glow. She could see lights from boats on the dark, shimmering river, the myriad lights of the Quarter, but she barely noticed any of it as she turned to look at Jake when he drew her closer to kiss her.

She wrapped her arms around his neck and kissed him. They stopped dancing and stood in the semidarkness, kissing while her heart raced. His kiss was deep, possessive, seductive.

His tongue stroked hers, slowly, driving her wild. Lights exploded behind her closed eyelids. His kiss closed out the world. She wanted Jake with a need that consumed her. Never had a kiss stirred the hunger that Jake's kisses did.

While kissing him she clung to him tightly, thrusting her hips against him. How could he do this to her so easily? The question came and then was gone. Her thoughts were on his strong, muscled body, his fiery kisses, and his words, which were tearing away the last barriers around her heart.

In return, she intended to reach his own guarded heart. She hoped to melt him into mush the way he did her.

Jake's fingers were warm at her nape. Continuing to kiss her, he slowly tugged down the zipper to her dress. Cool air washed over her back and shoulders, then lower. Her hands went to the buttons of his shirt to twist them free.

She wanted the obstacles of clothing away, desired him with a need that amazed her. Unfastening his belt, she couldn't control a tremble in her fingers as she hurried. She let her hand drift down over his trousers, feeling his hard shaft. This moment was the last that she could turn back. She gave it a fleeting consideration. It was still possible to stop, to end this and be safe.

He groaned and kissed her, pushing her dress off her shoulders, sliding it over her hips to let it fall around her ankles. Holding his shoulders, she stepped out of the dress and kicked off her shoes.

Jake's hands went to her hips to hold her away and his gaze drifted slowly, taking a thorough perusal that might as well have been his hands on her.

Aching to be back in his embrace, she wanted to kiss him. "Jake," she whispered.

"Shh, Caitlin," he said softly. "Let me look at you. You're gorgeous and I can never get enough." He unfastened her wispy bra and dropped it. His hands drifted down to her lace panties, which he peeled off. His chest expanded as he inhaled.

With deft touches, he peeled down her thigh-high stockings, first one and then the other, his hands caressing her as he removed them.

"Jake," she gasped, each light caress an exquisite torment, fanning fires.

She unzipped his slacks and let them fall, pushing away his low-cut briefs to free him completely. "Jake," she whispered, caressing his thick rod.

He groaned again, pulling her to him and kissing her hard, his warm naked body pressed against hers.

Need was building fiercely as she trailed kisses across his chest and then down his flat belly.

With a gasp he swept her up into his arms. He kissed her as he carried her to a bedroom, placed her on the bed and stretched out beside her. He pulled her into his arms, against his heated body.

"I want you and I want to love you all night long. I want to kiss you from head to toe," he whispered.

Breathless from his words, she kissed him, silencing him, just wanting to love him.

As they kissed, his free hand roamed lightly down her back. When his hand slipped between her upper thighs, she spread her legs slightly to give him access to her.

Tumbling down in an ocean of sensation, she desired him more with each caress. There was no turning back now. She had made her commitment, focusing on loving him, turning loose all caution and restraint.

He shifted to cup her breast with one hand, scooting so he could take the taut bud in his mouth, his tongue circling the tip slowly, driving her wild with need. All Caitlin knew was Jake's hands and mouth and how badly she wanted to make love with him.

His fingers stroked between her thighs, while her hips thrust. She clung to him, suddenly shifting, pushing him down and straddling him to take his thick rod in her hand. She kissed him, her tongue driving him to groan with pleasure, until he pushed her down and pleasured her once again.

He opened her legs, letting his fingers tease and drive her wild and then his tongue followed until she was thrashing beneath his touch, the pressure building. "Jake, love me," she cried, drawing him closer.

Her eyes flew open. "Jake, I'm not protected," she whispered.

He moved off the bed and she watched, drinking in the sight of his bare body, his arousal that declared his desire. He returned to open a packet and put on a condom and then his hands caressed her until he lowered himself and eased into her.

"Caitlin!"

She heard the shock in his voice as he withdrew. She locked her legs around him and held him. "Love me, Jake. I want you now," she cried. "I know what I want."

"You're a virgin," he said, frowning.

She raised up partially to run her tongue over his chest while her hand played between his thighs and her other hand stroked his rod lightly.

As she fell back on the bed, pulling him with her, she met his gaze.

"Love me, Jake, now," she whispered.

He eased into her again, bending his head to kiss her, going slowly. Pain tore at her, bringing a moment of clarity, but it was gone swiftly. Desire had built beyond control or pain. Drawing him closer, she held him as he filled her. He eased carefully, until pain diminished, transforming to pleasure as she moved with him. With slow, deliberate strokes he made love until his control shattered.

Kissing her hard, he held her and pumped faster. She thrashed with him, ecstasy suddenly filling her while she climaxed with a white-hot burst of pleasure.

She cried out his name, unaware of what she had done. Her cries muffled his words as he said her name and endearments until he shuddered, reaching his climax.

She had no idea how long they loved, knowing only that she wanted him more than she had ever dreamed possible. To her surprise, she experienced satisfaction that went beyond any expectations she had.

As they slowed and their breathing gradually became normal she held him tightly. For a moment she hoped she had bound Jake to her in a manner he would never forget her, but then she realized that was an absurd hope. This idyll was a magic spell that held her. She didn't want it to end. Not yet. She held Jake's long, hard body close against her and stroked the back of his head.

Soon he rolled over and took her with him, holding her close with their legs entwined. He gazed at her with worry clouding his blue eyes. "Why didn't you tell me?"

"I don't see why it matters."

"It matters, Caitlin. First of all, I never wanted to hurt you."

She was silent a moment, wondering if he would say the same thing when he told her he was not going to sell her home back to her.

"The hurt was fleeting. Still a little, but not bad."

"It makes our loving special."

"And that's a bad thing?" she asked, feeling disappointment welling up, knowing they were not in love and all he wanted to do was seduce her.

"Not bad, just special, more than I usually am involved in," he said slowly, choosing his words carefully. He looked at her intently. "You're not hurting now?"

"Only slightly," she said, stroking his face. "And it *was* special, Jake."

He pulled her close to kiss her deeply. Her heart now belonged to him. She faced her feelings. She was hopelessly in love with the one man she should have guarded her heart against at all costs. When he released her, she placed her palm on the side of his face, gazing into his blue eyes while he stroked strands of hair away from her face.

"Caitlin, loving you was incredible."

"Even the way it turned out?" she asked.

"Even the way it turned out," he repeated, showering light kisses on her temple and cheek. "Beyond my wildest expectations." He rose up to look at her. "Stay here with me. Let's go back Sunday. I can't let you go now."

"Yes," she whispered, knowing in that moment she was falling in love with a man she not only had intended to avoid falling in love with, but a man she might be furious with in the future. If only he wasn't a Benton. That was a flight of fancy wish because that was the one thing they had between them and the one thing that had brought them together. They had the ranch, past history, old angers and hurts, and now new ones between them.

"You have twisted me around to do what you want," she added softly.

"I think you're the one doing the twisting. It's been worth it." He kissed her lightly again.

Releasing her he slipped out of bed, and leaned down to pick her up. "Let's go to the spa tub."

She wrapped her arms around his neck, momentarily unable to believe what was happening that seemed like a dream. Except the strong arms holding her were real, as real as the hard body she was pressed against.

Jake carried her into an enormous, lavish bathroom with a sunken tub, plants, mirrors and a bearskin rug. Grecian columns graced the decor.

"This is beautiful."

"Absolutely," he said, looking at her and once again, he wasn't talking about the bathroom. He climbed down in the tub, turned on faucets and pulled her close with her back against his chest.

Warm scented water soon filled the tub while he sponged her off and she turned to do the same for him, watching water glisten on his sculpted muscles. "You are one handsome hunk, Jake."

He grinned. "I'm glad you think so, but I believe when it comes to looks, you win, hands down. Speaking of hands down," he said, cupping her breasts with his wet, warm hands.

She gasped with pleasure, closing her eyes as his thumbs began to circle her nipples, so lightly, slowly drawing circles that ignited desire instantly.

"Jake," she whispered, opening her eyes to look at him. He was aroused, his shaft thick and hard. She leaned forward to kiss him as desire burst into flames.

Soon Jake stood and pulled her up with him, water splashing around both of them.

He climbed out of the tub and lifted her up to set her in front of him while he grabbed a towel and began stroking her slowly, drying her.

She clung to his shoulders. "Jake," she said, reaching him to pull him up. "Come here. I want to kiss."

"Shhh, this time we go slowly. I want to pleasure you. I want this to be better."

"Kiss me, Jake. It is better," she whispered, not knowing what she was saying to him and not caring. Desire was hot, an intense need that surprised her because she thought she wouldn't have this driving need again so quickly.

Lifting her in his arms, he carried her to bed and loved her slowly, a sweet torment that built in her until she was trembling. This time when he entered her, pain was fleeting. In seconds pleasure was all she felt, sensations carrying her higher and higher, each stroke building until she plunged into ecstasy, moving rapidly with him as they climaxed together.

"Jake, love me now," she cried. He held her tightly as they arched together, locked in making love. For this moment all was perfect between them. *If only it could last* was a fleeting thought she had. She cried out again in pleasure, rapture enveloping her.

Holding each other, they crashed after the peak. She listened to Jake gasping for breath as much as she was.

Finally, he rolled them both over and combed her hair back from her face while he showered light kisses on her. "Ahh, Caitlin, you're perfect. Marvelous, beyond my wildest dreams. I don't want to leave this bed this weekend. Stay here with me all weekend."

Another invitation. Another decision. Another tie to bind her to him in a manner she had never intended. Yet, how could she say no, given how she felt about him—even stronger now that they'd made love?

I want to stay with him, even if he won't sell my home to me, she realized, the thought scaring her more than the reality. Because I'm falling in love with Jake Benton.

She took a deep breath, then looked into his eyes. "Yes," she whispered, realizing she was taking more chances than ever before in her life.

"Yes, I'll stay the weekend."

He kissed her deeply, another kiss that made her feel special, his woman. A kiss that she hoped wasn't an illusion.

He raised up. "This has been a great night. What I've dreamed about all the past week, but I never knew it would be this stupendous."

"You're insatiable, Jake," she said, smiling at him and he smiled in return, filling her with warmth as they shared this special time between them. If only it held meaning, she couldn't help wishing.

"What are you thinking?" he asked.

"That I wish this could last," she admitted truthfully, watching him to see how he reacted.

"It's going to last for a long time if I have my way," Jake

declared. "I'm not letting you go now that I've found you. Beautiful woman, you don't know what you do to me."

She had to smile, but she wondered if he was even thinking about what he said to her. It couldn't last. Unless...he *had* to sell her the ranch, for intimacy to last between them. Otherwise, how could she stay in his life when he denied her something so important to her?

"I think you're given to exaggeration," she managed to tease, tangling her fingers in his chest hair.

"Not at all. You destroy me. You make me want you all the time. In minutes I'll feel as if we've never made love and want you desperately. You will never know how desperately."

She smiled again at him, running her finger over the tiny stubble beginning to appear on his jaw.

"I stand by what I said about you and exaggeration. But I'm glad you want me and you'll be desperate to love."

"Also, I'm beginning to suffer acute hunger. Since room service takes time, why don't we turn in an order?"

Jake climbed out of bed and she watched him walk across the room and disappear in the living area. Sitting up, she pulled the sheet up beneath her arms to wait. When he returned, he had a towel wrapped around his middle and two thick menus in his hand. He climbed into bed and pulled away her sheet.

"Jake!" She grabbed the sheet, but he gripped her wrists and kissed away her protests and in seconds, as they made love again, menus slipped forgotten to the floor.

It was two hours later when Jake called room service. It had closed for the night, but with a substantial tip promised to the kitchen staff and bellhop, Jake had no trouble placing their orders.

"I'm a loyal customer so they try to keep me happy."

"I'm trying to keep you happy," she said, smiling at him.

"You want to keep me really happy now, you'll come sit in my lap."

She crossed the room to him, wrapped her arms around his neck and kissed him. Jake's arms circled her waist and he held her close as he kissed her in return.

They spent the weekend in the hotel suite until Sunday afternoon when she pulled on her red dress and high-heeled sandals, feeling as if it had been months instead of only a couple of days since she had worn them before.

"Jake, we both have to get back to real life," she said, going to the living area to find him dressed once again in his suit with his phone in hand while he sent a text.

"I know we do," he said. He pocketed the phone and crossed the room to slip an arm around her waist. "Will you go out with me next weekend?"

She gazed into clear blue eyes that held desire even after a weekend of constant loving. She wanted to say yes more than anything. But she couldn't. If he decided not to sell her her family home, her heart would be broken. "Jake, I'm glad that you want to be with me again next weekend. But, let's hold off talking about the future for now. Our relationship is tenuous at best, something unplanned, and impossible to continue if we are poles apart on your decision. This isn't a threat because our relationship isn't that vital." *To you,* she added silently, her heart squeezing. "Anyway," she continued. "I'll see you Monday in Dallas."

"You could go home with me tonight and then you wouldn't have to fly up commercially."

"Thank you, but I already have my ticket, so I should stick to my plans that I've made. We'll know tomorrow where we stand," she added "Unless you can tell me now."

For an instant there was silence between them. A tense

moment when she could hear a grandfather clock tick and nothing else.

Then Jake shook his head. "I still have two men to hear from and then I'll give you an answer. Sorry to put you off so long."

She could read nothing from his expression, so she merely nodded. "Then we better go," she said, picking up her small purse and walking to the door.

Jake gripped her wrist and turned her to face him. He pulled her tightly against him and kissed her, a breathtaking kiss that reminded her of the intimacy they had just shared.

Her heart pounded. Desire ignited again, as hot and strong as before. Longing tore at her and made a knot of her insides. It was a possessive kiss as well as a goodbye kiss. In that moment, she felt certain he was going to refuse to sell to her. She hurt while at the same time, she wanted him more than ever.

Just as she had expected, loving had created new demons for her to fight. She just hoped it created some for him, as well.

She suspected it wouldn't be enough because he had been through all this before and had breakups under his belt. He would move along without much hurt.

She, on the other hand, could be losing her roots, the welfare of people she loved, as well as Jake himself.

She stood on tiptoe and again, poured herself into the kiss, trying to bind him to her by sensuality, the one way to reach him.

He released her, gazing at her intently. "Think about next weekend."

"I'll think about it," she answered, knowing she wouldn't be able to forget his invitation. "We should go now."

He nodded and held her arm as they walked to the limo.

On the flight to Houston, they both were much more silent.

She no longer felt like talking, definitely not like flirting with him. She could feel a chasm opening between them. Maybe it had been there the whole time and hope had blinded her.

At her door he kissed her goodbye again. She watched him walk back to the limo in long strides, climb in and vanish.

With a long sigh she entered her empty condo.

The phone rang and she tossed aside her purse and went to get it. When she answered, she heard Kirby's voice on the line.

"I've been trying to get you," he said, sounding nervous.

Nine

"**I** was out of town and just walked in the door." From the solemn sound of his voice something had happened and instantly she thought of Cecilia who was getting up in years. "Kirby, is Cecilia all right?"

"She's fine. That's not why I'm calling. Sorry if I scared you about her. Caitlin, Benton Drilling hit oil in that well they're drilling near the house."

Caitlin's insides clenched and she turned cold. "Oh, Kirby," she said, sitting because she felt weak-kneed. "Oh, I hate that. Jake will never sell now."

"Hell, no, he won't. There should be oil right under the house. They'll tear the home place down. I'm sorry to bring the bad news to you, honey, but better from me than from any of the damned Bentons. You still have an appointment on Monday with Jake Benton?"

Hot tears stung her eyes. She had given herself—completely—to Jake. And now, even if he *wanted* to sell to her, he couldn't. It wasn't about her house anymore. It was about business. Money. And the Benton family.

She should have known better.

And he should have, too, she thought. Her blood ran cold for a moment.

"Kirby, when did this happen? When did the Bentons *know?*"

"Saturday morning," Kirby answered grimly. I've been trying to reach you ever since we heard, but your phone just rang and rang."

Oh, no. She'd turned it off so that she and Jake would not be interrupted. And she'd been so deeply involved with him over the weekend that she'd forgotten to turn it back on at all.

"I'm sorry I missed you, Kirby. I still have an appointment tomorrow morning with Jake. I'll call you afterward."

"Sure, honey. Caitlin, don't worry about us. We'll get along and so will you. The old house isn't the world. You don't spend a lot of time in it any longer and it served its purpose well."

Her heart clenched. "I know, Kirby."

"Honey, we love you and don't you worry about us."

"I love all of you, too, Kirby. I'll call you in the morning."

She replaced the handset and gave vent to tears, feeling alone and heartbroken and betrayed as well, although she had only herself to blame for their lovemaking, yet it was not all regrets. She loved him and she had wanted the weekend with him. Oil so close to the house. Jake would want every inch of the land now.

The minute Jake left Caitlin and was back in the limo, he called Gabe. He looked again at the curt text message that simply read: Oil. He had received it Saturday and hadn't read it until Sunday before they left for home.

He tried to get his brother on the phone or by text, but was unsuccessful. He left messages and gave it up until he heard back from Gabriel, but it was obvious they had found oil.

The well was within three miles of Caitlin's house. When he had left town on Friday he had been all set to tell Caitlin no, that he would not sell the land back to her. Then the weekend had happened.

The weekend had been one the greatest. He had to admire her for fighting for those people. She was caring, understanding. They had shared laughter, friendship and easy conversation. She had placed her trust in him and made love when she had known he might not sell. She was the sexiest woman he had known. Thinking about her, he could easily get aroused. Right now if she called him back to bed, he would turn around and go right back to Houston. He wanted her in his bed. He wanted her in his life.

The minute he told her no, she would be gone. She had said as much and he was certain that's exactly what she would do. Friday, he had been prepared to let her go out of his life. Now he wasn't. Each time he thought about telling her goodbye, his insides twisted and a bad feeling swamped him.

"Dammit," he swore aloud, feeling helpless and a loss of control and hating having to sit in the limo without even driving to distract him. He didn't want to tell Caitlin goodbye. Not now.

He mulled over the dilemma and thought of the possibility of offering her a far corner of the Santerre place and moving the house, but there actually were two more men who would report to him in the morning about the possibilities of wind turbines on the ranch and about drilling for oil. Gabe would see him tomorrow. He was certain the decision would be to turn her down.

Tell her no and get over her, he told himself. The prospect was untenable. He didn't want her out of his life. Not yet.

Ten minutes after Jake arrived at his condo, Gabe showed up.

He was casually dressed in Levi's, Western boots and a long-sleeved Western shirt with sleeves rolled up. His dark brown hair was tousled and he had a slight beard as if he had missed a day of shaving.

"Did you get my message?" he asked, following Jake into a living area.

"Yes, I did. So the well came in."

"Yes and a good one," Gabe said, sounding jubilant as he withdrew folded papers out of his back pocket and dropped them on a table for Jake. "Here are figures and information and you can look it all over. I wanted to make sure you knew before you see Caitlin Santerre tomorrow, even though you intend to refuse to sell to her. That old house where she was raised may be in the middle of an oil field. I always told you I thought there was oil on their ranch."

"Well, you were right. We have the mineral rights to the Santerre ranch whether I sell the house or not."

Gabe looked up sharply from the text he was reading on his cell phone.

"You're not changing your mind about selling to her, are you?"

"I'm still debating," Jake said, bracing for the storm that was coming.

"The hell you say. You weren't 'debating' last week." Gabe's blue eyes narrowed. "What did you do this weekend? You didn't answer the text I sent you until Sunday afternoon."

"You didn't answer the one I sent you—period."

"I've been out at the ranch and just got back to Dallas. Where have you been?"

"I was in New Orleans with Caitlin."

Gabriel groaned. "Dammit, did you sleep with her?"

"I don't see that's any of your business," Jake snapped, becoming annoyed with his younger brother's interference.

"Oh, hell. That means you did. That's why you're debating. If you tell her no tomorrow, she won't let you back in bed with her. That's what has you hot and bothered and 'debating.'"

"Gabe, it's none of your damn business what I do with Caitlin and if I decide to sell the land back to her, we still have rights to drill and you know it."

"It would sure as hell complicate things though in a lot of ways. They won't like the trucks, the noise, the drilling. Not to mention if we want to drill close to that shrine of a house she has. Look at the maps I brought you. You're going to let some sentiment interfere with your business sense and a lot of money?"

"There's a lot of land. You know it wouldn't have to be right in that one place."

"Jake, if we're close, it'll be just as bad. What's the deal? You know plenty of good-looking women and you barely know Caitlin Santerre. Dump her and go out with someone else. Someone you know and like."

"Thanks for the keen advice, Mom," Jake remarked dryly.

Gabe leaned forward to place his elbows on his knees and stare at his brother. "She probably slept with you just to get you to sell to her. You sell and she may disappear just as quickly out of your life. Knowing your luck with women, you probably can't even imagine such an event."

"Gabe, you're getting on thin ice," Jake said, trying to hang on to his temper. "Drop the subject of Caitlin."

"I can't believe this. You're letting a Santerre cloud your judgment. After you had already reached a decision about what you would do. She must have been really hot."

Jake stood, his fists clenched, and took a deep breath.

"Look, I'll make a decision and you'll have to live with it, which you can do. Now you're pushing me, Gabe. If I want to sleep with someone, that's my business and selling land back to her is not the end of the world or even a dime out of our pocket. I'll put a steep price on it because she'll pay it, but you stay out of my private life. No more remarks about Caitlin, either."

"I can't believe I'm having this conversation." Gabe leaned back and put his hands behind his head, studying Jake. Jake was angry, fighting it because part of the anger was with himself, part with Gabe, and part with Caitlin for getting him tangled up in her life.

"Want me to tell her?"

"What do you think?" Jake asked.

"Tell her no, Jake. By a month from now, you will have forgotten all about this. You let her keep that land, you'll have nothing but trouble and she could will it back to her half brother."

"She won't do that. There's no love between Will and Caitlin."

"You *care* about her. Damnation, Jake, you *care* about a Santerre. You've hated them all your life. What the hell happened?"

"I got to know her and I like her. I feel sorry for those people who've worked for her grandmother—"

"Oh, no. No, no," Gabe said. "You didn't feel sorry for them last week when you were planning on giving them the boot. Oh, no. That has nothing to do with it and don't tell me it does."

"All right," Jake snapped, his temper rising again. "It's Caitlin. It's land I acquired. The company is drilling on it, but I, personally, bought it and own it, so I can do with it as I damn well please," he told Gabe.

They stared at each other a long, tense moment. Jake

could feel the clash of wills that sparked the air. Then Gabe stood.

"I have to get going. You're right of course. It is your land to do as you please. So we just go from there and see what we can do. In the meantime, we'll make a tidy sum on this well."

"Good deal, Gabe. Thanks for what you've done."

Gabe shook his head. "You're loco, Jake. A Santerre is nothing but trouble. You'll see. She's just using you."

Jake shrugged, curbing the flash of anger he felt. "Time will tell, Gabe."

"Yeah, twenty-four hours of time. Well, it's your choice. You're all grown up now and know what you want to do."

"Thanks for coming by," Jake said.

"Sure. You keep thinking about it. You've had a complete turnaround."

"I'll think about it," Jake said, wondering if there would be a moment when he could let go thinking about it.

Gabe left and Jake closed the door behind him. He picked up the papers Gabe had brought and sat to read them, finding his mind wandering to Caitlin often.

Finally he pushed the papers aside and reached for the phone, wanting to talk to her, missing her and longing to hold her. He released the phone and sat back, thinking about tomorrow. He should tell her no. He had been all set to do so.

She had been a virgin—he was the first man in her life. He felt a mixture of emotions about that. She had to care about him and to have wanted to sleep with him to give up her virginity to him at age twenty-eight.

Had she done it purely to get him to sell to her? He didn't think she had. If he sold to her, would she get out of his life and not want to see him? As a Santerre, would she try to run the drillers off the property?

The logical thing was to refuse to sell and go on with life.

Each time he reached that conclusion, he couldn't face carrying it out. He wasn't any happier with the choice of letting her keep the land because he had looked at the maps Gabe had given him. Her house would more than likely end up in the middle of oil rigs. She wouldn't be happy. By then she might have to move anyway. He should tell her no and he could explain why.

He paced the room restlessly, arguing with himself for another hour before he left to work out and hoped to forget for a few minutes the problems looming in his life.

More than anything, he missed Caitlin and wanted to talk to her.

Monday morning Caitlin dressed with care, trying to look sophisticated, appealing and all business. It hadn't been twenty-four hours since she'd seen Jake but she missed him, missed his company, his kisses, his humor, his flirting, his sexy loving. Today his answer would be no and she had already started doing what she could to find places for Kirby, Cecilia and Altheda.

She hurt because she was in love with Jake, furious with him at the same time, yet she could see from a business standpoint why he would want the old house, buildings, people and animals out of the way. She ached, wanting to be with him. She felt torn in two.

She had rearranged her calendar and booked a hotel room in Dallas since she would be dealing with Realtors over the next couple of days. She intended to spend the afternoon trying to locate a suitable place to move Cecilia and Altheda. Kirby already had job offers from other ranchers. Most likely, Altheda might. They were all comfortably set from the money left to them by her grandmother, but Kirby and Altheda both liked to keep busy.

She pulled on the jacket of her charcoal suit. She wore a matching silk blouse and matching pumps and had her hair pinned on her head. She had already had one call from Cecilia to reassure her to not worry about them. Kirby had received two job offers.

She gazed in the mirror and fought back tears. She was holding on to Cecilia, Kirby and Altheda because they were a substitute family for her—the only one she had. They had been there for her all her life, Kirby teaching her to ride, to care for her horse and later, to develop an eye for a good horse. She couldn't ever let go or lose her love for the three of them and now they were all older with physical problems beginning to be part of their lives. She didn't want them worrying about jobs or income or having to lose each other. Kirby's wife had died ten years earlier. The other two had lost husbands years earlier, before they came to work for her grandmother.

Jake could never understand her close relationship with them because he had a big, close family, even if he did fight with his father on occasion.

She thought about how Jake spent money and the fortune he was giving up because he was too stubborn to do what his father wanted. That didn't bode well for her.

She gave one last look at herself, picked up her briefcase and purse and headed to the airport for her flight to Dallas. She would be in Jake's office in only a few hours. She just wanted to get the meeting over and get away. She was determined to keep control of her emotions because she never wanted Jake to know how deeply she felt for him. Hopefully, after today, all those feelings for him would vanish because it hurt to be torn in two over him.

If he could turn down his father's fortune without hesitation, he could just as easily turn down selling land back to her.

When she landed in Dallas, she rented a car and drove to

Jake's office. Taking a deep breath, she walked into his office after his secretary had announced her.

Jake stood and closed the door behind her. She barely glimpsed a luxurious, spacious office with a balcony, walls of books, leather furnishings, a big-screen television and bar. All she saw was the tall, brown-haired man at the door. His riveting gaze met hers and held. Her heart thudded and her first reaction was to want to walk into his arms and kiss him. He was breathtakingly handsome in a navy suit that made his eyes appear a darker blue.

"Come in and have a seat," he said and his greeting confirmed her guess that he would refuse to sell. His coolness hurt as if nothing had happened between them and the past weekend hadn't existed.

She fought back tears that threatened, determined to avoid letting him see how upset she was over his cold reception. This morning he was all business. She still wondered how much was revenge against the Santerres, driving them totally out of the county and away from him.

Had he seduced her to amuse himself? Or to add his own touch of Benton success over the Santerres?

She sat in a leather chair in front of his desk and crossed her legs. He pulled a chair to face her.

"Let's get this over with, Jake," she said, glad her voice sounded as calm as if she discussed the weather. "Kirby called me as soon as I got home. He had been trying to reach me over the weekend, but of course I didn't take my calls. One more mistake. He told me about the oil. Congratulations to you and Benton Drilling and your brother who predicted this."

"Thanks. My brother is delighted to see that he was right when he said he would find oil."

"That makes your victory over the Santerres so much

larger. You found the oil when my father couldn't. I know you are not selling back to me."

"Caitlin, would you want to buy the house knowing we're drilling right by it? With all the machinery, smells, noise and men working? I've thought about other possibilities. I can get the house moved."

"I've looked into that. It's a three-story old home—over a hundred years old. They've told me it would damage it structurally to move it. There may be a company out there who will tell me something different, but that possibility exists. I'm not moving it," she said, mollified slightly that he was looking at an alternative and trying to work something out. Maybe he cared more than she had realized. "Maybe before the past weekend together, but now I want more from you, a real commitment that you could best show by allowing me to buy the place." She took a deep breath.

"Caitlin, dammit," he said, placing his elbows on his knees and gazing intently at her. "That's moving where I'm not ready to go. I'm offering you hope of saving the house by moving it. I know what this means to you."

"I'm not surprised, Jake. When you put me off so long, I figured this was where we were headed. Then when your brother found oil, I knew the answer. I know you're giving me the best business answer, the most practical one from your standpoint. At one point, a compromise of moving it would have been acceptable. But now I want more from you. More than you can give me. I don't see any point in discussing it further." She stood, feeling a sensation of suffocating in his office that had sunlight streaming through glass, one sliding glass door open with cool fall air pouring in.

He stood, too. She gazed into darkened blue eyes.

"This isn't what I wanted and this isn't the way I want things between us to end," he said in a tight voice. He moved closer to her, placing his hands on her shoulders.

She inhaled, wanting him in spite of her anger and hurt, while at the same time furious with him and wanting him out of her life. "I wish I had never gone to your ranch and tried to get you to sell the land back to me," she said, fighting more than ever to keep from letting tears come. "Get out of my way, Jake. Out of my life. We don't have one thing to say to each other now except you won. The Bentons wiped out the Santerres and you did it single-handedly, seducing a Santerre in your dealings."

That was all their "relationship" had been to him. A game of seduction. And he'd won.

She brushed past him. Before she could reach the door, he caught her, spinning her around to wrap her in his arms. Her protest was destroyed by his mouth covering hers as he kissed her, bending slightly so she had to cling to him.

His tongue thrust deep in a passionate kiss that stormed her senses and brought the weekend swirling back.

The hurt she had experienced all morning skyrocketed. The man she loved was kissing her as if she was totally essential to his life. She wanted him physically, aching for his hands, his kisses and his loving. At the same time, she was enraged with him, wanting to get him out of her life and never see him again no matter how much she hurt in doing so.

He kissed her passionately while one hand caressed her nape, drifting down her back to cup her bottom against his hard arousal.

"No, Jake," she said, twisting out of his arms.

They both gulped for air as they stared at each other. Passion had been hot and desperate.

"Stay out of my life," she said. "I'll get everyone off your ranch and may you enjoy your millions you'll make from the oil discovery."

While her words poured out, she shook with rage and pain.

"Do you really want me to sell it back to you and you and

your people will live in the center of an oil field? Kirby can't run his cattle there. There will be lights and noise and trucks at all hours of the day and night, not to mention the smell. Have you even thought this through?"

"I've thought it all through and faced up to my mistakes in succumbing to your seduction, which I hope to blank out of my memory. Stay away from me, Jake, although I should save my breath. I suspect you have done exactly what you set out to do and you have no further use for me."

"That's damn well not true and you know it. The kiss we just shared makes that plain."

"Get out of my way. We don't have one thing to say to each other now except you won. The Bentons wiped out the Santerres and you did it single-handedly, seducing a Santerre in your dealings," she said, striking out blindly because she hurt.

"Take the time you need," he said gruffly.

"Thank you for your generosity," she couldn't resist replying. "I'm going. You can celebrate your victory, your fortune and one more meaningless seduction. I hope we never see each other again."

She rushed past him wanting to get out while she still had shed no tears. In the elevator, the tears came, blinding her and making her angrier at herself for succumbing to Jake, for falling in love with him, for ever hoping for any concession from a member of the family that had fought with hers for generations.

In the car she tried to gather her wits and get over the emotional upheaval in order to drive to her hotel. Taking deep breaths, she finally got control, wiping away her tears. She tried to shift her thoughts to what to do next.

When she felt she could focus on her driving, she left. Jake had never intended to sell one inch of the ranch back to her and had played her along until he could seduce her and then toss her aside.

She thought of the fiery kiss. Had he hoped for another quick lovemaking in his office? Or that she would let him stay in her life and sleep with him until he tossed her out?

She had no idea what his intentions were, only her own. No matter how badly it hurt, she would get over him. Determined to focus on her problems, she attempted to shove thoughts and memories of Jake out of mind. Jake could live with his conscience now.

The thing she dreaded was telling Cecilia who was an optimist, always hoping for the best and giving everyone the benefit of the doubt. Kirby already expected the inevitable outcome and Altheda was as much a pessimist as Cecilia was an optimist, so she expected the refusal from the start.

As soon as she let them know, she would make her plans, deciding to look into some kind of senior assisted living for Cecilia and Altheda.

The minute she closed the door to her hotel room and was alone, Caitlin gave in to her emotions once more, putting her head in her hands to cry. She loved Jake and she wasn't going to stop loving him any time soon no matter how angry she was with him. His rejection hurt badly and memories were a torment that would only grow worse as she began to miss seeing and talking to him. Had their time together meant even the slightest thing to him? Or had he just been another Benton getting even with a Santerre for past history? Jake hated the Santerres because of his sister. He could easily have done everything in revenge, but it was Will the revenge should have been directed against. Not her. She had been an innocent bystander.

Shocked when she looked at the time, she saw she had cried for an hour. She tried to ignore a pounding headache as she went to the bathroom to wash her face and place a cold cloth on her temple and then at her nape.

She picked up the phone to call Kirby because he would be the easiest call to make of the three. He expected the refusal and had already been thinking about the future.

"Kirby, I'm back at the hotel," Caitlin said, seeing Kirby, probably with his phone while he sat on a bale of hay or perched on a fence.

"He refused, didn't he?"

"Yes, just as you thought he would."

"I don't know why he strung you out, Caitlin. Well, I do know. He wanted to go out with you because you're a beautiful woman now. You probably won't see him again."

"I definitely won't. I told him as much—to stay out of my life."

"Is that what you want?" Kirby asked and she thought she detected curiosity in his tone.

"Definitely. I don't want to see him again," she said, the words hollow and making her hurt more.

"I hope you mean that," Kirby said.

"I'm going to look at assisted living places this afternoon for Cecilia and Altheda. Is there anything I can do for you?"

"Thanks, no. I've had four good job offers. Caitlin, one is down near El Paso. I won't see any of you as often, but I'm thinking about it, because it's a great job."

"Kirby, do what you want. We'll see each other. We don't see each other for months at a time now. Just don't worry about me. I'll be fine."

"I know you will. I'll go check on Cecilia and Altheda and see that they're okay after you break the news. Cecilia is as sentimental about that house as you are. Maybe even more. You'd think she had grown up in it."

"I know. This won't be easy."

"Caitlin, you forget Jake. Go on with your life."

"I will," she said.

"I'll get back with you," Caitlin said and broke the connection. She dreaded telling the women, debating whether to go to the ranch to let them know. Finally she made the call, hurting and crying when Cecilia started to cry. In minutes they concluded the call and Caitlin shed more tears, but she was relieved by Kirby's positive outlook and knew she could count on him to cheer Cecilia and Altheda.

Making a string of calls, Caitlin set up appointments, feeling the only hope for getting over her unhappiness was to immerse herself in work and in getting everyone off the ranch as soon as possible.

Her thoughts shifted to Jake. Was he going out tonight to celebrate with his brother? Or with a woman? How soon would another woman be in his life? For all Caitlin knew, there could have been one in his life all along.

The phone rang. She had told few people where she was staying, giving her cell number to the Realtors. She was surprised to hear her friend's voice. "Ginny, hi. I suppose you called to learn the outcome. It was what I expected."

She received another surprise to hear Ginny say she was in the hotel and wanted to come up and see her.

In minutes Caitlin let her tall, blonde friend into the room. Ginny carried two frosty malts and handed one to Caitlin. The minute she closed the door, Ginny gave her a hug.

"I'm sorry, Caitlin."

"Thanks. Come sit and we'll talk. What are you doing in Dallas? I thought you were at home in Houston."

"I wanted to be with you. I thought you'd need a friend this morning." Worried brown eyes gazed at Caitlin who smiled at her closest friend.

"You're the best. Thanks for the malt."

"You look as if you need it. It was worse than you expected, evidently. When do you have to get everyone off the ranch?"

"There's time. I have one more month. They struck oil and that's that. My house could eventually be in the middle of an oil field. It would be bad even if he sold it back, but he doesn't want to do that, of course. I don't think he ever intended to. I think he was just stalling because he wanted to go out with me."

"You had a good time with him."

"Yes, I did, but now I wish I'd never gone to his ranch. I gained nothing." *Except memories and a broken heart,* she added silently.

"You would have had regrets if you hadn't tried," Ginny said.

"You're right. I would have. If it hadn't been for the oil, I might have had a chance. On the other hand, he's a Benton and he's bitter about Will and his sister."

"I remember that and all the wild stories, that Brittany Benton was carrying Will's baby and he wouldn't marry her. That Will murdered her. That she tried to run him off the road and lost control and was killed. No one will ever really know what happened. I'm sure Will won't ever change his story. He was under oath."

"Will swore to my grandmother that he was telling the truth. He *always* told her the truth. He feared Grandmother."

"He might have feared prison more," Ginny remarked dryly and for a moment was silent. "Will you see Jake again?"

"No. I don't ever want to see him again," Caitlin said and Ginny studied her.

"Caitlin, when I talked to you before you went out with him last weekend, you sounded happy, really happy. Did you fall in love with him?"

Caitlin looked up to meet Ginny's curious stare. "I cared,

but I'll get over it," she said, unable to deny the truth to her closest friend.

"You did fall in love with him," Ginny said. "I knew it. Oh, my. That makes everything so much worse."

"Yes, it does, but I'll get over it," she repeated more firmly, wondering how long it would take to stop hurting.

"Next weekend I'll make plans and we'll keep so busy, you won't have time to think about Jake Benton."

Caitlin had to smile. "You do that. I may be busy anyway, trying to get everyone moved."

"All right. Let's see how I can help you get places lined up."

"Ginny, what a friend you are," Caitlin said, feeling slightly better, knowing Ginny would help take her mind off Jake for a while. "I know you're taking time from your work."

"I can do it. I took a few days off. Let's see your list of things to do and what I can help with."

As they went over tasks, Caitlin stared at the phone numbers, scratching out Jake's, recalling this morning and his fiery kiss.

"Caitlin—"

Startled, she looked up and saw Ginny frowning. "I'm sorry, what?"

"You haven't heard anything I've said to you for the last ten minutes. You're worse off than I thought."

Caitlin felt her cheeks burn and hated the blush that caused it. "My mind drifted, sorry."

"Drifted to one Jake Benton. You're really in love with him."

"No, I can't be, Ginny. When I talk to Kirby and Cecilia— no, I'm not," she said, lost again thinking about Jake with a tight knot in her throat.

Was he celebrating now? Was he going to forget her easily and go right on with his life, jubilant with the discovery of oil, never even thinking about what he had done that had been hurtful?

Had their time together meant anything to him?

Ten

Jake had a busy morning. At noon he planned to leave for an hour workout at his condo because he didn't feel like eating lunch. He had made mistakes during the morning—not heard things that were said to him, lost his train of thought in the middle of a meeting and stopped listening several times on business calls.

He had to get a grip on his feelings. Never in his life had he minded a breakup. He had never intended to sell the land back to Caitlin. At first, he had just wanted to go out with her to make love to her. Then he had liked being with her and he admired her. She became someone he enjoyed, someone who set him ablaze and the mutual attraction had been intense.

He had known it would be bad when he turned her down and he had expected her anger, but never had he thought he would care to this extent. He didn't even understand his own reactions. He'd told women goodbye before. A couple had walked out on him, but it hadn't disturbed him greatly. Or even a little. He had simply moved on.

That wasn't happening this time.

He reminded himself it had only been a few hours since she had walked out of his life, but that shouldn't make any difference. He wanted her back. He missed her. He wanted to look forward to going out with her again. When had she become important to him?

Why had she been so damned unforgiving? He already had the answer to his own question. Those people in the Santerre house were the only people she had. She had no family left except Will and she couldn't count Will Santerre as family. He treated her as if she didn't exist. Jake mulled over her remarks about wanting more now. She had been talking about love, not land or house or money. He drew a deep breath. How important had she become in his life?

As Jake left the building to drive to his condo, Gabe approached.

"I was just coming to see you," Gabe said. "Want to go to lunch? We can talk then."

"I'm going home and for a workout."

Gabe's eyes narrowed. "It must have been bad this morning. You don't skip lunch for exercise. Let's go talk. You can run a little later."

Jake nodded and walked beside his younger brother. They both went to the car in silence that was unbroken until they were seated on the patio of a restaurant.

"All right. You look as if you got kicked by a horse. What happened?"

"Dammit, Gabe. What do you think happened? I wrecked Caitlin's life this week. Well, not hers exactly, but she has to put those people out of the only home they've known for the past—I don't know how many—years. Long before she was born. She loves them because they are the only family she has."

"She can love them on another ranch. Let them move. She's got money and Kirby has a reputation in the area as being the best foreman, bar none. We've got a damned good one, but people say that about Kirby. The man knows horses. They still have two fine horses Kirby bought for them. She'll survive and she'll get over this and so will they."

"Maybe. I still felt like a heel."

Gabe waved his hand. "When trucks get to rumbling across that ranch at all hours, she won't be sorry. I don't think she'll be there much anymore, anyway. She'll forget her anger with you after they get settled into a new place."

"I don't think so, Gabe. That old house means something to her. They've got a month to vacate, but leave it standing until I say otherwise."

"What the hell for?" Gabe asked, studying his brother. "Are you going out with her this weekend?"

Jake had a stabbing pain in his middle. "No," he answered. "I don't know why I let you talk me into this lunch. I'm not hungry and I don't want to talk about it."

Gabe stared at him until Jake looked away. "That's what this is about. You're not angry over having to say no to her. You're undone because she won't go out with you again. You want to see her and she won't agree to it."

Jake clamped his jaw closed and wished he had gone ahead with his exercise and stayed away from Gabe who was making him feel worse.

"Lord, help us," Gabe said. "You're in love with her."

Jake jerked around to look at Gabe sharply. "I am not in love."

"Could fool me. You don't want to eat. You were out of it when you talked to Fred this morning because he told me that he got an answer from you, but that it didn't make sense.

Didn't to me, either. I told him to call you back and get it straightened out between you. He said he would this afternoon by two at the latest. Has he already called?"

"I don't remember."

"Damnation, you've fallen in love with her."

"No, I haven't."

"You wouldn't know. You've never really been in love in your life. In love with a Santerre. Jake, that's terrible."

"Thanks for your vote of confidence in this. Get off my back. I'm not in love with Caitlin. I'm not even going to see her again. She doesn't ever want to see me."

"Uh-huh. I'm willing to bet on that one. Unless she was faking interest to get the sale out of you."

"She wasn't faking interest," Jake said, his thoughts more on Caitlin than his conversation with his brother. Was he in love with her? Was this what love was like? This all-consuming need to see and be with someone? "Let's drop this subject because I'm tired of hearing about it."

"Sure, okay by me," Gabe said, switching to talk about a purchase of land they had made in New Mexico.

Relieved to get his mind on something else, Jake tried to focus intently on his brother's conversation only to drift back to thoughts of Caitlin and wishing he would see her after work this week. Was he in love? If he was, what would he do to get over it? How long was the hurt going to last?

By the following week Jake was in a sour mood, quiet at the office, burying himself in work in an effort to shut Caitlin out of his thoughts, but he couldn't do it. He thought about her constantly and he missed her more with each passing day. The empty weekend had been hellish. He had asked someone out Saturday night, hoping to take his mind off Caitlin. Instead, he could barely remember to be courteous and he had ended the evening early. Now he couldn't even remember which woman he had called to go out. To Jake's relief, Gabe hadn't mentioned Caitlin after that first day at lunch.

He missed her, wondered about her and what she was doing. He had reached for his phone to call her repeatedly, each time stopping because there was no point in it and she wouldn't want to talk to him.

Late Thursday afternoon the first week in November, over a week and a half since he had last seen Caitlin, Gabe came by with papers for him to sign.

"You could have sent these over and not brought them yourself," Jake said as he signed them.

"I didn't want you to lose them. I want them signed and back promptly."

"Since when have I lost papers?"

"Since you've been in love with Caitlin Santerre," Gabe snapped. "Where is that Turner contract I sent over Tuesday?"

Startled, Jake stopped signing. "Tracie asked me about that and I told her to find it and get me to sign it. I don't recall hearing from her again."

"Tracie isn't forgetful and you know it. Don't lay this one on her. You've lost it. I can get another contract, because it originates with us. I'll bet it's in your basket or somewhere around your desk."

"I'll get her to look for it," Jake said, making a note. "Then I'll get it to you."

"Jake, you're in a fog and I know it's over Caitlin. Have you called her?"

"No, and it wouldn't do any good to do so."

"Maybe. You don't know until you try. She may be suffering as much as you."

"She's too angry to go out with me."

"Call her and see. You're going to mess up some big business deal if you keep on this way."

"No, I won't," he said, wondering if he could keep his promise. *Call her,* he told himself. He longed to hear her voice.

To his relief Gabe finally left him alone. Jake sat in his empty office with his thoughts on Caitlin. Was he really in love? Should he call her? What did she feel for him? If this was love, under the circumstances, what could he do about it?

For the next four days, he debated with himself whether to call her or not. Finally he decided he would fly to West Texas to look at the new well.

While he was there, he met with Kirby. Then he visited both Cecilia and Altheda. He returned to his ranch, spending a quiet, solitary night thinking about Caitlin and the future. The next day he flew to Houston to go to her office, a public place where she would have to be civil to him.

He learned she was at her gallery. When he drove up to the gallery, which held a bronze statue outside in a landscaped bed, he looked at two black-and-white pictures on easels inside the shop window. One black-and-white was of two small girls. The picture held a bit of whimsy with kites in the background. The girls each had an ice cream cone. Their features were clear and they looked filled with happiness and the innocence of childhood on a summer day. He moved on to the next picture, which was artistic with interesting textures and shapes. It was a building from the French Quarter of New Orleans, he was sure.

Reminding him of time spent with her. Of how he felt about her.

He pulled out his cell and called her.

Caitlin looked up from a ledger on her desk as her cell phone rang. Her pulse jumped when she saw the number. Instantly, anger followed. She was tempted to not even take the call, but curiosity won and she raised the phone to her ear.

"Caitlin." Jake's deep voice was clear. She hated the reaction she had to the sound of his voice. Her pulse raced and she wanted to end the call, but she didn't have the willpower to do so.

"What is it, Jake?"

"I'm in front of your gallery. I want to see you."

Startled, she looked up. She was in her office and couldn't see the large windows out front. "Why? We don't have anything to discuss."

"We might. Do you want to go somewhere or do you have a place where we can talk?"

"Come in, Jake. I'm in my office."

Her heart raced and she glanced down at the blue shirt and slacks she wore. Her hair was in one long braid. It didn't matter how she looked, she reminded herself. Then Maggie, her receptionist, showed Jake into the office and she gazed into his blue eyes, feeling as if she had been struck by a lightning bolt.

Jake wore chinos, a white shirt open at the neck and Western boots. He took her breath and her heart raced and she hated her reaction more than ever.

He glanced around only briefly, gazing intently at her as he closed the door. "Nice gallery and nice pictures in front."

"Have a seat. Why are you here?"

"I want to see you and I want to talk to you." He crossed the room and sat in a chair facing her across her desk. She was happy to keep the desk between them, wanting barriers, hoping to get him out of her office quickly. She didn't want him to know the effect he still had on her and her fury was difficult to keep in check. Beneath the fury was her galloping heart that still melted at the sight of him.

"How've you been?"

"I'm fine. Why are you here?" she repeated, wanting the visit over and done.

"I've been to your ranch to talk to Kirby, Cecilia and Altheda."

Another jolt of surprise hit her. "You have?" she said without thinking, so startled by his statement. "Whatever for?"

"I've hired Kirby to work for me. It seemed a simple solution. He can stay right where he is."

"Kirby agreed to this? And he hasn't even told me?" She stared at Jake in shock.

"He agreed and I asked him to let me tell you. I talked to him yesterday. I went to see Cecilia and Altheda and told them they could stay in the house, that it would not be torn down. It will still be near oil wells and drilling and there will be noise and everything that goes with the drilling, but they can stay where they are."

Stunned, Caitlin sat immobile while she mulled over what he had just told her. "Why did you do this?"

"I want you back in my life," he said. He stood, walking around her desk and her heart thudded as she watched him. She couldn't get her breath. Were his feelings changing? Was he doing this to continue sleeping with her? Or was he feeling something deeper?

"I've been through too much emotionally." He reached to grip her wrist and pull her to her feet. Her pulse raced and questions besieged her.

"Caitlin, I've missed you." He took her wrist again, holding his thumb against her. "Your pulse is racing. We had something great between us and I want you back. I've been miserable without you."

She thrilled to what he was saying and wanted to throw herself into his embrace. At the same time, she couldn't.

"Jake, I have resolutions I've lived by. I tossed them aside that weekend for you. I've missed you terribly—"

"Ah, Caitlin, come here," he said, reaching out again. She pushed his hand away and shook her head.

"I told you when we met that I am not into casual relationships."

"Dammit, this won't be a casual relationship."

"Are you proposing?"

He had been reaching for her again, but with her question, his hand stilled. "I'm not into marriage and you know it."

"While I'm not into a relationship without a binding commitment. Can they stay in the house with that answer from me? Are you doing this to get me back into your bed?"

"It's much more than that. I like being with you. I miss you. I like talking and doing things together. Yes, I want you in my arms in my bed, but I want to be with you, too. Can't we go out together and see where the relationship goes?"

She ached to say yes, but she had spent a lifetime determined to never end up the way her mother had—an affair, an unanticipated pregnancy and the man turning his back on her. While Jake's words thrilled her, she wanted so much more from him.

"Caitlin, if I marry this year, my father will have won his battle," Jake said when she remained silent without answering his question. "My dad will be running my life and he'll continue running it forever. This is a big one. I have strong feelings for you," Jake said and her heart thudded. All her being longed to throw her arms around him, kiss him and forget this conversation, but if she did, she would be more lost than before. And there would be no permanency in her life.

She hurt as if cut by a knife, but now was the time to abide by what she wanted even if it cost her Jake in her life. She would never be happy the other way. It would be fleeting and then she would want more and be more in love with him.

"Jake, your words are magic, but I can't go into a relationship without a commitment. I won't do it, not even after our weekend together."

"Dammit, Caitlin, I love you and I want you," he said, grinding out the words and pulling her into his embrace to kiss her. Unable to resist, she responded, clinging to him and kissing him wildly with all the longing she had suffered over empty, sleepless nights.

"I love you...." Magic words that thrilled her and were another assault against her resistance. She wanted him with all her being, wanted his total commitment forever. She wasn't ever again going through what she had just been through, thinking he was out of her life, seeing their lovemaking turn into memories.

She held him tightly, pouring love, longing into her kisses, running her hands over him, wanting him and aching to lock her door and make love here in the office.

"Go out with me, Caitlin. I've dreamed about you," he whispered, showering kisses on her. "I can't work, I can't sleep, I'm forgetting things I shouldn't, making poor decisions. I want you back in my life. It'll be a commitment."

She looked up at him, framing his face with her hands. "Is that a proposal?"

He looked pained. "You know I will not marry. Dammit, you know why I won't. I refuse to give in to my dad on this because it's a giant, life-changing ultimatum that will make him think he can do the same thing again and again where I'm concerned. No, I can't marry, but I can promise a lasting relationship."

She stepped away from him, trying to gather her wits and her resolve. "If your father told you to forget what he said, whether you marry or not wouldn't matter, would it change how you feel?"

He blinked and looked surprised for a fleeting moment, as

if the prospect had never occurred to him. "I hadn't thought about it that way. And it's pointless to because he's here, in my life and meddling in the worst possible way." Jake's gaze was steady. "I love you, Caitlin."

"I've loved you since before our weekend together," she replied, thrilling to his words that made her want to kiss him, to forget everything else. She clung to fighting for what she wanted.

"If you really love me, you'll marry me," she said. "Don't you see, you're letting him run your life by not marrying if you're really, deeply in love."

"The hell I am. That would be doing just what he wants." Jake walked away, jamming his hands into his pockets, standing in silence with his back to her. She guessed he was thinking about what she had just said and her heart raced.

He turned back to face her, gazing solemnly at her. "Marriage is a giant step, but I've never felt this way before. I'm in love with you. Would you become engaged now and marry me when this year is up? That's not long."

She shook her head. "No. If you truly love me enough to make a binding commitment, then you are allowing his desires to come in the way of our love for each other. I want the marriage, Jake. When we parted, it hurt more than I dreamed possible."

"Caitlin—" he said, taking a step toward her and reaching for her, but she put up her hand. He paused, his eyes narrowing.

"Don't, Jake. I'm sorry. I won't settle for less. You wouldn't want to wait if you were deeply in love with me. At this point in our lives, we both should get over what we feel for each other unless it is one of those loves for eternity that songs are written about. And if it is that kind, we'll know in time because we won't forget or want anyone else. In the meantime,

I think you're allowing your father to control your life and I'm not going into a casual relationship. I refuse to."

"Caitlin, I'm asking for a Saturday night dinner date—"

"No, you're not," she replied quietly. "You want more than that. You want to make love again."

He inhaled and stood staring at her with his fists clenched.

"You don't want that, too?" he asked in a husky voice.

"Yes, I do," she said, seeing him take a deep breath, "but I won't. It hurt, more than you'll ever know, when we parted ways before. I'm not going through that another time. No. I thank you for what you've done for Cecilia, Kirby and Altheda. It will mean a lot to them. I love you, really love you, Jake. Maybe that kind of love that is for a lifetime. While it feels that way now, only time will tell on that one. This is goodbye. I think you will have a bitter, empty victory with your dad."

"You're sure that's what you want?" he asked.

"Yes, I am. Jake, thank you for what you've done for Cecilia and the others."

Nodding, he turned and left, pausing a moment at the door to look at her. Her heart was breaking for a second time over him. She fought the temptation to call him back. He looked at her one last time, then closed the door behind him.

Weak-kneed, she sat down and let tears come, not caring if she was at work. She loved him and he loved her, but not enough to rise above his dad's ultimatum, unless he was simply using that as an excuse. Whichever it was, he wouldn't even offer marriage right now and she had had one weekend of loving without commitment and she never wanted that again because it had meant heartbreak.

Did Jake truly love her? It was a question she would never know the answer to because she was certain he was gone for good this time.

Her thoughts turned to Cecilia, Altheda and Kirby and what Jake had done for the three at the ranch. She wiped her eyes and picked up her phone to call and see if they were truly happy with their new situation.

The house was there. It wasn't hers because Jake didn't sell it to her, but she could go there as long as Cecilia and Altheda lived in it. By the time they were gone, he might have a change of heart and sell that patch of land back to her. The fact that he had taken care of the others made her think his declarations of love might have been heartfelt. Those were not the actions of a man who wasn't in love or had his eye on the dollar. A month ago, Jake would not have agreed to that, much less thought it up himself. He wouldn't have a week ago. Was he really a man in love?

"You did what?" Gabe asked, pacing up and down in front of Jake in the living area of his Dallas condo.

"You heard me," Jake remarked dryly without looking up from an envelope he was addressing. "I've hired Kirby and I'll hire the women at Caitlin's house to work for me. The house stays and they stay and Kirby has two employees who will also go on my payroll and he has cattle that I've bought. In short, only the belongings in the house are Caitlin's. Otherwise, all the rest is mine and my employees."

"You've lost it, Jake. So is she back in your life?"

"Caitlin? No, she's not."

"I don't get this. Why did you hire them then? You don't need them. You didn't want the house to stay. You didn't want those people to stay the last time I talked to you. What the hell happened?"

"I had a change of heart."

Gabe raked his fingers through his thick hair. "I don't get it," he said, repeating himself. "So when are you seeing Caitlin?"

"I'm not. She won't go out with me."

"This gets more complicated. Why won't she go out with you?"

Jake finished and dropped his pen on the desk to lean back in his chair and stretch out his long legs. "She wants marriage."

Gabe snorted. "Well, at least this I understand. You're not a marrying man. This year in particular when you've vowed you won't marry because that's exactly what Dad has told you to do. Well, okay. I'll leave the old house. We have plenty to do where we are right now. Caitlin's out of your life. Who's in?"

"No one at present."

"Ditto here. I've been too busy with work to have a life." He glanced at his watch. "Speaking of, I have an appointment early in the morning. I need to get going now because I have some errands tonight before I go home. See you next week, Jake," Gabe said, picking up a briefcase and hurrying out, closing the door behind him.

Jake stared into space, missing Caitlin, wanting to call her, glad there wasn't a bad feeling between them even if she wouldn't go out with him.

Since he had last seen her at her office, he had thought about what she had said to him. Was he still letting his father run his life, by not marrying? Or was that an excuse? Marriage and commitment had always scared him. He missed her more each day instead of less. He had been surprised by how badly he missed her. It was still as if their weekend of loving had just happened and there was not a growing length of time since then.

He wanted her more by the day. He stood, restlessly pacing the room, feeling alone, wanting her laughter, her warmth, her passion. How deep was his love for her?

He thought about losing her, hearing Cecilia or Kirby someday tell him about Caitlin's wedding.

At the thought, something twisted and hurt inside him. He didn't want Caitlin to fall in love with someone else. Was he really deeply in love, the once-in-a-lifetime kind of love that he didn't think actually ever happened?

He loved her, he wanted her, and he was going to lose her. He swore softly and clenched his fists. Was he letting his father run his life by refusing to marry when he was in love? Was she right about that?

What if his father wasn't in the equation?

For the rest of the night Jake pondered that question, still mulling it over in the morning when he worked out. He finally came to a conclusion.

Eleven

Caitlin placed her camera in her Range Rover and climbed in, turning on the rugged road. She glanced back at the palatial mountain home with a backdrop of spruce and aspen. People stood in the yard and waved to her. She waved in return and then drove around the circle and headed down the mountain to drive back to her home in Santa Fe.

The job had come up suddenly and she was thankful for it because she had been miserable since she had told Jake goodbye. She thought about the pictures of the family she had taken today. It had been a busy, interesting day with some pictures that had pleased her and she hoped when they were finished, her work would please the family.

She inhaled the cool mountain air. It was mid-November now. Snow covered the mountain slopes and she wanted to get to a lower elevation because she didn't want to get caught in any sudden storm.

Two hours later, she turned into the drive of her adobe

house, startled to see a sleek black car parked there. She frowned, wondering who was waiting for her. The car door opened and Jake stepped out.

Her heart missed a beat. She stopped her car beside his and climbed out to face him.

"What are you doing here, Jake? How'd you find me?"

"Cecilia. You always let her know where you are."

"I had a photography job near here. Come inside," she said, turning to go in through the back door. He followed her into the kitchen.

"What brought on this visit?" she asked.

He walked up to her and took her coat off her shoulders, shedding his own jacket and dropping them on a chair before turning back to her.

"I've missed you." Her pulse still raced and his statement kept it galloping. She waited in silence.

"I've thought about what you said. I don't like life without you."

Her resolve slipped a notch. "Jake," she whispered, wanting to reach for him. He looked incredible, exciting, sexy, virile. He had filled her dreams while memories of him tormented her through each waking hour.

"I've given a lot of thought to what you said about my dad controlling my life. Maybe you were right," he continued. She wanted to kiss and hold him, to love him. She trembled and doubled her fists and waited to hear what he had to say and if his stand had changed in the slightest.

Now was not the time to toss aside all her resolutions because she couldn't take another heartbreak. Something had brought him to Santa Fe and she intended to hear him out.

"So," she prompted when he was silent. She held her breath, waiting to see what he would say.

He reached in his pocket and pulled out a ring. "I brought

this for you, Caitlin. Will you marry me? Right away if you want."

"Jake!" She had wanted a proposal, but when he actually asked, she couldn't believe what she was hearing. "You've been so set against it."

"I think you're right. This is what I would do if we pulled my dad out of the equation. I've got to stop thinking about Dad and what he wants me to do or not do. I have to stop reacting to his edicts. It's been pure hell without you. I love you and want you."

His words poured out swiftly as he wrapped his arms around her. She flung hers around his neck, kissing him wildly, joy making her cry. Her heart pounded with happiness while she ran her hands over Jake, wanting him with a consuming need. She twisted free buttons on his shirt, unaware of his hands at her buttons, clothing fell and was tossed away until she was naked in his arms and his hands were everywhere.

Once he paused to run his fingers on her cheek. "Tears, Caitlin?"

"Tears of gladness," she whispered and pulled his head closer to kiss him. In a few more minutes he paused again.

"Bed?" he whispered, picking her up as he kissed her. She twisted free long enough to point. "That way. Turn right," she whispered. "Jake, I've missed you more than you can ever imagine," she said before returning to kisses, running her hands over his shoulders.

"Not half as much as I've wanted you, darlin'. I love you with all my heart, Caitlin. I should have told you sooner, but I didn't recognize it myself. I've never been in love before."

"You know full well that I haven't, either," she whispered and then all words were gone as he kissed her passionately and made love with her.

Hours later she lay in his arms on her bed. She was on her

side, facing him. "Jake, I recall seeing you hold up a ring, but I don't have that ring."

"Damn, I think I dropped it when I kissed you. I'll go find it."

"I'll go with you if I can move. You've demolished me."

"You stay where you are. I'll be right back."

Jake returned, crossing the room to wrap his arm around her.

"Did you find it?" she asked, running her hands over his chest.

He held out the ring. "Darlin', I love you. Will you marry me?"

"Yes," she replied, her heart pounding with joy as she held her hand out to him and watched him slip a sparkling emerald-cut diamond on her finger.

"Jake, the ring is gorgeous," she said. "It's huge."

"So is my love."

She kissed him and he carried her to bed to make love again.

It was in the early hours of the morning when she was in his arms. A small light burned and she held her hand out to admire her new ring. "Jake, I love my ring. And I love you."

"Good. And I love you, too. I want to marry soon."

"What's soon?" she asked, thinking of jobs she had booked in the next few months.

"Tomorrow would be nice."

"Tomorrow!" she said, laughing. "How about a Christmas wedding?"

"Sounds good. But the sooner the better. And then a long, long honeymoon afterward."

She laughed. "What about your parents?"

"I'd be lying if I told you they will welcome you, but I think they'll adjust and when they get to know you, they will love you, too."

"I hope. We've had enough dissension in my family."

"Would you consider marrying in Dallas?"

She thought about it. "That would be fine. Houston is not that far away."

"Great. We'll have a lot of people."

"I can imagine," she remarked. "I can tell you who we will not have."

Jake looked into her eyes. "Your half brother."

"That's right, Jake. I think I've seen and heard the last of Will because he wouldn't attend our wedding if I asked him."

"Do you care?"

She shook her head. "Sadly, no. I don't miss him at all. He'll never come back here and he won't acknowledge that I'm related to him."

"If you don't care, then I can tell you, I'm glad he won't be here. I would find it really difficult to welcome him to my wedding."

"I understand. No problem there."

"Now, we've discussed Will. Let's close the door on that one. I don't want even a discussion about him to put a damper on tonight or any other time between us."

"Impossible," she said, smiling at him. "I'll look at my ring and think about my handsome hunk of a husband-to-be and the wedding we'll have. What else is there? If you can't get him out of mind, then I'll have to do something to take your thoughts elsewhere." She smiled at Jake.

He rolled over. "For a woman who was a virgin, pure and sweet only a short time ago, you are a wanton sex kitten."

"Kitten? That's not good," she said, rolling again on top of him. "Tigress, now that would be a good description. I'll have to earn that one," she said and kissed him. As his arms closed around her to hold her tightly, she was swept away by passion.

Twelve

The second weekend in December Caitlin stood in the lobby waiting to walk down the aisle. Dressed in white silk, she was on Kirby's arm. Cecilia and Altheda were seated where her grandmother would have been.

"Kirby, thank you for doing this," she said, looking at the man she had known all her life. Dressed in a tux, his weathered skin was still deeply tan even though it was winter. His brown hair was thick with gray strands. He smiled at her.

"Caitlin, I just wish your grandmother Madeline could see you. She loved you from the moment you came into this world. She always said your dad made the mistake of his life by not raising you, but it was the blessing of her life that he didn't."

"I miss her. I loved her with all my heart."

"Jake's a good man, Cait. He'll be good to you. He did right by all of us."

"That he did and I think he's a good man. So are you."

"It's time to start now," the wedding coordinator said, kneeling to smooth Caitlin's train that was spread behind her.

Caitlin and Kirby began the walk down the aisle. When she looked at Jake, he smiled and her heart beat with happiness. She loved her handsome husband and now she would be married to him. Someday she would have her own family, hopefully soon, because she wanted elderly Cecilia and Altheda to know her children.

She forgot everything else as she drew closer to Jake and looked into his blue eyes that were filled with love.

They said vows and prayers, he kissed her and finally they were introduced to guests as Mr. and Mrs. Jacob Benton.

When they walked back up the aisle, she paused to hand roses to Cecilia and Altheda. She smiled at Jake's parents and received only a faint smile from his mother and a flat stare from his father. Walking with Jake, she laughed with joy. "I can't believe I'm a Benton now."

"You are definitely a Benton now and forever," Jake said, smiling at her.

It took another hour for pictures before they could get to the country club for the reception.

When toasts were given, Gabe stood up and raised his champagne flute high. "A toast to Caitlin and Jake, who have helped bring a beginning to the end of a family feud that started with the first Bentons and Santerres to settle in Texas. A toast to them for bringing peace to two families, and a wish for a wonderful future filled with love for them."

Jake looked at Caitlin and smiled as he hugged her lightly. "No feud between this Benton and Santerre. Far from it."

She laughed. "Absolutely, love."

Later in the afternoon, Jake stood with his brother and friends. "Okay, Jake," Nick said, grinning. "You didn't keep your part of our pact to avoid marriage. Now you have to put a million in the pot because you've definitely lost the bet and Tony is our winner."

"Thank you, guys. The pot is welcome."

"At least both of you are happily married and not pushed into something you didn't want to do," Tony said. "I told you I would outlast you."

"I knew I'd outlast all of you," Gabe said.

"Only because you're younger."

"And more leery of marriage than anyone. Our dad will be on you now about it," Jake said.

"He thinks I'm too young. He's told me," Gabe stated with a grin. "I agreed absolutely, so we're both happy. But now I don't get that giant inheritance all to myself. You can well afford to lose this bet with Tony and Nick because you are back in Dad's good graces. Someday you'll be enormously wealthy. I couldn't imagine you holding out until the year was up."

"I could," Nick remarked dryly. "Jake can be stubborn as a mule."

"Well, I hadn't planned on Caitlin coming into my life." He turned to Tony.

"Okay, Tony, so what will you do with the money you've won?"

"First, I'll have a party. Gabe, you're invited even if you didn't participate in the bet. I'll find a fun place for a weekend. Nick, can you and Jake tear yourselves away from your wives?"

Jake glanced across the room at Caitlin.

"Never mind. I'll find something where the wives can come," Tony said.

"You'll have more fun if they're there," Nick said.

"You mean *you'll* have more fun," Gabe said, laughing. "Thanks for including me."

"You've always been a tag-along, you might as well continue," Tony said and the others laughed.

"I think I've been away from my bride long enough," Jake said, excusing himself and moving away from his friends to get Caitlin to dance.

"This is the only way I can get close to you," he said, holding her in his arms and dancing to a ballad.

"I thought you'd never come back."

"I'll always come back," he said. "I figure about one more hour here and then we're gone."

She smiled at him. "It's wonderful, Jake. It's a dream come true in my life."

"It is for me," he said solemnly. "It scares me when I think how close I came to losing you."

"Not really," she said. "I don't think you could have ever lost me. I was so in love with you."

"I want you to show me. I'm not sure I can wait that hour."

"Yes, you can and we will," she said, bubbling with joy. "I have to be married to the most handsome man in the world. You look wonderful, Jake."

He smiled at her. "I'm glad you think so. I believe you're a bit biased. While I, on the other hand, am coolly objective when I look around and then tell you that you are definitely the most beautiful woman ever."

She laughed with him.

"Ah, Caitlin, I will never forget that first moment I saw you on my porch and couldn't believe my eyes. A beautiful woman, mysterious, unexpected, waiting on my porch. My life has never been the same since."

"It never will be again," she said, smiling up at him. "I'll always remember that moment, too, when you stepped out and we looked into each other's eyes. Maybe I fell in love right then."

"I'm the one that did the falling in love then. I just didn't know it. So here we are—starting a life together."

"We have a lot of friends here. I've enjoyed getting to know Nick's wife, Grace. When we get back from our honeymoon, we're getting together with them. She had Michael and Emily with her for a few minutes at my shower before they were picked up by her aunt. Michael is an adorable little boy who looks just like Nick. Emily looks a little like him."

"Only Michael isn't Nick's baby. Michael's biological father was Nick's brother who died shortly after Michael was born. He never saw Michael and never married Michael's mother who also died shortly after Michael's birth," Jake said.

"That's sad, but Nick and Grace love him as if he's their own."

"He is their own in every way and he does look like Nick."

"Emily is really precious."

"You're showing a high interest in babies. Cool it until I've had a few months of having you all to myself."

"Of course, just someday in the not-too-far-distant future—"

"I know and I agree," he said. "Right now, I have other plans."

"One more hour."

"I'll try," he said as the music changed to a fast number and she moved out of his arms to dance.

It was over two hours when Jake finally held her hand and they rushed to the waiting limousine to be whisked away to Jake's private jet.

After a stop in New York for three days, they flew to Switzerland for their honeymoon, moving into a chalet Jake had leased.

The view of snow-covered mountains was breathtaking, but

her attention was captured more by her handsome husband as he pulled her into his embrace.

"At last, I have you all to myself and we are going nowhere for days."

"I feel the same," she said, wrapping her arms around his neck. He kissed her and she closed her eyes, standing on tiptoe, holding him, feeling his heart beating with hers. "I love you, Caitlin," he whispered and returned to kissing her.

Joy filled her and she kissed him passionately, certain her life would be filled with happiness with Jake. She already loved him with all her heart, unable to imagine life without him. "That family feud just died completely, Jake," she whispered. "I intend to seduce a Benton tonight and make mad, passionate love and there will never be bad moves between the Santerres and the Bentons again."

"Absolutely not. Love, sexy love. Let me show you," he said, his head dipping down as he showered kisses on her and began to unfasten her buttons.

"I have to be the happiest woman on earth," she whispered, certain it was so, holding him close to her heart and knowing he would be there for all her life.

* * * * *

Nothing could have prepared Ethan for the need that took over his body.

In that moment he captured her mouth with a desperate possession that fueled his fire as it had never been fueled before. He wanted to devour her alive.

A part of him couldn't believe that she was in his arms and that he was enveloping her mouth as if it were the only one left on earth, which for now, for him, it was.

He couldn't control the rush of physical hunger consuming his entire being. His tongue tangled with hers with a voracity that sent pleasure spiking throughout both of their bodies. He was kissing her with hunger, as if he were seeking out some forbidden treat that he was determined to find.

Moments later, only because they needed to breathe, he released her mouth and stared into her stunned gaze. Refusing to allow her time to think again, he lowered his mouth once more and at the same time swept her off her feet and into his arms. Before the night was over, his touch would be imprinted on every inch of her skin.

STAR OF
HIS HEART

BY
BRENDA JACKSON

Published in Great Britain 2012
by Mills & Boon, an imprint of Harlequin (UK) Limited,
Eton House, 18-24 Paradise Road, Richmond, Surrey TW9 1SR

© Harlequin Books S.A. 2010

ISBN: 978 0 263 89114 0

51-0112

Harlequin (UK) policy is to use papers that are natural, renewable and recyclable products and made from wood grown in sustainable forests. The logging and manufacturing processes conform to the legal environmental regulations of the country of origin.

Printed and bound in Spain
by Blackprint CPI, Barcelona

Brenda Jackson is a die "heart" romantic who married her childhood sweetheart and still proudly wears the "going steady" ring he gave her when she was fifteen. Because she's always believed in the power of love, Brenda's stories always have happy endings. In her real-life love story, Brenda and her husband of thirty-six years live in Jacksonville, Florida, and have two sons.

A *New York Times* bestselling author of more than fifty romance titles, Brenda is a recent retiree who worked thirty-seven years in management at a major insurance company. She divides her time between family, writing and traveling with Gerald. You may write Brenda at PO Box 28267, Jacksonville, Florida 32226, USA, by e-mail at WriterBJackson@aol.com or visit her website at www.brendajackson.net.

To Gerald Jackson, Sr. You're still the one
after all these years!

To my Heavenly Father. How Great Thou Art.

A good name is to be chosen rather than great riches,
loving favor rather than silver and gold.
—Proverbs 22:1

Chapter 1

"Quiet on the set!
"Take one!
"Action!"

The director's voice blared from the bullhorn and the words sent a pleasurable thrill up Rachel Wellesley's spine. She had known before she'd uttered her first words as a child that she had an overabundance of artsy bones in her body.

The only problem was that as she got older, her choice of an artistic career would change from week to week. First she had wanted to become a painter, then a writer. Later on she had considered becoming a fashion stylist. But at the fine arts college she'd attended, after she took theory and practicum classes on beauty, she had finally decided on a career as a makeup artist and wardrobe designer. This was the life she lived for and what she enjoyed—being on the set of a movie. Or in this case, the TV set that was taping the popular prime-time medical drama *Paging the Doctor*.

It was day one of shooting for the second season. All the cast members from last season had returned except for Eric Woods, who'd played Dr. Myles Bridgestone. No one had been surprised to hear his contract was not renewed, especially with all his personal drama last season. The well-known Hollywood movie star had evidently felt it beneath him to do TV and to play a role other than a leading one. But the ratings of his last few movies had plummeted. Everyone who worked with him last season had been aware of his constant complaints. Eric was an egomaniac and a director's worst nightmare.

Rachel had managed to get along with Eric, but she couldn't say the same for others who considered him a pain in the rear end. But then, her older sister Sofia claimed Rachel could get along with just about anybody, and she would have to agree. It took a lot to rock her boat. She was easygoing by nature and was an all-around nice person. She figured some things just weren't worth the hassle of getting high blood pressure and stress.

A slight movement out of the corner of her eye made her shift her focus to the actor she'd heard would be added to the show this season in the role of Dr. Tyrell Perry. His name was Ethan Chambers.

He had been in Hollywood only a couple of years

and already, at twenty-eight, he had taken the town by storm. And most noticeably, over the past few months, he and his playboy behavior had become quite the talk in the tabloids and gossip columns.

She gave him an appreciative glance. The only thing she had to say was that if the producer added Ethan to the show to boost the ratings, then he had hit the mark. Ethan was definitely eye candy of the most delicious kind. There was no doubt in her mind he would stir the interest of their female viewers, young and old, single or married.

And she couldn't help noticing he had already stirred the interest of several of the females on the set. He seemed oblivious to the open stares as he talked to a man she assumed was his agent. Although she found Ethan extremely attractive, she was too much of a professional to mix her private life with her professional one. And the one thing she detested above all else was being in the spotlight, which was something he evidently enjoyed since he'd managed to garner a lot of publicity lately.

She thought that his flashing white smile was as sexy as they came and figured he would be perfect for any toothpaste commercial. He was tall, probably six foot two, and powerfully built with broad shoulders, muscled arms and a masculine chest. He did a whole lot for those scrubs he was wearing. The company that manufactured the medical attire should be grateful, since he practically turned them into a fashion statement.

And last but not least was his cocoa-colored face with those striking blue-gray eyes—a potentially distracting pair for any woman fool enough to gaze into them too long—and his ultrasexy dimpled jaw. She had to hand it to him, he was as handsome as any male could get in her book, hands down.

A soft smile lifted the corners of her lips as she thought that this was bound to be an interesting season. Already a number of the women on the set were vying for his attention. The show's director, Frasier Glenn, would just love that.

"Cut! Good scene, everyone. Let's move on!"

Frasier's words had Rachel moving quickly toward the producer, John Gleason, and Livia Blake, a model and budding actress who would be guest-starring on the show for a few episodes as Dr. Sonja Duncan. The scene they had just filmed was an emotional one in which Dr. Duncan had broken the news to a devoted husband that his wife had died of cardiac arrest.

Livia would be in the next scene as well and it was Rachel's job to refresh her hair and makeup. And since Rachel was also the wardrobe designer for the show, she needed to verify John's request for a change in the outfit Livia would be wearing in the scene they would be shooting later today.

Rachel flashed a look back to Ethan Chambers, and her gaze raked over him once again. The man by his side was doing all the talking, and for a quick moment she detected a jumpy tension surrounding Ethan. She had been around enough actors on their first day on the set to tell he was nervous. That surprised her. If anything, she would think a man with his looks would be brimming over with self-confidence, even arrogance. If he wasn't, than he was different from Eric Woods in more ways than one.

Ethan Chambers took another sip from the water bottle, wishing it was a cold beer instead. He couldn't believe he had finally gotten his lucky break and was here, on the set of *Paging the Doctor,* playing the role of a neurosurgeon. He wasn't a hospital maintenance man or a victim who needed medical care but a doctor. He had landed the role of a lifetime on what was one of the most top-rated shows.

He would even go so far as to pinch himself if there weren't so many people around, and if his agent, Curtis Fairgate, wasn't standing right next to him, smiling, gloating and taking it all in. And of course, Curtis was ready to take credit for the whole thing, as if Ethan hadn't worked his tail off to get where he was now.

He thought about the three years he had studied acting abroad while doing some well-received but small theater gigs. He could finally say he was now building an acting career. Even his older brother, Hunter, who had tried pressuring him to stay in the family business, was happy for him now. And that meant a lot.

"You do know your lines, don't you?"

Ethan lifted a brow, not believing Curtis would ask such a thing. "Of course. I might be nervous but I'm not stupid. I'm not about to screw up my big break."

"Good."

Ethan pulled in a slow breath, wondering how he and

Curtis had managed to survive each other for the past two years. Hollywood agents were known to be pushy, cynical and, in some cases, downright rude. Curtis was all three and then some. Ethan only kept him around because they had a fairly decent working relationship, and Curtis *had* managed to land him a spot on this show by talking to the right people. But Curtis probably would not have managed that if the sister of one of Ethan's former girlfriends hadn't been the current lover of one of the show's writers.

Curtis began talking, rambling on about something Ethan had no desire to listen to, so he glanced around, fascinated at how things were going and what people were doing. He had been on the set of a television show several times, but this was his first time on one that Frasier Glenn directed, and he couldn't help but admire how smoothly things were running. The word around Hollywood was that Frasier was a hard man to work for, a stickler for structure, but he was highly respected in the industry.

Ethan was about to pull his concentration back to the conversation he was supposed to be having with Curtis when his gaze settled on a gorgeous petite woman wearing a cute baby-doll top and a pair of wide-leg jeans. She was gorgeous in a restrained sort of way. He figured she was an actress on the show and wondered what role she played.

She couldn't be any taller than five foot two, but he thought she was a sexy little thing with her short dark hair and exotic looks. And she was smiling, which was a change of pace since everyone else seemed to look so doggone serious.

"Ethan!"

Curtis snapped his fingers in Ethan's face, cutting into his thoughts. "Don't even think it, Ethan," the man warned.

Ethan blinked, and an annoyed expression showed on his face as he met Curtis's gaze. "Think what?"

"About getting involved with anyone on this set, especially that hot little number over there. I know that look."

Ethan frowned. He liked women. He enjoyed sex. He did short-term affairs better than anyone he knew. The women he was involved with weren't looking for long-term any more than he was. "Why?" he finally asked.

"Frasier usually frowns on that sort of thing on his set, that's why."

Ethan took another sip of his water before asking, "Are you saying that he has a fraternization policy?"

"No, but a workplace romance isn't anything he gets thrilled about, trust me. It can cause unnecessary drama, and Frasier doesn't like drama since it can take away from a good day's work."

Ethan didn't say anything as his gaze found the object of his interest once again. For some reason, he had a feeling she would be worth any damn drama that got stirred. He shook his head, thinking he needed to put his player's mentality in check for a while, at least until the end of the season. Making his mark on this show was his goal, and now that he was in the driver's seat and pursuing his dream, the most important thing was for him to stay focused.

Although the urge to hit on the sexy pixie was strong, he would keep those longings in check. Besides, she probably wasn't even his type.

"I have a feeling you're going to be a big hit this season, Ethan."

Ethan glanced over at the woman who had introduced herself earlier as Paige Stiles, one of the production assistants. "Thanks."

"And like I said, if you ever need help with your lines after hours, just let me know. I will make myself available."

"I appreciate that, Paige." The offer seemed friendly enough, but he recognized it for what it was. The woman had been coming on to him ever since they had met earlier that day. She wasn't bad looking, in fact he thought her rather attractive; but she hadn't stirred his fire the same way the sexy pixie had.

Once the show had begun taping one scene after another, the petite brunette had all but disappeared. If she was an actress on the show then her segment was evidently being shot later. He was tempted to ask Paige who she was but thought better of it. The one thing a man didn't do was ask a woman who was interested in him about another woman.

"So where are we headed?" he asked as they moved away from the set toward an exit door.

"To the makeup trailer. That's also where wardrobe is located since the same person handles both."

He lifted a brow. "Is there a reason for that?" he asked, since that wasn't the norm, especially for a show of this magnitude. It was a lot of responsibility for one person.

"None other than that she wanted to do both, and Frasier obliged her. But he would since her last name happens to be Wellesley."

Ethan immediately recognized the last name. The Wellesleys were the brilliant minds behind Limelight Entertainment Management, one of the top talent agencies in the world. Their clientele consisted of some of the best in Hollywood, although in recent years they had expanded to represent more than actors. The firm now represented an assortment of talent that included big-name singers, set designers, costume designers, writers and makeup artists.

"Wellesley?" he asked.

"Yes, the high-and-mighty."

Ethan had the ability to read people, women in particular, and had easily detected the scorn in her voice. And because he knew about women in particular, he decided to change the subject. "How long have you worked for *Paging the Doctor?*"

She began talking and just as he'd done to Curtis earlier, he nodded while he tuned her out. His thoughts drifted back to the woman he'd seen earlier and he wondered if and when their paths would cross again and they would finally meet.

* * *

Finally a break, Rachel thought, sliding into a chair that was now empty. She had been in the trailer for the past five hours or so. She had sent one of her assistants out on the set to do those second-by-second touch-ups as needed while she hung out in the makeup/wardrobe trailer, making sure those actors shooting their scenes for the first time that day went through their initial makeup routine.

A couple of the scenes being shot today showed the doctors out of the hospital and in a more relaxed atmosphere either at home or out on dates, which called for a change from medical garments to casual wear.

John had approved her choice of outfits, and she felt good about that, especially since the outfit she'd selected for Livia hadn't been on John's preapproved list. And some of the artwork being used as props were her own creations. Other than Frasier and John, few people knew that when she left here at night she became Raquel, the anonymous canvas artist whose work was showcased in a number of galleries.

Her sister was worried that with being a makeup artist and wardrobe designer by day and a painter at night, Rachel had no time for a love life. But that was the least of Rachel's concerns. She was only twenty-six and wasn't ready for a serious involvement with any man.

In her early twenties she'd dated a lot, but to this day she couldn't admit to ever falling in love. She would like to believe such a thing could happen for her. Her aunt and uncle had a loving relationship, and she'd been told her parents had had one, too. Regrettably, they had been killed in a plane accident before her second birthday.

Rachel eased out of her chair when she heard conversation outside her door and glanced at the schedule posted on the wall. She wasn't supposed to work on anyone for another hour or so. Who could be infringing on her free time?

There was a knock on the trailer door, followed by a turn of the knob. Rachel fought to keep the frown off her face when Paige stuck her head in. The twenty-four-year-old woman had gotten hired during the middle of the first season. For some reason they had rubbed each other the wrong way that first day and things hadn't improved since. Rachel still didn't know the reason Paige disliked her, but figured it had to do with Rachel's amicable relationship with Frasier and John.

"So you're here," Paige said in a voice that for some reason gave Rachel the feeling Paige wished she wasn't.

Determined to present a friendly facade despite Paige's funky attitude, she smiled and said, "Yes, I'm here. Was there something you wanted?"

"Frasier wants to go ahead and shoot the next scene as soon as lunch is over, which means you need to get started on this guy right away."

Paige came inside the trailer, followed by the hunky and sexy Ethan Chambers. The moment Rachel's gaze clashed with those blue-gray eyes of his, she knew for the first time in her life how it felt to be totally mesmerized. And nothing could have prepared her for her hormones suddenly igniting into something akin to mind-blowing lust.

Chapter 2

So this was where his sexy pixie had gone to, Ethan thought, entering the trailer and glancing around. He pretended interest in everything inside the trailer except for the woman who'd been in the back of his mind since he'd first seen her that morning. And now here she was.

"Rachel, this is Ethan Chambers and starting this season he'll be a regular on the show as Dr. Tyrell Perry. Ethan, this is Rachel Wellesley, the makeup artist for the show. She's the wardrobe designer as well."

Again Ethan picked up a bit of scorn in Paige's voice, although she had a smile plastered on her face. But then it was evident her smile was only for him.

He crossed the room and extended his hand. "Nice meeting you, Rachel."

"Ditto, Ethan. Welcome to *Paging the Doctor.*"

The moment she placed her hand in his he was tempted to bring it to his lips, something he had gotten used to doing while living abroad in France. And when she smiled up at him the temptation increased. She had such a pretty smile.

"John wants him ready for his scene in thirty minutes. I'll be back to get him, so make sure he's on time."

Both Ethan and Rachel glanced over at Paige and watched as she exited the trailer, leaving them alone. Ethan returned his gaze to Rachel once again and couldn't help asking, "What's got her panties in a wad?"

Rachel couldn't help the laughter that flowed from her mouth, and when he joined in, she knew immediately she was going to like this guy. But then, what wasn't there to like?

Up close, Ethan Chambers was even more handsome than he had been across the room earlier. With him on the show, this would be a pretty good season. She couldn't wait to see them shoot his scene.

She finally answered him. "I have no idea," she said. "But we won't worry ourselves about it. My job is to get you ready for your scene."

"But what about your lunch? Shouldn't you be eating something?"

"I should be asking you the same thing, but to answer

your question, usually I bring lunch from home and eat while taking care of business matters," she said, thinking about the order she had downloaded off her iPhone. *Libby's,* an art gallery in Atlanta, had just requested several of her paintings to display.

He nodded. "I'm too nervous to eat so I asked if I could go ahead and get the makeup part taken care of. I apologize if I'm infringing on your time."

She waved off his words. "You're not, so just go ahead and take the chair while I pull your file."

"My file?"

"Yes. Sorry, I can be anal when it comes to being organized, but there's no other way to work with Frasier and John. I have a file of all the scenes you'll be doing today, what you'll need to wear and the extent of lighting needed for that particular shot, although the latter is definitely changeable on the set. That gives me an idea of what kind of makeup I need to apply."

She tried not to notice how he slid into the chair; specifically, how his muscular thighs straddled it before his perfectly shaped backside came in contact with the cushioned seat. She grabbed the folder off the rack and tried to ignore the dark hair that dusted his muscular arms. However, something caught her attention. A tattoo of a cluster of purple grapes draped above his wrist.

"Grapes?" she asked, meeting his gaze and finding it difficult to breathe while looking into his eyes.

"Yes. It's there to remind me of home."

"Home?" she echoed, breaking eye contact to reach over and hand him a smock to put on.

"Yes. Napa Valley."

She recalled the time she'd visited the area years ago as part of a high school field trip. "I've been to Napa Valley once. It's beautiful."

"Yes, it is. I hated leaving it," he said after putting on the smock.

She glanced over and met those killer eyes again. "Then why did you?"

He would be justified to tell her it wasn't her business, she quickly thought, but for some reason she knew he wouldn't do that. They had met just moments ago, but she felt she knew him, or knew men like him. No, she corrected herself. She didn't know any man like him, and how she could say that with such certainty, she wasn't sure.

"I left to pursue my dream. Unfortunately, it wasn't connected to my family business," he said.

Now that she understood. Her sister and uncle always thought she would join them in the family business, but she hadn't. Limelight Entertainment Management had been founded by her father, John Wellesley, and his brother Jacob. It had been the dream they shared and made into reality, with the purpose of representing and building the careers of African American actors during a time when there were many prejudices in Hollywood. Today the company was still very highly respected and had helped many well-known stars jumpstart their careers.

"It's a nice tattoo, but I'll need to use some cream to completely cover it for the shoot. Dr. Perry doesn't have a tattoo," she explained, pressing a button that eased the chair into a reclining position

"That's no problem. Do whatever you have to do, Rachel."

It wasn't what he'd said but how he'd said it that sent sensuous chills coursing through her. For a timeless moment, they stared at each other as heat flooded her in a way it never had before. As the flames of awareness licked at her body, somehow a part of her—the sensible part—remained unscathed. In a nagging voice it reminded her that she needed to get back on track and prep Ethan for his scene.

She swallowed and broke eye contact with him again as she turned to reach for her makeup kit. "Comfortable?"

"Yes."

"Then why are you so nervous?" she decided to ask him while checking different tubes of makeup cream for one that would work with his complexion and skin type. It was August, and although the air conditioner on the set would be on full blast, all the lighting being used would generate heat. She needed to prevent any facial shiny spots from showing up on camera.

He shifted in his seat and she glanced over at him. "This is the first day on the job of what I see as my big break," he said, straightening in the chair. "This is what I've worked my ass off for since the day I decided acting was what I wanted to do. I've done small parts in theater and guest spots on a couple of shows and was even an extra on *Avatar,* but being here, getting this opportunity, is a dream come true."

She nodded, knowing just how he felt. She had wanted to step out on her own without any help from her family's name. She had submitted her résumé to Glenn Productions and had gotten called in for an interview with both Frasier and John. Although Frasier had been a friend of her father's, and both men were well acquainted with Sofia since she was Uncle Jacob's partner in the family business, Rachel was convinced she had been given the job on her own merits and hadn't been given any preferential treatment.

This was her second season on the show and she worked doubly hard to make sure Frasier and John never regretted their decision to give her a chance. So, yes, she knew all about dreams coming true.

The first thing she thought as she applied a light brush to Ethan's face was that he had flawless skin with a healthy glow. He had perfect bone structure and his lips were shapely and full. She bent toward him to gently brush his brows and was glad he had closed his eyes since crazy things were going on in the pit of her stomach. A tightness was there that had never been there before. She drew in a deep breath to relieve the pressure. His aftershave smelled good. Almost too good for her peace of mind.

"So tell me, Rachel, what's your dream?"

She smiled. "What makes you think I have one?"

"All women do."

She chuckled. "Sounds like you think you know us pretty well."

"I wouldn't say that, but I would think everyone has at least one dream they would love to see come true."

"I agree, and this is mine—being a makeup artist and wardrobe designer."

"You're good at it. Very professional."

He opened his eyes to meet hers and she was aroused in a way that just wasn't acceptable, especially for a woman who made it her motto never to mix business with pleasure.

"Thanks," she said, taking a step back and reaching over to grab a hand mirror to give to him. "You didn't need much. I don't believe in being heavy-handed with makeup."

"I can appreciate that."

She had made up enough men in her day to know if they had a choice they would gladly skip this part in preparing for their scene. "Now for that tattoo. I have just the thing to blend in with your skin tone that won't rub off. And later you can wash it off."

"Okay."

He held out his arm and she began applying the cream. Against her fingertips, his skin felt warm, slowly sending her body into meltdown. She could feel his eyes on her but refused to glance up and look at him for fear that he would know what touching him was doing to her. Instead she tried concentrating on what she was doing. This time, though, she was too distracted by other things, such as the feel of his strong veins beneath her fingers and the rapid beat of his pulse. Her body responded with a raging flood of desire that seeped into her bones.

Not being able to resist temptation any longer, she looked over at him. For a long, achingly seductive moment, they stared at each other. She wanted to look away but it was as if he controlled the movement of her neck and it refused to budge. She swallowed the panic she felt lodged in her throat as she slowly released his hand. So much for being a firm believer in the separation of business and pleasure. For a moment, no matter how brief, thoughts had filled her mind about how it would be to take her hand and rub it down his chest and then move her hand even lower to—

There was a quick knock at the door before it opened and Paige walked in. And for the first time ever, Rachel was glad to see the woman.

Chapter 3

"If he's as hot as you say he is, then maybe you should let him know you might be interested, Rachel."

Rachel wiped paint from her hands as she glared at the phone. If her best friend since elementary school wasn't there in person to see her frown, transmitting it through the speakerphone was the next best thing. "I'm not interested."

And because she knew Charlene would belabor the point, she went on the defensive and said, "Look, Cha, I thought you of all people would understand. You know I don't like mixing business with pleasure. Besides, I have plenty of work to do."

Charlene laughed. "You always have plenty of work to do. If becoming involved with a man is a way to slow you down, then I'm all for it. It's time you started having fun."

Rachel rolled her eyes. "I could say the same for you."

"Face it. Men aren't drawn to me like they are to you."

Rachel pulled in a deep breath knowing there was no use telling Charlene just how wrong she was. Her words would go in one ear and out the other. For once she wished Charlene would be the one to face it and see that she was beautiful and sexy.

Charlene had to be the kindest and sweetest person Rachel knew, but she always slid to the background when it came to dating and romance. Rachel blamed Charlene's parents, since they always thought their older daughter, Candis, was the "pretty one" and had always put her in the limelight. As far as Rachel was concerned, Charlene had a lot going for her, including a beautiful singing voice.

"I'm in no mood to argue with you, Cha. You know how mad I get when you put yourself down."

"I'm not putting myself down. I'm just stating facts."

"Then let me state a few of my own," Rachel said. "I'm the one on set every day surrounded by gorgeous men. The only problem is that those men are checking out the tall, slender actresses, not me."

When Charlene didn't say anything, Rachel had a feeling there was more going on with her friend. "Okay, Cha, what's wrong?"

There was another long moment before Charlene replied, "I talked to Mom today."

Rachel slumped down into a chair. Mrs. Quinn was the mom from hell, and that was putting it kindly. She'd always managed to boost one daughter up while at the same time tearing the other one down. "And?"

"And she wanted me to know that Candis made the cut for the *Sports Illustrated* swimsuit edition next year and will be staying in Paris for a while."

"That's great, and I'm sure you're happy for her." Rachel knew she could say that because deep down she knew Charlene was. Candis and Charlene had a rather good relationship despite the competitive atmosphere created by their mother.

"Yes, of course I'm happy for her."

"And?"

"And what?" Charlene asked.

Rachel pulled in a deep breath; her patience was wearing thin. "And what else did Mrs. Quinn say?"

"Just the usual about she still doesn't understand how Candis could be so pretty and me so plain when we had the same parents. She ended the call by even suggesting that maybe she and Dad got the wrong baby from the hospital. She said it in a joking way but I knew she was dead serious."

Rachel bet the woman had been dead serious as well, but she would never tell Charlene that. That was the kind of garbage she'd had to put up with all her life. "She wasn't serious, Cha. You and your mother look too much alike for you to be anyone's baby but hers."

Evidently Mrs. Quinn never took the time to notice the similarity. Or maybe she *had* noticed and since she'd never been happy with her own looks, she was passing her insecurities on to Charlene.

Rachel thought about her own situation. She had been raised by her uncle Jacob and her aunt Lily after her parents had been killed. Rachel had been only one year old and Sofia had been ten. Her aunt and uncle were wonderful and had raised her and Sofia as their own children, since unfortunately they'd never had any. The one thing Uncle Jacob and Aunt Lily didn't do was play her and Sofia against each other. Everyone knew that Sofia wanted to follow in their father's footsteps and take his place with Uncle Jacob at Limelight.

Although her uncle and sister would have loved for her to join them in the family business, Rachel had never been pressured to do so. She chuckled, thinking it was enough to have Sofia as her agent.

"Hey, let's do a movie this weekend," she suggested, thinking her best friend needed some chilling time.

"Sounds super, but don't you have a lot to do?"

Rachel laughed. "I always have a lot to do, but I need a break to have fun, and it sounds like you do, too."

A short while later, Rachel made her way to the kitchen, hungry after missing lunch. On the way home she had stopped by a restaurant owned by one of the cameramen's parents. She considered Jack Botticello her buddy, and his parents were truly a godsend. Whenever she dropped by their Italian restaurant, Botticello's Place, for takeout, they always gave her more food than she could possibly eat in one sitting. There would definitely be enough lasagna left for tomorrow's dinner.

As she sat down at the table to enjoy her meal, she recalled everything that had happened on the set that day, especially the scenes that included Ethan Chambers. She couldn't help but remember the moment he had walked into a patient's hospital room. To say he swaggered into the room would probably be more accurate. And when he began speaking in what was supposed to be a northern accent, all eyes and ears were on him. There was no doubt in her mind he was a gifted actor. It was as if the part of Dr. Tyrell Perry had been created just for him.

She couldn't wait for the airing of the show in a few weeks to see how he would be received by the viewing audience. It would probably be no different than the way he'd been received on the set. Women were all but falling at his feet, doing just about anything to get his attention.

He had mentioned to a member of the camera crew in between scenes that he was going to get a cup of coffee. The three women who'd overheard him had all but broken their necks racing across the room to the coffee cart to get it for him. She could tell he'd actually gotten embarrassed by their antics. That surprised her. Most men would be gloating about all the attention. But then, this had been his first day on the job. There was no doubt in her mind that eventually his media-hungry playboy tendencies would come out. It was only a matter of time.

Unbidden, the memories surfaced of what had happened during their makeup session that day. Had he deliberately tried to unnerve her? Break down her defenses so she would behave the way Tina, Cindy and Nina had done today with the coffee incident? It wouldn't surprise her to discover he was just as superficial as all the other playboys in Hollywood. And to think for a short while today she'd actually been attracted to him. But with his make-you-drool looks, the attraction couldn't be helped. It had a way of vamping your senses the first time around.

And his family had money. He'd mentioned his roots were in Napa Valley, but it was only later that day when she'd overheard some of the camera crew talking about how wealthy he already was that she realized he was one of *those* Chamberses. There were two African American families whose roots and vast financial empires were in Napa Valley. The Russells and the Chamberses. Both families' vineyards were known to produce some of wine tasters' finest.

So, okay, she had let her guard down and let herself be affected by him. But tomorrow would be better. She had gotten used to him and would be more in control.

With that resolved, she proceeded to finish her meal.

"Do you promise, Uncle Ethan?"

Ethan couldn't help but smile. "Yes, I promise."

"Truly?"

"Yes, truly."

His six-year-old niece, Kendra, had him wrapped around her finger and probably knew it, he thought. When his parents had mentioned to her that Los Angeles was close to Disneyland, she had begun asking him questions. Mainly she wanted to know if he'd seen any princesses.

Just to hear her voice was a sheer delight because Kendra hadn't done much talking since her mother had died three years ago in a car accident. She had pretty much been withdrawn and quiet much of the time. But she would always talk to her Uncle Ethan.

"Daddy wants to talk to you, Uncle Ethan."

"Okay, sweetheart, and always remember you're Uncle Ethan's cupcake."

"I remember. Nighty-night."

He then heard her hand the phone over to his brother, Hunter, after telling her daddy nighty-night, too and after exchanging an "I love you" and an "I love you back." It was only then that Hunter placed the phone to his ear. "What's going on, kid?"

Ethan couldn't help but chuckle. There was an eight year difference in their ages, and Hunter never let him forget it. But even with that big variation, they'd always gotten along. Like all brothers, they'd had their disagreements, but they'd never lasted more than a few hours. Except for that one time a few years ago when Hunter had tried pressuring him into staying in the family business and getting all those ideas out of his head about making it big in Hollywood.

Ethan had left home anyway to pursue his dream.

It was only after the fatal car accident that claimed Hunter's wife's life—an accident that Hunter and Kendra had survived—that Hunter had understood why Ethan had to do what he did. He'd learned that life was too precious and fleeting to take for granted. Tomorrow wasn't promised to anyone.

"Nothing much is going on. Kendra talked a lot tonight," he said.

"Only because it's you. She loves her uncle Ethan. Besides, she wanted to ask you all about princesses."

Ethan grinned. "Yeah, I noticed. What's up with that?"

"*The Princess and the Frog.* She's seen it five times already. I should blame you since you're the one who got her the DVD as soon as it went on sale."

"Hey, there's nothing I wouldn't do for my cupcake," he said, meaning it.

He talked to Hunter for a few minutes longer before his brother passed the phone to their folks. In addition to the winery, Hunter and his parents ran a small four-star bed-and-breakfast on the property. It was always good to call home because he truly missed everyone, and updates were priceless.

"And you're eating properly, Ethan?"

He cringed at his mother's question, knowing he would have to tell her a little white lie, especially when at that very moment the timer went off to let him know his microwave dinner was ready. He had a beer to drink and his dessert would be a bag of peanut M&M's he'd grabbed out of the vending machine when he'd left the studio today. Paige had invited him to her place for dinner but he had declined.

He removed his dinner from the microwave and said, "Yes, Mom, I'm eating properly."

"Met any nice girls you want to bring home?"

She has to be kidding. The last few girls he dated weren't any he would dare bring home for his parents, brother and niece to meet. But then the face of his sexy pixie flashed across his mind and he couldn't help but think that she would work. For some reason he liked her, and the sexual vibes between them hadn't gone unnoticed, although it was evident she'd tried ignoring them.

Besides, he didn't have time to meet girls—nice or any other kind. He had lines to study every night, especially tonight. Frasier had been impressed with him today and had added another scene to his schedule for tomorrow.

"No, Mom, so don't go planning a wedding for me yet."

Later that night when he slid into bed, he couldn't help but think just how blessed he was. Both of his parents were alive and in good health. As the oldest son, Hunter had taken on his role with ease and was the perfect businessman to manage the family's vast wealth. And Hunter had had the insight to utilize the property surrounding the winery to build the bed-and-breakfast, which was doing extremely well. The reservation list was always filled up a year in advance.

As much as he'd loved Napa Valley, Ethan had

known it wasn't in his blood to the extent it had been in Hunter's. After college, he returned home and tried working alongside Hunter and his parents, but he hadn't been happy. Hunter had said it was wanderlust and that eventually he would get over it, but he never did. A year later he had made up his mind to pursue his dream.

So here he was, living in a nice place in L.A. and building the career he'd always wanted. Money was no object, thanks to a trust fund that had been set up by his grandparents as well as the financial standing of the winery, in which he was a stockholder. Of course, every once in a while some smart-ass reporter would ask him why an independently wealthy person would want to work. He was sure Anderson Cooper was asked the same question often enough, too. Ethan wasn't privy to Anderson's response, but his was simply, "Wealthy or poor, everyone has dreams, and there *is* such a thing as continued money growth."

He reached over to turn off the lamp light, thinking that things had gone better than he'd expected on the set today. His lines had flowed easily, and for a while he had stepped into the role of Dr. Tyrell Perry. To prepare, he had watched medical movies and had volunteered his time at a hospital for ninety days. He had come away with an even greater respect for those in the medical industry.

As he stared up at the ceiling his thoughts shifted to the woman he'd met that day, Rachel Wellesley. There had been something about her that pulled her to him like a magnet. Something about her that he found totally adorable. Even among the sea of model-type women on the set, she had somehow stood out.

And when she had leaned over him to apply whatever it was she brushed on his face, he had inhaled her scent. With his eyes closed, he had breathed it all in while imagining all sorts of things. It was a soft scent, yet it had been hot enough to enflame his senses.

So he had sat there, letting her have her way with his face while he imagined all kind of things, especially the image of her naked.

More than once during the shoot, he had had to remind himself that he didn't really know her and that it would be crazy to lose focus. But he would be the first to admit that he hadn't counted on being bowled over by a woman who had to tilt her head all the way back just to look up at him. He smiled, remembering the many times they had looked at each other and the number of times they had tried not to do so. And nothing could erase from his mind the sight of the soft smile that had touched her lips when she'd seen his tattoo and when he'd told her why he had it. If he had been trying to impress her, he would definitely have garnered brownie points. But he wasn't trying to impress her.

He shifted in bed, knowing he had to stay focused and not let a pretty face get him off track. All that sounded easy enough, but he had a feeling it would be the hardest thing he'd ever had to do.

Chapter 4

"Quiet on the set!
"Take four!
"Action!"

Rachel sat quietly in a chair and watched the scene that was being shot. When she heard two women, Paige and another actress on the set named Tae'Shawna Miller, whispering about how handsome and fine Ethan was, she had to press her lips together to keep from turning around and reminding them about the no-talking-during-a-take policy. But that would make her guilty of breaking the rule, too.

So she sat there and tried tuning them out and hoped sooner or later they would close their mouths. It didn't help matters to know that Paige was one of the women. Rachel figured she of all people should know better.

Rachel turned her attention back to the scene being filmed and couldn't help but admire the way Ethan was delivering his lines. He was doing a brilliant job portraying Dr. Tyrell Perry, the sexy doctor with a gruff demeanor that could only be softened by his patients. And from the looks of things, a new twist was about to unravel on the show with Dr. Perry being given a love interest—another new doctor on the hospital staff, the widowed Dr. Sonja Duncan.

Rachel had been on the set talking to one of the cameramen when Ethan arrived that morning, swaggering in and exuding rugged masculinity all over the place. The number of flirtatious smiles that were cast his way the moment he said good morning had only made her shake her head. Some of the women were probably still wiping the drool from their mouths.

Why did women get so silly at the sight of a good-looking man? She would admit she had been attracted to him yesterday like everyone else, after all she was a woman, but there was no reason to get downright foolish about it.

"Freeze! No talking on the set!"

Frasier was looking straight at Paige and Tae'Shawna and frowning. He knew exactly who the noisemakers were, and to be called out by the director wasn't good. They had caused time to be wasted, and everyone knew Frasier didn't like that.

"Unfreeze!"

This time around, everyone was quiet while the shooting of the scene continued. In this scene, Dr. Tyrell Perry and Dr. Sonja Duncan were discussing the seriousness of a patient's condition. It was obvious in this scene that the two were attracted to each other. The television viewers would already know through the use of flashbacks that Sonja's late husband, also a doctor, had gotten killed when an L.A. gang, intent on killing a man being treated in the hospital, burst into the E.R. and opened fire, killing everyone, including the doctor, a nurse and a few others waiting to be treated.

Rachel figured since Livia was only a temporary member of the cast, there would not be too much of a budding romance between the two doctors, although it wasn't known just how Livia's exit would be handled. Frasier was known to leave the viewers hanging from scene to scene, so it would be anyone's guess what he had in mind. She couldn't help but wonder if the chemistry the two generated on the set would extend beyond filming.

She hadn't gotten a chance to get to know Livia. During the makeup and wardrobe sessions there hadn't been much conversation between them. Her initial impression was that Livia was just as shallow and self-absorbed as the other Hollywood types Rachel had met. She'd seen no reason for that impression to change. Livia had a reputation of being a party girl and as much the tabloid princess as Ethan was the tabloid king. So it would stand to reason the two would be attracted to each other both on and off the set.

"Cut! Good scene! Let's enjoy lunch. Everyone take an additional hour and be back to start again on time."

Rachel smiled, grateful for the extra time. It seemed a number of people were in a hurry to take advantage of Frasier's generosity…in more ways than one, she thought, when out of the corner of her eye she noticed several women bustling over in Ethan's direction. She rolled her eyes. My goodness, did they have no shame? Interestingly, Livia walked away in another direction, as if the attention given to Ethan didn't concern her one bit.

Shaking her head, Rachel walked back to her trailer to grab her purse. She had a few errands to do before lunch was over.

Ethan watched Rachel leave before forcing his attention back to the two women standing in front of him. Tae'Shawna had all but invited him over tonight to go skinny-dipping in her pool. Of course he had turned her down. Paige had offered to come over to his place to help him go over his lines. He turned her down as well. For some reason, he wasn't feeling these two. If truth be told, he wasn't feeling any woman right now. Except for the one who'd just headed off toward her trailer.

"So what are you doing for lunch, Ethan? We would love for you to join us," Paige invited, interrupting his thoughts.

"Thanks, but I have a few errands I need to take care of," he said, knowing it was a lie as he said it. But in this case, he felt it was justified.

"No problem. Maybe we can help with your errands and—"

"Thanks again, but that's not necessary," he said, pulling his keys out of his back pocket. He had planned to wait until the weekend to shop for Kendra's gift, but now was just as good a time since these two were beginning to make a nuisance of themselves.

"I'll see you ladies later. I need to leave so I can be back on time."

For a second Paige looked like she was going to invite herself along. Instead she said, "Then I guess we'll see you when you return."

He only smiled, refusing to make any promises as he headed toward the exit. He was grateful for the additional hour and planned on making good use of it. Moving quickly, he reached for the door at the same time someone else did. The moment their hands touched he knew the identity of that person. Her scent gave her away.

"Excuse me."

"Excuse me as well," he said, taking a step back, opening the door and holding it for her to pass through. "You're taking advantage of the extra hour, I see."

Rachel smiled up at him. "I think everyone is." She glanced back over his shoulder. "Where's your fan club?"

His gaze scanned over her face and he saw a cute little mole near the corner of her lip. How could he have missed it yesterday? "My fan club?"

"Yes."

They were walking together as they headed toward the parking lot. "Trust me, there are some fans you can do without."

"And you want me to believe you're not flattered?" she teased, speaking in a low tone when a crew member passed them on the sidewalk.

He slowed his pace as they got closer to where the cars were parked in the studio lot. "Yes, that's exactly what I want you to believe."

She stopped walking and so did he. "Why? Why does it matter what I think?"

Ethan thought she had asked a good question. Why did it matter what she thought? He knew the answer before he could pull in his next breath. He liked her, and if he had the time he would try to get something going with her. The thing was he didn't have the time. He had to stay focused and doubted he would have time to pursue a relationship, serious or otherwise, with any woman anytime soon. He kept reminding himself that this was his big break, and he wasn't about to mess it up by trying to get between any woman's legs. He had gone without for six months, and he could go another six months or more if he had to.

But that didn't mean that he and Rachel couldn't be just friends, did it? It would be nice to have someone who wasn't interested in anything more than friendship. The little attraction that had passed between them yesterday couldn't be helped. After all, she was a nice-looking woman and he was a hot-blooded man. But as long as they kept things under control, being just friends would be fine.

"It matters because I like you and I'd like for us to be friends," he said.

She pushed a wayward strand of hair from her face as she looked at him. "And why would you want us to become friends?"

Providing an answer to that question was easy enough. "The one thing I noticed yesterday was that you're genuinely a nice person." He chuckled then added, "Hey, you didn't rag on me about being nervous. And it's obvious everyone on the set likes you, from the maintenance man all the way up to the bigwigs. I figure with that kind of popularity, you can't be all bad. Besides, you and Livia are the only two females on the set that I feel pretty comfortable around."

She lifted a brow. "Livia?"

"Yes."

She tilted her head back as if to give him her full attention. "Not that it is any of my business, but I thought that maybe something was going on between the two of you."

He smiled. "There is, on the show. But it's all acting. She's supposed to be my new love interest for the next few episodes."

She nodded. "Your scenes earlier were pretty convincing."

He chuckled. "We're actors. They were meant to be convincing."

Ethan glanced at his watch. "I'd better get going. I

want to pick up something for my six-year-old niece from the Disney Store. After watching *The Princess and the Frog* she's into princesses, so I thought I'd pick her up a Princess Tiana doll."

A smile touched the corners of her lips. "You have a niece?"

"Yes, Kendra. She's my older brother's little girl and, I hate to say it, but she's perfect."

She chuckled. "I believe you. And there's a store in walking distance on Hollywood Boulevard. I'm headed that way myself to pick up something from the art supply shop."

He turned the idea over in his mind only once before asking, "Mind if I tag along?"

He did his best not to watch the way her lips were tugged up in a smile when she said, "Sure, you can tag along, as long as we don't talk about work. We need to give our brains a break."

He jammed his keys in his pocket as he resumed walking by her side. It was a beautiful August day, and he had a beautiful woman strolling alongside him. Things couldn't get any better than that. "So what do we talk about?" he decided to ask her.

She slanted her head to look at him. "You."

"Me?"

"Yes."

"Hey, we talked about me yesterday."

Her mouth twitched in a grin. "Yes, but all I know is that you're from Napa Valley and you have a niece."

She chuckled. "I guess I could go by what I've heard and—"

"Read in the tabloids," he said, finishing the statement for her.

"No, I don't do tabloids. It would be nice if others didn't do them either, then they would go out of business."

He glanced over at her and laughed. "You don't like the right of free speech?"

She laughed back at him. "More like the right of sleazy speech. Ninety percent of what they print isn't true, but then I guess that's the price of being a star."

He smiled, liking the way the sunlight was bouncing off her hair, making it appear even more lustrous. He liked the short cut on her. "Yes, it's one of the detriments, that's for sure. I just go with the flow. As long as I know what's true about me and what's not, I don't lose any sleep."

She didn't say anything for a while, and then replied, "I hate being in the spotlight."

She kept looking ahead, but he'd heard what she said. Clearly. If that was true, he wondered how she managed it, being a Wellesley. The company her family owned was so connected with this industry, and had been for close to thirty years, they were practically an icon in Hollywood.

He had researched information on Limelight when he'd returned to the States from abroad. He had even considered contacting them to handle his affairs before he'd chosen Curtis, who'd been a friend of a friend to whom he'd owed a favor. But he wouldn't hesitate to consider them again when his contract with Curtis ended. Lately, he'd begun feeling as if he was making his own contacts. Everyone he knew handled by Limelight was pleased with its services. Not once had they ever been made to feel like they were a passenger instead of a driver.

"Being in the spotlight doesn't bother me," he decided to say. "It comes with the territory. But then, my family is well-known in Napa Valley, so I got used to having a mike shoved in my face, only to be quoted incorrectly." He could recall a number of times when he'd been referred to as "the playboy Chambers" while Hunter had always been considered the one with a level head. The responsibly acting Chambers.

"And it doesn't bother you?" she asked.

He met her gaze. "A distortion of the truth will bother most people, and I'm no different. However, I don't lose sleep over it," he said, shifting his gaze to study her features.

But he had a feeling she would.

There had to be a reason, and the question rested on the tip of his tongue.

But he had no right to pry. This woman owed him nothing, had no reason to divulge her deep, dark secrets and innermost feelings. Not to him. They weren't husband and wife. They weren't even lovers. Nor would they ever be.

No, he reminded himself, he was trying out the friendship thing.

Chapter 5

Rachel could feel the power of Ethan as he walked beside her. And although it sounded strange, she could feel his strength. Not only did she feel it, she was drawing from it.

The very thought that such a thing was possible should be disconcerting, but instead the knowledge seemed to wrap her in some sort of warm embrace. That in itself was kind of weird since they'd decided to just be friends. She was fine with that decision. In fact, she refused to have things any other way. She didn't mix business with pleasure and she had too much on her plate to become involved in a serious relationship.

The last guy she had gone out with that she'd truly liked had been Theo Lovett. That had been a couple of years ago. They had dated for almost six months before she'd found out the only reason he'd been interested in her was as a way into her family's business. Luckily, she'd overheard him bragging to a friend on the phone when he'd thought she was in the shower and out of hearing range. Theo's explanation that he'd only been joking with his friend hadn't made her change her mind when she had kicked him out that day.

She stepped out of her memory and into the present. Apparently she'd missed some of what Ethan had said while she'd been daydreaming, because he'd changed the subject and was talking about his family.

"My older brother's name is Hunter. There is an eight year difference in our ages."

She glanced over at him. Despite the fact he was a lot taller than she, walking side by side they seemed to fit, and their steps appeared to be perfectly synchronized. How was that possible with his long legs and her short ones? He'd evidently adjusted his steps to stay in sync with hers. It was a perfectly measured pace.

"There is a nine year difference in me and my sister's ages," she said.

"Really? Was your sibling as overprotective as mine while you were growing up?"

Rachel made a face. "Boy, was she ever. She was ten when our parents were killed in a plane crash, and I was one. Our aunt and uncle became our legal guardians, but somewhere along the way my sister, Sofia, thought I became her responsibility. It was only when she left for college that I got some breathing space."

"Are the two of you close now?"

"Yes, very. What about you and your brother? Are the two of you close?"

"Yes, although I would be the first to admit he was somewhat of a pain in the ass while we were growing up. But I can appreciate it now since he covered for me a lot with my parents."

She could imagine someone having to do that for him. She had a feeling he'd probably been a handful. "Was your family upset when you decided not to enter the family business but to forge a path in a different direction?"

The corners of his lips lifted in a wry smile. "Let's just say they weren't thrilled with the idea. But I think it bothered Hunter more than it did them," he said. "The Chamberses have been in the wine business for generations, and I was the first to pull out and try doing something else. He lay on the pressure for me to stay for a while but then he backed off."

He placed his hand at the center of her back when others, walking at a swifter pace than they, moved to pass them. She could feel the warmth of his touch through her blouse. She breathed in deeply at the feeling of butterflies flapping around in her stomach.

"What about your family?" he inquired, not realizing the effect of his touch on her.

"Once I explained things to Uncle Jacob and Aunt Lily, they were fine with it. They wanted me to do whatever made me happy. But Sofia felt it was part of our father's legacy, that I owed it to him to join her and

Uncle Jacob at Limelight. I had made up my mind on how I wanted to do things with my future, so instead of letting there be this bone of contention between us, she backed off and eventually gave me her blessings to do whatever I wanted to do with my life."

She chuckled. "As a concession, I am letting Limelight Entertainment handle my career. I'm one of their clients."

They paused a moment when they reached the security gate. They had deliberately walked the expanse of the studio lot to avoid running into the paparazzi that made the place their regular beat. Now that they were no longer in safe and protected territory, she noticed Ethan had slid on a pair of sunglasses. He had kept on his medical scrubs and had a stethoscope around his neck, and she wondered if anyone seeing him would assume he was a bona fide doctor walking the strip on lunch break.

She pulled her sunglasses out of her bag, too, although it had been years since she'd had the paparazzi on her tail. When she was younger, they'd seemed to enjoy keeping up with the two Wellesley heirs. She'd always found the media's actions intrusive and an invasion of her privacy. She could recall all the photographs of her as a child that had appeared in the tabloids. That was the main reason she much preferred not being the focus of their attention again.

She glanced over at Ethan when his hand went to the center of her back again. It was time for them to cross the street, and he was evidently trying to hurry her along before traffic started up again. Her pulse began fluttering, caused by the heat generated from his touch.

They increased their pace to make it across the street. She checked him out from the corner of her eye and saw how sexy the scrubs looked on him. They had agreed to be just friends, she reminded herself. And it meant absolutely nothing that they had a few things in common. Like the fact that they were both renegades. That they were both members of well-known families. That they both had siblings who'd chosen to go into the family business. Overprotective, older siblings who meant well but if given the chance would run their lives.

Rachel inconspicuously scanned the area around them and breathed a sigh of relief when she saw the paparazzi was nowhere in sight. But then they were known to bounce out from just about any place. Hopefully she and Ethan looked like a regular couple out on a stroll during their lunch hour.

A couple who were just friends, which was something she could not forget.

"You are such a good uncle."

Ethan glanced at Rachel while accepting his change from the girl behind the counter at the Disney Store. Had he used his charge card his cover would have been blown. Even through his sunglasses, he could see the woman was looking at him, trying to figure out if he was a doctor or someone she should know.

He smiled at Rachel. "I'd like to think so, especially

since I doubt very seriously that Hunter will have any more children," he said, accepting the bag the cashier was handing him.

"Why is that?"

"He lost his wife in a car accident," he explained as they headed for the exit. "He took Annette's death hard and hasn't been in a serious relationship since. It's been three years now."

"Oh, how sad."

"Yes, it was. Hunter and Kendra were in the car at the time of the accident and survived with minor injuries," he said. He paused a moment and then added, "Kendra was three at the time and very close to her mother. She felt the loss immediately and withdrew into her own world and stopped talking."

The eyes that stared into his were full of sorrow and compassion. "She doesn't talk?"

He released his breath in a long and slow sigh, wondering why he was sharing this information about his family with anyone, especially to a woman he'd only met yesterday. But there was something about Rachel that was different from most women he'd met. For one, she wasn't trying to come on to him or jump his bones. It was as if she saw him as a person and not some sex symbol, and he appreciated that.

"She talks now, but not as much as she should for a child her age," he responded. "And she talks more with some people than with others. I happen to be one of those she will talk to most of the time. But it took me a while to gain that much ground again after the

accident." He recalled the time he had come home from
France to give his brother and niece his support. "But a
part of Kendra is still withdrawn and so far no one has
been able to fully bring her back. She's been seen by the
best psychologists money can hire. They practically all
said the same thing. Kendra suffered a traumatic loss,
and until she's convinced in her mind that she can love
someone again, become attached to that person without
losing them all over again, she will continue to withdraw
into her own little world."

He checked his watch and figured they needed to
head on back. Prior to stopping at the store, they had
stopped by an art supply place and picked up some new
brushes. She'd told him that she liked dabbling with
paints on canvas every once in a while and had promised
to show him some of her work one day.

As they began retracing their steps back toward the
studio lot, he had to admit he had enjoyed his time with
her and knew that he was going to enjoy having her as
a friend. An odd thought suddenly burned in his brain.
What if they became more than just friends? He quickly
forced the notion out of his head. The fact of the matter
was they were just friends, or at least they were trying
to be.

He glanced at her and saw her scan the surrounding
area. He could tell she was nervous about the possibility
of being seen by the paparazzi. So was he, but only
because it bothered her. Despite the fact that only
minutes ago he'd vowed not to pry, he couldn't stop the
question now.

"Why do you avoid the spotlight, Rachel?" He could tell his question surprised her and suspected her reasons were deep-seated.

"I just do," she said.

She tried to act calm, like his question wasn't a big deal, but he sensed that it was. "Why?"

She frowned up at him, and the first thing he thought was that he'd made her mad. He hadn't meant to, but a part of him wanted to push her for an answer.

"Well?" he asked.

She didn't say anything as they kept walking. She had stopped glaring at him and was staring straight ahead. He'd almost given up hope for a reply when she began speaking. "I told you my parents were killed before my second birthday. Since my uncle and aunt who adopted us couldn't have any kids of their own, my sister and I became known as the Limelight heirs. For some reason we made news, and the paparazzi followed us practically everywhere we went—school, church, grocery stores... you name it, they were there. I couldn't tell you how many times when I was a little girl that I got a mike shoved in my face or my braid pulled by a reporter to get my attention. It was...scary.

"Things only got better when I went away to college. By the time I returned, the media interest was on someone else, thank goodness. But every once in a while someone tries to connect the dots to see what Sofia and I are up to. She doesn't mind being in the spotlight and uses it to her advantage."

Ethan took in what she said. The thought of someone

harassing a child to get a story angered him, and knowing the child had been Rachel angered him even more. It was interesting that he felt such protective instincts for her.

A flicker of some sort of alarm flashed through his brain but he chose to ignore it. No matter what his mind thought, there was no way he would get in too deep with Rachel.

Chapter 6

Rachel stood by the window in her uncle's study and gazed out at the ocean. The sun was going down and she enjoyed watching it. Just like she had enjoyed being on the set the past two weeks.

Frasier and John were pleased with the tempo of the series. Ethan was working out perfectly as Dr. Perry, and the blossoming on-the-air love affair between the gruff doctor and the resistant Dr. Duncan had pretty much heated up. They had shot a love scene yesterday that had pushed the temperature on the set up as hot as it could get for prime-time programming.

She could definitely say she was pleased with this assignment and looked forward to going into work each day. The more time she and Ethan spent together during filming, the more they talked and bonded as friends. She found him fun to be around, and the two of them would laugh together about some of the actresses' hot pursuit of him. A few had tried some outlandish things to get his attention. Like the time Jasmine Crowder summoned him to her trailer to help rehang a photo that had fallen off the wall. Instead of going, Ethan had sent one of the cameramen, Omar Minton, in his place. Poor Omar had walked into the trailer to be met by a half-naked Jasmine draped across the sofa.

That had been just one of many times during the past week that Ethan had had to foil seduction plots. Just the fact that he'd done so impressed Rachel, and she would be the first to admit that she was seeing him not as the superficial playboy she'd originally thought he was but as a focused, hardworking actor. That was another thing they had in common. They believed in professionalism on the job.

"Lily said I'd probably find you in here."

Rachel turned at the sound of her uncle's deep voice and smiled. Since she'd been only one year old when her parents had gotten killed, she didn't have a solid memory of them the way Sofia did. But what she did remember was her aunt and uncle being there for them, raising her and Sofia as their own. Rachel appreciated having been part of a family in which she'd always known she was loved and always been encouraged to use her talents in whatever way she wanted to do.

She'd learned from her aunt and uncle that her mother was a successful artist, and several of Vivian Wellesley's paintings were on the walls in this house as well as in a number of art galleries across the country. Vivian had passed down her talent and love of painting; Rachel really enjoyed the time she spent putting color to canvas. She was definitely her mother's daughter.

And Sofia was definitely her father's. She had stepped into the role of the savvy and successful businessman that he'd been. And because Sofia had been the only child for almost nine years, she had been the pride of her parents' life and definitely the apple of her father's eye. Sofia had worshipped the ground their father had walked on and was still doing that same thing even though their parents had been dead for twenty-five years. Sofia thought John Wellesley was the most amazing person to have ever lived.

The man standing before Rachel was John's identical twin.

"Uncle Jacob," Rachel greeted, crossing the room to give her uncle a hug. She'd seen pictures of the brothers from years past, and to see one was to see the other. That said, she knew if her father had lived he would have matured into a rather handsome man. And at fifty-five, her uncle was definitely that, with a charm and charisma that should be patented. Ethan had told her about the close relationship he had with his niece, and she had fully understood because such a relationship existed between her and her uncle.

"And what honor has been bestowed upon me for this visit?" he asked, leaning back and scanning her from head to toe. "Hmm, I don't see anything broken or in need of repair, although I still keep plenty of bandages around."

Rachel could only laugh. While growing up she had been a handful, a tomboy in her earlier years. And anytime she got hurt, she would run to her uncle to fix her boo-boo.

"C'mon, Uncle Jacob, it's not like I never come to visit," she defended herself, laughing.

"No, but since you've moved to the other side of town we barely see you these days."

Rachel nibbled on her bottom lip. In addition to the enormous mansion her aunt and uncle owned in Beverly Hills, they also had this place, a luxurious oceanfront hideaway on Malibu Beach. A few months ago she had purchased a condo in the gated community of Friar Gate that was located on the outskirts of Hollywood. Before moving, she had lived in a condo that had been within walking distance of Rodeo Drive. It was fine until one of the Jonas Brothers had moved into the complex. There was no peace with the paparazzi, and she'd figured it was just a matter of time before they added others to their list to harass.

"I needed more space," she said and knew her uncle would understand. It was no secret she didn't like being in the spotlight.

He nodded. "And when will I get invited to your new place for dinner?"

She threw her head back and laughed again, knowing that was a joke since she didn't cook. The few times she'd tried, she had made a complete mess of things and decided there were too many restaurants serving good, tasty food to put herself through the agony of following some recipe.

"Just as soon as I get everything in its proper place. I still have a few boxes left to unpack, but I've been so busy on the set. And then there's that painting I want to finish before the gallery hosts that charity event next month."

"I understand," Jacob Wellesley said, leading her to the nearest sofa so they could sit down. "You are a very busy lady, just like your mother was. We would try and convince her there were but so many hours in the day, but she was always determined to stretch them anyway."

Rachel couldn't help but smile. She always liked hearing the stories her uncle and aunt would share about her parents.

"And how are things going for you at work? Frasier isn't working you too hard, is he?" he asked.

Frasier Glenn was not only an old friend of her father's but he'd been close to her uncle as well and had been one of Limelight's first clients. When she'd interviewed for the position of makeup artist and wardrobe designer for *Paging the Doctor,* Frasier had been up-front and let her know it was her own merit and work ethic, not the long-standing friendship he had with her family, that had gotten her the job. She had appreciated that.

"No, both Frasier and John are wonderful, and I'm learning so much from them," she said, leaning back against the sofa's cushions.

"Good. I understand Eric Woods's contract didn't get renewed."

"No, but we were expecting it with his behavior last season. I hear he's mouthing off to the tabloids that he had no idea he was getting the ax."

Jacob shook his head. "Oh, I'm sure he knew. Frasier doesn't work that way. When he makes a decision to let you go, you know why. Eric's just trying to save face. Everyone in the industry knows his last few movies bombed out, and because of his temperament, it's hard to find a director in Hollywood with the patience to take him on."

Rachel nodded. "This season is going to have a new twist. They brought in a new doctor and I think his appearance will boost ratings."

"Really? Who is he?"

"Ethan Chambers."

A slow smile touched Uncle Jacob's lips. "I've never met Chambers but I've heard of him. Word's out that he's an actor who's going places. He received good reviews from the guest spot he did on CSI that one time last year. And there was that rumor earlier this year that he was being considered for *People*'s Sexiest Man of the Year. That didn't hurt. There hasn't been an African American male to get that honor since Denzel and that was close to fifteen years ago."

Rachel could see Ethan being considered. He was definitely a hot contender in her book.

"And how is Chambers working out?"

"I think he's doing a great job. It is difficult, though,

to get the females on the set to concentrate on what they are supposed to do instead of on him. He has a way of grabbing your attention and holding it."

"Mmm, does he now?"

She smiled, knowing what her uncle was probably thinking. "Okay, I admit he's hot, but I'm beyond fawning over any man, Uncle Jacob. Besides, Ethan Chambers comes with something I could never tolerate."

Jacob Wellesley lifted a thick brow. "What?"

"The spotlight."

Later that night, after spending time in front of the canvas for a good part of the evening, Rachel's phone rang. She reached out and picked it up without checking caller ID, thinking it was either Charlene or Sofia.

"Hello?"

"Save me."

She blinked upon hearing the sound of the ultrasexy, masculine voice. "Ethan?"

"Yes, it's me."

She was surprised. They had known each other for two weeks now, considered themselves friends and had even exchanged phone numbers one day on the set, but he'd never called her before and she'd never had a reason to call him. And what was his reason for calling her now? Had he said something about saving him?

"What on earth is going on with you?" she asked, putting him on speakerphone while she dried her hands.

"I need a place to crash for the night. I came home

and found the place swarming with paparazzi. Luckily they didn't see me, and I made a U-turn and headed in another direction. So, will you have pity on me and put me up for the night?"

She tossed the hand towel aside as she leaned against the kitchen counter. "Ethan, you know how I detest being—"

"In the spotlight. Yes, I know," he said interrupting her. "And that's the reason I hesitated calling you, but I need this favor, Rachel. I've been driving around for a few hours now and have periodically checked my rearview mirror to make sure no one is following me. They're probably still parked out front waiting for me to come home. They wouldn't think of looking for me at your place."

That was an understatement, Rachel thought. They probably figured he was somewhere warming some starlet's bed. He was single, sexy and a man who probably had needs that any woman would love filling. In that case, why couldn't he go back to his lady friend's place instead of putting her privacy at risk?

She began nibbling on her bottom lip. Tomorrow was Sunday and they were due back on the set Monday morning at eight. All she needed was for someone to get wind that Ethan had stayed overnight at her place, no matter how innocent it might be, and make a big deal of it.

Everyone on the set knew the two of them had become friends, but no one thought anything of it since she was friendly with just about everyone…except for Paige, who still had her panties in a wad for some reason. Besides, no one would assume something was going on between them because she wasn't the type of woman Ethan would be interested in. She was definitely not model material.

But still, she didn't want anyone assuming anything or, even worse, the paparazzi hunting him down at her place. Jeez, she didn't want to even think of that happening. One good thing was that she had a two-car garage, so his car wouldn't be seen parked in front of her place. And her gated community was known for its privacy and security.

"Rachel?"

She drew in a deep breath. "Fine, but if anyone from the media gets wind of this and starts harassing me, Ethan, you're dead meat."

She heard him laugh. "I don't want to be dead meat, Rachel."

She folded her arms across her chest and tapped her foot. "Well?"

"All right, I'll take my chances."

"With the paparazzi?"

"Heck no," he said. "I'll take my chances with you. I'm hoping our budding friendship will keep you from actually killing me. Besides, I've been around you enough to know that you do have a soft heart."

She either had a soft heart or a foolish mind, Rachel thought an hour later when she opened her door to Ethan. She also had a bunch of erratic hormones. The tingle started in the pit of her stomach when she looked at him, and it took a full minute to catch her breath. Not only did Ethan look good but he smelled good enough to eat.

She was caught off guard by her reaction to him. They'd agreed to just be friends, but at the moment friendship was the last thing on her mind. She couldn't stop her gaze from roaming all over him. He was leaning in the doorway in a sexy stance, wearing jeans and a button-down shirt with the top four buttons undone. She glimpsed his chest beneath, poking out like a temptation being dangled in front of her. If this was the way he showed up at his woman's home, no wonder he was in such high demand. And no wonder a rush of adrenaline jolted through her.

"And you're sure you weren't followed?" she asked, taking a step back to let him in. She figured conversation between them would distract her long enough to get her mind and body back under control.

He gave her a wry smile as he entered, moving over the threshold and filling the room the same way he'd filled the doorway…with dominating sexiness. "I'm positive. I drove around an additional twenty minutes or so to be sure. Those were good directions you gave me, by the way. I found this place without any trouble."

She nodded as she closed the door. That was when she noticed the shopping bag in his hand. When she gave him a questioning look, he said, "I made a pit stop at a store to pick up a few toiletries."

"And you weren't recognized?" she asked, moving away from the door.

"No. I had my disguise on," he said, pulling a baseball cap and a fake mustache out of the pocket of his jacket.

Rachel lifted a brow while fighting back a smile. "That's the best you can do?"

He gave her a flirty smile. "Depends on what we're talking about."

He was flirting with her.

On a few occasions over the last couple of weeks, he'd turned on the charm and flashed his devilish smile that lit up his blue-gray eyes. But she'd just rolled her eyes at him. Tonight was different. Tonight she couldn't help her body's reaction to his flirting.

As much for herself as for him, she said, "We're talking about your disguise, Ethan."

"Oh." He glanced down at the items he held in his hand. "There's nothing wrong with my disguise. It served its purpose."

With a suddenly sweaty palm, she pushed her hair behind her ear and met his gaze. "We can only hope."

Then he flashed that devilish grin that she'd tried so hard to avoid. And something slammed into her. Awareness. Attraction.

Uh-oh, said the one remaining rational part of her brain. *You've made a big mistake.*

She had to agree. Letting Ethan stay overnight just might be the biggest mistake she'd ever made.

Chapter 7

Ethan gave Rachel a hot look because there wasn't any other type of look he could give her. He was totally taken with seeing her again. Had it been just yesterday when they'd last seen each other? Just yesterday when he had been alone with her in her trailer, reclining in the chair while she applied his makeup?

She had leaned over him and her scent had almost driven him crazy. They had agreed to be just friends, and God knows he'd tried keeping his desires under control with her on the set. But at night, alone in his bed, his dreams had been another matter. She was his friend by day and his dream lover at night. And the things that went on inside those dreams were enough to make a man stiff just thinking about them.

No woman had ever dominated his thoughts like she had.

As he'd told her, he had driven around a couple of hours before finally deciding to call her. There were a number of women he could have called, but she was the one he knew he could contact and not worry about anything getting leaked to the tabloids. But now he had to be honest with himself and admit the real reason he had sought her out. He had wanted to see her.

He pulled in a deep breath, and instead of standing there staring at her like she was a nice juicy steak he couldn't wait to eat, he glanced around, needing a distraction as much as he needed a cold beer. He saw several boxes and then recalled her saying she'd only been living in this place a few months. Obviously she hadn't finished unpacking yet. But it was a nice place, large and spacious and her choice of furnishings hit the mark. "Your place is tight, Rachel."

"Thanks. You want to see the bedroom?"

At his raised brow, she said, "I mean the one you'll use tonight. The guestroom."

He'd known what she meant but thought she looked cute when she blushed. He liked seeing her get all flustered. "Sure. But you didn't ask if I wanted something to drink, and I'm thirsty."

She rolled her eyes. "Are you going to be a pesky houseguest?"

"I'll try hard not to be but I do have another confession to make. I'm hungry, too."

Rachel shook her head, chuckling. "Then you're at

the wrong place. I can give you something to drink, but for a meal you're out of luck."

"Why is that?"

"I can't cook, and before you ask, my aunt and uncle always had live-in cooks and I never had a desire to learn."

He chuckled. "No problem. I know my way around a kitchen."

She laughed. "That's all nice but there's still a problem."

"What?" he asked.

"I don't have any groceries."

He lifted a brow. "Nothing?"

"Well, my best friend did feel sorry for my refrigerator and went to the store last week and picked up a few items like eggs, butter and bread. The basics."

A smile touched his lips. "That's all I need. Just lead me to your kitchen."

"That was simply amazing," Rachel said, leaning back in her chair. "If I hadn't seen it, I would not have believed it."

Ethan leaned back in his chair as well and laughed. "It was just an egg sandwich on toast, Rachel. No big deal."

"Hey, I beg to differ. I never got the hang of cooking an egg. Or anything else for that matter."

"Why would your friend buy eggs if you can't cook them?" he asked, taking a swig of his beer. He'd found several bottles behind all the art supplies she kept in her refrigerator.

"They can be boiled, you know," she said, taking a sip of her own beer, right from the bottle. "And I know it was just a sandwich but it was still good. I hadn't realized I'd gotten hungry."

"Hadn't you eaten dinner?" he asked, getting up and grabbing their plates off the table. They had used paper plates and plastic utensils so all they had to do was trash them. No dishes to wash. How convenient. That had been a good idea on her part.

"I had lunch with my aunt and uncle earlier in the day and when I got home, I started painting and lost track of the time." She got up from the table as well. "If you hadn't called, I probably would have ordered out for a pizza or something eventually."

He watched her stride across the floor to the sink to rinse out her beer bottle before tossing it into a recycle bin. She was wearing a pair of shorts and a top and looked pretty in them. He glanced down and thought she even had cute bare feet with polished toes.

"My uncle knows you or at least he's heard of you," she said, causing him to shift his gaze to her face. "He was very complimentary."

"Was he?"

"Yes. He believes you're a person who's going places."

A broad smile touched his lips. "That means a lot coming from the likes of Jacob Wellesley," he said before finishing off his beer.

He joined her at the sink and she slid over to give him room when he proceeded to rinse out his own beer bottle. She smelled good, he thought, pulling in a whiff of her scent through his nostrils. She smelled better than good. She smelled like a woman he wanted.

He smiled over at her and she glared at him. "What's wrong?" he asked, moving to place the beer bottle in the recycle bin. "I assured you that no one followed me over here."

"That's not what's bothering me, Ethan."

He leaned back against the sink. "Then what is bothering you, Rachel?" He had an idea but wanted her to tell him.

She had moved back to the table and stood with her arms crossed over her chest. "I think we need to reiterate a few things, like the fact that two weeks ago we decided to be friends and nothing more."

"I thought we were."

"I thought so, too," she replied. "But…"

He lifted a brow and tried looking baffled. "But what?"

"I'm getting these vibes."

"Really? What kind of vibes?"

When she didn't say anything, he crossed the room to her. "Rachel, just what kind of vibes are you getting?"

He was staring at her and those gorgeous eyes of his were probably seeing a lot more than she wanted them to. A lot more than she needed them to see. And that put her on the defensive.

"None. Forget I said that," she said.

"Not sure I can do that now," he said, eyeing her up and down the way he'd done the first day they'd met. Before they'd decided all they wanted between them was friendship. Her mind scrambled as she tried to recall that day. It had been his second day on the set. Had it really been two weeks ago already? They had walked to the Disney Store and Art World. He had purchased a Princess Tiana doll for his niece, and she had picked up some art supplies.

They'd both agreed they were not involved in serious relationships and wanted to keep things that way. Besides, she had painstakingly explained to him that she didn't mix business with pleasure. He had understood and said the same rule applied to him. That should have settled things…so why didn't it?

Why was he looking at her now in a way that made her so aware of her sensuality while at the same time reminded her that it had been a long time since she'd been with a man? Nearly two years, to be exact, and even then it hadn't been anything to brag about.

"You have no choice, Ethan," she heard herself say.

"I don't?"

At the shake of her head, he said, "And what if I told you I'm getting those same vibes, and that if we don't at least share a kiss, there will always be curiosity between us?"

Heat circled around in her stomach at his admission and his suggestion. "Maybe for you, but not for me," she said, lifting her chin.

He took a step closer. "And you want me to believe that you aren't curious?"

Of course she was curious. What woman wouldn't be when there were lips that looked like his? "No, not in the least," she lied while looking him straight in the eye.

Unfortunately, those eyes were staring right back at her, as if seeing straight into her. Heat crawled all over her skin and her heart thumped faster. And when the corners of his mouth eased into a sexy smile, she inhaled sharply.

She broke eye contact with him, not liking the look on his face. It was taunting her and tempting her, all at the same time. She nervously licked her tongue across her top lip as a sudden case of panic gripped her.

God, how he'd love to try out that tongue.

Thrumming heat raced through his gut. Funny the difference a couple of weeks could make. His first days on the set, he was ready to push everything aside to focus on his role on *Paging the Doctor*. But now that he felt comfortable playing Dr. Tyrell Perry, he no longer went to bed with his lines infused into his brain. Instead something else—or should he say someone else— occupied his thoughts. And that person was standing right in front of him.

"You know what I think, Ethan?" she asked, interrupting his thoughts.

"No, what do you think?"

"You being here, claiming you needed a place to crash

for the night, is part of some manipulating scheme." He could hear the sharpness in her tone and could see the fire in her eyes.

"Not true. I called you for the reason I told you. I didn't have anyone else to call."

"C'mon, Ethan. Do you honestly expect me to believe that? Of all the women you've been linked to, do you really assume I'm that gullible enough to think none of them would have let you stay overnight at their place?"

"I imagine one of them would." He paused a moment and then said, "Let me rephrase what I said earlier. There are others I *could* have called but you are the only one I *wanted* to call." Boy, if only she knew how true that was.

She got silent and he knew she was thinking, trying to make heads or tails of what he'd said. Then she simply asked, "Why, Ethan? Why was I the only one you wanted to call?"

He saw the frustrated expression on her face. But it was what he saw in her eyes that captivated him. Desire. Although she might wish it wasn't there, it was and it was just as deep as what he was feeling.

But Rachel was a logical person who would not accept anything less than a logical and straightforward answer, so he said, "Because you are the only one I want."

Chapter 8

Speechless, Rachel could only stare at him while all the sexual desires she'd had for him since day one came tumbling back. Why was he trying to make things so difficult? Why was he forcing her to admit the one thing she had tried to deny? She was attracted to him something awful.

It would be so easy to let her guard down and walk across the room, wrap her arms around his neck and give in to temptation and indulge in a heated kiss. A kiss that would probably curl her toes and then some.

But she had to think logically. He threatened something she couldn't risk losing—her privacy. Any woman he was involved with would become just as much news as he was. The paparazzi would make sure of that.

He was a man who spent his life, both personal and otherwise, in front of the camera, a place she tried to avoid.

She shook her head. Things were going all wrong. They had decided they wouldn't go down this road, so why were they? They were friends and that's all they would ever be. He knew it and she knew it, as well. If he refused to do what was best, then she would.

Rachel backed up and nervously tugged at the hem of her T-shirt. "C'mon, let me show you where you'll sleep tonight. I think you'll like this room since it has its own private bath."

He held her gaze and, for a moment, she felt a weakening she didn't want to feel. Those eyes were the reason and she understood what was happening. Ethan had invaded her space, both mentally and creatively. And she couldn't deal with it.

Instead of saying anything else, she walked off and drew in a deep breath when she heard him falling in step behind her.

Walking behind her had its advantages, Ethan thought, watching the sway of Rachel's curvy hips and the lushness of her backside in her shorts. She probably hadn't figured out yet that he was enjoying the back view, and it was just as well since he definitely needed to think.

Contrary to what she thought, when he had shown up tonight it hadn't been with the intent of jumping her bones, although he found such a possibility a very enticing prospect.

He followed her up the stairs and once they reached the landing, he glanced around. The second floor was just as large and spacious as the first. There were a number of hung paintings and he couldn't help but admire them.

"Are these your creations?" he asked when she turned around after noticing he had slowed down.

She followed his gaze from wall to wall and smiled. "Some of them." She pointed out those that were. "The others are my mother's. She was a successful painter. A few of her pieces are on display at the L.A. Museum and various others."

"They're all beautiful. You inherited her gift and it shows in your work."

"Thanks."

They began walking again and as before, he followed. When she paused by a door he moved ahead and glanced inside. It was a huge room with a small bed. But it was a bed and tonight he wasn't picky, although he would much prefer hers.

"This is it," she said, entering the room. "The bath is to your left and there are plenty of towels and washcloths. Everything you need for your overnight stay."

He didn't miss her emphasis on "overnight." She intended for him to be gone in the morning. "Thanks, I appreciate it, and no matter what you think, Rachel, I didn't have an ulterior motive for coming here tonight."

Instead of saying she believed him like he'd hoped, she merely nodded, turned and walked away. Instinctively, his gaze went to her backside, and a sizzling heat began building inside of him. Hell, he was a man and tonight he was reminded of just how horny he was.

A few hours later, Rachel curled up in her favorite spot in her king-size bed. Ethan had been in her home only a few hours and already her house smelled of man. And as much as she hated admitting it, she liked the scent.

She couldn't help but notice it after rechecking the doors for the night and walking up the stairs to get ready for bed. She had heard the sound of the shower and the fragrance of his aftershave had floated through the air. Immediately, tremors of desire had rippled through her, and upon reaching the landing she had quickly hurried to her room and closed the door.

While getting dressed for bed, she had heard him moving around. The sound of someone else in her house felt strange because other than Charlene or Sofia, she rarely had houseguests.

All was quiet, so she could only assume Ethan had settled in for the night. That was just great. He was probably sleeping like a baby, and here she was, wide awake and thinking about him and the fact that he'd wanted to kiss her. She could now admit to herself—although she would never admit such a thing to him—that she had wanted to kiss him as well and that she *was* curious. However, being curious wouldn't benefit either one of them. It would serve no purpose.

Yes, it would…if it didn't lead anywhere.

Rachel rolled her eyes. *Not lead anywhere? Yeah, right.* There was no doubt in her mind that kissing Ethan would probably lead right here to her bedroom. And they had agreed to be nothing more than friends, she reminded herself.

But since he seemed quick to break the rules, why couldn't she break a few of her own? As long as the kiss and anything that followed after the kiss was all there could ever be and they knew where they stood with each other, would it really hurt for them to indulge in something that her body was telling her she both needed and wanted?

Her ears perked up when she heard the sound of Ethan moving around. A smile touched her lips. It was two in the morning and she felt grateful he couldn't sleep any more than she could.

She sat up in bed when she heard his bedroom door opening and then picked up the sound of him going downstairs. Being hungry at this hour would serve him no purpose since she didn't have any food in the house, unless he was planning to make another egg sandwich.

Before she could get cold feet, she eased out of bed, deciding if a kiss was what he wanted, then a kiss was what he was going to get.

* * *

With a deep sigh, Ethan closed the refrigerator door after pulling out a bottle of beer. He was hot and needed to cool off. He'd tried to get some sleep only to be awakened with dreams of him and Rachel together in some of the most explicit sexual positions possible. If those dreams kept coming, they could possibly ruin him for future relationships—at least until he discovered how close his dreams were to the real thing.

After screwing off the beer bottle top, he took a huge swig, appreciating how the cold liquid flowed down his throat and hoping some would keep moving straight to his groin.

"I see you couldn't sleep either."

Ethan spun around. Rachel was the last person he expected to see. After showing him the guest room, she had made herself scarce, basically hiding out in her bedroom.

She crossed the room toward the coffeepot, and he wished he could ignore the tantalizing view of her bare legs and curvy backside in a pajama set that consisted of clingy shorts and a spaghetti strap tank top.

"No, I couldn't sleep," he answered, before taking a final swig of beer while wishing it had been something stronger.

"Why?"

He looked over at her after placing his empty beer bottle on the counter. "Why what?"

"Why couldn't you sleep?" Her expression grew

troubled, showed her concern. "Isn't the bed comfortable enough?"

For a moment he thought about telling her the real deal, then decided she probably couldn't handle it if he did. "The bed is fine."

"Then what's your problem?"

He crossed his arms over his chest. "What's yours?"

Ethan hadn't meant for his tone to sound so gruff. Nor had he meant for his eyes to shift from her face to slide down to her thighs. But they did. Heat settled in his gut before he returned his gaze to her face. Just in time to see the corners of her lips lift in a wry smile. "Something amusing, Rachel?"

"You tell me." She began walking toward him and her scent—lush, exotic, jasmine and womanly—preceded her. He watched her as a sharp, tingling hunger swept through his groin, and suddenly, memories of the dream that had awakened him had his skin feeling like it was being licked with tongues of fire.

He never took her for a tease and hoped that wasn't her intent because he was not in a teasing mood. It wouldn't take much to push him over the edge right now. When she came to a stop directly in front of him, he inhaled and filled his lungs with her scent. And his testosterone level shot sky-high.

"Remember earlier when you asked me about those vibes, Ethan?" she asked.

"I remember," he said while thinking her mouth was almost too luscious for any woman's face.

"Well…"

He refused to let her get all nervous on him now. "Well what, Rachel?"

Ethan watched her take a long, slow breath. "You were right about that curiosity thing."

He didn't intend to make it easy for her. "What curiosity thing is that?"

She cleared her throat. "That curiosity thing about kissing."

He nodded slowly. "So are you admitting to being curious?"

"Umm, just a little," she said.

He went silent, deciding to let her think about what she'd said and, more importantly, what she planned to do about it.

Standing there facing Ethan, not all in his face but probably less than two feet away, Rachel concluded she had never felt anything close to the stomach-churning heat that had taken over the lower part of her body. It didn't help matters that he was shirtless with his jeans riding low on his hips. His muscular physique dominated her kitchen and reminded her that she was very much alone with a very sexy man.

And apparently he was a man who didn't forget anything, especially her evasiveness from earlier when she'd refused to elaborate on these vibes she was sensing. She was smart enough to know Ethan had no intention of letting her off the hook and was making her work for anything she got. That was fine with her, since she'd always considered herself a working girl.

He was a man who knew women. So he had to know she wanted him to kiss her. She hadn't been ready earlier tonight and hadn't been accepting. Now she was both ready and accepting. Nothing would change between them with one kiss. She was convinced of that now. Why would it? She wasn't his type and he definitely wasn't hers. Sharing a kiss wouldn't produce a marriage license or any document that said they would have to take things further than that. Monday, on the set, they would go back to being just friends. Nothing more. Nothing less.

"You think too damn hard."

She blinked upon hearing Ethan's blunt words and had to agree that she did think too hard. But then she'd always been the type of person to weigh the pros and cons before she acted. This was one of those times she had to really consider whether the pros outweighed the cons.

She quickly concluded that they did.

A smile touched her mouth when she took a couple steps closer to him, fascinated by the blue-gray eyes watching her. Now she *was* all in his face and decided it was time to do something about it. Granted, she wasn't the typical kind of woman he became involved with; however, she intended to show him that good things could come in small packages. With a pounding heart, she stood on tiptoe, reached out and placed her arms around his neck.

"Now, are we in accord?" Ethan asked, placing his hands at her waist, drawing her closer and lowering his mouth toward hers, hovering mere inches from her lips.

She drew in a deep, unsteady breath, barely able to contain the heated passion taking over her body, filling her with all kinds of sensations. She had never responded to a man this way. Had never been this affected and bold. "Yes, we're in accord."

Fueled by a degree of desire she'd never felt before, she leaned farther up on tiptoes and whispered against his lips, "So, let's go for broke."

Chapter 9

Nothing could have prepared Ethan for the need that took over his body at that moment. Unable to hold back, he captured her mouth with a possession that fueled his fire in a way it had never been with another woman. He wanted to devour Rachel alive.

A part of him couldn't believe that she was in his arms and that he was taking her mouth like it was the only feminine one left on earth. For now, for him, it was.

For some reason, he couldn't control the rush of physical hunger consuming him. His tongue tangled with hers with a voracity that sent pleasure spiking throughout his body. He was kissing her hungrily, as if he was seeking out some forbidden treat and was determined to find it.

Moments later, only because they needed to breathe, he released her mouth and stared into her stunned gaze. Refusing to allow her time to think again, he lowered his mouth once more and at the same time, he swept her off her feet and into his arms. Before the night was over, his touch would be imprinted on every inch of her skin.

Somehow he managed to get them up the stairs. Upon reaching the landing, he moved quickly toward her bedroom. She wanted to get it on and he was determined not to let anything stop them. Though he had wanted her from the first moment he'd laid eyes on her, he'd thought he would be satisfied with them just being friends. Well, he'd been proven wrong.

The moment he placed her on the bed, he joined her there, wanting to keep her in his arms, needing his lips to remain plastered to hers with his tongue inside her mouth and doing things so wicked it made his skin shiver. The kiss really had gotten ridiculously out of hand because never in his life had he been so damn greedy. So hard up to make love to a woman.

In an unexpected move, she pulled back, breaking off the kiss and drawing in a ragged breath. Her gaze latched on to the mouth that had just thoroughly kissed her, and he felt his rod pulsate when she took her tongue, that same tongue he'd tried to devour, and licked her top lip before saying, "I think we should get out of our clothes, Ethan."

He couldn't help but smile as he pulled up on his haunches. "I think you're right." He moved away from the bed to pull the jeans down his legs while flames of desire tore through him. He pulled a condom pack out of his wallet and ripped it open with his teeth. Sheathing his aroused member was an exercise in torture.

Without wasting any time, he returned to her. With a ravenous growl and a need he didn't want to question, he reached out and began removing the clothes from her body. The moment she was completely naked, the lusciousness of her feminine scent filled his nostrils and further stimulated every nerve in his body, making his protruding erection that much harder. He intended to stake a claim on every inch of her body. Beginning now.

He lowered his head and captured her mouth at the same time his hands reached around and began caressing her back and pulling her closer to the fit of him, his hard arousal pressing into her stomach.

He broke off the kiss and his mouth trailed lower, planting kisses over the soft swell of her breasts before taking a nipple into his mouth and sucking it with an intensity that made her groan.

Without losing contact with her nipple, he tilted his head and gazed up at her, saw the heated desire flaming her pupils. Returning his attention to her breasts he began kneading the other while continuing to torment the one in his mouth. He liked the feel and the taste of her and realized his desire for her was intrinsically raw.

"Ethan…"

He liked the sound of his name from her lips, and his erection throbbed mercilessly in response. "Tell me what you want, Rachel," he coaxed softly, planting kisses across her chest while his hands remained on her breasts. "Tell me what you like."

When she didn't say anything but let out a tortured groan, he blew his breath across a moist nipple. "You like that?"

She didn't hesitate, responding, "Yes."

"What about this?" he rasped in her ear before shifting, letting his wet, hot and greedy mouth slide down her body. She arched her hips the moment his mouth settled between her legs, and he could taste the honeyed sweetness of her desire on his tongue.

Her eyes were closed, her breathing was heavy. He knew she was feeling every bit of what his mouth was doing to her. With his hands he widened the opening of her legs as her taste consumed him and made him want to delve deeper into her womanly core. Her unique and sensuous flavor drove him to sample as much of her as he could get.

But he wanted to do more than that. He wouldn't be satisfied until he shattered her control the same way she had shattered his.

When he felt her body tremble beneath his mouth, he released her and pulled his body up and then over hers, easing between her legs and caging her hips with the firmness of his thighs just moments before thrusting into her. The force alone made her scream out her orgasm mere seconds before he released his.

A pulsing and fiery explosion rocked his body, which subsequently rocked hers. He leaned down and captured her mouth and knew what it felt to truly want a woman in every sense of the word.

Next time around they would go slow. And there would be a next time. He would make sure of it.

An aftermath of sensations consumed Rachel as she lay there, unable to move. Ethan excused himself to go to the bathroom, and she could barely nod in acknowledgment of what he'd said. Nor did she have the strength to turn over off her stomach and onto her back. She felt completely drained. And it wasn't because it was her first orgasm in two years. It was all about the man who'd given it to her.

Moments later, she heard him return and opened her eyes, only to see his naked body walking out of the bathroom. The dim light from the bedside lamp didn't miss his engorged erection. How could he be hard again so soon when she could barely catch her breath? And she couldn't help noticing he had on another condom. He couldn't possibly assume she had strength for another round.

The bed dipped beneath his weight as he slid in next to her. His hands began gently caressing the center of her back and the rounded curves of her buttocks. She closed her eyes again, enjoying the feel of being touched by him. When he replaced his fingers with the tip of his tongue and licked up and down her spine, a moan of pleasure escaped her lips.

Now she understood how desire could get stirred all over again so soon and gave herself up to the pure joy of it in his hands and mouth. She drew in a deep breath and then breathed out slowly, reveling in the passion building in every part of her body. It was a primitive force she didn't want to yield to again so quickly. She wanted to prolong the enjoyment.

"Turn over, baby."

She pulled in another deep breath and whispered, "Can't. Too weak."

"Then let me help you."

She heard his soft chuckle moments before he gently eased her onto her back. She stared up into his gaze, and the look in his eyes stroked something she hadn't counted on—intense desire even in her weakened state. Desire she couldn't resist or deny. She'd never wanted a man this much, so this was a first for her. And when he leaned down and claimed her mouth in a way no man had ever done before, a shiver of intense heat rode up her spine, renewing energy she didn't think she had. Her heart began pounding in her chest. At the same time, her body started shuddering with sensations she felt all the way to her toes.

With a burst of vigor that was rejuvenating every part of her, she lifted her arms and wrapped them around his neck while his mouth continued to mate with hers in a kiss that progressed from hot to scalding with a stroke of his tongue.

When he finally released her mouth it was only to shift his body between her thighs. She moaned, knowing he was about to soothe the ache at the juncture of her legs.

He reached out, cupped her bottom, lifted her hips and thrust deep inside of her. For a moment he didn't move. It was as if he needed to savor the feel of his erection planted so profoundly inside of her, pulsing, thickening and growing even larger while her inner muscles clamped down on him tightly.

Then, finally, he began moving in and out at a rhythm and pace that had every cell in her body humming, trembling and shuddering in pleasure. The muscles in his shoulders bunched beneath her fingers when he lowered his head to breathe against her mouth. Her breath hitched in her throat and then her lungs cleared in a precipitated slam.

"Ethan..."

He tasted her lips with his tongue as he drove into her. His hard thrusts made her bed shake, the springs squeak and the headboard hit against the wall. Not only was he drawing out a need and desire within her, he was fulfilling it to a degree that had her meeting him, thrust for thrust.

With one final thrust into the depth of her, her body spun into an orgasm of gigantic proportion. As she reveled in her climax, he kissed her with an intensity that elicited moans from deep in her throat.

At that moment, there was only one thing she could think of. So much for them being just friends.

* * *

Ethan eased from the bed and slipped into his jeans. Once he had snapped them up, he glanced back over his shoulder at the woman asleep in the bed. Never had any one woman touched him the way she had, in and out of bed.

And that was the crux of his problem.

He pulled in a deep breath and leaned down to brush a kiss against her temple and then quickly pulled away when he breathed in the scent of her, which had the power to render him helpless.

He rubbed a hand down his face. What the hell had he gotten himself into? Rachel had made it clear, exceedingly so and on more than one occasion, that she had no intention of getting involved with anyone she considered to be in the spotlight, anyone who would put the media on her tail. If she became involved with him, she ran the risk of that happening. He knew if there was any ounce of decency within him, he would grab his stuff and leave and when he saw her tomorrow he would pretend last night never happened.

Easier said than done.

He couldn't do that.

Something was forcing him to not only acknowledge that it happened but to do whatever he could to make sure it happened again.

He shook his head in dismay as he left the bedroom, closing the door behind him. Wasn't it just a little over two weeks ago that he'd made the vow to focus on his career more than anything else, certainly more than any woman? But there was something about Rachel that called out to him at every turn.

He had gone back into the bedroom he should have been occupying to freshen up when his cell phone on the nightstand rang. He released a deep, annoyed breath when the caller ID indicated it was his agent.

"Yes, Curtis?"

"Ethan, where are you?"

He rolled his eyes. "Is there something you need, Curtis?"

"The paparazzi can't find you."

"That's too bad," he murmured with agitation clearly in his voice. "And how did you know they were looking for me?"

His agent paused a second before saying. "It's my job to know everything that's going on with you."

Ethan frowned. Was Curtis somehow responsible for the media hounds hanging around outside of his house last night? It wouldn't surprise Ethan, since his agent liked keeping him in the news. In the spotlight, as Rachel termed it. The thought that Curtis could be connected didn't sit well with him. "Your job is to advance my career, not fabricate lies about me and my love life."

"It's never bothered you before," his agent countered.

The man was right. It hadn't bothered him before. "It does now, and it would behoove you to remember that. Talk to you later, Curtis."

Ethan then disconnected the call.

* * *

The sound of a ringing telephone worked its way into the deep recesses of Rachel's sleep-shrouded mind. Without lifting her head from the pillow, she reached out and grabbed her cell phone off the bedside table. "Hello," she said in a drowsy voice.

"I can't believe you're still in bed."

Rachel forced one eye open upon hearing her sister's voice. "What time is it?"

"Almost noon. You weren't at church today, and Aunt Lily wanted to make sure you were okay since it's not like you to miss service."

Rachel moaned, which was followed by a deep yawn. "I'm fine, Sofia." *Am I really?* "I overslept." That wasn't a lie.

She slowly pulled herself up in bed, surprised she had the energy to do so. Taking part in lovemaking marathons wasn't something she did often, and thanks to Ethan, her muscles had gotten one heck of a workout.

Ethan...

She glanced at the rumpled spot beside her in the bed. It hadn't been a figment of her imagination. He had been there. His masculine scent was still in her bedcovers. And she could hear him moving around downstairs, which meant he was still there.

She closed her eyes as memories of their lovemaking flowed through her mind. There were the memories of his hands all over her body, his tongue licking her nipple, his head between her legs, his—

"Rachel?"

She snapped her eyes back open. "Yes?"

"I asked if you wanted to do a movie later."

Sofia was a workaholic and any other time Rachel would have jumped at the chance to do something fun with her sister, but not today. But she knew better than to tell her sister the real reason. "Can I get a rain check? I want to finish this painting so it can be ready for the gallery's opening day."

"Sure, just let me know when."

They talked for a few more minutes and then Sofia had to take another call. Rachel disconnected the call and stretched her body in bed, thinking that as much as she had enjoyed making love with Ethan, it couldn't happen again.

She eased out of bed, knowing they needed to talk.

Few people knew that cooking was one of Ethan's favorite pastimes, so he wasn't taken aback by the look of surprise on Rachel's face when she walked into her kitchen. Her sexy-pixie expression was priceless.

Something else that was priceless was the way she was dressed. She had showered and was wearing a printed sundress with spaghetti straps at the shoulders and a cute pair of sandals on her feet. On anyone else the simple outfit would have been so-so, but not on her. It gave her an "at-home" look that couldn't be captured any day on the set.

There were a number of reasons for him to make that conclusion. Heading the list was the fact that this was the first time he'd seen her out of bed since they'd made love, so in his book she could have worn a gunnysack and she still would have looked good to him.

"Ethan, what are you doing?" she asked, glancing around her kitchen.

"I'm preparing brunch. I figured you'd be hungry when you finally woke up." He didn't have to say why he'd expected her to sleep late. Last night had been quite a night for them. He doubted either of them had gotten a full hour's sleep.

"But where did you find the stuff to prepare this spread?"

He smiled. "I went to that grocery store on the corner, and before you ask, no, I wasn't recognized. I wore my disguise and quickly went in and out."

"But your car…"

"I drove yours." At the lift of her brow he said, "I left a note just in case you woke up while I was gone."

"Oh." The thought of his male scent infusing the interior of her car was almost too much to think about. Now she would drive her car and think about him.

"You like cooking, I gather," she said moving across the room to the coffeepot. The coffee smelled good but she smelled even better. There was a sensuality to her fragrance that could reach him on a masculine level each and every time he took a whiff of her.

He chuckled. "You gathered right, although I didn't get an interest until college. It was a quick and easy way to get a girl up to your dorm room."

She glanced at him over her shoulder. "I'm sure getting a girl up to your room wasn't hard, Ethan."

A grin formed on his lips. "Should I take that as a compliment?"

"You should take it for whatever you want. I know it to be true. Most women would find you simply irresistible."

He tilted his head and looked at her. She was reaching up to open one of the cabinet doors, which was an almost impossible feat for her without stretching and standing on tiptoes. What flashed through his mind at that moment was a reminder of a position they had used last night when they'd made love standing up. Those same feet had been wrapped around him, locking him inside her body. "Do you find me irresistible, Rachel?"

She turned around to face him, leaning back against the kitchen counter as she did so. Her gaze roamed over him, up and down, before coming to settle on his face where she gave him her full attention. His stomach tightened at her perusal since it seemed as intimate as any physical caress could get. She pushed a few strands of hair behind her ear before a smile touched her lips. It was tantalizing in one sense but frightening in another.

"Yes, but not the same way that other women do."

Her words, spoken both seriously and honestly, had a profound effect because a part of him knew they were true. She had a way of seeing beyond what the media described as the "killer-watt" smile, past the persona of a jaw-dropping Hollywood leading man. In the two weeks they'd known each other, she'd shown him that she had the ability to get to know the real Ethan Chambers. She knew that what you saw was not always what you got.

And that made *her* irresistible.

Needing to touch her, wanting to kiss her, especially at that moment, he moved toward her and pulled her into his arms. She came willingly, without preamble, filled with all the grace and refinement that most women didn't possess. She had the ability to change the physical to the sensual the moment her lips locked with his. She also had the intuition to know that when it came to an attraction between them, he needed more.

And more importantly, she was willing to give it.

He pulled her closer, wanting to seal every inch of space between them. She leaned up, wrapped her arms around his neck and tilted her head back automatically to meet his mouth that came swooping down on hers. He needed her in the way a man needed a woman.

A woman he was beginning to think of as his.

Nobody kisses like Ethan Chambers, Rachel concluded when she could manage to think again. She loved being held captive in his strong grip, loved being the recipient of his lusty and marauding tongue. And she loved the feel of her breasts pressed against the hard and firm lines of his chest. The same chest she had kissed every inch of last night. Even then she had felt the strength of it beneath her lips. Ethan had a body that was an artist's dream, and she would love to paint him one day, capture the essence of all his masculine beauty on canvas.

"Brunch has to wait."

Those words were barely out of his mouth before he swept her off her feet and into his arms. Once again she had managed to drive him out of control and she enjoyed every single moment of doing so. It was only last night that she had discovered her ability as a woman and the pleasure-filled places that skill could take her.

It might have been his intent to take her back to bed, but somewhere between the kitchen and living room he decided they couldn't make it that far. He headed for her sofa.

Her heart began beating rapidly because with Ethan she had discovered you never knew what you would get, but the one thing you could expect was the most intense pleasure any man could deliver. And that knowledge caused an intense ache between her legs that only he could appease.

She caught her breath when she felt the sofa cushion touch her back, and he spread her out as if she was a sampling for his enjoyment. He would soon discover that he was also one for hers. His musky and ultrasexy scent was devouring all common sense in her body and replacing it with a spine-tingling need that had her moaning out his name.

"I'm right here, baby," he whispered while quickly removing the clothes from her body and then from his. When he stood over her naked, fully aroused and looking as handsome as any man had a right to look, she was filled with a craving that had her moving upward, launching herself at him and toppling them both to the floor.

He cushioned their fall, and they ended up with their legs entangled and her stretched out over him. Just the way she wanted. Some deep, dark emotion, an intense hunger he had tapped into last night, consumed her and she began licking him all over, starting with his broad shoulders and working her way downward.

Moving past his tight abs, she cupped his erection in her hands before lowering her head and taking him fully, needing the taste, texture and total length of him between her lips and as deep in her mouth as he could go.

"Rachel!"

His palms bracketed her head, his fingers dug into her scalp and his moan became music to her ears while she proceeded to torture him. She felt his shaft swell deep inside her mouth and she stretched to accommodate its size.

"I'm coming, baby."

And he did.

She appeased every deep craving she ever had, using her throat to prolong his orgasm. He seemed lost, powerless as he gave himself over to the magic she created. And she reveled in the control as she never had before.

When he could draw another breath, he pulled a condom pack from his jeans, sheathed himself and entered her. Quick work but thorough.

He began moving in and out of her, thrusting hard

and deep, taking her to the brink where she'd led him moments ago. No matter what would come tomorrow, she knew she would have these memories of their lovemaking. Memories that would comfort her and tear at her heart long after he was no longer a part of her life.

But for now, for today, he was and because of that, she was satisfied.

It was time for him to leave.

After making love on her living room floor, they had returned to the kitchen and eaten the brunch he had prepared before going back up to her bedroom and making love some more. When they were spent, they had showered together, returned downstairs to devour the apple tarts he'd made for dessert, then he'd gone upstairs to gather his few belongings.

"Do you think the paparazzi have gone now?" she asked, walking him to the kitchen door that led to her garage where his car was parked beside hers.

"Yes. I spoke with the manager of my condo complex and she apologized profusely. The one thing I was assured of when I moved in was that my privacy would be protected. She doesn't understand what could have happened." He paused. "I think I do."

She lifted a brow. "What?"

"My agent. He thinks one of the ways to build my career is for me to stay in the spotlight, to keep my name in the news."

He could tell her mind was at work. Making that

statement had made her remember her one argument as to why there could never be anything but friendship between them. For that reason, he was not surprised by her next statement.

"I refuse to think of this weekend as a mistake, Ethan, but it's something we can't allow to happen again. You are who you are and I am who I am. We live different lives and reside in basically different worlds."

"It doesn't have to be that way, Rachel."

"Yes, it does. I could never ask you to give up your dream for me, like you can't expect me to do the same for you."

He paused for a moment and then asked, "So where do we go from here?"

A sad smile touched her lips. "Nowhere. Let's chalk it up as nothing more than a one-night stand. This weekend is our secret. And it's up to us to know it was just one of those things that can't happen again."

He glanced down as if studying the floor and then he looked back at her. "What if I said I don't agree? That there has to be a way?"

A bittersweet smile touched her lips. "Then I'd say don't waste your time trying to figure one out. It doesn't exist. We are as different as day and night."

Ethan pulled in a deep breath and felt a tightening in his gut because he knew, in a way, she was right. Becoming a successful Hollywood actor was his dream, and it was a dream that didn't mesh with hers.

He leaned down and kissed her hard and deep. Only one thought pierced his mind then and again moments later when he walked out her door. How on earth was he going to give her up?

Chapter 10

"Quiet on the set!
"Take three!
"Action!"

Rachel could hear the sound of Frasier's booming voice carrying all the way into her trailer. Today they would be shooting mostly medical scenes, and several doctors from an area hospital were on the set to make sure that aspect of the show was done correctly.

She had arrived at work early, mainly to have herself together by the time Ethan got there. Like she'd told him yesterday, although she hadn't regretted any of it, their time together could not be repeated. For twenty-four hours she had let herself go and had made love to a man who had pleasured her body in ways probably not

known to most men. All women should be made love to
the way Ethan had done to her. Memories of their time
together still made her skin hot whenever she thought
about it.

When he had arrived this morning, he had not given
her any more of his time and attention than he always
had. There was no way anyone seeing them interact
together would suspect they'd spent practically the entire
weekend behind closed doors. There had been so much
red-hot chemistry between them and they had taken
advantage of it time and time again.

Although no one on the set had a clue, each and
every time he glanced her way or gave her a smile,
heat would begin simmering in the pit of her stomach.
One look into Ethan's eyes had the power to send a
rush of desire spiking through her. That was why she
was letting Theresa work out on the set today, brushing
up the actors during shooting, while she remained in
her trailer applying the makeup for those in the next
scene.

"You're quiet today."

Rachel blinked, remembering where she was and
what she was doing. There never had been a time when
thoughts of a man had interfered with her job. She
looked down at Tae'Shawna Miller, the model-turned-
actress from last season who played a nurse on the show.
Tae'Shawna was known to be moody and self-centered
and, not surprisingly, months ago she'd begun hanging
around Paige.

Rachel wasn't sure what Paige might have told her,

but lately Tae'Shawna had been acting even moodier where she was concerned. She'd even gone to John saying Rachel had applied her makeup too heavily last season and that she wanted to bring in her own makeup artist. John had denied her request.

"It's Monday," Rachel said, hoping that would end things. It was a joke on the set that although Wednesday was considered hump day, Monday was pretty low-key with everyone trying to recover from the weekend.

"I hear you, girl. I could barely pull myself out of bed. If it wasn't for Ethan calling to wake me up this morning, I probably would have been late coming in today."

Trying to keep her hands steady and acting as nonchalant as she could, Rachel continued applying Tae'Shawna's makeup and asked in a casual tone, "Ethan Chambers?"

A smile touched the woman's lips. "None other. We spent some time together this weekend. I'm only mentioning this to you because I know you're the soul of discretion. Ethan would be upset if he knew I told anyone. He wants to keep things quiet since we're both working on the show."

The woman gave a naughty smile before adding, "Needless to say, I had to all but force him to leave last night."

Rachel managed to remain calm as she dissected the woman's words, hoping what Tae'Shawna was saying was more wishful thinking than gospel truth, especially since Ethan had been with *her* from Saturday night to late yesterday afternoon.

But she couldn't help wondering if he had left her bed and gone directly to Tae'Shawna's. And where had he been before coming to her place on Saturday night? She'd felt it hadn't been her place to ask. However, now the woman in her couldn't help wondering if Ethan had shared his weekend with her *and* Tae'Shawna.

That question was still on her mind hours later. For the moment, her trailer was empty and she slid into the chair to take a breather, trying to fight the green-eyed monster of jealousy consuming her. She pulled in a deep breath, wondering why the thought of Ethan being involved with Tae'Shawna bothered her and how she could get beyond it.

The odds had been high when he'd shown up at her place Saturday night that he would probably spend some of his weekend with another woman. It would have made perfect sense that he did. After all, he was a known playboy around town. It really shouldn't concern her since they had used protection every time they'd made love, so she wasn't at risk. But still…

It disappointed her that, on the set, Ethan portrayed himself as a man not giving any of the women who came on to him the time of day. Although he was always friendly to them, she'd had no reason to assume that things had been any different after hours. Was it only an act? Was he involved not only with Tae'Shawna but others as well, possibly even Paige?

She eased from the chair and began pacing. She told

herself she should not be bothered if he was also seeing other women. They hadn't set any rules or guidelines regarding their relationship. A frown deepened her brow when she reminded herself they didn't have a relationship. What happened this weekend was just a one-time deal. She had made that clear to Ethan. But why had he bothered to make it seem as if he hadn't had sex for a while, certainly not that same day? Men!

She knew when it came to sex, men would get as much of it as came their way and still want more. A part of her couldn't help feeling somewhat disappointed to discover he was one of those men and wasn't different at all.

"Looks like you're thinking too hard again."

She spun around to find the object of her deepest and most disappointing thoughts leaning against the trailer door. She hadn't heard him enter the trailer.

"And what's it to you?" she asked in a tone that sounded pretty snippy to even her own ears.

He shrugged. "With that attitude, nothing, I guess. Frasier gave everyone an additional hour for lunch again, and I was wondering if you'd like to take a walk over to—"

"No." And then because she knew there was no reason for her to have an attitude, she said, "Thanks for asking, but I have a lot to do here."

He nodded slowly as he continued to look at her. She wished he wouldn't do that. And she wished it didn't bother her, didn't make her feel those vibes again, especially when he probably looked at Tae'Shawna the same way. Not only Tae'Shawna but all the other women with whom he was probably involved.

"Is that why you haven't been out on the set today?"

"You could say that."

Avoiding his gaze, she moved around the trailer, picking up items to repack in her various makeup kits, as well as hanging up items of clothing that cast members had discarded.

"Is something wrong, Rachel?"

She glanced over at him. "No. What gives you that idea?" She then returned to what she was doing, basically presenting her back to him.

Moving away from the door, Ethan strode through the space separating them and came to stand in front of her, forcing her to look up and meet his gaze. "Hey, I knew yesterday you were serious about continuing this 'friends only' thing and, although I prefer more between us, I will respect your wishes."

"Do you?"

He had a confused look on his face. "Do I what?" His tone was low, gruff, with more than a hint of agitation.

"Do you prefer more between us?"

He released a frustrated sigh. "I told you I did."

She nodded slowly. "And what did you tell Tae'Shawna?" The moment the words left her lips, she wished she could take them back. She probably sounded like a jealous shrew. And she had no right to be that way, considering she had told Ethan there would be nothing between them. Ever.

She stared up at him to see even more confusion settle in his features when he asked, "Is this supposed to be a trick question or something?"

"Not a trick question, Ethan, just a curious one."

He crossed his arms over his chest. "And what does Tae'Shawna have to do with us?"

A shiver ran through her when he said the word *us*. Although when it came to them there was no "us," just hearing him say it did something crazy to her. "By 'us,' you mean you and Tae'Shawna?" she asked.

A smile that didn't quite reach his eyes touched his lips. "Was that question supposed to be a joke, Rachel?"

"What do you think?" She made a move to walk away but he reached out and gripped her arm, not too tight, but enough that the heat of his hand felt like a flame licking her skin. *Amazing,* she thought. Even when she wasn't happy with him, he had the ability to make her want him.

"Explain what you meant by that," he said. She thought she heard somewhat of a growl in his tone.

He was staring at her, and she returned his stare with no intention of breaking it. And she had no problem explaining what she'd said as well as elaborating on what she'd meant. "When I worked on Tae'Shawna's makeup earlier today, she took me into her confidence and shared information about you and her."

His expression seemed thoughtful. "Me and her?"

"Yes."

"And what did she say?"

She shrugged and then said, "Nothing more than that the two of you spent part of the weekend together and that you didn't leave her place until late last night and that you were her wake-up call this morning. I know you were with me from Saturday night until yesterday afternoon, but—"

"You're not sure about the time I wasn't with you?" he said, finishing her statement for her.

"Yes, but it really doesn't matter. Saturday night just happened between us. And it's not like I didn't know about your reputation."

He nodded as he held her gaze. "My reputation that you know about from a tabloid you *don't* read. Right?"

It was easy to see his expression had gone from thoughtful to rigid, as if he was struggling to contain the anger she could actually feel radiating from him. She was smart enough to take a step back when he took one forward, and she noticed the eyes staring at her had turned a stormy gray. Not a good sign.

She took another step backward only to have her spine hit a wall. He caged her in when he leaned forward, bracing his hands against the wall on both sides of her face. If his aim was to get her attention, he had it.

She lifted her chin and met his glare with one of her own. "What is this about, Ethan?"

"You tell me, Rachel."

"I told you. And I also told you that you don't owe me an explanation about Tae'Shawna because—"

"I wouldn't repeat it if I were you," he interrupted in a tone gruff enough to make her heed his warning.

He didn't say anything for a moment. He just stared at her. Then finally he said, "First of all, when I made love to you Saturday night, it was the first time I had been intimate with a woman in over six months."

She couldn't stop her mouth from dropping open. Nor could she disguise the flicker of surprise in her eyes. Both were probably what made him continue on to say, "This weekend I needed to get away, so I got up early Saturday morning and drove across the border to Tijuana. Alone. When I got back later that night, I discovered the paparazzi camped out at my place and called you. When I left your apartment Sunday afternoon, I went straight home. I don't know what make-believe game Tae'Shawna is playing but, unfortunately, it's not the first time and probably won't be the last time that some woman claimed we were together or involved in an affair when we weren't. That's how those tabloids you *don't* read are sold."

"Ethan, I—"

His sharp tone interrupted her. "The only thing I want to know from you now is whether you believe me or Tae'Shawna."

She frowned. "Does it matter?"

"To me it does."

She took a deep, uneven breath as she stared into his eyes, still jarred by his admission that their night together had been his first time in over six months. Her heart was pounding because he indicated what she believed mattered to him. And although she didn't quite understand why, she was glad that it did.

As odd as it might seem, she didn't want him to be involved with women like Tae'Shawna, women who would go so far as to invent a relationship with a man. Or even worse, women like Paige who would try anything to get him into their beds.

There was one thing that was actually making her feel somewhat warm inside—the fact that he hadn't wanted any of the model types. He had wanted her. And the strangest thing of all was that she didn't want any of those other women to have him either.

She couldn't explain the thought processes that supported her reasons, especially not to him when they were still somewhat foggy to her. But what she could do was give him the answer he was still waiting for. "I don't believe you're involved with Tae'Shawna, Ethan."

Ethan hadn't realized he was holding his breath until he released it after Rachel had spoken. Why what she believed mattered so much he wasn't sure, but it did. It might have everything to do with that bond he felt with her. A bond he'd never felt with any other woman. That bond had strengthened when they'd made love. He wondered if she realized it. If she didn't comprehend it now, he was certain she would later.

Needing to kiss her, he reached out and pulled her into his arms and captured her mouth with his. All the reasons this weekend had meant so much to him came roaring back to life like a living thing with a mind of its own. It had the ability to push him closer to her even when she wanted to keep him at a distance.

He tried to steady his heart rate and had almost succeeded until she wrapped her arms around his neck and pressed her body closer to his while returning his kiss with equal fervor. Her response was what he had hoped for and definitely what he was enjoying. It wouldn't take much for him to take her like this, standing up against the wall. He fought the temptation. Instead, he continued to make love to her mouth with a hunger that seemed relentless. The feel of her hardened nipples pressing against his chest was sweet agony, as was the rough texture of her denim jeans rubbing against his hard erection. He continued to fight the temptation, knowing what his body wanted would only lead to trouble.

That fight was taken out of his hands when they heard the sound of conversation right outside the trailer door and they quickly ended the kiss. He took a deep breath while forcing his body to cool down, which seemed nearly impossible to do.

He reached out and flicked the pad of his thumb across her bottom lip. "I know what you said last night, but I think we'll be doing each other an injustice not to explore what could be, Rachel. There will be risks but I intend to convince you they will be worth it."

He leaned down and swiped a quick kiss across her lips before moving toward the door.

Chapter 11

"Let me make sure I got this right." Wide-eyed, Charlene spoke in a low tone of voice as she leaned across the table while they waited in Roscoe's for their food to be served. Lower still, she said, "You spent the weekend with Mr. Drop-Dead Gorgeous himself? Ethan Chambers?"

At least Charlene hadn't blurted it out in a loud voice, Rachel thought, grateful for that, although it was evident Charlene was stunned. "Only *part* of the weekend," she quickly clarified. "He arrived around eight Saturday night and left Sunday afternoon around five. That's not even a full twenty-four hours." What she didn't have to say, and what Charlene could figure out on her own, was that a lot had happened during that period of time.

"Wow!" Charlene said, still clearly stunned. "Two weeks ago you said the two of you were nothing more than friends. What happened?"

Rachel drew in a deep breath, wondering how she was going to explain to her best friend that lust happened. The man was simply irresistible, both in and out of bed. "Well, it happened like this…"

Charlene leaned even farther over the table. Not only were her ears perked but her eyes were bright with curiosity. Rachel figured she was more than ready to take in all the hot-tamale details. "Yes?"

When Rachel didn't say anything, Charlene lifted a brow. "Well?"

A smile touched Rachel's lips. "Well what?"

Charlene gave her a don't-you-dare-play-with-me-like-that look. "Tell me what happened."

"Whatever you can imagine probably did happen, Cha. The man knew positions that are probably outlawed in most states, and he has more staying power in bed than Peyton Manning has on a football field."

A huge grin lit Charlene's face as she sat back in her chair. She exclaimed proudly as she looked at her with envy, "What a woman."

Rachel shook her head as she recalled the past weekend. "No, what a man."

And she seriously meant that. Ethan had her considering taking risks she normally would not take. He said he would make it worth her while and, considering this past weekend, she had no reason not to believe him. After that incident in the trailer a few days ago, she had been trying to keep a level head around the set and handle things decently and in order. In other words, although she didn't try to avoid him, she didn't do anything to seek him out either. But she was well aware that he was waiting for her to make the next move.

She glanced over at Charlene. "What have I gotten myself into?"

Charlene smiled naughtily. "His pants, for starters."

"Girl, be serious," Rachel protested.

"I am."

Rachel chuckled. Yes, her friend was serious and also right. She had gotten into his pants and was looking forward to getting into them again. How shameful was that?

"It doesn't make sense," she said. "You know what a private person I am and how I hate being in the spotlight. Anyone involved with Ethan will have their face plastered all over the tabloids. There's no way to get around that unless we sneak around."

"And how do you feel about doing something like that?"

That was a good question and one she needed to think about. Were earth-shattering, toe-curling orgasms worth all of that?

"You know what's wrong with you, don't you?" Charlene asked, smothering a giggle.

Rachel took a sip of her iced tea. "I don't have a clue."

"You went without a hot male body too long. Trust me, I know how it feels."

Rachel hated to admit that Charlene was probably right. In the past, she'd always had enough on her plate to keep her mind occupied so she didn't think about sex. She was just as busy now as she was before, so what was there about Ethan that made her want to make him a top priority on her "to do" list? It wasn't like she wasn't routinely surrounded on the set by gorgeous, sexy men. Why had her body decided Ethan was the one?

Before she could offer any more input to the conversation, her cell phone began vibrating. Caller ID indicated an unknown number. Normally she refused to answer those kinds of calls, but she felt a warm sensation in the pit of her stomach. She excused herself from the table and quickly headed toward the ladies' room.

"Yes?"

"This is Ethan. I want to see you."

So much for him waiting for her to make the next move.

The sound of his voice plunged her into a sea of desire so deep she felt herself going under. "Why? Do I need to save you again?"

"No, but I do need you to make love to me like you did last weekend."

If she hadn't been drowning before, she was certainly drowning now and there was no one around to throw her a life jacket.

"Ethan, I think—"

"You do too much of that."

For a moment she struggled with the possibility that maybe he was right. "One of us needs to."

"No, we don't. Just consider it something we both deserve. We work hard, so we should get to play harder."

He did have a point. Didn't he?

She drew in a deep breath, wondering where her logical mind was when she needed it the most. It had probably taken a flying leap with that first orgasm Saturday night. "We're risking the chance of you being followed."

"I have everything under control."

Including her, she thought, when she tried summoning the gumption to deny what he was asking. But then all she had to do was to remember Saturday night or the kiss they'd shared in her trailer earlier in the week. His lips had teased her mercilessly, and his tongue had nearly made her short-circuit.

"Rachel?"

"Yes?"

"Will you meet me?"

She nervously licked her lips. "Where?"

He rattled off an address that was followed by a brief set of instructions. "Do you need directions?"

"No, I'll use my GPS," she said, tucking the piece of paper she'd written on back in her purse.

Moments later, she hung up the phone with her heart pounding in her chest. Emotions she refused to put a name to stirred in her stomach, and she knew she was falling deeper and deeper into lust.

* * *

Slow down, buddy. The last thing you need is a ticket while racing across town for a night of hot and heavy sex.

Ethan flinched at the thought of that because he knew his meeting with Rachel was more than that. She was different and not just because she wasn't a woman anxious to blast their affair to all who'd listen.

And they were involved in an affair because neither of them was looking for any sort of heavy-duty relationship right now. He was satisfied to keep things under wraps as much she was, especially since he knew how she felt about the matter.

He had actually been followed for a short while after leaving his place. He had driven his car to the private parking garage of condos owned by a friend of Hunter's from college. If the person tailing him thought he was smart, Ethan intended to show he was smarter.

Ethan had parked his car in a designated spot and had donned his disguise before getting out of his car and getting into another vehicle—one owned by that same friend of Hunter's who was presently out of the country for the next month or so.

He had smiled upon leaving the garage and bypassing the photographer who was parked across the street, waiting for Ethan to come out. No doubt, the man would be there for some time while trying to determine what woman and at what address Ethan was visiting at this particular condo complex.

Ethan couldn't ever recall going through this much

hassle to keep his interest in a woman hidden. If he wasn't so concerned about Rachel's feelings, he truly wouldn't give a damn.

But he needed tonight. He needed her. This had been one hell of a week, with Frasier in rare form, demanding more than perfection from everyone. The rumor floating around the set was that the man and his partner were having problems. Although Frasier's policy demanded all of them leave any and all personal matters at the door and not bring them on the set, evidently that rule didn't apply to Frasier.

Luckily, so far none of Frasier's tirades had been leveled at him but at a number of others, including Tae'Shawna when she had messed up her lines. After the lie she'd told to Rachel, the woman hadn't gotten any pity from Ethan.

He had come close to confronting Tae'Shawna on more than one occasion about the lie she had told. However, Rachel had asked him not to say anything. She worried that Tae'Shawna would resent her for breaking a confidence and possibly even retaliate in some way.

Ethan exited off the interstate and noted a lot of cars on the road for a Thursday night. He was in Industry, a city in the San Gabriel Valley section of Los Angeles. His destination was an old warehouse owned by Chambers Winery that was used to store bottled wine shipped from the vineyard. In other words, it used to be their off-site wine cellar. More than once he had considered the idea of fixing up at least part of the place as a possible hideaway when he needed peace from the media's scrutiny. This week he had acted on that idea, and after a few phone calls and explicit instructions, he had received word that the place was good to go. He couldn't imagine not bringing Rachel here to help christen the place.

More than once during the drive over, he had glanced back in his rearview mirror to make sure he was not being followed. Satisfied that he had not been, he pulled into the drive and around the side of the building that was away from the street.

Grabbing the pair of wine glasses off the seat beside him, he got out of the car and closed the door behind him. It was a beautiful August night with bright stars lighting the sky. The perfect night for a romantic rendezvous.

He had made good time, intentionally arriving ahead of Rachel. As he headed for the entrance with the wine glasses in his hands, he smiled. So far so good. His evening was going according to his plans.

Rachel pulled into the parking lot of the huge vacant building to park next to the vehicle already there. Her heart began pounding and her hand on the steering wheel began trembling somewhat.

She glanced around through her windshield. She had followed Ethan's instructions to the letter, and the huge building looming before her appeared dark and scary. But she knew somewhere inside, Ethan was waiting for her.

She opened the car door and glanced around as she

got out. It had been hard for her to consume her dinner knowing what her plans were for afterward.

If Charlene suspected anything was amiss, she hadn't let on. Rachel would give her best friend all the details later. But for now, the plan for tonight was something she hadn't wanted to share. She didn't want to take the risk of anyone talking her out of doing something she really wanted to do. She didn't want anyone to knock the craziness out of her and force her to go back to being her logical self.

She pushed the door and, to her intense relief, it opened, just like Ethan had said it would. The moment she stepped over the threshold, the smell of vintage wine consumed her nostrils. She could probably get intoxicated just from the scent alone.

The place was dark. The only light was a bit of moonlight shining in through one of the windows. She'd never been afraid of the dark but there was something eerie about this place. Her heart rate increased, and she fought back a nervousness that was about to consume her as she took a step back and bumped against the hard, solid wall of a masculine chest.

She gasped when a pair of strong, muscular arms reached around to enclose her within a powerful embrace. The familiar scent of him surrounded her and she breathed it in and relaxed against him. She could feel his hot breath at her neck, close to ear, when he whispered, "Welcome to my lair."

Her heart rate steadied when another type of response took control—not fear of the unknown but apprehension of the known. She knew why she was here, why he had asked her to come and how tonight would end up.

She released her breath with a shaky sigh when he turned her to face him and leaned forward to give her a more physical display of welcome, one she had no problem receiving.

His tongue tangled hotly with hers while his hands seemed to roam all over her, finding her bare skin not covered by her short skirt. And he was caressing her backside in a way that only he could execute. When he finally pulled back, she was grateful for his hands around her waist because her knees seemed to buckle beneath her, and she felt herself swaying against him.

He held her tight as he continued to rain kisses all over her face while his hands gently massaged her back. They stood that way for a while as their heartbeats and breathing returned to normal. But she was completely aware of the way her hard nipples pressed against the hard wall of his chest.

"Come on, let me show you around," he whispered against her temple.

He took her hand in his, and using a flashlight that he pulled from his pocket, he led the way. She glanced from side to side and saw rows and rows of wine bottles and immediately knew this was a place his family owned.

"There's usually a security guard around," he said. "Clyde has worked for us at this place for years, making sure no one runs off with anything. I thought I'd give him the rest of the night off."

Instead of saying anything, Rachel nodded and

merely followed him through another door and up a flight of stairs. She tried pushing back the question rushing through her mind. Why was she here and not at home in her own bed getting a good night's sleep? After all, it was Thursday and tomorrow was a workday for the both of them. But she knew the reason. Ethan had called and said he wanted them to make love again. She wanted them to make love again as well. For what other reason would she be here?

She knew getting involved with him, secretly or otherwise, was probably not a good idea, but then she could do casual dating just like the next man or woman. She wasn't looking for everlasting love. She liked her life just fine the way it was.

He used a key to open another door and it was only then that he put the flashlight away and flipped on a switch. She nearly closed her eyes at the brightness but not before she saw the immaculate-looking office.

She continued to glance around when he locked the door behind them. And when she gave him a questioning look, he smiled before taking her hand again and leading her through another set of doors.

She gasped when she saw what was in front of her. It was the most beautifully decorated room she could imagine, one designed as a lovers' hideaway, complete with a king-size bed and all the other matching furnishings. There was even an expensive throw rug on the floor and several beautiful paintings on the wall, lit candles around the room and a vase of roses sitting on a dresser.

She lowered her head when an errant thought hit her. Was this where Ethan brought all his conquests when he needed privacy? She glanced over at him and apparently the question was there, looming in her gaze, because he said, "I called and had this place renovated just a few days ago. I'm pleased with what they've done in such a short period of time."

And then in a voice that had thickened, taken on a rough edge in an ultrasexy sort of way, he said, "And let me go on record as saying that you're the only woman I've ever brought here, Rachel. I consider this place as ours."

Her breath caught in her throat as she took in all he said and all he meant. He had created this place for them? Did he assume there would be many more secret rendezvous for them? So many that they would need a place to slip away to and be together without prying eyes or stalking photographers hell-bent on fueling the tabloid frenzy?

The thought of such an idea—Ethan being so into her—was ludicrous. She could see him taking advantage of her willingness to engage in no-strings-attached sex a couple of times, but did he honestly think it would become a long-term affair? No, he probably knew that it wouldn't be and would be satisfied with the here and now. When she ceased being his flavor of the hour, he would replace her with someone else, someone more his style. More than likely it would be one of those leggy models his name was usually hooked up with. A woman who enjoyed being in the spotlight just as much as he did.

She fought the thick lump blocking her throat. Not wanting to put a damper on the mood he'd set for them tonight, she let her eyes roam around the room. The decor was simply beautiful in the warm glow of candlelight. Then her eyes lit on the glasses and the bottle of wine on a nightstand beside the bed.

"That's Chambers Winery's finest," he leaned over and whispered close to her ear. She glanced up into the depths of his eyes, saw all the desire embedded deep within them, and an unfamiliar sensation overtook her. It ran through her like a burning ball of heat and settled in the pit of her stomach as if it belonged there and had no intention of going away.

Mentally she weighed her options. She could take tonight and accept it for what it was—a night two sexually charged individuals wanted to enjoy each other. Or she could go along for the ride as long as it lasted and as long as they took all the measures necessary not to get caught—providing it was all enjoyment and no emotion. There *had* to be a no-emotional-attachment policy.

Deciding which option she would go with, she eased closer to him and said, "I can't wait to have a glass."

The tips of her nipples were beginning to heat up, and she intentionally rubbed against him to bring her breasts in contact with his chest. The hitch in his breath let her know she'd made a hit. It seemed Hollywood's newest heartthrob wasn't immune to her charms. Just the thought that she had enough to hold his interest made her heart pound and her entire body begin to tremble inside.

The look in his eyes told her that he knew exactly what she was doing and was willing to let her take the lead for now.

"And there's something else I can't wait to have," she said, tilting her head back to meet his gaze.

"What else do you want, Rachel?"

The huskiness of his voice made a shiver ripple through her. She lowered her gaze to his chest and then lower still to his crotch. She'd never been fascinated with the makings of an aroused man before, but now she couldn't help marveling at what a fine specimen of a man he was. His erection nearly burst through the zipper of his jeans, and she felt proud of herself that she had caused his intense arousal.

"I want this," she said, reaching out and groping that part of him. She heard his low growl and glanced up. His eyes could not hide the desire she saw in them.

"Sweetheart, I'm going to make sure you get everything you want." And then he swept her off her feet and into his arms and carried her over to the bed.

There was something about Rachel's scent that got to him every time. It was an intimate fragrance that seemed to beckon him on a primitive level that even now had every muscle in his body rippling in a way he found tormenting.

He undressed her and then undressed himself. He

had seen the way she blushed when he tossed several condom packets on the nightstand and took a step away from the bed to put one on. She watched him sheath himself and the thought that she was doing so sent a rush of blood to his loins.

Silence dominated the room and for a heartfelt moment he wished some type of music was playing to set the mood. Too late now. But next time…

And there would be a next time. He was going to make sure of it. Like he told her, this was *their* place. When he'd made the arrangements on Monday, it had been with her and only her in mind. He hadn't wanted any other woman in that bed with him.

He flinched at the thought, like he always did when his mind would begin thinking of more than sex between them. During those times, he would do whatever was needed to get his thoughts back in check. The only reason he and Rachel were drawn to each other was their intense sexual chemistry. And they were well aware that the attraction could never go beyond what they were sharing now. Neither of them had plans of ever falling in love.

He moved back toward the bed and she shifted on her haunches and met him, reaching out and taking hold of his throbbing erection. She tilted her head back and stared into his eyes for a long moment. Something was passing between them, and he felt it in the hands holding him as well as in the eyes locked with his.

"Tomorrow will we be able to pretend tonight didn't happen?"

Her question broke the silence. "Yes, it's going to be hard but we'll manage it."

She leaned up and licked the side of his face. "You think so?"

"Hell, I hope so, but I'll be the first to admit, every time I see you on the set, I want to tear your clothes off."

He heard her snort at that. "You would have a hard time convincing me of that with that love scene you did today."

He lifted a brow. Love scenes were staged and she was well aware of that. Surely she didn't think any part of them meant anything to him. He was simply following the script. Did he hear a bit of jealousy in her voice?

"Then I need to do whatever it takes to erase that scene from your mind," he said, and for emphasis he reached out and pulled her closer toward him.

He felt the shiver that passed through her and, in response, a slew of emotions flowed through him, nearly taking his breath away. A need for her filled him to capacity, and for a moment he could imagine her with him even when he was in his eighties.

At the thought, he went momentarily still. Where had that come from? He knew there was no way he could consider anything with her beyond this affair.

He reminded himself of that again as he captured her mouth with his and lowered her body to the bed.

There was something about being pressed into the mattress by the man you wanted. A man who was holding her gaze as he entered her slowly, as if he was savoring the journey.

The last time they'd made love he had taken her hard and fast, and now the slowness was driving her mad. She could only ask, "Why?"

He knew what she was asking and said throatily, "There's no rush. We have plenty of time and I want to take things slow, draw it out and make you scream. A lot of times."

She could feel the hardness of him grow inside of her and knew he intended to make some point. Being the skilled lover he was, he'd succeed in making all his wishes come true.

Chapter 12

"Quiet on the set!
"Take one!
"Action!"

Rachel fought back the rush of jealousy as she watched yet another love scene being shot between Dr. Tyrell Perry and Dr. Sonja Duncan. Did Ethan have to appear to be enjoying it so much?

Usually she stayed in the trailer working with the actors, but today she decided to venture out and would be the first to admit a part of her had wanted to see Ethan. More than once he had accused her of hiding out in the trailer, so today she had decided to be seen.

Although, she thought as a smile touched her lips, hiding out in the trailer hadn't stopped him from seeking her out on occasion and making the find worth his while. He had introduced her to quickies. She didn't want to think about the risk they took of someone discovering their secret. So far no one had, and she was thankful for that.

It had been a week since that night when they'd started their secret rendezvous. Most of the time they would meet up at their hideaway haven but on occasion he would come to her place. So far he was still outsmarting the paparazzi.

She smiled, thinking about how Ethan had bought her a disguise—a honey-blond wig and green contacts. And because she was a makeup artist, it hadn't been difficult to add her own camouflage to make herself unrecognizable when they'd made a decision to branch out beyond the bedroom to grab something to eat. They had even risked going to a movie together.

On more than one occasion she had found herself thinking just how a normal relationship with him would be, one where they wouldn't have to sneak around to be together. But she knew such a thing wasn't possible.

"Cut!"

The production crew rushed around trying to get the props changed for another taping, and it was then that Ethan glanced over at her. When he winked and smiled, she couldn't help smiling back. Last night they had spent the night together at *their* place, and he had surprised her by having an easel with art supplies waiting for her when she had arrived. After having made love, he reclined on the bed while she painted him, something he had surprised her by agreeing to do. It would be her own personal painting of him in all his naked splendor to be shared with no one.

She had returned to the trailer when her cell phone went off. Caller ID indicated it was Charlene. "Yes, Cha?"

"I know you don't read the tabloids so I feel I should give you the scoop."

She raised a brow. "About what?"

"Ethan. He's driving the paparazzi crazy by eluding them every chance he gets. They've begun wondering what's going on with him and who the woman he's intent on hiding is."

Rachel felt a knot in her stomach. "Do they have any idea? Did they mention a name?"

"No, but they have vowed to find out, so you might want to cool things with him for a while."

Rachel began nibbling on her bottom lip. Yes, that would be best, but it would be hard to do.

"The media can be relentless when they want to find out something," Charlene added.

Rachel knew that to be true. "Thanks for keeping me in the loop. I appreciate it."

"What are you going to do?"

Rachel drew in a deep breath. She had few options and knew there was only one thing that she could do. Regardless of whether she liked it or whether she was ready for it to happen, their affair had run its course. "I'm going to talk to him."

"And if the two of you meet up somewhere to have

this talk, you might want to be looking over your shoulder. Disguise or no disguise, the two of you will have the media hounds on your heels for sure."

Ethan glanced in his rearview mirror. He was being followed. A deep frown set into his features. He'd been trying to elude the guy now for a full hour without any success.

He was to meet Rachel at *their* place and he couldn't do so as long as this reporter was still on his tail. Even switching cars and donning his disguise hadn't helped. This guy was on to him and seemed intent on letting him know it.

When his cell phone rang, he almost snatched it off his belt and his frown deepened when he saw the caller was Curtis. He had been trying to avoid his agent for a week or so now. "Yes, Curtis?"

"Damn, Ethan, are you trying to mess up a good thing?"

Ethan glanced into his rearview mirror, getting more agitated by the minute. He needed to get rid of this reporter so he could hook up with Rachel at their scheduled time. "What are you talking about?"

"The tabloids. You've become elusive over the past few weeks, annoying the hell out of several tabloid reporters who even claim you've purposely given them the slip."

Ethan rolled his eyes. "And?"

"And they are wondering why and just who you're trying to hide. Someone has connected you to a nameless married woman and has vowed to uncover her identity."

Ethan's hand tightened on the steering wheel. That was not what he wanted to hear. He of all people knew how tabloid reporters could make a pest of themselves more so than usual when they thought they were on to a story.

"I'd like to see them try to uncover anything," he said, almost in a growl, knowing he would do whatever it took to protect Rachel's identity.

"So you're admitting to being involved with a married woman?"

"I'm not admitting to anything, but if I were, it would be my damn business," he responded.

"Not here in Hollywood, Ethan, and not while we're trying to build your career. You were doing a great job wining and dining the ladies, causing others to take notice and earning the title of this town's newest heartthrob. All of that is what we need to continue to build your image the way we want. I know how important that is to you."

Ethan pulled in a deep breath. Yes, it had been important to him at one time, but now…

"And in that same vein, I have a suggestion for a date for you on Saturday night."

Curtis's words pulled Ethan's concentration back into the conversation. "Excuse me?"

"I said that I have a suggestion for a date for you on Saturday."

Ethan frowned. "What are you talking about, Curtis?"

"I'm talking about Faith Pride. I got a call from her agent who suggested it might be a good idea if the two of you attended the event together."

"I know nothing about an event next Saturday night."

"Sure you do," Curtis insisted. "I sent you the invitation with a mailing confirmation so I know you got it."

He might have gotten it but, like the rest of his mail, he hadn't opened it. His time and the majority of his attention had been given to his sexy pixie, with no regrets. He looked back in his rearview mirror. The man was still there. Damn.

"I'm not going anywhere Saturday night, Curtis."

"What? You can't be serious, Ethan. You have to go. You're hot news and expected to be there. If I didn't know better I'd think you didn't give a damn about your career anymore. I assume you still want one, right?"

"Of course I do!"

"Good, but it sounds like you have a distraction and that isn't good. Get rid of her."

"Come again?"

"I said get rid of her, Ethan. I don't know who she is and frankly I don't care. She's interfering with your life in a negative way. Your actions in keeping her a secret mean she isn't someone you want to be seen with." Curtis paused a moment then said, "Oh, hell, please tell me the person is a she and not a he."

Ethan fought the urge to tell his agent just where he could go. Instead he said, "Bye, Curtis."

"Hey, you didn't answer me."

"And I don't intend to. If you don't know the answer to that then it's time I start looking for another agent."

"Wait, Ethan, I think we—"

Angrily Ethan clicked off the phone. He then glanced back in his rearview mirror and saw the bastard was still on his tail. Deciding he'd had enough, he figured it was time to seriously lose this guy. Increasing his speed, he darted in and out of traffic before making a quick exit off the interstate, only to make a quick right and then a quick left into the parking lot of a car wash.

He smiled, thinking it was his lucky day since there weren't many cars around and immediately drove around the side of the bay. A glance in his rearview mirror showed his stalker speeding by. Backing up, Ethan quickly pulled out and headed back toward the interstate, satisfied for the time being that he'd lost his tail.

Rachel continued to pace the bedroom floor. Ethan had called to say he was on his way but would be late due to "unforeseen circumstances." He hadn't elaborated.

She paused by the bed and drew in a deep breath, remembering her conversation with Charlene. Rachel's common sense was basically telling her that continuing to take risks at this point would be acting irresponsibly. She was an intelligent woman and Ethan was an intelligent man. They had enjoyed each other's companionship but both fully understood that they could not have a future together of any kind. And that was where their similarities ended. Their connection over the past three weeks had only been physical. He didn't love her and she didn't love him.

Then why was the thought of not being with him, not sharing stolen moments any longer, causing her heart to ache?

She began moving again, pacing the floor. He would know something was bothering her the moment he saw her. For one thing, she still had her clothes on, and usually if she was the first to arrive, she would be naked in the bed waiting on him.

She turned when she heard the sound of footsteps and felt the fluttering in her chest when the door slowly opened. She couldn't deny the excitement and joy she felt when her gaze met his blue-gray eyes. It was the same moment of elation she felt whenever she saw him.

He closed the door and leaned against it, holding her gaze for a moment, and then he began slowly unbuttoning his shirt. She knew she should stop him, tell him what she'd heard and that they needed to talk about it.

But she couldn't now.

Her hands automatically went to her skirt and undid the zipper, then slowly shimmied out of it before pulling her blouse over her head. She then kicked off her sandals and by the time they met next to the bed they were both completely naked.

As they tumbled together on the bed, one thought ran through her mind. *So much for talking.*

Chapter 13

An hour or so later, a very satiated Ethan was stretched out in the bed with Rachel in his arms and their legs still entwined. Mentally he was ordering his heart rate to slow down, but it wasn't listening. And his brain cells, which had gotten scrambled after a couple of back-to-back orgasms, were still a jumbled mess. But he didn't mind. In fact, he couldn't imagine it any other way. He was precisely where he wanted to be and was with the one person he wanted to share his time.

He raised her hand to his lips to kiss it and in response she snuggled even closer to him. Her body felt warm all over, and he liked the feel of spooning her backside, cradling her hips.

"So tell me," he leaned down and whispered close

to her ear. "Why were you still wearing clothes when I got here?"

He noticed the exact moment her body stiffened and he tightened his arms around her. Only a man who had been a lover to this woman could detect at that moment she was bothered by something. He shifted his weight, turned her in his arms to face him and his eyes met hers. "What's wrong, Rachel?"

For a moment he wasn't sure she would answer him, and then in a soft voice she said, "My friend Charlene called today."

He was sure there was more. "And?"

"You were in the tabloids. It seems reporters are trying to figure out who's your flavor of the month."

"They wouldn't have to try and figure it out since I'd be glad to tell them, if you would let me."

She stared at him through long lashes, surprise showing in her eyes, and he understood why. This was the first time he'd ever suggested they take their affair public. The only reason he'd never done so was because he knew her feelings on the matter.

"Ethan," she breathed out in a regretful tone. "I can't."

In other words, you won't, he thought and fought back the frustration he felt. He thought about the party and knew he didn't want to take any other woman but her. He pulled in a deep breath, wondering at what point he had decided he wanted more than a fling with her. When had sneaking around with Rachel become something he did only because that was the way she wanted it?

"Okay, you can't," he said, trying to keep the sting from his voice. "What does a tabloid reporter have to do with you having your clothes on when I got here?"

She turned her head to look at the painting of him that she had done and hung on the wall. It was a good thing they were the only ones with keys to this room in the building. He would hate for anyone to ever walk in and see that painting of him. She called it art; he thought of it as borderline X-rated. The only thing keeping him from being completely nude was the very thin piece of cloth that covered a certain part of his body at the juncture of his legs.

"Rachel, you're thinking too much again."

She returned her gaze to his. "Tabloid reporters are trying to figure out who you're spending your time with. You and I know if they keep snooping then it's only a matter of time before they find out, and I can't let that happen, Ethan. I can't risk being placed in the spotlight ever again. And then there's my career I have to think about. I've worked too hard building myself as a professional in the industry to risk losing everything."

He pulled in a deep breath. Those damn reporters had definitely done a job on her when she was a kid for her to have this intense fear. He could just imagine the hell she went through. He pulled her tighter to him, trying to imagine life without her. He would still see her on the set but he had begun thinking of these interludes with her as their time. He looked forward to them. In a way, he needed them. They had stopped being just sexual escapades a while ago. There were those times like these where he would hold her in his arms and savor what they shared, both the physical and the emotional.

"You won't lose anything, Rachel. I told you our secret is safe. No one knows about us or this place."

"For now, but how long will it be before they—"

"Once they see I'm no longer worth their time and effort, they will leave me alone," he interrupted her. "Hmm, as much as I don't want to attend that function Saturday night, maybe I should."

Rachel lifted a brow. "What function?"

"Some charity function Curtis wants me to attend with a date to calm the waters with the tabloids. Maybe if they see I'm a boring person who's gotten so absorbed in my career and nothing more, they will move on to someone else."

He could tell by the look in her eyes that she was confused. "But I thought you wanted to court the media, build your career that way as a playboy."

He studied her features. *I thought so, too,* he said to himself. And instead of trying to determine why he'd had a change of heart, he said, "There are other ways."

He pulled her closer into his arms. "Come on, we've talked enough. Let's get some sleep."

She pulled back. "Sleep?"

He smiled. "Yes, but if you prefer that we didn't…" He leaned over and kissed her in a way that had her body quivering. And when she responded by returning the kiss he proceeded to deepen it.

This was what he wanted and what he needed. Tabloids or no tabloids he intended to keep her by his side, even if they had to continue to sneak around to do it.

Rachel wrapped the sheet around her as she sank into the chair across from the bed. She needed to think and she couldn't do so wrapped in Ethan's arms. She had to have distance.

She closed her eyes and could clearly recall how it felt to be accosted by a crowd of reporters shoving mikes in your face, pulling on your hair to get your attention and all but screaming questions at you. She would try hiding behind her aunt and uncle, and later behind Sofia, but they would get relentless, their questions more demanding, the hordes of reporters even bigger. Then there was the period where she'd had nightmares about them and how they would all enjoy making her life unbearable.

And it had kept up that way until after she'd finished high school and then decided to travel abroad for a while. When she returned home, all the attention had shifted to other heiresses and up-and-coming starlets and actors. They forgot about her, practically left her alone, except for those times when the Wellesley family appeared together at a social function.

Over the years she had worked so hard to avoid that, as well as strived to be taken seriously in the industry as a makeup artist and wardrobe designer. To land a job on one of the most popular television shows was definitely a feather in her cap, one she refused to lose.

But she didn't want to lose Ethan either. She glanced at him, asleep in the bed. She enjoyed these times with him when she could be herself. Although they made love, they spent time talking as well. He had become her lover but he was still her friend, a very good friend. And it was a friendship that she cherished.

"Rachel?"

She heard the sound of her name and glanced toward the bed again. Ethan had awoken and had stretched his hand out to her. Without a moment's hesitation, she eased from the chair, dropped the sheet and went to him.

He gathered her into his arms and whispered, "You're thinking again and that's not a good thing."

She pulled back and looked up at him and smiled. "It's not?"

"No."

"Well, then, can you come up with a better pastime?"

He rubbed his nose against her neck. "Um, I think I can," he said throatily before capturing her mouth.

He released her mouth and eased her down on the

bed. "Yes," she managed hoarsely, as her body began shivering in a need only he could satisfy, "I believe you can."

A few days later Rachel looked down into the face of the actress reclining in her makeup chair and smiled before handing the woman the mirror. "There you go. Your makeup looks good on you, as always."

Livia studied her features in the mirror and smiled. "And, as always, you did a wonderful job, Rachel. You certainly know your stuff."

Rachel thanked her. Livia Blake was always giving her compliments about her work. Unlike Tae'Shawna Miller. The woman was still living in a fantasy world, still weaving the story of a secret affair with Ethan. Rachel figured she was the only one the woman had probably shared her lie with, probably because she figured Rachel was the only person gullible enough to believe her.

"You're one of the few people I'm going to miss when I leave the show," Livia said, easing up in her chair and handing the mirror back to Rachel.

Rachel knew she was going to miss Livia as well. Over the past weeks, she'd discovered her earlier assumptions about the woman had been all false, especially when she'd taken time to compare her to Tae'Shawna. Both were beautiful women who turned men's heads without much effort. But their attitudes and the way they treated people were totally different. Livia wasn't shallow or self-absorbed at all. Tae'Shawna took all those honors.

"You know how directors are. They may decide to rewrite the script and keep you on."

Livia shook her head sadly. "I doubt that will happen, although it would be wonderful. I'm thirty and nearing the end of my modeling career and although it's been a good one, it's time I moved on, although I haven't figured out to where just yet. *Paging the Doctor* has been a stepping-stone in the right direction. I've met some good people on the set, and—" she threw her head back and chuckled "—a few not so good ones."

Rachel smiled. Livia didn't have to tell her who the "not so good ones" were. Everyone had figured out by now there were several women on the set who were jealous of Livia's beauty, with Tae'Shawna heading the list.

"Well, I wish you the best," Rachel said sincerely.

"And I wish you the best, as well." Livia paused and then said, "Can I offer you some advice, though?"

Rachel raised a brow. "Advice about what?"

"Not what, but who. Ethan Chambers."

With effort, Rachel kept her features expressionless as she continued to pack away her cosmetics. "Ethan?" she asked, fighting to keep her voice steady. "And what kind of advice do you want to offer me about him?"

Livia paused, as if trying to choose her words carefully, and then she said, "I know the two of you are fiercely attracted to each other and..."

When Rachel began shaking her head, trying to deny it, Livia waved her off. "Hey, I felt the vibes between the two of you, even during his hot and heavy love scenes with me."

"But I—"

"Want to deny it," Livia said, smiling. "I don't know why you would want to when you're both beautiful people. Look, I'm sorry if mentioning it got you all flustered. That wasn't my intent. I just don't know why the two of you are keeping it a secret."

Rachel dropped down in the nearest chair, totally outdone. She and Ethan had worked so hard not to give anything away on the set, yet Livia had picked up on it. She met Livia's curious gaze. "Do you think others noticed?"

Livia shrugged. "Probably not. I'm just good at reading people and picking up vibes. I doubt Tae'Shawna noticed, since she's under the illusion he's all into her, and Paige isn't any better. Those are the only two still hanging on, hoping he'll give them some attention. I think the other women on the set have decided he's truly not interested."

Rachel didn't say anything for a moment, and then asked, "What did we do to give ourselves away?"

Livia chuckled. "The way the two of you look at each other when you think no one else is noticing, and I'm sure no one else is noticing but me, only because I have a tendency to notice everything. But I still don't understand why the two of you are keeping it a secret."

Rachel nibbled at her bottom lip. "It's complicated. I prefer not being in the limelight and he's a person who can't help but be there, dead center."

"Well, I hope things work out for the two of you because I think you're a good match, and you and Ethan truly deserve each other. Since I've gotten to know the both of you, I can easily see you're good people."

Livia glanced down at her watch. "It's time for me to get ready for my next scene. I'm not sure how they plan to write in my exit from the show since I'm supposedly Dr. Perry's love interest with emotional baggage. I think I'm supposed to pack up and leave when things between us get hot and heavy because I haven't gotten over my husband's death."

Rachel nodded. It was either that or killing Dr. Duncan off, but she couldn't see them doing that. Still, on the set, you never knew how things would go.

"Ethan, can I see you for a moment?"

Ethan kept the annoyance out of his face as he turned around. "Yes, Tae'Shawna, what is it?"

She smiled up at him. "I have tickets to the premier of *Saturday's Hussle*. Would you like to go with me tonight?"

Ethan knew just where he planned to be tonight, and Rachel's arms were far better than any movie premier. Even if he and Rachel hadn't made plans to meet up later, Tae'Shawna would be the last woman he'd go out with. "Thanks, but I have plans already."

"Oh. Maybe next time."

He doubted it. In fact, he knew for certain there wouldn't be a first time or a next time. "I'll see you later," he said, turning to leave.

"Umm, you don't know how I wish on that one, Ethan."

He kept walking, refusing to turn back around and respond to her flirty comment. His workday had ended, and for him, the fun was about to begin with the woman he wanted.

Chapter 14

Rachel glanced over at Charlene as they got out of the car. They were at a karaoke bar for a girls' night out. It was Saturday night and Ethan had decided to go to the charity event solo, against his agent's wishes. He'd insisted he would not take a date.

"Are you ready to have some fun?" she asked her friend. Rachel knew she needed to cheer Charlene up since her mother had hit again, calling her and telling her younger daughter all the reasons why she couldn't get a man.

"Yes, although you should have let me spend the weekend alone getting wasted."

Rachel laughed. "Neither one of us can handle too

much booze and we both know it. Come on, let's enjoy ourselves."

A few hours later they were doing just that. Rachel was trying to talk Charlene into competing in the singing contest to win the five-hundred-dollar prize. Everyone knew what a beautiful voice she had.

"You really think I should?" Charlene asked.

Rachel smiled. Charlene had a dynamite voice but she'd always had this thing about singing in public. She much preferred staying behind the scenes, working as a voice coach at one of the local schools. "Hey, so far I haven't been impressed by the others I've heard. The sound of your voice has spoiled me. Personally, I think you have a good shot at winning. Just think of what you could do with the money." And Rachel could see from her best friend's expression that she was thinking the same thing.

"I don't know, Rachel."

"Well, I do, so just think about it. You have time to make up your mind. We're going to be here for a while."

And she meant it. She wasn't ready to go home to sit around or go to bed wondering if Ethan was having a good time at that event without her. No doubt there would be plenty of women there throwing themselves at him. She pulled in a deep breath. By mutual agreement, they were in an exclusive relationship. She knew she hadn't dated anyone else since they'd begun sleeping together and he'd said he hadn't either.

"Okay, I'm going to do it!"

Charlene's exclamation interrupted Rachel's thoughts and she smiled over at her friend. "Good. I have a feeling that you won't regret it."

The hounds were on Ethan the minute he got out of his car.

"Chambers? Where have you been hiding?" a reporter asked as a mike was shoved in Ethan's face and cameras went off from all directions.

Stepping into his role, he smiled for the cameras. "I haven't been hiding."

That began a series of other questions and he answered every last one of them with the intent of diffusing their curiosity and getting them interested in his role in *Paging the Doctor* instead. After a while it worked, although there were still a couple of reporters who seemed determined to dig into his personal life. Years of being one of the heirs to the Chambers Winery had taught him how to handle that kind.

"No date, Ethan?" one of the two resilient reporters asked.

"No, no date. Is there anything wrong with a man coming alone?"

"Not when he doesn't have to," was the other resilient reporter's quick comeback.

Ethan smiled. "I call it freedom of choice."

He answered a few more questions before bidding the reporters good-night. He knew he would be tailed when he left the event, but he figured eventually they would reach the conclusion he was no longer newsworthy and go find someone else to harass.

"I can't believe I won!"

Rachel smiled brightly over at Charlene who was holding a bottle of champagne in one hand and a check for five hundred dollars in the other. "I told you that you would. I keep telling you that you have a beautiful voice. Maybe one day you'll finally believe me." Charlene had done a beautiful rendition of "Bridge Over Troubled Water" and brought everyone out of their seats. "You sounded like a young Aretha."

Charlene waved off her words. "You're my best friend, so of course you'd think so, and you know how much I love me some Aretha."

Yes, Rachel did know, but no matter what Charlene thought, she was dead serious.

"Excuse me, ladies."

Both Rachel and Charlene glanced at the man standing by their table. "Yes?" Charlene asked.

"I hate interrupting, but I wanted to congratulate you, Ms. Quinn. You did an outstanding job. And I want to introduce myself. I'm Jason Burke, a talent scout," he said handing Charlene his card. "Please call me. I would like to discuss a few things with you. The company I represent would love to bring you on board."

Rachel could tell from the look on Charlene's face that she wasn't taking the man seriously. Playing along with him, Charlene slid his card into her pocket and said, "Sure, I'd love to contact you. Will next week be soon enough?"

The man smiled brightly. "Yes, and I'll look forward to that call." He then walked away and out of the club.

Charlene rolled her eyes. "Does he really think I'm going to call him?"

Rachel took a sip of her drink. "You said that you would."

"That was to get rid of him. Please. I can sing but not that good. And he's probably not who he's claiming to be."

"Let me see his business card." Rachel waited while Charlene dug it out of the pocket of her jeans.

Rachel studied the card. "I think you should call Sofia and let her check him out to see if he's legit. If he is, I would follow up with him if I were you."

Charlene waved off her words. "Whatever. Hey, let's forget about Jason Burke and have a good time. We need to get on the dance floor and celebrate my win."

Rachel laughed as she followed Charlene onto the floor to shake their booties for a while.

It was past three in the morning by the time Rachel had showered and slid between the sheets. She was about to turn off the lamp when her cell phone rang. Thinking it was Charlene still on a high from that night's win, she answered the phone saying, "Hey, haven't you gotten enough already?"

"Of you? Never."

Her body immediately began throbbing at the sound

of the deep, husky voice. Her eyes clouded over in desire just from hearing it. "Hey, lover boy, haven't you heard it's not nice to call a girl after midnight?"

His soft chuckle came through the phone and touched her in places she'd rather leave untouched. But since he was going there, she might as well let him finish. "I prefer being there in person but some ass is parked outside the complex, waiting for me to leave. So I guess I'll stay in and engage in some sex talk with you."

She chuckled. "Sounds like a winner to me. Speaking of wins, Charlene won a singing contest at the club tonight. A whopping five hundred dollars and a bottle of champagne. And a talent scout approached her afterwards."

"I'm happy for her."

Although Ethan and Charlene had never officially met, they knew a lot about each other thanks to Rachel. "I'll tell her you are." There was a pause, and then she asked, "And how was your night?"

"Boring."

"Did you change your mind about taking a date with you?"

"No."

Rachel tried not to feel giddy at that one single word but couldn't help it. She had convinced herself that she could handle it if he'd decided to take a date. After all, they were nothing more to each other than occasional bed partners. She drew in a deep breath, not wanting to think about it or how depressed she'd get when she did.

"So what are you wearing?"

His question made her smile. "What makes you think I'm wearing anything?"

He chuckled. "You only sleep naked when you're with me."

"Says who?"

"Says me. The man who has made love to you a lot of times."

"Hmm, how many?" she asked in what she hoped was a sexy, low tone. And he was right. He had made love to her a lot of times.

"Was I supposed to be counting?"

"I was."

He laughed. "Okay, then how many?"

"Tally up your own numbers, Chambers."

"If I were there, I would tickle it out of you."

"If you were here, Ethan, I'd make sure you put your hands to more productive use."

When Rachel hung up the phone an hour later she drew in a deep breath. Ethan's smooth, hot talk had almost made her come several times, it definitely had made her consider leaving her house and meeting him somewhere. But luckily her common sense held tight. They had agreed to throw the paparazzi off their scent by not meeting at their place anytime during the coming week. That meant when they did get back together for some bed time, they would have a whole lot of making up to do.

Ethan left his home on Sunday morning to go to the diner for some coffee and a roll. When he walked out with his purchase, he noticed one of the reporters from last night was waiting on him, braced against Ethan's car. The man was Joe Connors and he was known to be as tenacious as they came.

Since he was wearing the same clothes as he'd worn yesterday when he'd followed him, Joe had apparently slept in his car. And because Ethan considered himself a good guy, while buying breakfast for himself he'd also grabbed something for Joe.

"Looks like you could use this as much as I can," Ethan said, handing the man the extra breakfast sack he had in his hand. "All the creamers, sugars and artificial sweeteners you'll ever need are in that bag," he added.

The man accepted the offering. He then took a sip of the coffee, drinking it black. "Good stuff. Thanks."

"You're welcome." Ethan took a sip of his own coffee and asked, "Now, why don't you be a nice guy and leave me alone."

Joe chuckled as he shook his head. "No can do. I have to make a living."

"Don't we all?" was Ethan's dry response.

The man eyed him curiously. "Since you're in a giving mood, Chambers, how about an interview?"

Ethan shook his head. "I gave you an interview last night. You asked your questions and I answered them."

"Yes, but you refused to talk about your love life."

Ethan smiled. "What makes you think I have a love life?"

The man shrugged. "I just figured you did. This time

last year you were dating anything in a skirt, and now for the past month you've been cooling your heels, so to speak, which can only mean you've been caught."

"Caught?"

"Yes. Some woman's got your heart. Is she married?"

Ethan threw his head back and laughed. "What is this obsession that I'm involved with a married woman?"

"What other reason would make you go to great pains to hide her?"

Ethan fought back the temptation to respond by saying he wasn't trying to hide Rachel. He would be perfectly happy if they made their affair public but...

"Um, look's like you started to say something and then changed your mind. Did I get close to the truth or something?"

"No."

"You sure?"

"Positive."

Joe looked at him for the longest time. "Then what was that funny look about?"

"Nothing. Eat your food, Joe. It's getting cold."

After pulling a warm croissant from the bag, Joe tilted his head and looked at Ethan. He grinned and said, "Hey man, you're not such a bad guy."

Chapter 15

"Have a nice evening, Rachel."

Rachel smiled over at one of her assistants. "You do the same, Loraine."

"And don't hang around here too late. They start killing the lights around seven," Loraine advised.

"Thanks for letting me know that."

There were only a few more weeks of filming left before the final shoot of the season. A wrap party was already being planned and Frasier was going all out to make it a monumental affair.

As she thought about the season ending, Rachel was happy that Livia's character was not killed off. It left the door open for a possible return next season. Just as she had predicted, Dr. Duncan was not emotionally ready for a hot and heavy love affair with Dr. Perry so soon after her husband's death. The season would end with her asking to be transferred to another hospital in Florida. That meant Dr. Perry would be free to pursue another love interest next season.

Livia would be joining her and Charlene for dinner over the weekend. Ever since Livia had mentioned that she was aware of her affair with Ethan, the two of them had become friends. Rachel appreciated Livia not gossiping about her and Ethan; apparently somebody in Hollywood could keep a secret.

Rachel's cell phone went off and she pulled it out of the pocket of her smock. "Yes?"

"Whooo, Rachel, you'll never guess what happened to me!"

Rachel couldn't help but hear the excitement in Charlene's voice. "And what has happened to you?"

"That guy Jason Burke is legit. Sofia checked him out. He works in A&R for the big music company that distributes Playascape."

Rachel lifted a brow. Playascape was a well-known recording company. One of the biggies. "Are you sure?"

"Sofia verified everything."

Then that settled it. Sofia knew just about everyone in the music, movie and television industry through Limelight Entertainment.

"And guess what?"

"What?"

"They want me to come in and meet with them."

Rachel couldn't help but be ecstatic as well. "Wow, Cha, that's fantastic."

"I think so, too, and Sofia suggested I send them a copy of that demo tape I did a while back."

"That's a smart move."

"Sofia's managing everything for me."

Rachel's smile widened. She knew her sister's abilities when it came to working deals. "Then you're in good hands."

Rachel heard a sound and turned around. Her breath caught in her throat when she saw Ethan. He had entered the trailer and was leaning against the closed door. Their eyes met and she watched as he reached behind him and locked it. The click sounded loud.

"Cha, that's good news but I need to call you back later."

"You okay?"

Evidently Charlene had heard the change in her voice. "Yes, I'm fine. I'll call you when I get home." She then clicked off the phone.

"Ethan, what are you doing here? I thought you'd left hours ago."

He crossed his arms over his chest. Instead of answering her, he had a question of his own. "And why are you still here?"

"I had some paperwork to do."

He checked his watch. "It's late."

"I know but I'm fine. The security guard patrolling the studio lot is still here."

He was still leaning against the door, but now

his hands were tucked into the pockets of his jeans. Although they saw each other every day on the set, they hadn't been together intimately for over a week thanks to that tabloid reporter dogging Ethan's heels. But they did talk on the phone every night and had made plans to try and sneak away to Tijuana this weekend.

"Go ahead and finish what you have to do. I'll wait and walk you out to your car."

She swallowed the lump in her throat. "That's not necessary."

"I think it is."

Instead of arguing with him she slid behind her small desk and began going over the paperwork she needed to give John in the morning. Out of the corner of her eye she saw Ethan had moved away from the door to straddle one of the chairs.

The air-conditioning system was working but she was beginning to feel hot. She was also feeling his eyes on her, singeing her flesh. In the quiet, she couldn't help but be aware of him. He'd been in the trailer with her lots of times while she'd applied his makeup, and because of where they were, things had always been professional between them. But she'd always been tempted with him reclining in one of her chairs and her over him and breathing in his scent.

Deciding the trailer was too quiet, she opted to share Charlene's good news with him. "Isn't that wonderful?"

"Yeah, I think it's great," he replied. "I hear they have a good outfit over there."

Rachel continued working, going through John's requests for the season finale. Out of the corner of her eye, she saw that Ethan had moved again. This time he'd gone over to the watercooler to get something to drink. She turned to look at him at the exact time he tilted the cup up to his lips to take a swallow.

The way his throat moved as water trickled down it did something to her. And when he licked his lips as if the drink had been one of the most refreshing things to go into his mouth, she actually began envying the water.

"How much longer before you're done?"

She blinked and realized he had spoken to her. In that case, he'd probably caught her staring. She drew in a deep breath as she looked down at the papers. "Not long. If you need to leave then I—"

"No, I don't need to leave. But I do need you."

Now *that* she heard. And upon doing so, she couldn't smother the heated sensations taking root in the pit of her stomach or the hot tingle between her legs. This was where she worked, her business sanctuary. Actors came and went and usually she was too busy, too involved to connect the insides of this trailer to any one particular person. But for some reason, she had a feeling that was about to change.

Deciding not to respond to what he'd said, she turned her attention back to the papers in front of her. Ten minutes later, she was signing off on the last sheet. She opened the top drawer to slide them inside.

"Finished now?"

She glanced over at him and met his gaze. He had gone back to straddling one of the chairs. "Yes."

"Good." He stood. "Come here, Rachel."

She continued to hold his gaze, felt the heat zinging between the two of them. She didn't have to ask what he wanted; the look on his face told her what he needed. It was there in his expression, in the chiseled and handsome features. Not to mention those beautiful eyes staring back at her.

Instead of putting up any fuss, not that she would have, she crossed the room without a word and walked straight into his arms. He pulled her to him and she felt it all. His heat, the pounding of his heart against her chest and the engorged erection pressing at the juncture of her thighs.

"It's been hell these seven days without you," he whispered against her lips.

"Actually, it's been eight but who's counting?" she said as her arms automatically went around his waist and she rested her head against his chest. She had to fight hard to keep from being overwhelmed by him. When she felt his erection throb against her thigh, she pulled back and glanced up at him.

"We'll be together Saturday," she reminded him.

He smiled down at her but she still saw the tension in his features. "I can't wait. I need you now."

As he spoke, he backed her against the wall. Already his hands at her waist were lifting her up. Instead of wearing jeans today she had decided to wear a skirt. *How convenient for him,* she thought.

And for her.

Her legs automatically wrapped around him and his hands were busy under her skirt, pushing her panties aside before unzipping his pants and freeing himself. By mutual consent, he had stopped using condoms when she'd told him she was on the pill.

His finger slid inside her as if to test her readiness, and the feel of his touch had her moaning.

"Shh," he whispered in her ear. "There's no need to bring the guard in here to check out things."

No, there was no reason, which meant she couldn't let go and scream. How was she going to stop it? He always made her scream.

His finger inside her was driving her to the brink. He'd said he needed her and he was taking his time to make sure that she also needed him. She should tell him doing so wasn't necessary. She did need him. She did need this.

"Baby, you're hot and your scent is driving me insane," he whispered before taking her mouth in a kiss that told her this was just the beginning.

He covered her lips, captured her mouth in a combination of hunger and tenderness that zapped her senses. And when his tongue began doing its thing, exploring her mouth as if it were conquering unfamiliar territory, she went weak in the knees. But he held her, making sure she didn't go anywhere. She had detected his hunger the minute he'd entered the trailer, and now she was experiencing it firsthand.

Her body was responding to him as it always did

and as it always would. Whenever it came to this kind of mutual satisfaction, they were always in accord. A deep, throbbing ache within her intensified and, of its own will, the lower part of her body rocked against his. She clung to him as his mouth clung to hers, plundering it, stirring sensations all the way down to the soles of her feet.

For one fleeting moment she felt the silky head of his erection probe her womanly core, then he entered her in one smooth stroke. She wrapped her legs around him to take him in fully.

She moaned into his mouth and gripped tightly to his shoulders, surrendering to the feel of him being embedded within her, stretching her wide. He deepened the kiss and at the same time he began to move, thrusting back and forth inside of her, feeding her hunger while making her skin tingle all over. Her breasts felt heavy, full and sensitive to the chest rubbing against them.

He was deep inside her and with each thrust he was going deeper still. As he rocked his hips against her, he used his hands to cushion her back from the wall.

He pulled his mouth away and whispered against her lips, "Come for me, baby. I need to feel you come."

As if his words were a command for her body to obey, she felt herself begin to shatter into a million pieces. She clenched her teeth to hold back her scream, and when his mouth came down on hers she gave in and felt every part of her body explode in a climax so intense she trembled all over.

"That's it, baby. Now I'm yours," he uttered huskily

right before his body ignited in an explosion as well. She felt the hot, thick essence of him shoot all the way inside of her in the most primitive way, and she called out his name.

He responded in kind, and the sound of her name on his lips sent everything within her throbbing for more. She only knew this kind of pleasure with him. She only wanted this kind of pleasure from him.

Sensation spiraled inside of her and she knew at that moment that Ethan Chambers had captured her heart.

Chapter 16

"Ethan, wait. I need to see you for a moment."

Ethan looked over his shoulder and turned around. "I was on my way out, Paige. What's up?"

Joe Connors had finally stopped being his shadow, but that didn't mean he and Rachel could let their guard down. They'd been careful since that amazing night in the trailer, not hooking up until last weekend in Tijuana. Their Mexican rendezvous had been special, and they'd made up for the time they'd lost. Now they would be spending the night at *their* place and Ethan couldn't wait. He didn't need Paige Stiles delaying him.

"Evidently you're up, big boy," she said in that flirty voice that annoyed the hell out of him. "I need a date to the wrap party."

He chuckled softly. "And?"

"And you're going to take me."

He was surprised by her bold statement. He had finally gotten Tae'Shawna out of his hair by his persistence in letting her know he wasn't interested. Paige, on the other hand, was not getting the message. He'd just have to be more explicit. "I'm not taking you anywhere."

"Yes, you are. At least, you will if you want me to keep your secret."

He felt the hair stand up on the back of his neck. "And just what secret is that?"

"You banging Rachel Wellesley. She never fooled me. I figured she had the hots for you just as bad as the next woman, and I was wondering how long it would take for you to be lured by her bait." The woman then chuckled. "Seriously, Ethan, are you *that* hard up? You couldn't do better than Rachel? If I was picking someone that you'd want to mess around with, it wouldn't be her. And don't deny the two of you are involved because I can prove it."

He drew in a deep breath, not sure if she could prove it but truly not caring. "No, I seriously don't think I can do better than Rachel. Now if you will excuse me, I—"

"I mean it, Ethan. You make plans to get something going with me or else."

"Or else what?"

She smiled sweetly. "Or else everyone, especially Frasier and John, will know that Rachel isn't the sweetie pie they think she is."

Now that pushed his anger to the top. "I don't know what game you're playing, Paige, but keep Rachel out of this."

"Sure, I'll keep her out of this, but only if you give me what I want. My name connected to yours will open doors. I not only want those doors opened, I want to walk through them."

"It won't happen."

She wiped the smile from her face. "Then I suggest that you make sure it does."

She walked away.

On the drive home, Ethan tried to figure out the best way to handle Paige. Reasoning with her was out of the question since the woman was vindictive and obviously intent on hurting Rachel. He had detected her dislike and jealousy from the first.

The one thing he'd learned growing up as a Chambers was to not let anyone bully, or in this case blackmail, you into doing something you did not want to do. He had no intention of taking Paige or any other woman to the wrap party. The only woman he would take was the woman he wanted and would always want. Rachel.

He thought about telling Rachel about Paige's threats, but he could just imagine what her reaction would be. He wanted to save her from that worry. And he wanted to save himself from seeing it. No, he would simply ignore Paige as he had Tae'Shawna and hopefully she would forget about her foolish threat.

He had no problems with his and Rachel's relationship going public and he'd pushed for that several times with

Rachel—only to meet a brick wall. For some reason she thought news of their involvement would diminish the professional career she had created, and then there was her intense desire not to be in the spotlight.

There was no one who could say his and Rachel's relationship on the set had been anything other than professional. And as far as her being in the spotlight, he thought she didn't give herself enough credit for handling things. He knew the media could sometimes be relentless, but because of their families, he and Rachel had been born into the spotlight anyway and the key was not avoiding it but dealing with it.

As he continued on the drive home, he finally admitted something else. Something he'd known for a while but just hadn't acknowledged. He had fallen in love with Rachel. And because he loved her, he didn't want to sneak around to be with her. He wanted everyone to know the woman he loved and adored, the woman who could make him smile just by being close to him. The woman he wanted to bring home to meet his family.

The woman he wanted to marry.

He wanted Rachel, and only Rachel, to become Mrs. Ethan Chambers. He wanted her to be the mother of his children. To walk by his side for always.

He gripped the steering wheel, knowing those thoughts were true. Every single one of them. But they were thoughts he could not share with Rachel. She didn't love him, and she didn't want to share a future with him.

* * *

Two days later Paige was back in his face again, reiterating her demands.

Ethan gave her his total attention, squaring off and looking her right in the eyes with an adamant expression. "Look, Paige, I told you once before that I'm not taking you to the wrap party and I meant it. My feelings haven't changed."

He saw the anger build in her features. Her jaw clenched and her eyes narrowed. "Then you leave me no choice. Now everyone will know what you and Rachel have been doing behind their backs."

Then she walked off.

Ethan got into his car, pissed but still positive he was handling the nagging woman the only way he could. He decided to forgo the air-conditioning on the ride home, preferring the warm breeze against his face. He imagined the stench of Paige Stiles being blown off him.

As if he'd warded it away, any thought of the encounter dared not enter his mind. Until the next night when his cell phone rang.

How Joe Connors, of all people, had gotten his cell phone number, Ethan didn't know and didn't waste his time asking.

"What do you want, Connors?" he asked instead.

"I like you, Chambers. You're different from most of the stars out there who can be anal, so I'm giving you a heads-up. You and your lady have been exposed. Not by me, but by a tip we received. And there are pictures, nothing sleazy, but pictures that will substantiate this person's claim. They are pretty damn excited over here, and I understand the article, pictures and all, hits tomorrow's paper."

Ethan felt his heart drop to his feet. He drew in a deep breath, knowing he had to get in touch with Rachel. She had volunteered to be a chaperone to Disneyland for a group of kids who attended the school where Charlene worked as a voice coach. She wasn't scheduled to return until late tonight.

When Ethan didn't say anything, Joe Connors continued, "I can't give you details but I can tell you the headline of the article isn't pretty."

Dread turned to anger, and it raced through Ethan. "Thanks for the heads-up."

Ending the call, he tried to reach Rachel. He had to prepare her for whatever the article said and assure her they would handle it, work through it and deal with it.

He only hoped she'd believe him.

Rachel finished taking her shower and was about to settle in for the night when she checked her messages on her cell phone. She lifted a brow. She had several missed calls from Ethan and just as many text messages and they all said the same thing: "Call ASAP."

Wondering at the urgency, she was about to punch in his phone number when there was loud knock at her door. After running downstairs she took a quick look through her peephole and saw Ethan. She quickly opened her door.

"Ethan, what is—"

He suddenly pulled her into his arms and kissed her, kicking the door closed behind him as he continued kissing her and sweeping her off her feet, into his arms.

She always enjoyed being kissed by him and today was no exception. His lips moved hungrily over hers and instinctively she melted against him, loving the feel of being in his arms. She whimpered his name when moments later he pulled his mouth away.

"Rachel, sweetheart, we need to talk."

She saw they were no longer at the door, but he had carried her across the room and had taken a seat on the sofa with her cradled in his arms. She had been so wrapped up in their kiss she hadn't noticed the movement.

It was then that she remembered the missed calls and text messages. "What about?" Her voice sounded wobbly from the impact of his kiss.

He continued to hold her tightly against him and when he didn't answer her, she glanced up into his eyes. She had been with Ethan long enough to know when he was deeply troubled. She pulled herself up. "What is it, Ethan?"

"I need to prepare you for something."

"What?"

"The tabloids know about us, thanks to Paige, and *The Wagging Tongue* is breaking the story tomorrow. Someone I know on the inside called and gave me a heads-up."

Rachel felt as if someone had just doused her with a pail of cold water right in her face. She jumped out of his lap. "What?"

"Yes, baby, I know. This is not how you wanted things, but together we'll deal with it."

She backed away from him. "No, no, this can't be happening..." Shaking her head as if to get her thoughts in order, she asked, "What does Paige have to do with it?"

Ethan rubbed his hand over his face. "Earlier in the week she approached me claiming she knew about us and threatening to go to Frasier and John if I didn't begin dating her. She figured her name connected to mine would take her places. I flatly refused and two days ago, when she approached me again and I refused again, she got mad. I guess this is her way of getting retaliation."

Rachel's head began pounding. "She approached you earlier in the week and you didn't mention it to me?"

He came to his feet and faced her. "I didn't want to upset you and I was hoping she would drop it."

Rachel pulled in a deep breath. "Paige is like a sore that only festers. She's never cared for me, Ethan. Jealousy is deeply embedded in any decision she makes about me. She's always wanted you, and for her to find out you and I have been involved in an affair, there's no way she would have dropped it. You should have told me."

"Maybe I should have, but I didn't want you upset."

"Well, now I am upset. I am livid. I am mad as hell."

He reached out for her. "The truth is out, baby, and we'll deal with it."

She pulled away from him. "It's not that easy, Ethan. It's my privacy and professionalism being threatened."

"And I still say we will deal with it, Rachel. When we're approached we'll tell them the truth."

"No, we won't! We will deny everything. They can't prove anything."

"I'm not sure about that. The person I talked to claims there are pictures."

"Pictures! Oh my God!" She dropped down on the sofa and covered her face with her hands.

Ethan went to her and pulled her into his arms. He'd never seen her this upset. "Rachel, the best thing to do is not to deny anything. We're two consenting adults who—"

"Should not have let things get out of hand. We should not have gotten involved in the first place since we knew what was at risk."

"But we did and we need to own up to it and not let the tabloids or anyone else control our lives or our relationship."

She jerked out of his arms. "No! You make it sound so easy and it's not. Don't you understand what I'll be going through, Ethan? Don't you understand? You like this sort of stuff. It makes you who you are, but it can only destroy me."

"Rachel, we can deal with it. Together."

"No! That's just it. We can't be together. That will just be more fuel for their fire. We have to end things between us now."

"That's not going to happen, Rachel. I won't give you up because of any damn tabloid," he said angrily.

She glared up at him. "You don't have a choice because I'm ending things between us, Ethan. I can't sacrifice a professional career I've worked hard to build or a private life I've tried hard to preserve. Besides, our affair was about nothing but sex anyway."

Her words were like a backhanded slap to Ethan's face and he felt the pain in the depths of his heart. "You don't mean that, Rachel," he said softly.

He refused to believe all the time they'd spent together had been about nothing but sex. Maybe that had been the case the first few times, but there was no way he would believe she didn't care for him the way he cared for her. No way.

"I love you, Rachel. Our times together weren't just about sex for me and I refuse to believe that's the way it was for you. And I won't deny what we shared to anyone. I won't make it into some backstreet, sleazy affair. I've never loved a woman before you, and I hope that you'll realize that our love—yes, our love—will be able to deal with anything. Together. You know how to reach me when you do."

He then turned and left.

Chapter 17

By noon on Saturday, Rachel was ready to have a stiff drink. The entire bottle, if necessary. Her phone hadn't stopped ringing. Some calls she had answered and some she had not.

Ethan's calls were some of the ones she had not.

It seemed everyone was shocked by the tabloid's allegations that she'd been having a secret affair with Ethan, but they were happy if she had. Uncle Jacob and Aunt Lily told her not to be bothered by the accusations. Sofia inquired as to how she was holding up but didn't ask any specifics about the affair. So far no one believed the tabloid's headline that she only got involved with Ethan to further her career. That was so far from the truth. She had already had an up-and-coming career before Ethan appeared on the scene. But the goal of the tabloids was to sell papers, and with those kinds of accusations and the photos of them kissing in the studio lot, they created the sensationalism they craved.

Thanks to Charlene, who'd shown up for breakfast with a copy of *The Wagging Tongue* in her hand, she'd been forced to see the article. She wished she could claim the picture plastered on the front page had been doctored, but it hadn't.

Evidently, Paige had been around that night Ethan had shown up in the trailer unexpectedly. After they'd made love, he had walked her to her parked car. Since it was late, they assumed everyone had left and, before getting in her car, Ethan had pulled her into his arms and given her a very heated kiss. What she considered a special moment between them had been reduced to something sleazy, thanks to Paige and her cell phone camera.

She looked up from the book she'd been trying unsuccessfully to read when her house phone rang. She hoped the caller wasn't Ethan again. She couldn't help but smile when she heard the voice of Carmen Aiken on her answering machine.

"Rachel, I know you're there, so pick up this phone!"

Carmen was an Oscar-winning actress who was married to director/producer Matthew Birmingham. She and Carmen had become good friends when Carmen, new to Hollywood at the time, had been cast in one of

Matt's movies. Rachel had been the makeup artist on the set.

She reached for the phone and answered, "Okay, so you knew I was here."

"You've been holding back on me, girl. Ethan Chambers! Why did you keep that hunk a secret?"

Rachel wished it had been a secret she could have shared, but the only people who'd known about her affair with Ethan had been Charlene and Livia. "You know why, Carmen."

"Yes, I know how brutal the tabloids can be. Remember, I was a victim of their gossip for a while. Even after Matt and I remarried, they claimed we did it as a way to get publicity for his next movie."

Rachel was aware of that lie. Carmen and Matt had been divorced for a little over a year and had remarried last month. Rachel was glad they had worked out their differences and had gotten back together. She didn't know of any couple who deserved each other more.

"It really doesn't matter what those reporters think. It's how you feel, Rachel. I can tell from the photo that was one hell of a kiss he gave you. You're probably the envy of a lot of women today."

Rachel drew in a deep breath. Charlene had said the same thing, but it really didn't matter. She wanted no part of the tabloids and no part of Ethan.

She couldn't help but remember what he'd said before leaving and in the messages he'd left on her answering machine and cell. He said he loved her.

Well, she loved him, too, but in this case love would
not be enough.

Carmen breached her silence. "I don't want you to
make the same mistake I made, Rachel, by letting the
tabloids rule your life."

Moments later when Rachel ended her call with
Carmen, she knew it was too late. The tabloids were
already ruling her life.

"What do you want, Curtis?"

"I like the publicity, Ethan, but you could have hooked
up with another woman. It would have benefited your
career a lot more had she been a model or an actress.
She's a makeup artist, for crying out loud, regardless of
the fact her last name is Wellesley."

An angry Ethan slouched back against the sofa with
a beer bottle in one hand and his cell phone in the other.
He didn't give a royal damn whether Curtis liked the
publicity or not. That last comment alone meant the
man's days as his agent were numbered.

When Ethan didn't say anything, Curtis continued,
"Now what we need to do is to play our cards right with
this publicity and keep it moving. But you need to get
rid of the broad in that picture and get someone more
newsworthy. Someone like Rayon Stewart. We can work
the angle that Rachel Wellesley was just someone you
were sleeping with while waiting for Rayon Stewart to
end things with Artis Lomax."

"Go to hell, Curtis."

"Excuse me?"

"I said, go to hell. By the way, as of now, you're no longer my agent. You're fired."

He then hung up the phone and took a swig of his beer. He refused to let anyone put Rachel down. She was the best thing to ever happen to him, and he loved *her* and not some model or Hollywood actress.

He reached for his cell phone and punched in her number. He knew she was at her condo hiding out. He'd tried calling her all day but she refused to take any of his calls.

Joe Connors had been right. The article hadn't been pretty and had made Rachel look like a schemer who had used their affair to build her career. No doubt that was the story Paige had told the tabloids and they had run with it. If anyone would have bothered to check, they would have known it was all lies fabricated by a jealous woman.

When Rachel didn't answer, Ethan clicked off the phone before standing and moving to the window. The paparazzi was out there and had been all day, waiting for him to come out with a story. Well, he didn't have one. At the moment, the only thing he had was heartache.

Rachel braced herself for work Monday, knowing everyone had probably seen the tabloid's article. She had decided the best thing to do was to deal with it and move on. She had worked too hard to build her career to do otherwise.

Ethan had continued to call her through late last night and had called her again this morning. By her not answering his calls, she hoped he now realized she hadn't changed her mind. Ending things between them had been the best thing to do. It was important that anyone expecting drama would get the professional she had always been.

She appreciated that the studio lot was private. But that didn't stop the paparazzi from being crowded out front with their cameras ready to get a shot of her when she arrived at work. A few even tried blocking her car from going through the gate.

From the way everything got quiet when she walked onto the set, it was obvious she had been the topic of conversation. She gave everyone her cheery hello as usual while heading toward the trailer, but she didn't miss Paige's comment, which was intentionally loud enough for anyone to hear. "And she actually thought someone like Ethan Chambers could be interested in *her?*"

Rachel refused to turn and comment, but she couldn't help the smile when she heard Livia speak up. "Evidently he was interested in her, since she's the one with him in that photo, Paige."

Livia's words had no doubt hit a nerve with Paige, since everyone on set had seen her flirting outrageously with Ethan. Tae'Shawna had been just as bad. Some people on set had placed bets on which of the two—Paige or Tae'Shawna—would finally get his attention. Neither had.

Rachel kept walking to her trailer, intent on not being around when Ethan arrived. It would be bad enough having to work with him on the set knowing they would be the subject of everyone's attention. She needed to get herself together before seeing him.

She appreciated her two assistants giving their support with words of encouragement and letting her know if she and Ethan were an item, that meant he had good taste.

For the next hour or so she went about her day as usual, and when it was time for her to go out on the set she left her trailer. The last thing she wanted was to give the impression she was hiding out.

Ethan and Livia were in the middle of a scene where Dr. Duncan was explaining to Dr. Perry why they couldn't be together and why they needed to end things. Boy, that sounded familiar.

Several people turned to look at her, including Frasier and John, who both gave her nods. If they believed the tabloid story, then they knew she and Ethan had broken the show's rule. In which case, she knew her job was in jeopardy. If they had to choose which of them to keep, no doubt Ethan would stay, since he was their star.

"Freeze! Rachel, kill that shine on Ethan."

At Frasier's command, she moved forward. The set got quiet and she knew everyone was looking at her. At them. She greeted him only with his name when she stopped in front of him.

He did the same.

Their greeting sounded stiff. Being the professional she was, Rachel was determined to do her job. She took her makeup brush and swept across the bridge of his nose. She tried to ignore his scent, something she'd gotten used to, and the sound of his heavy breathing.

But she couldn't ignore the blue-gray eyes that seemed to watch her every moment. Emotions stirred within Rachel but she fought hard to keep them at bay. Making sure she didn't take any more time than necessary, she gave him a smile and said, "All done." And then she quickly walked away.

"Unfreeze!"

They resumed shooting the scene, and when she glanced over at Paige, there was a malicious smirk on the woman's face. Paige doubtless assumed it was Ethan who ended things between them and not the other way around. She was probably also thinking that although she might not be his date at the wrap party, neither would Rachel.

She didn't want to be the object of discussion and speculation. But since she was, she would do everything she could to stay professional and put her and Ethan's affair behind her.

No matter how much it hurt.

"Ethan, wait up."

He glanced around and saw Tae'Shawna approach with a smile on her face. Out of the corner of his eye, he saw Paige watching. She'd had the good sense to avoid him today.

"What is it, Tae'Shawna?"

"I see you're scheduled for makeup with Rachel tomorrow."

"And what of it?"

"If you're uncomfortable about it, I'll speak to John for you to have one of her assistants do it."

He didn't need Tae'Shawna to tell him of his schedule. He knew Rachel would be doing his makeup, which meant they would be alone in the trailer for a short while. But he figured to keep talk down, Rachel had already arranged for one of her assistants either to do his makeup or be there with her when she did it. He doubted very seriously they would be alone.

He looked at Tae'Shawna. "Why would I be uncomfortable with Rachel doing my makeup?"

She shrugged. "I just assumed since the news is out about how she came on to you to boost her career that you are leery of her now. Coming on to you was unprofessional on her part."

Ethan put his hands in the pockets of his jeans and he didn't care one iota about the fierce frown that settled on his face. He was sick and tired of people assuming the worst of Rachel. Bottom line was he had pursued her, he had wanted her. He still wanted her.

"First of all," he told Tae'Shawna, "anyone with good sense knows most of what's printed in those tabloids isn't true. Second of all, Rachel is one of the most professional women I know. She didn't have to come on to me because I found her attractive from day one. I saw in her something I haven't seen in a lot of woman lately."

Tae'Shawna lifted her chin and he could tell his words had hit a nerve. "And what is that?"

"Unselfishness. She is not self-absorbed and I doubt that she has a shallow bone in her body. In fact, she never came on to me, but *you* did, many times, right here on the set. So who should I think is the professional one? Now if you'll excuse me, I need to call it a day."

A few hours later, in the privacy of his home, Ethan sank down on his sofa frustrated as hell. He hadn't tried making any type of contact with Rachel while on the set but he had called her several times since getting home, and she still would not accept his calls. If the paparazzi were on her tail like they were on his, he could imagine what she was going through, but that was no reason to block him out of her life.

Considering everything, he had expected her to withdraw for a day or so, but he hadn't expected her to put up an emotional wall that he could not penetrate.

For the last three days on the set she had been cordial yet distant, as if to prove to everyone that they were not together. When she looked at him, it was as if she was looking straight through him. He knew she was trying hard to maintain a mask of nonchalance where he was concerned, determined to avoid any situation that would compromise her professionalism.

He had tried not to be angered by her actions but a part of him couldn't help it. And now in the comfort of his home, lonely as it was, his anger was turning into intense hurt.

Why was he letting her do this to him?

Because, as he had told her, he loved her and a part of him believed she loved him back. And he believed that one day she would realize that nothing, not the paparazzi and not the threat of jeopardizing her career, was worth sacrificing their love.

Rachel cuddled on her sofa and pressed the replay button to pick up her last call.

"Rachel, this is Ethan. I know what you're going through but I wish you would let us go through it together. When you hurt, I hurt. I love you and I know you love me. Baby, please don't do this to us."

She glanced over at the beautiful bouquet of flowers that had been delivered to her from Ethan by way of Charlene. Her best friend had dropped by with the flowers earlier that evening. The card attached simply said:

I love you.
Ethan

Tears rolled from her eyes. She didn't think it would be so hard giving him up. She hadn't counted on the agony and the pain, the feeling of loneliness and heartbreak. It was hard during the day to see him and try to ignore him. Alone in her trailer, she would feel alienated. Even after three days, everyone on the set was still abuzz about her and Ethan breaking the rules, but so far neither Frasier nor John had approached her or Ethan. She figured they were probably waiting for one of them to approach them first, so tomorrow she would.

Tomorrow… Tomorrow she was scheduled to do Ethan's makeup. Typically they would be alone in her trailer, but she didn't want everyone speculating about what they were doing or saying behind closed doors. To have one of her assistants fill in for her would indicate she wasn't professional enough to handle a controversial situation. So in a way it was a "damned if you do and damned if you don't" situation.

Livia had come to her rescue. She volunteered to be the buffer by being in the trailer at the same time Ethan was there, on the pretext of repairing a broken nail or something. Rachel hoped the ploy worked.

Ethan knew all eyes were on him as he headed for Rachel's trailer. No doubt there were some who had their watch set to see how long he stayed inside alone with her.

"Ethan, wait up." He stopped and glanced around. Livia was walking toward him. She was one of the few women on set who hadn't tried coming on to him. Like Rachel, she was a specialist in her craft. Even with all those love scenes they'd done, they had still maintained professionalism.

"I need to see Rachel a minute myself," she said, smiling. "Broken nail."

He smiled, seeing through her ploy. Rachel was her friend and she was making an attempt to avoid gossip and speculation.

From the look on Rachel's face when they entered her trailer, Ethan knew for certain that Livia's appearance had been planned. Rachel showed no surprise at seeing them both walk in.

"Hello, Ethan, you can take my chair. And Livia, I'll fix that nail in a minute, just as soon as I finish with Ethan."

"No problem," Livia said, smiling. "I'll just sit over here."

"You can go ahead and take care of Livia and then do me," Ethan suggested. Only after the words had left his mouth did he realize their double meaning.

"No, Livia can wait until I finish with you," Rachel insisted.

"And I don't have a problem with you doing her first."

Before Rachel could open her mouth to retort, Livia spoke up. "Look, guys, evidently you two need time alone to clear up a few things."

"No, we don't."

"Yes, we do."

Livia shook her head. "Since the two of you can't agree, I'll make the decision for you," she said. "Rachel, you can work on Ethan while I excuse myself a minute to go to the ladies' room." Livia then headed toward the back of the trailer where the dressing room and bathroom were located.

Rachel watched her friend's retreating back.

"You can take care of me now, Rachel."

Rachel turned and glared at Ethan. "Do you not care about my career?"

His face rigid, he returned her glare. "And do you not care about my heart? Or yours?"

Her stomach twisted with his question, and she forced

herself to ignore the stab of pain that ripped through her. "I care, but there's nothing I can do about it, Ethan. Please just let me make you up so I can be ready for the next person."

"Fine, get to it then."

He reclined in the chair and she stood over him. She hesitated a moment and looked into the eyes staring back at her. Just like always when she looked at them, she was in awe of their beauty, but this time she saw the anger and pain in their depths.

Drawing in a deep breath, she brushed foundation across his cheekbones, then around his mouth, and she couldn't help but focus on his lips. Lips she had kissed so many times. Lips she wanted to kiss again. But she fought doing so.

Those lips moved and she heard the husky but low tone of his voice. "I love you, Rachel."

She dropped the brush from her hand and took a step back. "I'm finished, Ethan."

He eased out of the chair, his long legs bringing him to stand directly in front of her. "You might be finished but I'm not, Rachel. At least not where you're concerned. What we've shared is too precious and I won't give up on us. Admit that you love me as much as I love you."

She looked up at him, her heart full, but was unable to say the words he wanted to hear. "Ethan, I—I can't say it."

He reached out and gently pulled her into his arms and she could not have pulled out of them even if she wanted to. He lowered his head and, of their own accord, her lips parted as she sighed his name. The moment his lips touched hers she felt soothed by something she had missed for the past couple of days, something her body had gotten used to having.

A sensuous shudder passed through her as his tongue reinstated its rights to her mouth, letting her know that no matter how she continued to deny them, put distance between them, there would always be this—a passion so intense and forceful, it would take more than negative publicity to destroy it.

When he angled his head to deepen the kiss, she stretched up on tiptoes to get the full Ethan Chambers effect. And it was worth every effort. He was kissing her like a starving man, and in kind, she was kissing him like a starving woman. Her heart swelled with every stroke of his tongue, and she knew in her heart what she refused to speak out loud.

He finally pulled his mouth away and tenderly touched her cheek. "One day you will tell me that you love me and I'll be ready to hear it when you do." His tone was raw and husky and sent sensuous shivers all down her spine.

He leaned down and brushed a kiss across her lips before turning to walk out of the trailer.

Chapter 18

Rachel's lips twitched in a smile when the limousine pulled up behind Amaury's, an exclusive restaurant in Hollywood whose doors usually were closed until eight every night. Only Sofia, with a list of connections and contacts a mile long, could make the impossible happen.

For the past week, other than leaving for work, Rachel had pretty much stayed in and not ventured out with the paparazzi breathing down her neck. Although the breakup between Rayon Stewart and Artis Lomax and rumors of another adoption by Brad and Angelina now dominated the headlines, there were a few reporters who just didn't know when to quit.

"We're here, Ms. Rachel."

"Thanks, Martin," she said to the man who'd been the limo driver for Limelight Entertainment for years. She could recall sitting in the backseat of the huge car, with him behind the wheel, while being transported to and from private school as a child of no more than eight or nine. During those days, he kept her entertained with his own rendition of the animated voices of Bugs Bunny and Daffy Duck. He used to be so good at it.

Moments later, he was holding the door open for her as she got out. Amaury Gaston met her at the door and gave her a big hug.

"Sofia is already seated and waiting on you, Rachel," he said in a heavy French accent.

"Thanks."

"I've prepared your favorite," he added.

Rachel licked her lips. Chicken cordon bleu, she guessed, and Amaury's was the best. "You like spoiling me and Sofia," she said, smiling.

"Yes, just like I used to enjoy spoiling your parents. They were two of my first customers, and your father proposed to your mother right here one night. It was very special."

Rachel had heard the story before but didn't mind hearing it again. According to everyone who knew them, her parents had been very much in love.

"And I know if they were alive, they would want me to treat their girls just as special as I thought they were," Amaury added.

Moments later, Rachel made her way toward the table where her sister sat waiting. Sofia saw her approach and smiled. With her beauty and tall, slender figure, Rachel thought Sofia could have easily been a model or actress. Instead, she had followed in their father's footsteps and had taken his place in the family business working alongside Uncle Jacob. Despite their age difference, she and Sofia had maintained a close relationship, especially now that Sofia wasn't as overprotective as she used to be.

Sofia stood and Rachel walked straight into her sister's outstretched arms. Then Sofia took a step back and studied her from head to toe. "Hmm, it doesn't look like the tabloids have beaten you up too badly, although I'm sure there are scars on the inside that I can't see."

Rachel felt a thickness in her throat. She hadn't intended to let Sofia know just how shaken up she really was. Ethan's kiss yesterday had done that enough. She had expected him to call last night, but he hadn't. She wasn't sure what she would have said if he had.

"Are you okay, Rach?" Sofia asked, looking into her eyes.

"Yes."

"You sure?"

Rachel forced a smile. "Yes, I'm fine. Come on, let's let Amaury know we're ready to be served. I'm starving," she said, moving to her chair and away from her sister's intense scrutiny.

"Okay, but don't think you're not going to tell me everything," Sofia said, taking her own seat again.

"Everything like what?"

Sofia held her gaze with that "let's get serious"

expression on her face. "Everything like how you really feel about Ethan Chambers."

"Maybe we ought to buy stock in those tabloids since you seem to be in them quite a bit these days, Ethan."

Ethan closed his refrigerator after pulling out a cold beer. He juggled the phone as he twisted off the cap. His heart had begun pounding in his chest when the phone had rung, in hopes the caller was Rachel. Instead it was Hunter. "That's a possibility."

"So is any of it true?" his brother asked.

"The only thing I will admit to is an involvement with Rachel. Her motives were exploited falsely. Our being together was mutual and she didn't need me to advance her career. She did that on her own."

"Pretty defensive, aren't you?"

"Can't help but be where she's concerned. I love her."

There was silence on the other end, and Ethan was well aware that his brother was recovering from what he'd said. In all his twenty-eight years, he'd never admitted to loving any woman. While his brother was pondering what he'd said, Ethan took a swig of beer.

"This is serious," Hunter finally said.

"I hope she realizes that it is. She's tabloid shy."

"And you're just the opposite," Hunter pointed out. "For as long as I can recall, you enjoyed getting in front of a camera."

Ethan shrugged, remembering some of his wild

escapades while in high school and college. "Not when they portray my woman in a bad light."

"Well, we're all looking forward to meeting her. And since things are that serious, don't forget the traditional Chambers vineyard weddings."

Ethan smiled. "I won't, but first I have to convince her that she loves me and that I will make her life with me worth anything the tabloids might put her through."

"Good luck."

Ethan drew in a deep breath. "Thanks." He knew he was going to need it.

Sofia took another sip of her wine. "And you think Livia Blake might be looking for another agent?" she asked.

"Yes," Rachel said, eager to keep her sister talking about something else other than her and Ethan. "Livia says at thirty her modeling days are coming to an end, and she wants an agent who will take her acting career to another level and run with it. Of course, she's heard about Limelight Entertainment and would love to talk to you, but she's heard how selective you are."

Sofia didn't deny what Rachel said. She *was* selective. "I've been keeping an eye on Livia Blake's modeling career for a while now and wondered if she planned on doing anything beyond that. Limelight is definitely interested, so have her give me a call."

Rachel looked at her sister and could tell she was bothered about something and that it was something other than what was going on with her and Ethan.

"You've been working a lot lately, Sofia. When do you plan on taking another vacation?"

Sofia smiled. "Hmm, a vacation sounds nice but I won't be going back to the islands any time soon. My clientele has doubled, and I have to find work for a lot of people." She took another sip of her wine, leaned back in her chair and asked, "Did you know Uncle Jacob is thinking about retiring?"

Rachel's eyes widened. "No. I talked to him a few days ago and he said nothing about that. But I can see him wanting to just chill, take it easy and travel. He and Aunt Lily have been saying they want to build that house in Barbados for years."

"Yes, I'd love for him to retire and enjoy life, too, but not if the rumors I'm hearing are true."

Rachel lifted a brow. "What rumors?"

Although there weren't others in the restaurant, Sofia leaned over the table and said in a low tone, "I've heard that he's thinking about selling his interest in Limelight to Ramell Jordan at A.F.I."

Rachel's expression denoted her surprise. Artists Factory Inc. had been a rival talent agency of Limelight Entertainment for years. In fact, Ramell's father, Emmett, had been a close friend of her father's, but for some reason they were not on good terms at the time of her dad's death. And because of Sofia's close relationship with their father, Rachel was not surprised that her sister would not favor a possible merger.

"What you heard is probably just a rumor," Rachel

said, hoping that would smooth her sister's ruffled feathers.

"I certainly hope so. I can't believe Uncle Jacob would consider doing such a thing."

Rachel could see why he would. Although her father and Emmett Jordan had ended on bad terms, Uncle Jacob and Emmett had remained somewhat friendly.

"Ramell Jordan is nothing more than the son of a backstabber after what Emmett did to Dad," Sofia said angrily.

Rachel lifted a brow. "And just what did he do to Dad?"

She'd always believed there was more to the story than either she or Sofia knew, but no one would ever say. In fact, Sofia was the only one who'd ever made such accusations about Emmett Jordan. All Uncle Jacob would say was that it had been a misunderstanding between the two men and that had her father lived, his and Emmett's relationship would have been restored to a close friendship.

"You're better off not knowing."

Rachel only shook her head. For years that had been the same response Sofia gave her whenever she asked. Maybe she was simply better off not knowing.

"And now that you've tried to get me to avoid talking about you and Ethan Chambers, I think that we need to finally get to the meat of your problem."

Rachel pushed away her plate. Dinner had been delicious and now she was ready for desert and coffee.

But she would wait awhile until after she answered the questions she knew her sister had for her.

"There's really nothing to tell, Sofia. You know how I detest being in the public eye and Ethan's popularity right now puts him there, as well as any woman he's involved with."

"So the two of you *are* involved?"

Pain rolled through Rachel. "We *were* involved."

Sofia studied her sister's features, saw the pain that settled in her face. "The two of you kept things between you a secret from everyone—including me—which evidently was working for a while. So what happened?"

Rachel took a deep breath, and then she told Sofia about what Paige had done.

A deep frown appeared on Sofia's face. "And this Paige person works on the set of *Paging the Doctor?*"

"Yes, she's a production assistant."

"Not for long," Sofia muttered under her breath. "Tell me something, Rachel. Did your affair with Ethan have substance or was it all about sex?"

Rachel met her sister's inquisitive gaze. It would be so easy to claim it had been nothing but sex, but this was Sofia and she'd always had a way of seeing through any lie Rachel told. Besides, she would tell Sofia what she hadn't told anyone, not even Ethan.

"I love him, Sofia. It wasn't all about sex."

Her sister stared at her for a long moment, and then a smile touched her lips when she said, "Then I can see no reason why the two of you can't be together."

Rachel rolled her eyes. In a way she was surprised at her sister's comment, since Sofia of all people knew how she guarded her privacy. "You know that's not possible, Sofia. Ethan is an up-and-coming star, and being the focus of a lot of attention is what will boost his career. I can't risk that kind of publicity with the career I tried so hard to build."

"And what else?"

Rachel gave her sister a confused look. "What do you mean what else?"

Sofia leaned in closer. "This is me, and I can read you like a book, Rachel. So level with me and tell me the real reason you and Ethan can't be together. Since I'm always on the lookout for potential clients, I'm well aware that Ethan Chambers is hot news. I'm also well aware that during the time the two of you were having your secret tryst, his name wasn't linked to any Hollywood starlet, which made the tabloids wonder exactly what he was doing and who he was doing it with. And when it seemed he had decided to just live a boring life, they backed off. When the news hit the papers about the two of you, the tabloids had basically given him a rest."

Sofia paused to take a sip of her wine and then asked, "And what's this I hear about you taking a temporary leave from the show?"

Rachel placed her wine glass down after taking her own sip. She didn't have to wonder where Sofia had gotten the news. Few people knew that Frasier considered himself as their godfather. "I thought it would be best, and I met with Frasier yesterday. He wasn't all that keen on the idea but said since there was only a week left for filming, he would go along with it. But he wanted me back on my job when they began the new season. I can handle that."

Sofia lifted a brow. "Can you? They aren't writing Ethan out of the script, so he'll be returning, too. Will you be able to handle that?"

"I don't have a choice."

"Yes, you do. For once you can fight for what you want, what you have every right to have."

Rachel was still surprised by her sister's attitude. She'd expected her to be the voice of reason and agree with her that the best thing was to put her career ahead of anything else. That was certainly what Sofia was doing these days. She couldn't recall a time when her sister had gotten serious about a man.

"You don't think my career is important, Sofia?"

Sofia waved off her words. "Of course I do, but your heart takes priority."

At Rachel's frown, Sofia reached out and captured her hand in hers. "Hear me out for a second, Rach." She paused and then said, "This is the first time I can truly say I believe you're in love. It shows on your face every time you say Ethan's name. You, little sister, are truly in love and I don't believe it's one-sided. I've been waiting to see how Ethan was going to respond to the tabloids. He hasn't denied the two of you are having an affair. In fact, he's gone on record with Joe Connors to say that you were not using him to boost your career. Other than that, he's been low-key about everything, which shows me he's doing whatever he can to protect you, and I like him for that. He could take all this publicity and run with it, but he hasn't. He's trying to fade to black."

Rachel had to agree with Sofia on that. Ethan was keeping a low profile these days.

"A man like that is worth keeping, Rach. And it's time you do what I haven't been able to do yet."

"And what is that?" Rachel asked, taking another sip of her wine.

"Stop hiding behind your career as an excuse to avoid falling in love. It's an unfortunate Wellesley trait. I'm guilty of it, too. We're both scared that if we love someone, they will abandon us like Mom and Dad did."

Rachel met her sister's gaze. Is that what she had been doing? Was that the reason she'd deliberately kept men at arm's length? Although she was barely out of diapers when her parents were killed, and her uncle and aunt had always been there for her, she had grown up feeling a tremendous loss. It had been hard during her early years when all her friends had had someone to call Mom and she had not. A part of her had always had that inner fear that to love also meant to lose. Wasn't it time for her to finally take a chance on love and believe she was deserving of a forever kind of love like everyone else? Did she want to live the rest of her life afraid of the unknown? Wasn't a life with Ethan better than a life without him? In her heart she knew that it was, and it was time for her to take a leap of faith and take control of her life.

A smile touched Rachel's face when she recalled the party planned for the cast and crew this weekend. "You're right. It's time for me to stop hiding."

Chapter 19

"You look simply beautiful, Rach," Charlene said, smiling as she gazed at her best friend from head to toe.

"And I feel beautiful," Rachel responded, looking at herself in a full-length mirror. She glanced over her shoulder at the woman who was smiling proudly at her handiwork. "Livia, I'm thinking that maybe I ought to be worried. You could take my job as a makeup artist."

Livia chuckled as she waved off her words. "You don't have to worry about that, and thanks to your sister I won't either. I appreciate you putting in a good word for me. It's a dream come true to be represented by Limelight Entertainment."

Rachel smiled as she looked at herself in the mirror

again. Sofia had gone shopping with her and helped her pick out her dress, Charlene had selected the accessories and Livia had done her makeup and hair. She felt like Cinderella about to go to the most important ball of her life. And her Prince Charming was waiting.

At least she hoped he was waiting.

She'd heard from Livia that Ethan had gone home to Napa Valley last weekend and that on the set for the season finale he had thrown himself into his work and pretty much kept to himself. More than once she was tempted to call him but decided to do things this way. Now nerves were setting in and all those "what-ifs" were stirring through her mind.

She turned to her two friends. "Are you sure he's coming to the wrap party tonight, Livia?"

Livia smiled. "I heard him assure Frasier that he'll be there to walk the red carpet."

Rachel nodded. "What if he brings a date?"

"I doubt that, and I even heard him tell Frasier that he's coming alone," Livia responded. "And just so you know, Paige was dropped from the show. All I know is that she got called to John's office and he told her she was no longer needed. So the only thing she gained by stirring up that mess with the tabloids is an unemployment check." Livia smiled and added, "And I heard she's having trouble finding a job. Seems like someone put the word out around town about her."

Rachel didn't have to guess who. Her sister was that influential.

"I think it's time for you to leave now," Charlene said, glancing out the window. "Martin just pulled up."

Nervous flutters raced through Rachel's stomach. Sofia had called her from London, where she'd gone to meet with a client, and given her another pep talk. Then Uncle Jacob and Aunt Lily had called and told her to follow her heart, and since they would be at the wrap party, they would see her later.

Rachel knew she was doing the right thing. Ethan had said he wanted her to tell him that she loved him and she was prepared to do that. And it no longer mattered who would be listening. She did love him, and she needed him in her life more than anything. It was about time that he knew it.

Ethan drew in a deep breath when the limo he was riding in alone pulled to a stop in front of the red carpet. The crowd was massive and, as usual, reporters were out in droves. People were standing behind the roped areas, and cameras were flashing from just about every angle.

More than anything, he wished Rachel would have been there with him, by his side, to bask in the moment of his accomplishments. He had worked hard to reach this point in his career and, more than anything, he wanted the woman he loved to be with him.

He had told her that he loved her and now the next step would have to be hers. And he could only hope that sooner or later she'd make it.

He had to believe that one day she would realize

that together their love was strong enough to withstand anything. Even this, he thought, glancing out the car window at the crowd that seemed to be getting larger by the minute.

As soon as he stepped out of the car, flashbulbs went off, momentarily blinding him, and he was immediately pulled center stage to be interviewed. The cheering crowd made him feel good, but nothing could heal his broken heart.

"Everyone, we have Ethan Chambers, who this season became known as Dr. Tyrell Perry on *Paging the Doctor.* And how are you doing tonight, Ethan?"

Ethan smiled for the camera while giving his attention to the red-carpet host for the evening, Neill Carter. "I'm doing great, Neill, and looking forward to a wonderful evening."

Neill laughed. "I can believe that, but you came by yourself, man. Surely there was a special lady who would have loved to make this walk down the red carpet with you."

It was Saturday night and, more than likely, millions of people were sitting in front of their television sets watching the festivities, including his family. He hoped Rachel was one of those watching because he intended to give her a shout-out. Even if no one else knew whom his message was meant for, she would.

"Yes," he said, looking directly into the camera. "There is a special lady for me and I want her to know that I…"

He stopped talking when he glanced over Neill's

shoulder and saw a woman strolling toward them. He blinked. She was beautiful, from the way her hair was styled on her head to the gorgeous red gown she wore—down to the silver shoes that sparkled on her feet.

His gaze returned to her face and for a moment he didn't believe what he was seeing. Rachel was here, in the spotlight, and it was obvious she wasn't there to make anyone up behind the scenes tonight. She was standing out and she was walking toward him.

All eyes were on her, including his. When she reached his side, she smiled and leaned closer and whispered in his ear, "I love you, Ethan. Thanks for waiting on me."

He couldn't help the smile that touched his lips. He had waited on her. And that wait had not been in vain. He pulled her into his arms and lowered his mouth to hers, kissing her right there in front of everyone. It was a move that caused the crowd to roar with excitement. Photographers snapped pictures, taking it all in. When Ethan finally released Rachel's mouth, he grinned down at her as flashes continued to go off around them.

"I take it you two know each other," Neill said with a teasing grin.

"Yes, we know each other," Ethan said, pulling her closer to his side. "This is my special lady, and she has something I've never given another female."

"And what's that?" Neill asked.

"My heart."

Later that night, Ethan opened the door to *their* place and swept Rachel into his arms. The party had been great. He'd made more contacts and had gotten numerous offers from new agents looking to fill Curtis Fairgate's place.

But the highlight of the entire evening was the woman in his arms, the star of his heart.

He tried to maintain control as he carried her to the bed. His hands began shaking as he slowly undressed her, hoping and praying this wasn't a dream and he wouldn't wake up to an empty room.

It was only after he'd gotten them both undressed and eased on the bed with her, right into her outstretched arms, that he finally accepted this was the real deal. He took her face in his hands and stared into the darkness of her eyes as his heart swelled even more. "I love you, Rachel."

Her smile brightened his whole world, and her voice was filled with sincerity when she said, "And I love you, Ethan."

For a suspended moment in time they stared at each other, and then he captured her lips with his as joy bubbled within him. He knew at that moment that he'd been made to love her, to be her shelter from the storm, to protect her, to honor her for always.

He deepened the kiss and felt her body tremble. When he settled his body over hers, he knew he was almost home.

He had wanted to take things slow with her, but it had been too long since they'd been together like this and his body was craving to get inside of her. When she moaned his name he knew he couldn't wait any longer.

He broke off the kiss to gaze down into her eyes at the same time he thrust inside of her, entering her with a hunger that shook every part of his body. As her scent swept through his nostrils and her inner muscles gripped him for everything they could get, he threw his head back and surrendered to her.

"Rachel!"

His sexy pixie was making her mark, and each time she lifted her hips to meet his thrusts, stroke for stroke, he was pushed even more over the edge. When he felt a mind-blowing explosion on the horizon, he glanced back down into her face and saw his passion mirrored in her eyes.

When the climax hit, he could swear bells and whistles went off. Their bodies exploded together, escalating them to the stars and beyond. They shuddered together as the power of love drenched them in an orgasm so potent he wondered if they would ever be able to recover.

But deep down he knew they would—only to take the journey over and over again, for an entire lifetime.

When their bodies ceased shuddering, he rolled to the side, pulled her into his arms and held her close to his heart. Just where she would always be.

Rachel lay contented in Ethan's arms. She hadn't realized how much she'd missed coming here, being here with him, until they'd stopped being together. But never again.

They had made love several times, and she kept

telling him how much she loved him because she loved hearing herself say it and he seemed to enjoy hearing it. And he told her how much he loved her as well. She knew now that together they could face anything. She was no longer afraid of what the tabloids might print or how her career could be affected.

Tonight Frasier had congratulated everyone and indicated that he expected them all back for the new season. Everyone except Paige, of course, who ironically wasn't invited to the wrap party she'd been dying to attend with Ethan. And Tae'Shawna Miller. Apparently she had whined one time too many, because rumor had it she'd been released from the show as well.

Rachel shifted her body to glance up at Ethan. "You're quiet. What are you thinking?" she asked him.

He smiled down at her. "I was thinking about how surprised I was to see you tonight. Surprised and happy. What made you come?"

She reached up and her fingers touched his cheek. "You. I knew I loved you and you kept telling me that you loved me, breaking down my barriers." She paused a moment and then said, "And I also realized Sofia was right. I was hiding my love on the pretense of protecting my career when I was really afraid to admit loving you. I was afraid I wouldn't be able to handle it if you were to leave me the way my parents did."

Ethan held her gaze. "I'll never leave you, sweetheart. And by the way, while you were talking to Frasier tonight, I got a call on my cell phone. It was my mother. She was watching the whole thing on television and heard me when I said you had my heart. So she wants to know when's the wedding."

Rachel laughed. "The wedding?"

"Yes. I told her I hadn't gotten around to asking you yet." He pulled her closer into his arms. "So, baby, will you marry me?"

She smiled up at him. "For better or for worse?"

He nodded. "And richer or poorer."

"In sickness and in health?"

He chuckled. "Until death do us part."

She leaned up and threw her arms around his neck. "In that case, I accept!"

He wrapped her in his arms and kissed her, sealing what he knew would be a Hollywood marriage that would last forever.

* * * * *

A sneaky peek at next month...

Desire™

PASSIONATE AND DRAMATIC LOVE STORIES

2 stories in each book - only £5.30!

My wish list for next month's titles...

In stores from 20th January 2012:

☐ Caught in the Billionaire's Embrace — Elizabeth Bevarly

& The Tycoon's Temporary Baby — Emily McKay

☐ The Proposal — Brenda Jackson

& To Tempt a Sheikh — Olivia Gates

☐ Reunited...with Child — Katherine Garbera

& One Month with the Magnate — Michelle Celmer

☐ A Lone Star Love Affair — Sara Orwig

& Falling for the Princess — Sandra Hyatt

Available at WHSmith, Tesco, Asda, Eason, Amazon and Apple

Just can't wait?

Visit us Online

You can buy our books online a month before they hit the shops! **www.millsandboon.co.uk**

0112/51

Don't miss Pink Tuesday
One day. 10 hours. 10 deals.

PINK TUESDAY IS COMING!

10 hours...10 unmissable deals!

This Valentine's Day we will be bringing you fantastic offers across a range of our titles—each hour, on the hour!

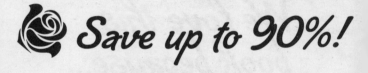

Save up to 90%!

Pink Tuesday starts
9am Tuesday 14th February

Have Your Say

You've just finished your book.
So what did you think?

We'd love to hear your thoughts on our
'Have your say' online panel
www.millsandboon.co.uk/haveyoursay

- Easy to use
- Short questionnaire
- Chance to win Mills & Boon®
  goodies

Visit us Online

Tell us what you thought of this book now at
www.millsandboon.co.uk/haveyoursay

YOUR_SAY